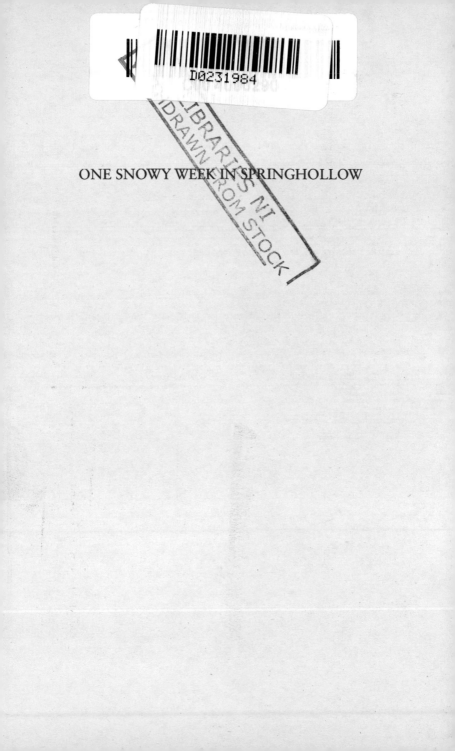

ONE SNOWY WEEK IN SPRINGHOLLOW

ONE SNOWY WEEK IN SPRINGHOLLOW

Lucy Knott

An Aria Book

First published in the the United Kingdom in 2020 by Aria,
an imprint of Head of Zeus Ltd

This paperback edition first published in 2021 by Aria

9 7 5 3 1 2 4 6 8

A CIP catalogue record for this book is available from the
British Library.

ISBN (PB): 9781801100342
ISBN (E): 9781800243316

Typeset by Siliconchips Services Ltd UK

Cover design © Lisa Brewster

Printed and bound in Great Britain by
CPI Group (UK) Ltd, Croydon CRO 4YY

Aria
c/o Head of Zeus
First Floor East
5–8 Hardwick Street
London EC1R 4RG

www.ariafiction.com

For my Nanna; the strongest Superhero
I have ever known

Prologue

December 2007

'*You really think I can do it?' I shout, my voice a touch skittish; trepidation in my tone, followed by an excited squeal. My fists are clenched, hovering by my ears in nervous anticipation. I bend my knees to give me some bounce as I balance on the tree branch without holding on. My arms are stretched out above my head, ready for take-off.*

'*Of course, you can do it, Scar; we're superheroes and superheroes fly,' Devon yells up from the safety of the grass. I don't think that now is the time to inform him that Captain America doesn't fly, and neither does Black Widow. That conversation probably should have happened earlier, so instead I close my eyes tight, squeeze my fists harder, do three small bounces on the balls of my feet with my knees bent and leap into the air with an almighty roar.*

When I open my eyes, I see the ground rapidly approaching. I start flapping my arms manically like a wild bird – totally not like Superman. Within half a second, I hear a loud crunch. I don't feel any pain, yet the ground is right under my nose and the thin blades of grass are tickling my eyelashes. I exhale all the air in my lungs and that's when it hits me.

I hear screaming but I can't quite tell if it's my voice, Devon's or both. The pain in my wrists is excruciating. Tears are flooding my face, forming a puddle in the snowy, slushy, muddy earth. I can't move. I register Devon shouting words at me but can't make out what he's saying. If he's asking me if I'm OK, he's lost his mind. I can't feel my hands. I think I'm going to be sick. For the first time in my twelve years of existence I think I'm going to faint, but worse than that – I don't think I believe in superheroes anymore.

My lips are pursed into an "o" shape and I am aware they have been stuck like this since my lunch arrived an hour ago because they are actually starting to hurt, but I'm allowed to pout. My world has drastically flipped upside down; being upset is natural.

'Open your mouth, Scar,' Devon says, frustration in his voice. I deepen the crease between my brows, pucker my lips a little more and defiantly shake my head. I will not open my mouth.

'Your cape got caught on a branch, Scar, that's all. I saw it. You jumped and it whipped you back, disabling flight mode,' Devon explains for the tenth time this afternoon. He's taking my no longer believing in superheroes pretty hard. I am too. I don't want to eat, and I am mad at both Devon and Superman for making me think I could fly. I wince as both my casted wrists tingle and prickle with pain. Devon tries again to feed me from the bowl of mush, which

has grown colder while we've argued. He brings the spoon up to my mouth.

My mum is sat at the base of my bed while Devon's is stood by the window. Both have their lips drawn thin, no doubt individually plotting more ways to keep me and Devon apart, and thinking how they can put a stop to Devon and I watching superhero movies for good. Our parents are not close; each blames the other for our behaviour and antics. This is, after all, our second trip to the hospital this month.

Only two weeks ago we were testing out Super Strength when Devon dropped a log on his foot, breaking two of his toes. But they healed quickly, just like Devon had told me they would, because it doesn't take Wolverine months to recover so it wouldn't take Devon long either. They were one and the same, being one of Devon's favourite superheroes and all; we accumulated our powers from our favourite heroes.

I shake my head again, not wanting to eat the mysterious gloop on the spoon or to talk to Devon. We'd been planning this one for months; studying our Superman DVDs, flicking through our comics and checking the aerodynamics with our action figures. We found the tallest tree and had my mum iron our capes. So what had gone wrong?

'Scar, you can't stop talking to me. I'm sorry you got hurt but we'll try again. I promise it was just the branch that got in the way.' Devon whispers so our mums don't overhear our plans to try this stunt again. Devon's brown eyes are watering. I hate making him sad; this is worse than the time I accidentally snuck his Thor figure into the wash because I'd somehow managed to get paint on him. The wash had worked but when my mum hadn't noticed and put Thor in the dryer I had feared my friendship would melt as quickly

as Thor did. However, I got lucky and Devon only cried for two days before he started talking to me again, though only after I gave him my Thor to make up for it.

'I don't really think superheroes are fake. That would be stupid. Who would be out there saving people and capturing the baddies?' I say, catching Devon's eyes and giving in to stop his tears. He wipes at his eyes with the back of his hand and smiles. All is right with the world again. I could never really stop talking to him, not forever.

'Best friends forever!' he says, holding up his spoon-free hand then thinking better of it and resting his hand on my bed. In my current state I am unable to perform our usual handshake, which would – you know – involve the use of both my hands.

'Best friends forever,' I agree as Devon takes the opportunity of my opening my mouth to shove the spoon of cold slush in.

'Superheroes have to eat, Scar,' he says with a shrug, his tone caring, but with a slight sly smirk on his face. 'And they don't really roar like lions when they fly.' With that he promptly bursts out laughing while I try not to spray mush all over the hospital bed sheets as giggles creep up my throat.

December 2011

'You don't think this is dangerous?' I shout to Devon who is standing at the base of the small hut that houses some equipment for the skatepark. I don't know why I'm even

4

asking him. I know beyond a shadow of a doubt that what I'm doing is dumb, not least because it's December and it's icy out, yet here I am. But this is what Devon and I do. It's a Friday night and after a day of being teased and taunted by Ruby and her gaggle of bullies at school we need to blow off some steam and, if I'm totally honest, I might be sixteen, but my childhood dream of being a superhero hasn't faltered. I can say the same for D too.

'No, you'll be fine, Scar – it's height that you need. Once you leap, tuck your board and you'll fly for longer,' D yells up at me. He has a beaming smile on his face, one that I notice – now that we're in year eleven – makes some of the girls at school go all googly-eyed at him, which is really annoying. I shake my head to focus and take in a few deep breaths. I can do this.

I plant my foot firmly on the board, so I don't roll before I'm ready, and I close my eyes to envision myself soaring into the sky, a symbol of what life will be like after seven more months of secondary school – but who's counting? When I open them, I push off with my right foot. The sloping roof allows my board to pick up the speed that I need to accelerate into the air before I land in the bowl.

The edge of the roof is in sight and, just as my board hits the air, I hear someone shout, 'What are you kids…' I don't hear the rest because the next second an all too familiar pain courses through my body, if not worse than the time before, and this time I immediately black out.

'So much for spending the Christmas break drawing,' I muse as I precariously lift my right arm, which happens to be my drawing arm, and wince as I take in my bright and shiny new cast. This time I added a broken arm to my fractured wrist.

'At least it's only one hand this time,' Devon retorts from his sitting position by my legs. Our mums are out in the corridor, having been unable to keep their anger in. They were full-on shouting at each other, until the nurse encouraged them not to do so in front of us kids.

'Well, it's all right for you – at least I can still hold a camera with one hand. We can still practise auditions and keep adding to your acting reel, but I might need you to sketch for me. I've got this really awesome idea for a superhero dinosaur that finds itself in the present day. I don't want to forget any visuals so I will have to make do with your terrible drawing skills,' I say with a laugh and a roll of my eyes. I'm only teasing but whereas acting is Devon's thing, I hate being in front of a crowd. Mine is art, so Devon knows I'm only playing. However, I notice that his shoulders are tense and he's not joining in with my laughter. Devon hit a growth spurt in year ten and his shoulders grew so broad they're hard to miss.

'You're acting funny. What's up?' I ask, wriggling a little in the hospital bed, suddenly feeling irritated, though I'm not sure why. There's just something off about Devon not looking at me, averting his eyes to the floor. He doesn't speak. 'D, since when do we keep secrets? Something's up. What is it? Don't worry about my mum, you know what she's like. They can't stop us hanging out. They couldn't when we were five and they've got no chance now. You're stuck with me, big guy,' I say, laughing again and sitting up so I can punch him in the bicep with my good hand.

But Devon still doesn't say anything. Instead he gets up off the bed and stands by my tray of hospital food – complete distraction technique.

'If you think I'm eating that again, you've got another thing coming,' I say, chuckling to lighten the mood, though I can feel my palms begin to sweat, which isn't pleasant for my right hand as it's already hot in my cast.

'Scar,' Devon starts and I notice there are tears in his eyes. A lump forms in my throat and I swing my legs over the bed faster than the speed of Mercury so I'm facing him.

'Scar, I'm leaving,' Devon whispers as the tears roll down his cheeks.

'What? Now? Sorry, D, I didn't mean to keep you. They're probably going to discharge me soon anyway. I won't be here much longer,' I ramble, feeling very strange at how our roles have reversed – Devon normally being the quick talker.

'No, I'm leaving like for good,' he mumbles, making me lean in closer to him to hear.

'I don't understand,' I say, feeling utterly confused. 'Leaving where? What?' My eyes scrunch up; my vision is going blurry. I'm not a crier but watching the tears tumble from Devon's eyes is killing me. I hate seeing him sad. It's always been my job as his best friend to make them go away.

'We're moving to New York. Mum and Dad enrolled me in a theatre school there. We're leaving Springhollow,' Devon tells me. His words are coming out fast now, like he's ripping off a plaster.

This is all too much for me to take in. I try to push myself up off the bed; I want to do something, to smack Devon in the arm playfully for pranking me with this ridiculous joke

– or maybe to run, run somewhere far away to break this nightmare, but I gasp as the pain shoots up my arm, having momentarily forgotten to not put pressure on my very recently damaged appendage. Devon steps closer to me, his thighs grazing my knees. 'It's the middle of term – you can't leave now,' I say, my voice coming out high-pitched.

'I'm sorry,' he mutters. 'I tried to argue my case. I don't want to leave but they gave me no choice. Dad got a great job there and they said if I'm serious about acting they'll support me, and I shouldn't be ungrateful for this opportunity. The high schools there are amazing for the arts,' he adds, wiping a stray tear from my cheek that falls without my consent. 'Don't cry, Scar, we'll keep in touch. Just think of it like we're going to different colleges or something. People go away to college all the time, and I'll be back.'

His hands are on my shoulders now and I feel my skin heat. Devon and I are no strangers to wrestling around but something in me shifts. My heart is pounding, and I feel as if it's being ripped from my chest. He's always been the closest thing to me in every way, joined at the hip most would say. I feel cold at the thought of him not being right by my side. 'How can you say that? You can't leave me to face school alone.' My stomach is starting to twist uncomfortably; just the thought of going to school without Devon makes me want to be sick.

'When do you leave?' I find myself asking in a daze. Devon drops his hands and shuffles a little on his feet. A few seconds pass before he speaks.

'Tomorrow morning,' he replies, barely audible.

I leap off the bed as the words register in my brain and I wince at the pain that shoots through my right arm but

I don't care in the slightest about my injury anymore. The coldness in my bones has turned to fire. My cheeks burn and anger boils in my blood.

'How long have you known?' I shout, pushing him with my good arm. This is not something you spring on your best friend.

The tears are streaming down Devon's cheeks fast and hard now, but I don't care. I don't care about anything.

'I'm sorry, Scar, I didn't know how to tell you. I don't want to go, but they won't listen to me.' He pleads and I just glare at him, my breathing now heavy. My tears have dried up, any remaining wetness on my face has been harshly rubbed away with the back of my hand.

'A month, they surprised me about a month ago.' He mumbles.

'You've known for a month? Get out,' I yell with all my might. 'Get out.' I don't have any control over it. The words just fly out of my mouth. I can't even look at Devon. Just then the door swings open and both our mums race in.

'What's going on?' I hear my mum ask, but I don't turn around, I keep my gaze on the window.

'Scar, please,' I hear Devon say from somewhere behind me, but again I don't look back.

'Just go,' I mutter, finding that breaking my arm and fracturing my hand was a lot less painful than the agony in my heart right now.

I

December Present Day

Istep in from the cold, pulling my hoodie over my head, and shake off the chill. Though the weather is wonderfully wintry outside, my brow is sweaty, my body hot from my walk around the village trail. 'Christmas is in the air, Eddie,' I say to my goldfish as I make my way into my cosy living room after a quick pit stop in my kitchen to fill up my watering can and a tall glass of water for myself. I balance my sketchbook and my glass in one hand before carefully placing them both down on my coffee table and turning on my Christmas tree lights. I stand back for a moment, just staring at how they sparkle, and take a deep breath to calm my breathing. The fresh air has done me some good, but the walk certainly quickened my heart rate. It was one way to get my adrenaline pumping these days.

I water my potted cacti, which are strategically placed either side of my pink accent wall to give the room a beautiful pop of colour and natural vibe, before I take a seat on my couch to see that I get enough water myself.

I nudge my sketchbook as I place down the glass and see Eddie looking at me through his little glass tank. 'I got nothing but trees, Ed. I tell a lie; I did draw a bird today too,' I tell my curious goldfish. He gives me a disapproving pout before swimming away. 'Well, that's not very nice.' I let out a small sigh at how well he knows me. 'It's just a teeny bit of a rut, Ed, that's all,' I say trying to justify myself. 'We'll be out of it soon,' I add quietly, more to myself than to my tiny golden friend.

By the time the sky has turned navy my sketchbook is safely stowed away, I'm showered, fed and curled up in my bed, going through my final idea for the Springhollow Christmas fair. Every company gets a stall each year to use as they desire. Our village likes to get creative. Where I work, at *The Village Gazette*, my boss encourages her employees to get involved to help decide what our stall will be. We each put forth our proposal and then put it to a vote.

I'm the person who has been planning and preparing since the beginning of November, allowing the excitement of the festive season to guide me. I'm feeling confident in my vision for this year, not because I have won the last three years in a row, but because I truly think this is my best idea yet to really bring the community together. With visions of gingerbread and fondant Santas dancing in my head, I place my notebook on my bedside table, glance out of my window and say a prayer for a white Christmas. It's been a while since we had a white Christmas and a little magic in the air.

My alarm clock rings out and when I sit up to hit the button, panic floods through me at the time displayed on the clock. How many times did I press snooze? I jump out of bed, make a dash for the bathroom and shower as hastily as I can, grateful that my short hair doesn't take up much of my time and thinking it might just have to be a no makeup kind of day. When I get to my wardrobe the efficient speed at which I am moving comes to a standstill as I look over my outfits. One side of my cupboard holds a small selection of awesome flares and vintage and faded tees, while the other is all lace and frills – appropriate workwear according to my mother. My eyes dart back and forth as I graze my hand over a particularly cosy-looking tee that I had purchased online one evening after dinner with my parents. My mum had spent the evening telling me that I should sign up for dance classes to put myself out there more and meet people. The shirt had been my way of rebelling. I have yet to wear it.

'Arrrgh.' I let out an agitated groan as I reach for a pink pencil skirt and white daisy print blouse. Rebelling will have to wait for another day. I'm going to be late.

I make it into work with five minutes to spare and make a beeline for my office. Candles are lit, the room is already toasty, satsuma essence is wafting itself around the air and my best friend, Hope, who also happens to be my boss, is already sat behind her desk tapping away at her keyboard with unsurprising alertness at this early hour of eight-fifty-five. When I walk in, she springs up from her chair and closes the door behind me.

'Scarlett, we have a problem,' she announces walking over to my vintage charity shop desk that's on the other side of the room by the window. I stop pulling out my laptop from my bag and look to her so she can elaborate, but she's taking her time, chewing her nails. Her eyes are wide behind her giant spectacles, which finish off her signature hipster meets casual businesswoman look. Her cropped linen trousers and loosely fitted white tee look super chic but she isn't exuding her usual girl boss demeanour.

I don't like being kept in the dark or when people build up to bad news; I'd rather they just spit it out and get it over with before my mind runs away from me with all sorts of horrible possibilities. I immediately start thinking about Hope's mum and dad. They were healthy and happy last time I saw them, as was Jess, my other best friend. 'Hope, what is it?' I ask urgently.

'I've been trying to figure it out myself for some time but we're struggling, Scarlett. The magazine is struggling. With so much information online these days people aren't buying it. Even some of the villagers have cancelled their subscriptions and I don't know what to do, so I need all hands on deck. I need everyone's ideas, including yours,' she tells me, squeezing her hands together in a prayer-like position. I visibly let out a breath.

'Jeez, Hope, I thought something had happened to Jess,' I say and continue with my typical routine of switching on my laptop and getting comfortable at my desk.

'I didn't say anything had happened to Jess,' she says shaking her head at me, her brow furrowed. 'Scarlett, this is just as serious. I love this place; we can't lose it. It's not the same reading things on your phone – people need print. I'm panicking a little, but you can't tell anyone out there. We can keep up the positivity, but encourage new input,' she adds, pointing towards the door and to the office floor.

'We have some time to salvage this thing, but I'm aiming for a solid plan that can take us into the New Year.'

'Don't panic, of course I won't tell anyone you're worried. We will save it. The villagers won't want to see it crumble; they love this place too much, even if some of them have forgotten. We'll think of something. Why don't you come to mine tonight and we can put our heads together?' I suggest. It was never my dream to work at *The Village Gazette* but it's Hope's dream and she has done so much for this magazine as well as making my working here a hell of a lot better than it used to be. As far as jobs go, it isn't bad. I'd hate to think of what my mum would make me do if this place fell through. I like my job being Hope's assistant. I get to work with my best friend. Who wouldn't want that? But at one point in time I was a little girl who dared to dream, and that dream didn't include copy-editing, organising schedules and doing general assistant work.

Springhollow being such a small village, Hope and I had applied to work at the magazine right out of college at the ripe old age of eighteen. Hope had always dreamt of being a journalist and overseeing the magazine one day, whereas I loved spending time with Hope and thought maybe a job at our village's only magazine would appease both my creative aspirations and my mother. I could focus on sophisticated pieces of writing, report the news and leave my silly dreams to professionals more suited to it than me. However, my previous boss didn't quite take to my writing style, for some reason. I tended to add my own twist and inspiration when it came to facts and what was going on in our small village; that may have included the odd alien or magic power.

Giving me the top stories or putting me out in the field

was not on his agenda. I was better suited to making coffee and seeing to it that the photocopier never ran out of toner, is what I was told. I take a deep breath and open up my emails. It's better these days, I've gotten used to organising meetings, scheduling appointments and helping Hope assign writers to their suited articles.

Since landing our jobs here at *The Village Gazette*, Hope has worked her way up from editing other people's articles to becoming a manager, and she is a businesswoman to be reckoned with. I on the other hand have remained the coffee runner, only now I'm getting to do it for Hope and not Alfred, an older man who always wore a grey suit to match his grey hair, and didn't much care for my creative flair. So really, I could take that as a win, maybe even say it was somewhat of a promotion, right?

'Thanks, Scarlett. You're the best. We're just like Clark and Lois working at the *Daily Planet*,' Hope says as she goes to sit down. I choke on the strong scent of satsuma and feign a smile, but I'm happy to be of service and to see that she's smiling now. That's what best friends are for.

'Speaking of superheroes, will you come and watch the new DC movie with me tomorrow night? Jess was going to come but he can't make it now – he has to attend his office's Christmas do until late,' Hope says looking up from her screen. Usually the minute the clock strikes nine she turns into business Hope until lunchtime. She must be feeling shaken by the possibility of the magazine closing, given the fact she is still talking to me at nine-thirteen. I'm determined to help her save it. At her question, I scrunch up my nose and try to compose my words gently, so as to not let her down.

'I'm afraid I can't,' I say, with an apologetic nod, before trying to look busy pressing some keys in hope that she won't try and persuade me.

'Not one superhero movie in the ten years I've known you. Whatever will it take to bring you over to the dark side? Are Jess and I too nerdy for you? Can you not be seen out in public with us geeks?' Hope says, mock pouting and wiggling her eyebrows my way. She knows this isn't true. They are two of my favourite people and were a godsend in my life when I went to college.

I can feel a trickle of sweat on my top lip and pray that Hope hasn't noticed that too.

'You know how much I love you, both of you,' I say forcing a causal laugh. 'But Eddie has an appointment,' I blurt out. For someone who once loved spending every day on other planets and using every bit of their imagination, I'm horrified by my lame excuse and cross my fingers under my desk hoping that Hope somehow buys it. She looks up at me over her laptop with a smirk on her face.

'Should I be worried about you, Scarlett?' she asks, the smirk fading slightly as a look of concern flashes across her kind features.

'Why would you need to be worried about me?' I ask, turning away and trying to focus on an email from Billy in horoscopes.

'Oh, I don't know, I'm just trying to think of all the possible reasons or events that would require a goldfish to have an appointment and I'm struggling to think of one,' she says, waving a hand in the air casually, her lips curving into a grin again. If I wasn't sweating under the pressure of getting out of movie night, I would probably be laughing right now too at the absurdity of what I just said, but there's no turning back.

'Oh, it's OK, just a general check-up. Now, stop distracting me. We've got work to do if we're going to save this magazine,' I reply with confidence.

Hope hesitates for a moment, as if assessing me, then she gets right back to typing away at her laptop. My shoulders relax a couple of inches from my ears and inwardly I sigh with relief.

If I'm going to score the Christmas fair project and come up with a plan to save *The Village Gazette* I can't lose focus and be out watching superhero movies. I love Hope and I can't let all the work she has done here at the magazine be for nothing and see her dream fade, because leaving your best friend to go into battle alone is not something that I would ever consider doing.

2

The office is now deserted. The hum of the photocopier silent. The shuffling of paper has settled and only the odd creak of the old and rickety pipes can be heard as we walk down the stairs. It had been a super busy day, especially once Hope had informed everyone of the status of the magazine, minus the scary detail that we were on an incredibly tight schedule for a miracle to happen, but she hadn't wanted them to fret over losing their jobs so close to the holidays. I had been answering questions with unwavering positivity and was so busy listening to people's comments and views that I didn't even get chance to nip out for mine and Hope's usual lunchtime treat and afternoon coffee.

'I'm proud of us for getting through the afternoon without our afternoon pick-me-up.' I grin at Hope. It's just gone five-thirty and we're finally stepping out of the office and into the December evening. Our building sits around the edge of the village square so from my office window I can see the shops below: Mrs May's Sweet Shop, Duncan's Hairdressing, the post office, the library, Jenny's Boutique, Kelly's Pizzeria and the grocery stall. I have everything I could ever need around me.

The grass circle that stands in the centre of the square has to be my favourite part. With its gazebos and benches and decorations to match each season, I never tire from looking at it. Right now they are busy building and constructing the Christmas spectacle. It will soon be home to the most extravagant Christmas tree and lights will be strung up everywhere. I can't help grinning as I gaze over at it while Hope locks up. It is also wonderfully convenient that my walk to and from work requires us to go past Mr and Mrs Rolph's bakery, especially when Hope and I are having a little get-together, albeit the working kind. It certainly helps to have chocolate.

Rolphs' Bakery has been a staple in Springhollow since 1947 when Mrs Rolph's parents moved to the village from Italy. They bought an empty shell of a shop, very much a small hole in the wall and at first, they only served the freshest most mouth-watering bread. But as it started to grow, and they built up loyal customers, they began sharing all sorts of Italian delicacies with the village, delicacies that Mable and Jonathan still make to this day with many Springhollow originals of course, what with Mable having been born here and Jonathan's family being born and raised here too. Jonathan became something of an honorary Italian after marrying Mable and passing the bread-making test. Despite my run-ins with Mrs Rolph when I was a kid, she's lovely and one of a kind, as is her husband.

'I think missing out on our treat means we can make up for it now,' Hope says with an exaggerated wink as she links my arm and we fall into step. I'm not one for watching my weight. I take regular walks and hikes over the weekend and I don't care for the diet fads and trends that come through via email asking about sponsorship and spots in our magazine, but I am becoming increasingly aware of getting older, mostly thanks to my mum. My body has remained lean since I was a child. Being outdoors all the time – skateboarding and running around, jumping off everything in sight – had done my body good. But my mum likes to remind me that getting older means your body has a mind of its own. Skateboarding used to be my activity of choice, but I gave it up along with most of my childhood joys many moons ago. Plus the idea of being the only twenty-six-year-old shredding makes me feel stupid, and the last hiding place my mum had hidden my skateboard sure was a doozy as I'm yet to find it.

We duck inside the bakery and are greeted with the most heavenly scent of the last few gingerbread men and chocolate-covered doughnuts that look as though they have been waiting in the display case just for us. The small square-shaped shop is simply decorated with family photos hung up on the light cream walls, an old-fashioned wooden counter where an Italian flag and a British one hang proudly from the ceiling above and to the right stands a wooden shelving structure that houses packaged goodies. It's the cakes and bakes that take centre stage in this place. Mrs Rolph smiles when she looks up from cleaning the empty trays.

'Evening, Mrs Rolph,' Hope and I say in unison.

She stops what she's doing by the big sink and walks over to the counter. 'Evening, girls, what can I get you?' she asks sweetly but I can't respond. My heart feels like it has fallen out of its cage and landed with a thud on the ground and my hair feels like it's sticking to my hot cheeks. I blink a few times and swat at my face, wondering if I'm dreaming.

Behind Mrs Rolph on the bakery wall there is a poster, a poster of a man in red spandex wearing a white cape and gold boots. His brown hair is short and he's baring a goofy bright smile.

For a ridiculous moment I think he's the spitting image of Devon Wood, my childhood best friend. I pinch the skin on the back of my hand, fearing I'm hallucinating; it has been a long day. But my skin stings with my pinch and I snap my eyes away and shake my head.

'Thanks, Mrs Rolph,' Hope says cheerfully as the old lady places our box on the counter. Hope must have ordered while I was busy having an internal panic attack. I nod my head and pretend to tip my non-existent hat and mutter a thank you when Mrs Rolph narrows her eyes at me. Then a warm smile spreads across her face as she turns around to look at the poster and then back to me.

'Have you not seen it yet, Scarlett dear?' Mrs Rolph says.

'Seen what?' I retort. 'Let me help you with that box, Hope. I've got it,' I add, fumbling to take the box out of Hope's more stable and secure grip, while taking a few steps back.

'Our village has its very own superhero,' Mrs Rolph answers, causing Hope to squeal with glee and me to hiccup in horror at her confirmation that the man on the poster was not just an uncanny lookalike but Devon himself. Shoot, so he did it, he really did it; he became an actor. Well good for him. I try to get my face to display a cool, relaxed, unbothered look but can't be sure I'm nailing it because my eyebrows feel very close to my hairline and my cheeks are heating by the second.

'Oh, Mrs Rolph, that movie looks amazing. I can't

believe I live in the same village where Devon Wood grew up. Did you know that this movie is his big break? He's been relatively unknown until now. How lovely is that; to get your big break in a comic book franchise? Did you know him, Mrs Rolph? I'm going to see it on Wednesday night. I've been trying to get Scarlett to come with me but she's no fun,' Hope tells Mrs Rolph with all the excitement of my twelve-year-old self, but I have no time to get lost in what once was. We need to get out of here quick. Hope knows nothing of my vigilante days or of my childhood with Devon and I'd very much like to keep it that way.

'Know him, the whole town knew him. Mind you I do hope he has grown up a touch and stayed out of trouble. He was always up to no good with this—' Mrs Rolph starts to regale us with a mix of pride and distain.

'Would you look at the time. Phew, it's getting late and we have so much to think about and plan, what with the Christmas fair and saving the magazine,' I blurt out while shooting Mrs Rolph an offended look. Devon and I were not always getting into trouble, getting into casts and hospital beds was more like it while trying to hone our skills in order to save the people of Springhollow from impending danger. With my words Mrs Rolph's face softens and her wrinkles deepen.

'What did you say about saving the magazine? Is it in trouble? Johnathan and I are happy subscribers; we'd hate to see it struggling, Hope,' she says and I realise in my freaked-out state I just put my foot in it and let slip about the magazine's possible demise, though my words have effectively distracted her from memory lane. I continue backing towards the door bowing with the box, needing to escape before I do further damage. Hope is looking at me with a befuddled look on her face.

'No, don't be silly. It's in no trouble. How can it be in trouble with Hope at the helm? But be sure to keep subscribing. Please pass on our love to Mr Rolph and thank you for the treats,' I say and push open the door, allowing the cool wind to chill my heated cheeks.

'Thank you, Mrs Rolph, and please don't worry about us. It's just been a long day,' Hope shouts after me as she walks through the door. She links my arm again in hers and doesn't speak for a moment. We really do have so much to think about tonight. I wasn't lying when I said we have tons to plan. With only two weeks until the Christmas fair, I need to bring my idea to Hope. I don't want to think about the poster and what it means but it seems Hope has other ideas.

'I truly can't believe I'm friends with someone who hates superheroes and can't keep a secret.' Hope chuckles and tugs at my elbow as we turn onto my street. I shiver with a mixture of guilt and the frosty air. 'Can you believe Mrs Rolph knew that guy? Did you know him growing up?' Hope adds. I think I may have left my heart on the floor in the bakery, for where there should be a rhythm of healthy beats there is only a hollow feeling and a complete sense of dread about lying again to my best friend.

'I can keep a secret just fine and she's none the wiser about the magazine. I recovered,' I say, crossing my toes and hoping that's true, and that Mrs Rolph will not spread any rumours about the magazine, which would only put more pressure on Hope. 'And err, nope, no, no not really. Our paths never crossed; he was one of the popular kids at school.' My eye twitches. I try a casual shrug to loosen my shoulders. Devon was far from popular; he was a nerd just like I had been.

'You know I was thinking,' I start as I open my gate and walk up my path, really wanting to enjoy the evening with my best friend and not talk about village heroes, 'that we should use this year's Christmas fair as a way of raising money for the magazine. Maybe we split the sales of a raffle or think of a fun way of enticing people to subscribe again. We could maybe even get some ideas going in the build-up, have some festive activities going on before it. I haven't quite sussed it all out in my head yet, but things are brewing and that way if we keep things fun the villagers don't necessarily need to know about us struggling,' I say with a smile, genuinely getting excited. Tying the fair and saving the magazine together might alleviate some of the pressure. Christmas is my favourite time of year. I love the Christmas fair because it is the one time of year when my creativity is actually needed, and I can indulge in all the crafts my heart desires away from my cramped and secret spare room.

For the past three years Hope has let me oversee our stall at the Springhollow fair and once the paint, glitter, sweets, and fondant come out, I'm a different person, like a fire has been lit in my belly. I can make this work.

'That sounds great,' Hope says matching my excitement as we enter the warmth of my house and shiver out of our boots and jackets. 'I can't wait. You always come up with the most crafty, bespoke and festive ideas. Sometimes I feel your talent is wasted being my personal assistant. Are you sure you wouldn't prefer being an artist, craftsperson, or something?' Hope's face suddenly goes from cheerful to sombre as she thinks about my career choices. She says this every Christmas and every year it makes me blink nervously.

'Don't be silly. This year will be the best year yet and the most important,' I say chirpily and hurriedly changing the subject from where my talents lie. I don't enjoy conversations about careers. While I appreciate that Hope sees and likes my crafts when it comes to the holidays, the "what do you want to be when you grow up" discussions only bring back hurtful memories, as I heard it enough from my mum when I was younger. Apparently, girls don't write comic books or spend their time drawing aliens and otherworldly creatures. They needed proper jobs.

My plans of leaving school at sixteen and becoming an illustrator had been well and truly flattened when I broke my arm, fractured my hand and Devon had left. I was angry. I boxed up every toy, every pencil, every remnant from our childhood and spent the Christmas moping around in my pyjamas, going to hospital appointments and rowing with my mum. I didn't want to do anything and totally failed my GCSEs as a result. I had no plans to go to college, not without Devon by my side, but my mother had other ideas. If I didn't go to college and retake my Maths and English, I would be required to work with my mum at the hair salon. I went to college.

As it turns out, it wasn't half bad, so long as I stuck with Jess and Hope who I met and instantly clicked with during the induction day. And though I was done with any notion of wanting to write superhero comics, I still loved creative writing and aced English in the end.

'I love my job and I wouldn't want to be doing anything

else,' I say as Hope walks into the living room. My mouth goes dry as the words leave my lips, but it's not entirely untrue. Like I said before, I do like my job; I mean I love my boss. Sure, it's not my dream job but then who actually worked their dream job? A vision of Devon in a white cape flashes across my mind as I hang up my coat.

'Hey, Eddie,' I hear Hope gush from the living room, which snaps me out of my thoughts. 'I hear you have an appointment on Wednesday. I didn't know goldfish got check-ups. I think it might be Scarlett who needs one, Ed.'

'I heard that,' I say, bringing in the treats and making myself comfortable on the couch.

Hope shoots me an innocent smile. 'There's something going on with you. I don't know what it is yet, but I don't believe it's got anything to do with outings with your goldfish. Are you lonely? Do we need to get you dating again? Or is it the magazine? I promise I'm not about to make anyone redundant. We've got a bit of time to pull something together – I'm sure of it,' Hope says, grabbing a cushion and hugging it.

'I'm not lonely. How can I be lonely when I have Ed here? And I believe in us. We can and we will save the magazine. Now, stop the doom and gloom. I'll plate up the snacks; you grab the notebooks and turn on the Christmas lights please,' I say before walking into the kitchen and throwing cold water on my face from the sink, still feeling a little shaken by the poster back at the bakery and with the stress of wanting to do my best for Hope.

My nerves disappear when I re-enter my living room and it's basking in twinkling Christmas lights. It is fully festive now. Hope and Jess helped me decorate two weekends ago.

We like to decorate at the end of November so that we can wake up on the first of December to Christmas lights and the first day of our chocolate Advent calendars. It's our tradition. Each year since we moved into our houses, we spend a full festive day at Hope and Jess's doing their house and decorating their tree and the next day we spend at mine transforming it into a cosy Christmas wonderland. My tree stands to the left of my fireplace by the small rectangular window. It's beautiful when the snow begins to fall outside, and the gold lights bounce off the glass. My couch is covered in Christmas throws and blankets, all homemade – some I have stitched myself, others made by our town's seamstress.

Even in the British summer my couch is littered with blankets and throws of every design and softness. Hope wraps herself up in a deep woollen navy throw with sparkling light blue snowflakes cross-stitched into it; this one I helped make at the Springhollow craft fair a few autumns ago and it remains a favourite of mine. I place the snacks and hot chocolate on the table.

'They look so much better than the protein snacks I've been researching this week,' Hope notes, reaching for a doughnut. I take a seat next to her and pick up a notebook.

'How's that going? And is this why you've been trying to figure out social media? Because the magazine is struggling? You should have told me sooner,' I say. Like me, Hope isn't a huge fan of technology; however, recently with work she has been trying to keep up with what is going on in the media in order to keep our magazine interesting and inform the people of Springhollow what is going on in the world around us – or at least that's what she had told me. She and Jess do get their weekly emails for the daily gossip in the comic book world, though Hope much prefers the subscriptions and newsletters that you can get in the post, so she's a little more knowledgeable about the internet than I am.

These little nuggets of social media have only been a small part and new addition to the magazine, but like with anything to do with her job, Hope takes it seriously. This month she has been diving headfirst into the world of media influencers. What that means I have no idea, but she wanted to add a feature for the younger generation, hoping to draw them to the magazine with things that they could relate to. Now I know why she has been taking it so seriously.

'I made these brownies with avocados that I saw an influencer post the other day and it was a giant no-no. I do not believe avocados should ever be cooked, baked, fried or served hot,' she says with a grimace, sticking out her tongue for good measure, then she takes a huge bite from one of Mrs Rolph's scrumptious doughnuts. 'Plus, I can't bake nearly half as well as Mr and Mrs Rolph, so I think I'm going to leave that one up to them. And I'm sorry I didn't tell you sooner. I didn't want to worry you with everything going on with the fair,' she adds. I give an "Mmmm" in agreement through my own mouthful of chocolatey goodness.

Suddenly, I reach out for a napkin and grab the pen and notebook. Talking about recipes has given me an idea.

'What if we collaborate with the baking competition? The winning recipe each week gets featured in the magazine and to enter you have to pay a pound. It adds an extra something exciting for the winner. We can ask Mr and Mrs Rolph if it's something they would be interested in offering,' I waffle to Hope, not having thought it through entirely but immediately thinking of the community spirit everyone shares each week. We might not raise a whole heap of money, but it would still be something. 'And I'm putting forth my idea for the stall, right now,' I say waving my hands in the air and crossing my toes. 'I'm thinking a giant gingerbread-building competition and tons of cookies for everyone to decorate,' I finish clapping my hands together.

'I love it,' Hope expresses, sitting up and reaching for her hot chocolate. 'I really love it. I mean I'll have to see what the others have come up with but you're winning right now,' she says with a cheeky grin.

We spend the next two hours on a sugar high from the doughnuts, gingerbread and hot chocolate, writing down, scratching out and scribbling good and bad ideas in our notebooks before Hope heads home around nine, leaving me and Eddie to sketch out a plan for the main stall. When I can focus on Christmas and avoid drawing any caped crusaders, drawing relaxes me.

3

I can't quite believe it's Friday. Tuesday evening saw me popping by my mum and dad's house to stock up their fridge with the usual essentials of milk, bread and eggs with them due back from their annual Christmas holiday next week. I escaped going to the movies with Hope on Wednesday. She had told me to try and make it after Eddie's appointment, but I genuinely lost track of time delivering some more food to my parents' house and then I'd gotten distracted by wandering across to the park. After three laps of the gorgeous paths and winding layout, I had made myself comfy on a bench, people-watching while drawing up my final design for the stall in all its gingerbread goodness.

Hope had informed me on Wednesday morning that my idea had won for the fourth consecutive year. It gave me a little buzz and something to feel proud of. But after I'd sat in the park for a while, I realised I had completely missed the movie's start time. Hope hadn't been too disappointed with my excuse due to its content and the fact that she had been way too distracted by how awesome the movie was anyway to care if I was there or not.

On Thursday evening I had purchased supplies for the fair and made a start on the stencils for my cookies and had fallen asleep on my notebook thinking of sustainable ways to keep *The Village Gazette* alive and kicking.

Now, I pull my beanie a little tighter over my ears as I lock up my front door. Today there is a frosty nip in the air, the wind letting me know that snow could be just around the corner. I love the snow and I love a cosy beanie, especially at this time of year. My snapbacks had made their way out of my wardrobe during my college years. No matter how much Hope stood up for me I quickly got fed up of the negative comments about my fashion sense and my mum's constant nagging that women don't wear caps and especially not backwards, but my beanies aren't going anywhere. Granted I'm wearing a light blue one with sparkly snowflakes on it that my mum bought for me, but at least this time she had acknowledged my love of beanies. Last year she had attempted to get me to wear some sort of French beret, telling me it looked sophisticated and demure. I am neither of those things, which displeases her greatly.

'You look beautiful, Hope,' my mum says as Hope and I walk into my house after college. I drop my bag on the kitchen table and look to my mum in shock.

'Mum, she's wearing a Star Wars tee,' I say, defiantly.

'Thank you, Mrs Davis,' Hope replies with a butter-wouldn't-melt smile.

'Oh, is that what that writing is. Well, it looks cute,' she adds, rubbing salt further into my wound.

'You won't let me wear graphic T-shirts,' I protest, choosing my words carefully. Hope doesn't know I have a hidden drawer of old superhero tees, for two reasons: one

being my mother and two because of ex best friends I don't wish to tell her about.

'But you never tuck them in or wear them with such delicate trousers. You're always trying to wear those ugly flares and boy cuts,' my mum argues. 'Can you please take your bag off the table,' she adds.

I roll my eyes and do as I'm told. I can't believe Hope has made her vintage Star Wars tee cool, not just to the girls at school, but to my mum as well. 'Don't worry, I'll pick up some more bits and pieces next time I'm out. You girls will be starting work soon – you will need to dress accordingly, Scarlett.'

I throw my bag over my shoulder and make for the stairs, feeling disgruntled. When Hope dresses in her vintage hippie way, she's stylish; when I do I receive funny looks and have to endure rants from my mother about growing up.

I'm not sure why I allow my mother to dress me. Our relationship has always been a little strained. Maybe I feel like it will make her like me more, either that or the guilt I have for ruining way too many frocks when I was a child has something to do with it. But really who in their right mind puts a six-year-old in white? And a six-year-old who loves skateboarding and eating mud pies for dinner at that?

And that is why I'm walking funny, sporting a stiff black A-line dress underneath my parka. The beautiful decorations that leap out from the village square distract me from the private disgruntled complaints about my mum that are going on in my head as I wobble along. A giant fir tree has replaced the autumn pumpkin patch in the middle of the green and the hay bales have been replaced by giant presents and a Santa sleigh. I can't help the grin that spreads across my face.

I walk past the library as Mrs Bride is opening up for the day and send her a wave. 'Morning, Mrs Bride,' I say loudly so she can hear me. She turns eighty-two next month and her hearing isn't what it used to be, but she turns around and smiles warmly.

'Hello, dear,' she says with a wave in return. 'Have you seen…' She starts to speak but is interrupted by Rex, Mr Thompson's dog, who barks his greeting at me and wags his tail at my feet. Mr Thompson is holding his lead from about four metres away, engaged in conversation with Elliot who's on his newspaper round. It takes a moment for him to notice where his dog has wandered and when he spots me, he chuckles and waves Elliot off on his bike so he can catch up with his dog.

'Morning, Scarlett, sorry about that. This fella is too fast for me these days.' He grins.

'Morning, Mr Thompson, and that's no trouble. I rather enjoy my morning cuddles,' I say, bending down with some difficulty, thanks to the cardboard-like dress, to scratch the adorable Jack Russell behind the ears.

'Hello, Mrs Bride,' Mr Thompson calls across the path as the old lady waves and ducks into the library.

'Well, I best get to work. Have a lovely day, you two, and thank you for the cuddles, Rex,' I say, feeling the festivity in the air as the weeks wind down towards Christmas. After the bumpy start to the week, today I feel like a new me. I have the Christmas fair to think about, my house smells consistently of gingerbread thanks to my baking, and I get to see my dad next week. I leave Mr Thompson and Rex to their walk and cross the green, taking in the sparkle of the larger-than-life presents and the twinkle of Santa's gold sleigh. I push open the door of Rolphs' Bakery and pass the aisle of freshly baked cakes when I notice a tall figure at the counter. My body freezes and goosebumps prickle my arms.

'Hold him still, D,' I demand as Mrs Rolph's cat is trying to scratch and claw at Devon's eyes.

'I'm trying, Scar, she doesn't like it,' D says his bottom lip pouting as he holds on to the cat for dear life so our plan doesn't fail.

'She'll love it when it's on properly. Hold still, Bonny, nearly done,' I say in a softer tone this time, trying to soothe the cat. I really want this to work but I also want D to keep his eyes too. 'OK, it's on.'

'Do I just let go?' D asks nervously.

'I think so,' I reply, peering over the scaffolding. We're not that high up – my dad won't let us climb higher than two planks.

'Do I just drop her?' D asks me like I have all the answers. I guess this was my idea; I suppose I should know what to do. But I thought Bonny would like it more. Her hissing is starting to freak me out.

'Maybe, or maybe we should put her on the ground first and let her jump,' I say undecided. Before D can give his thoughts on my lack of direction, Bonny shrieks and leaps out of his hands. She soars into the air, her cape floating up behind her, then lands on all fours on the dusty concrete. I stand with my mouth open in awe.

'Whoa, did you see that?' Devon exclaims, his eyes just as wide as mine.

'That was so cool,' I reply. 'Now it's our turn,' I add, grabbing D's hand.

'What?' Devon says aghast. His hand is clammy in mine.

'Oh, come on, D, it's not that high. If Bonny can do it, so can we.' My seven-year-old brain is determined. 'Together, after three. one, two, three...'

The till chimes and instantly knocks some sense into my head. I leap behind the largest cake stack and peer over the cherries on top of the Bakewells, carefully checking to see if the figure is still there.

Thankfully, he is still facing away from the shelves and is deep in conversation with Mr and Mrs Rolph. Really, I can't be certain that it is who I think it is by only looking at the back of his head. It's been ten years since he was in this village and we all know movie posters are Photoshopped. But so much for my morning coffee. There's no way I can move, just in case it is him. Do I race to the door now and pray he doesn't see me, or do I wait it out until he leaves? I wish my brain was more decisive sometimes.

Before I can make a decision, the man moves. My tongue immediately turns to sandpaper as I see his side profile. He has a strong jawline with rounded cheekbones and long eyelashes and there's no denying it. He still looks like my Devon but more manly and distinguished and big. I feel like Peggy Carter in that scene where Steve Rogers first comes out of the chamber. Wait, what am I even thinking? I gulp.

As he moves towards the door with a much more

confident stride than sixteen-year-old nerdy Devon, I move like a crab along the rows of packed bakes, ducking between the cinnamon rolls, stretching over the breadsticks and squatting down by the reindeer-shaped cookies, all so he doesn't see my face but so I can keep my eyes on him. What on earth is Devon Wood doing back in Springhollow?

When finally he disappears out the door, I exhale a shuddery breath, slowly stand and smack my hand against my chest. 'What was that all about?' I whisper angrily to my heart. I have spent the best part of ten years getting over my friendship with Devon Wood. As far as I'm concerned, we have nothing to say to each other. The village is big enough, sort of, kind of, that I can avoid him for however long he is here.

Oh gosh, how long is he going to be here? Has he moved back? He can't possibly be moving back, not if what Hope said the other night is true. Why would an actor move back to their tiny hometown after getting their big break? I'm no expert on Hollywood etiquette but that doesn't add up.

The smell of the cinnamon rolls snaps me out of my trance as someone rustles them to purchase a packet. I make eye contact with Trisha, one of my mum's friends, who eyes me suspiciously. I give her a closed-mouth grin. Right, new plan, I will just have to get my coffee from another coffee shop, from the village two miles out every morning, until I know our village is safe again, or I can just have coffee at work, the instant one that tastes, well, that tastes like instant coffee. I shudder and look around triple-checking the space before I move.

Mrs Rolph is staring at me with an amused expression on her face when I register I am still hovering by the breads. I nod, shake my head and quick-march to the door. No coffee, not even her peppermint coffee, is worth the questions I know she was about to ask.

I make it into work a good fifteen minutes late after using my best ninja-like manoeuvres to navigate the street corners, cross the green and walk past the shop windows, just in case Devon was inside one. My beanie has ensured that my hair is gorgeously matted with sweat and I know my cheeks are bright red from the cold wind and endurance needed to duck, dive and squat my way here, and because when I walk in to our office Hope looks at me with a worried expression, her eyebrows lowered, her eyes narrow.

'What happened to you?' she says pointing at the hair that has frizzed and waved around my beanie. I won't be taking it off today then.

'Oh nothing. My alarm didn't go off and I had to run back as I forgot to feed Ed and then I had to jog to get here,' I ramble, spewing whatever my brain thinks of on the spot. I muse for a moment that it isn't half bad.

'No coffee this morning?' she questions, looking a tad deflated, which makes me feel bad. We never miss a peppermint coffee from Mrs Rolph in December. If Hope knew that I had just had a near miss with an evil villain she would certainly be on my side, but I daren't bring up Devon; after all, in her eyes he is this badass superhero who she and Jess no doubt want to meet at the next Comic Con.

'I'm so sorry – the line was so long, and I was already running late. We can stop by after work, OK?' I say and Hope seems to buy my excuses as she waves off my verbal diarrhoea and starts jumping up and down. She gets in five jumps by the time I sit down at my desk. I'm relieved to not be further interrogated but I'm extremely confused by her lack of sophistication in the office. Her giddiness and happy dances are usually saved for out of work hours and when Marvel announce their next action flick.

'We have an interview this afternoon. I know it's last minute but I got the call this morning. I already know what I'm going to ask, but don't panic, I have the next few hours to research too and cross-check all my facts. Can you run through all the articles for the Christmas issue and double-check my ads and we can get it sent over before we leave?' Hope asks, while she moves side to side, from foot to foot. She's created enough air with her flapping hands that my cheeks are beginning to cool.

'Yes sure, no problem. Who's the all-important big celebrity that schedules interviews so last minute on Fridays?' I say sarcastically with a chuckle, knowing celebrities never pass through Springhollow and the last person Hope and I went to interview was Louis at the grocery stall for growing the largest courgette the village had ever seen – and even he had the courtesy to be interviewed on a Wednesday. But by the time Hope lands her sixth jump and the last word leaves my lips, my stomach hits the floor as I think back to the bakery. I want to take my joke back, either that or pray to the gods that the world has been flipped on its head and that growing the world's largest courgette now trumps being an actor or a musician. I will gladly interview Louis again, on a Friday morning, afternoon or evening. I'll even come in on a weekend, if Hope doesn't say the name I think she's going to say.

'Devon Wood. His publicist rang at seven this morning. I'm glad I got in early today,' she says before doing one more jump with an open-mouthed smile and going to sit at her desk. I momentarily forget my struggle to breathe as I take in the bags under Hope's eyes. She might be wearing a ridiculously wide grin and a dot of concealer, but I can see that my best friend is tired; her skin is grey with worry. She shouldn't have been in so early. She's going to run herself into the ground.

'Hope, what were you doing in so early? You need to rest. I told you not to worry about the magazine and I'm here to help with whatever you need, please don't wear yourself out. We don't want a repeat of last Christmas, do we?' I say sternly tilting my forehead to her.

'I'm not going to get sick. That was just the once. I promise, I plan on enjoying all the Christmas festivities with you and drinking all the hot chocolate and peppermint coffees this year,' Hope replies, grinning and then turning back to her screen. 'Now, get to work. I have important research to do.'

I sink back in my chair. 'About that, Hope, I'm really sorry but Eddie was looking a little green this morning. I might need to go home early and check on him,' I say, opening my eyes wide and mustering the saddest face I can.

'You just said you're here to help me. Think about it, Scarlett, this interview will be amazing for the magazine. It will be sure to give us a huge boost in sales. It's Devon Wood, back in his hometown, newest addition to the superhero franchise. It's going to fly off the shelves. It's just what we need for the first January issue of the New Year. We need this,' she says, looking over at me, her sorrowful face besting mine. Then she turns back to her work as I try and rack by brain for another casual excuse. 'And besides, that goldfish has had more check-ups than you. I think he's healthier than the two of us combined,' she adds, not taking her eyes off her screen.

Touché, I think to myself while trying not to sulk and draw attention to the situation. It's no big deal. It's just two professionals going to interview another professional. That's all, there's nothing to it.

'Wait, Devon wasn't a part of the group of popular kids who bullied you in high school was he, Scarlett?' Hope suddenly pipes up. It's nearing ten o'clock now and the fact that Hope is still talking makes this morning all around unsettling in every way.

'Oh God no,' is all I can manage. No, Devon wasn't anything like the kids who bullied me. He was the exact opposite and would never hurt me. Well up until the point where he did hurt me, big time, I think to myself.

'OK good,' Hope replies. 'Because gorgeous celebrity superhero or not, if he ever hurt you, I'd kick his ass.'

4

I'm hoping there were no grammar mistakes or missing articles when I sent the magazine to print only ten minutes ago. I've spent the morning and the whole walk over to the village pub contemplating which headline would be more exciting and sell the most copies. The one that reads: 'Superhero Devon Wood is no match for tiny villager who attacked him standing up for her best friend' or whatever happy headline about Devon's homecoming Hope is thinking about for the first January issue.

I choose the latter and think better of divulging my entire childhood to Hope right at this moment. It's for the best. All we have to do is go in, ask a few questions and come out, and then my world can return to normal. I shuffle behind Hope into the pub. It looks stunning this time of year with its beautiful stone fireplace, pine-cone-decorated large plump Christmas tree off in the corner, and tinsel dangling from every beam, except the man in a black suit bearing sunglasses and an earpiece throws off the feng shui a tad. He's standing guard to the party room at the back of the pub.

*

'Oh, now this is sad. I thought you had some friends, but it turns out it really was just Devon who put up with your weirdo vibes,' Ruby says with a cackle as she waves a delicate hand up and down my frame, to the delight of her posse. Devon has been gone for two days and I can't say Ruby's wrong; I don't know how to speak to people without him taking the lead in his nerdy chatterbox way.

'Whatever, Ruby,' I mumble, pushing past her with my head down.

'What is that smell?' she exclaims, holding her nose, which her gang copy through their sniggers. She spins on her heel to face me as I try and walk down the corridor to get away from her. 'You might need to get that cast cleaned; you smell like a sweaty farm animal,' she calls after me. Their howling reverberates off the cold school walls.

She's not wrong there either. It's hard to maintain cleanliness when your armpit down to your fingertips is covered in plaster and the anxiety over coming to school each day for the next six months without your body armour is making you sweat.

I nervously pat down my beanie and stray hairs and casually try to check if I smell funky or if I'm sweating through my too-tight dress when a smart lady in a black pant suit ushers us over to the door of the party room. I nod at the suit-wearing man, but he keeps his position looking straight ahead. The usual long oak table that takes centre stage in the middle of the room is pushed up to one side and has been replaced by spotlights and cameras dotted around, in addition to a wall of green screens.

It takes a second for my eyes to adjust to the dim light. On my third blink I register the posters dangling from the ceiling. There's the same one Mrs Rolph had up at the bakery, but twice the size, as well as different prints that are pinned to the walls – walls that once held pictures of Devon and I for our tenth birthday party – but on these posters I am nowhere to be seen. It's just Devon's face staring back at me. Something flutters in my belly.

Hope nudges me forwards but I struggle to take my eyes off the colourful prints and with one step trip over a cable taped to the floor and promptly fly into a life-size cut-out of my former best friend. Is it just me or is the air getting thin in here? I can feel my forehead sweating under my beanie but I'm too frozen stiff to remove it.

I feel like the sweat is leaking out of me in buckets. Before I can plan my escape route another lady in a straight black dress, like mine, though I'm positive she chose to wear it, unlike me, and a man in cargo shorts holding a clipboard come over.

'Can we have you both sign these forms please? We're doing a documentary on Devon Wood, so we're going to be filming segments of the interviews today. We will credit your magazine for any footage of you we use,' the lady informs us authoritatively, while the man passes us the clipboards.

My ears are ringing, and I fear that everyone is going to hear the mad flapping of wings with the number of butterflies I have in my stomach. Hope is grinning broadly. I can see the cogs ticking in her brain over how much of a big deal this is for our small-time magazine. I bite my tongue and steady my breathing. I can do this, for Hope.

Once the forms are signed. I place my bag down and tell

myself that it's like any other day at the office, just another man and his enormous courgette, as we are signalled towards the spotlight, where there are four cameras all facing the back wall. I walk behind Hope who turns around just before we reach the neon platform, gives me an evil glare and swipes my beanie off my head, throwing it off to the side. Distracted by the sweep of hair that falls in my face in a mess of static, mixed with the blinding, uncomfortable light, I trip up for the second time over more of the cables that litter the floor and perform a spectacular dive that results in me headbutting my ex BFF in the chest, when he leaps out of the chair to catch me.

Hope lets out a gasp. I take a sharp intake of breath. When did Devon's chest get so hard? I'm bent over now gazing at his lower half and immediately regret telling myself to think of courgettes. I blink and toy with the idea of looking up. Do I have to? But my forehead is throbbing.

When I go to rub my bruised noggin, I realise Devon's hands are gripping my shoulders. My arms freeze in a way that makes it look like I'm about to perform the robot. I sense he's trying to keep me from further damaging him, myself or any one of the very expensive-looking cameras that surround me. It takes me a minute before I finally surrender to the fact that I must look up. It takes me a further minute to meet Devon's gaze – I don't remember Devon being this tall – but when I do I feel as though I have been transported back ten years, looking into the eyes of my sidekick, my partner in crime, my best friend who was supposed to be with me through it all, but wasn't.

Emotion bubbles up inside of me. I feel like a kid again.

I feel joy mixed with anger and pain and it's a dangerous combination.

Suddenly Hope springs from her chair. 'Are you OK?' she asks. The question isn't aimed at me but at Devon. It breaks the spell and I stand up straight, brush my hair from my face, smooth down my dress, hold my head high and elegantly take a seat in the chair next to Hope's. Devon's eyes shoot to Hope as he clears his throat and gives her a disarming smile with a small nod. He waves our little incident off and encourages her to sit back down, but I notice his cheeks are flushed and then he gives me a strange look.

'Is everyone OK?' the lady from earlier asks, the cameramen are all staring, opened-mouthed in shock.

'Yes, yes, everything's fine,' Devon announces with a chuckle, keeping his eyes trained on mine. Hope is breathing rather heavily beside me, but I can't bring myself to look at her, fearing the whole "if looks could kill" scenario. That and it's hard to take my eyes off Devon. He has the same deep brown eyes as my former best friend, the same lips and goofy smile, but he seems different and his gaze is intense.

'Is this clean?' I ask D as I pick up a T-shirt that's crumpled up on his bed.

'It sure is,' he replies, not looking up from his Ant-Man comic to even consider what shirt I am enquiring about.

'Do we really have to go to this thing?' I ask, my voice coming out in a whine as I disappear into Devon's cupboard to replace my tighter girls' Thor tee with his baggier Superman one.

'My mum says we need to make an effort and that it will be fun,' D informs me, putting down his comic.

'What will be fun about hanging out at Ruby's house and celebrating all things Ruby turning sixteen?' I groan, tucking my hair behind my ear, then untucking it again when I see Devon staring at me as I emerge from the cupboard. 'What?' I say suddenly feeling awkward under his gaze. I sit down on the edge of his bed to flick through a comic book that lies open on top of the covers.

'Nothing, you just look cute,' Devon says and promptly turns the shade of Superman's cape. Then he clears his throat. 'I mean, are you not going to wear a dress or something?'

I fear my glare might burn a hole in the comic strip. My cheeks are on fire. I concentrate on the tiny words on the page for a moment before clearing my own throat and jumping off the bed. 'We best go.'

We charge past each other to see who can get through the door first – some childhood competitions will never die. 'Oh, and I'll wear a dress the day you wear a suit,' I add, shoving Devon as we exit his bedroom, me winning as I get my foot on the landing first.

I hear my name in a hushed, annoyed whisper and turn to Hope. Out of the corner of my eye I see Devon retract his hand, bringing it to his chin. He props an elbow up on the edge of his chair, a finger resting over his lips. He looks over my dress for a moment before turning his attention to Hope. Did I just miss handshakes? *Concentrate, Scarlett,* I scold myself, *you're doing this for Hope.*

Hope shuffles her papers and goes through her usual

spiel of "Thank you for sitting down today with *The Village Gazette*; we're thrilled to have you," before asking a bunch of questions about Devon's work. Devon responds politely, his answers charming, humble and rather sophisticated. There are no hand gestures or fast-talking, occasional high-pitched tone or nervous deep laugh. He's not the Devon I knew. Hope is beaming as bright as the spotlights that are starting to give me a headache, but I sit up straight, doing a pretty spot-on impression of one of those nodding dogs you see in the back of cars.

I ignore the urge to reach out and ruffle Devon's short hair, which looks like it's sporting gel or hairspray as it's not moving, just to see if the man before me is real, as I listen to Devon's next answer. His excitement over realising his dream of being a superhero comes through in his megawatt smile and my heart begins to hammer at a very painful speed. It's hard not to be drawn in by his joy and the positivity that radiates off him, but my gosh if it doesn't hurt.

They discuss every single detail about Devon's spandex-clad bod, his workout routine, and the awesomeness of his cape, while I silently applaud Hope for asking such great questions. She really is a natural at these interviews and knows the perfect questions to ask. I think she's right: this article will no doubt do our small magazine wonders. It's hard not to get washed away by all the movie buzz and behind-the-scenes sneak peeks that Devon is giving us.

I find myself drifting in and out of the past and present, excitement zipping through my veins when it hits me that Devon is a part of one of the movie franchises we used to watch growing up. Hope's passion has created this relaxed and safe space and I wonder if this, if the three of us sat chatting like this, would have made the rest of high school and college a happier experience for me. With that thought a pain pierces my chest, slicing through any daydream of what could have been and reminding me of what is and what was.

'So, Devon, you grew up here in Springhollow and moved to New York when you were sixteen. What was your childhood like?' Hope asks in her confident and velvety voice, surprising me with this much more personal question. The topic of superheroes, though a part of me secretly loved hearing about it all, was painful enough.

Devon's eyes glance over at me for the first time in over twenty minutes and for the first time in ten years I feel as though someone is looking at me, like really looking at me, but I feel like a fraud. I'm wearing a dress my mum bought for me and the days of knowing every move a superhero makes are long since behind me, and I have no idea who this suave and well-dressed man in front of me is. We've finished talking about superheroes now; surely we can leave. I shift uncomfortably in my chair and tug at the hemline of the stiff dress. Why isn't he as sweaty and awkward as I am?

I try to cross one leg over the other, suddenly feeling inadequate sandwiched between my glamorous best friend and refined ex best friend. I interlace my fingers over my knee. My back has gone surfboard straight. 'Did you have a rough childhood, Mr Wood? Did our lovely town here suffocate you, threaten to hinder your talents; your need for big and better opportunities sending you on your way?' The questions tumble out without my consent and very much without Hope's. I hear her gulp beside me. I barely recognise the tight and angry tone in my own voice. Who knew I could be so mean? But I'm starting to feel extremely off-kilter and claustrophobic with Hope's change in direction, though I know I've just made it worse. I glare at Devon, struggling to keep the light smile on my face.

He meets my gaze and that blush creeps back into his cheeks, then he checks his watch. A stir of anger swishes around in my belly. A moment ago, I wanted to get out of here, but for some reason now I've asked the questions, I want answers. I want to hear the painful truths even if it's only going to hurt me more. Him checking his watch and wanting to run makes me clench my fists.

Hope lets out a nervous giggle and attempts a subtle elbow to my bicep. It stings but I ignore it, waiting for Devon's answer.

'You would be right, Hope. I lived in a house opposite the park, which was where I spent most of my days, playing superhero. I loved it here. I was sixteen, yes, when my parents decided to move to Long Island,' Devon answers smoothly, taking his eyes off me and giving his full attention back to Hope. He completely ignores my questions and that only makes the rustles of anger in my stomach grow.

'It's such a beautiful park. Do you miss Springhollow? Did you miss it when you were a kid, or did New York instantly win you over?' Hope asks, her tone keen and interested.

Devon's lips purse. He does that thing again where he brushes his knuckles over his pout indicating he's thinking. He used to do the same thing when we were teenagers when he was deep in scheming our next stunt.

'Our town seems rather dull in comparison to the bright lights and glam of New York, wouldn't you agree? I mean you've been gone for ten years. I'm sure New York had everything you ever needed. You had no reason to look back, I assume?' I ask, my voice hard. I receive another elbow from Hope for my input, which hurts worse the second time – I will definitely have a bruise there in the morning – but this time Devon doesn't look at me. His eyes stay trained on Hope's.

'I do, I miss it very much and I missed it back then too, but New York certainly has a magic to it that pulls you in,' Devon responds before making a subtle swirling motion with his hand that I take to mean "can we wrap this up?" because as soon as he does this the man behind the camera makes a hand gesture to Hope, which Hope registers, shuffles her papers and launches into her closing monologue.

'Well, thank you so much for talking with us today, Devon. Good luck with your movie and we hope you can enjoy some of the magic Springhollow has to offer, for old time's sake, during your stay.'

What was that? Do people now just bow down to Devon's every whim? He didn't answer all our questions and I know for a fact his parents brought him up better than that. How rude. People rustle over, unclipping microphones and praising Devon for his answers.

'You did great.'

'Perfect, warm, charming – the village will eat it up.'

I'm gobsmacked.

The minute I'm relieved of my tiny microphone I jump out of my chair. The lady with the clipboard pulls Hope aside with nothing but compliments and I move away quickly from the spotlight. As I bend down to pick up my beanie from where Hope threw it, a shadow looms over me.

'You're wearing a dress,' Devon says softly.

His words catch me off guard and for all the frustration, confusion, and heat coursing through my body, I freeze. I turn around, coming face to chest. I forget that now I have raise my gaze to the heavens if I want to look Devon in the eye.

'No sh...' I go to say but Devon is waving his hands over his suit and there's something different in his smile that wasn't there in front of the cameras. Then my brain clicks. He remembered.

'And you're wearing a suit,' I reply, stammering over my words. He's wearing slim grey trousers and a grey blazer over a white shirt. It's fitted and shows he has filled out. Something flutters in my belly and I hurriedly look away as someone shouts to Devon before bustling over and tugging at his arm to try and take him away, taking no notice or bother of me or the fact that we might have been talking. I'm reminded of my irritation and the fact that Devon is no longer the boy I once knew.

'I'm not a fan of suits,' I say quickly and quietly and turn to secure my bag. I rush to the door, exit the party room and wait for Hope at the bar. The air in the pub feels a lot less stuffy than in the back room and my shoulders instantly uncurl.

'Just like old times, huh?' I look up from staring at my feet and see Ryan leaning on the bar, a rag over his shoulder and a grin on his clean-shaven boyish face. Ryan went to the same primary school and high school as Devon and me. His family own this pub so he always knew he would take over one day, having helped here since he was old enough. He's the kind of cool guy who got on with everyone back in school. He was even nice to me and Devon, though we had nothing in common and the other popular kids liked to tease us. He didn't exactly stand up for us, but he never joined in.

'Something like that,' I mumble.

'I have to admit I used to think you guys were a little geeky, but I give credit where credit's due – your man's made a name for himself,' Ryan says, with a cool chuckle and a contemplative tilt of his head. 'Who would have thought? Hollywood,' he adds, shaking his head in disbelief.

I'm about to argue that Devon is not my boy, my dude nor my friend and certainly not my man, when Hope bursts from the room, looking like a Christmas angel, her eyes starry, happiness radiating off her and like she has an aura of white light surrounding her. I blink. 'What took you so long?' I ask, agitated. She turns to wave at Ryan and links my arm, finally guiding us out of the pub and into the refreshing air.

'Devon just wanted to thank me again and ask a few questions of his own,' she says like Christmas has come early. I feared she was going to be mad at me for my outbursts and butting in but she's walking with such a giddy spring in her step that I'm struggling to keep up. 'I have to go and tell Jess everything,' she exclaims when her road comes up. She lives on the street before the bakery while I live on the street after it.

'OK, have fun,' I say, as she hugs and kisses me quickly and dashes down her street, making me think I got away with my high-brow interview input.

'We'll talk on Monday about your interview etiquette,' she shouts as I watch her run up her path. Shoot, maybe not.

'Sounds good,' I shout back before walking the short distance to my house, feeling grateful that goldfish can't talk because I have a giant headache.

5

I pull my duvet off my head, grateful that it's Saturday and I have nowhere to be. The sky outside is a hazy light blue with a grey tinge and I cross my fingers for snow. It's been years since we had a white Christmas. I glance at my alarm clock: six-thirty. I mustn't stay in bed for too long as today I have to bake. What I'm planning is shaping up to be quite the task and, so far, I've only made a small dent. I wriggle and do a happy horizontal dance at the thought of filling my house with the smell of gingerbread and spending the day in my winter wonderland with nothing but Christmas on my mind. The bitter taste that yesterday left on my tongue shall be washed away with a homemade iced peppermint latte and some Christmas tunes.

A hammering on my front door startles me, disrupting my leisurely state as I shoot upright and my heart rate spikes. Who on earth is making such a racket this early on a Saturday? The hammering is growing louder and incessant and fear floods my whole body. Has something happened to Hope or Jess? Oh God, my parents, when did they say they were they flying home? Planes make me nervous.

I clamber out of my cosy king bed and cross my bedroom in two strides. My bedroom is my favourite room in my house. It consists of my giant bed and that's pretty much it – well that and potted cacti plants in each corner and hundreds of hand-sewn and stitched cushions and pillows, a few throws and a couple of candles adorning my window ledge. It's my safe place, my haven, and I adore it, but the knocking is throwing off its usual calming ambience.

I bolt down the stairs to the door as fast as I can, my cool wooden floorboards chilling my feet with every step.

The knocking isn't relenting so I shout, 'I'm coming, I'm coming,' before opening the door mid-sentence, 'Hope, is everything al…' My voice trails off when I clock that it's not Hope or Jess stood at my door but all six foot four inches of Devon Wood, new Hollywood heartthrob, celebrity, superhero and my former best friend.

I tense from my shoulders down to my toes. My eyes simply cannot get used to seeing Devon dressed in tailored trousers, which are a deep grey and black gingham this morning, and a fitted blazer to match. He fills my doorframe. I know for sure I am doing a fine impression of a howler monkey. I can't close my mouth. What's wrong with me?

'Sup?' Devon says, in a dorky, awkward way, his shoulders hunching a little as he breaks the silence.

I snap my mouth shut and shake my head. I used to hear those words every day from a nerdy, hoodie-wearing boy, with wavy hair and enough energy for the both of us. The words don't match the mature, cool man in front of me.

'What are you doing here?' I manage, as the wind whips around me and chills my lungs.

'Hope gave me your address and I had to see you,' Devon replies, with a touch less chill and sophistication in his tone than he had yesterday. He crosses his arms over his chest making his blazer strain against his biceps. I had been praying for snow this morning. He looks cold and my legs feel as though they have turned to icicles with the door wide open.

I shakily step aside and gesture for him to come in. He hesitates slightly then moves his eyes away from mine, looking ahead like he's nervous, before stepping into the hallway. My hand trembles as I close the door behind me while Devon takes his shoes off.

Once he's placed them neatly by my shoes, I lead him into the living room. It's still relatively dark so I walk over to the coffee table and turn on the lamp before walking over to my Christmas tree and turning it on too.

'When I'm big, I'm going to buy all the awesome superhero ornaments in the shops that my mum never lets me buy,' I tell Devon as we sit at the base of my tree and ogle the presents underneath it, trying to guess what they are with our x-ray vision.

'Me too. When we have our own house, it will be so cool. No one will tell us what to do. Our Christmas tree will be the best,' Devon replies, flicking an ordinary gold bauble with his finger and watching it sway on the branch. My mum likes her tree elegant and themed; it's always all gold and silver, and it's rare that she lets my sticky six-year-old fingers help decorate it.

I absent-mindedly graze my fingertips over a plain silver bauble before turning to look at Devon. Strangely enough, something about him and his broad frame making my modest living room seem tiny makes me feel like all is right with the world once more. He adds something to my colourful, clean space but I'm not exactly sure what.

'What was all that about yesterday, Scar?' he asks, interrupting my thoughts. The only person who has called me "Scar" in the last ten years has been my dad. I move to the couch and take a seat, picking up a cushion and cuddling it to my chest as I tuck my feet up underneath myself in need of comfort and security. I don't feel Ed would appreciate me scooping him out of his bowl for cuddles.

'What was all what about?' I retort, with a whole mix of stubbornness and fake innocence. If he's referring to my outburst of questions, I stand by that I had every right to ask them.

Devon stays put, standing by my coffee table, his brown eyes wide, glaring at me.

'It was a professional interview with cameras present and media personnel. You can't do that,' he explains, a hardness to his voice that I'm not accustomed to hearing from him.

'I'm very sorry that I embarrassed you in front of a room full of people. I have absolutely no idea what that feels like,' I say, my voice coming out a little higher, with sarcastic undertones, as memories of high school come flooding back. I squeeze my cushion tighter.

'What do you mean? I've never embarrassed you.' Devon's voice comes out softer; concern flashes across his face. In one stride he's sat on the couch next to me. I kick my feet out from underneath myself.

'Really, D? You think that when you left, high school became a delightful paradise and all of a sudden Ruby took pity on me and her days of embarrassing me were magically over?' I scoff, looking over to my tree. The headache from last night that I had managed to cure this morning with wonderful Christmassy thoughts is returning.

'I don't know,' he replies, slowly. The care in his voice irks me. I focus on the glittering tinsel. 'I just thought, maybe with growing up…' he starts.

I turn back to look at him. 'What? That they'd all just snap out of it, be nice to me and accept me?' I enquire, gripping the cushion tighter still, trying to resist the urge to whack Devon across the head with it. I don't think the new and mature Devon would appreciate that, though the urge is terrifyingly strong.

'People can change,' he offers in return; his hands look as though they are about to reach out and touch my knees before he thinks better of it and retracts them. I let out a breath that had apparently got stuck as I watched his movement. I shrug, not having a response to that. Thanks to the man before me, I'm not all that keen on change. While yes, the idea of Ruby changing overnight into someone whose main objection in life was not to make fun of me would have been pretty swell, I'd have preferred some things to have simply stayed the same, like my protection and sidekick not up and deserting me.

'You seem like you've done well for yourself though. You work at the magazine – that's cool. Are you drawing for them? I've kept an eye out for your comics, but I wasn't sure if you'd changed your name. Do you have a pen name?' With each question Devon asks, I get a glimpse of the old, enthusiastic Devon, who loves to talk and often does so with his hands. It's unnerving. It can't be this simple; opening up, chatting as if we were still sixteen, skirting over the fact that our lives are now worlds apart and have been for ten years. Am I supposed to just fill in the blanks and forget the past?

'D, I can't do this. Congratulations on your movie, on your life. I'm so happy it's all worked out for you. I really am, but you left,' I say, standing up and making towards the living room door. 'You left and we're different people now,' I add, as I get to the door. Him thinking that my life turned out exactly as I had planned makes the disappointment I have in myself stir in my gut; it's extremely unpleasant.

'You never wrote back,' Devon says, his words coming out quiet and vulnerable, making something twinge in my heart. I stop moving and go to retaliate, to make an excuse. He's the one who hurt me, who lied and didn't tell me he was leaving, but I come up empty. It had been too hard. I didn't want to be pen pals; I wanted him with me. I couldn't skateboard, deal with the school bullies or go to parties with a pen pal.

'It was easier that way,' I mumble, barely audible, not quite believing myself. Had it really been easier living a life pretending that Devon didn't exist? No superheroes. No comic books. Had it all been worth it? If life had been better without him then why did I still think about him? Why did I struggle every year on the anniversary of his departure?

'Easier?' he scoffs. 'Easier, for who?' D murmurs. I don't turn around; his voice sounds so defeated and hurt and it's all because of me.

'I'm going to make coffee,' I splutter and shuffle into the kitchen. My familiar friend guilt is back. When I was sixteen, I hadn't thought about how hard it would have been for Devon to leave. All I had heard was great opportunity this, fantastic opportunity that, and that New York had the most amazing schools. I didn't listen to Devon saying he would miss me. I skimmed over the part in the letter where he talked about visiting. All I knew was that the person who had been by my side for sixteen years wasn't by my side anymore and that it was painful, for me. He had hurt me.

'Sssh, just don't tell her, Scar,' D pleads in a whisper.

'She's going to ask where your pocket money went and what am I supposed to say to my mum now?' I ask, annoyed.

'Just keep him hidden and don't say anything. I'll come and get him tomorrow. It won't take long to clean my room.' D goes over his spontaneous and terrible plan as he passes the hamster cage up to me whilst I'm balancing on the large tree branch outside my bedroom window. I could now add hamster smuggling to the list of things my mum could mark against me should she find out.

'If my mum finds out, I swear I'll...' I start but D interrupts me.

'Hey, this is all your fault in the first place. She wouldn't be monitoring me cleaning my room if you hadn't decided we try and make our own fireworks last week. Now she thinks I'm hiding all sorts of dangerous objects.'

I try and hide a laugh as I climb over the ledge and secure the hamster cage in my cupboard. I cover it with my clothes, leaving just enough light for the tiny creature when Devon walks through my bedroom door, his hands tucked inside his rustling pockets. I move to close the door behind him.

'We did it. Right I've got to go, Scar. Please look after him,' Devon says, handing me the little ball of fur.

'*You don't have to worry about a thing, I've got your back. If I go down…*' I say, confidently.

'*I'm going down with you,*' Devon finishes with a nod. I smile. '*Bye, Steve Rogers,*' Devon says to the hamster in a squeaky baby voice before heading home.

The words 'I'm going down with you' rattle around in my head as I stir lashings of cold milk and peppermint syrup into two mugs of coffee. I breathe in the aroma to try and calm my nerves. I never thought I'd be nervous around Devon but then I didn't think I would ever see him again either and here we are. I tentatively walk back into my living room and hand Devon his coffee.

'Thank you,' he says, taking the handle. I place mine on the coffee table and sprinkle a few flakes into Eddie's bowl, having not fed him yet this morning.

'What's his name?' Devon asks as I give Eddie a one-finger wave through the glass before taking my seat.

'Eddie,' I say, leaning over to get my mug. I take a hearty sip. Devon quirks an eyebrow. It's not exactly the Steve Rogers of names I know, but I like it. I keep my answer short as I watch my once-upon-a-time best friend in his smart attire smell the mug before hesitantly taking a sip. 'Don't tell me you've gone off peppermint coffee? We used to get it from Rolphs' Bakery every Christmas,' I say, somewhat amused by Devon's actions.

'It's been a while,' he replies, puckering his lips at the sweetness. The elephant in the room returns with a heavy thud. A part of me wants to brush ten years under the rug and it's a huge part of me. I just want to let it all out and chit-chat, but the other part of me is terrified to do so.

'I've missed you, Scar,' Devon tells me after a minute's silence. His eyes are trained on his coffee mug.

'When do you leave?' I hear myself asking and it comes out harder than I had intended. My wall goes up immediately, reminding me that catching up is not a good idea, not when I assume Devon is only visiting for a short while to make his documentary. Suddenly Devon's bottom lip juts out slightly, which is the tell-tale sign that I may have gone too far, that Devon is sad, and he is close to tears. Devon is more emotional than me; he always has been. It takes a lot to make me cry, like my best friend leaving without warning, but I'd never let anyone see my tears. But Devon is not my best friend anymore. His tears won't affect me now; my best friend duties are in the past.

'I leave next Sunday,' Devon informs me and I feel like I'm sixteen all over again. I pass my mug back and forth between my hands, taking turns to wipe away their clamminess on the cushion. 'Maybe we can hang out?' Devon pipes up, looking at me with his puppy-dog brown eyes.

I raise an eyebrow and slurp my coffee, going over this proposition. My thoughts are currently at war with each other. On the one hand I can't fake the ease that keeps sneaking into my heart or the buzz of joy that keeps fluttering around in my stomach with being in Devon's company again; just like old times. And on the other hand, how can I trust that this is a good idea?

I can feel my inner child fighting to get out, ready to throw a tantrum if I don't stop being so stubborn and not let Devon in. When he looks at me with those familiar eyes it makes me want to pull out my Superman cape, tie it around my neck and believe I can fly; then a second later I want to tie it around Devon and strangle him with it.

'I don't know if that's a good idea,' I say, trying to sound diplomatic, not wanting to cause any more hurt, to either of us.

For a moment silence descends on my cosy living room as we sit and stare at each other.

'You don't want to hang out with a superhero?' Devon says, a playful smile threatening his lips, a sparkle breaking through the shadows in his eyes.

'I'd only feel inferior. I'm no superhero,' I say matter-of-fact, my lips twisting into a small grin. I'm happy for him, of course I am. I can't deny the sting that we didn't do it together, but my former best friend is a bloody superhero with cardboard cut-outs, posters bigger than me and full spandex attire.

'Yeah, well superheroes wear pants, Scar. You should probably start with those,' Devon says with a mischievous smirk and a twinkle in his eye. I look down and suddenly become conscious of my outfit: my oversized tee is resting at the top of my thighs, my tiny boy shorts visible. I jump up off the couch, lobbing a cushion at Devon as I do so. He shoots his hands out in front of him to stop my attempt at thumping him in his grown-up muscled bicep. His hands are large and too strong to get past and so I give up and race to my bedroom to grab a pair of shorts. My cheeks feel flushed for no reason as I rummage through my wardrobe. It's just Devon, it's not exactly a big deal – we used to have baths together.

'You just let me sit there the entire time, you...' I shout, halfway down the stairs, a nervous giggle creeping up my throat as I make my way back into the living room. The minute I walk through the door I freeze.

Devon has a shy smile plastered on his face and is stood awkwardly next to the couch, one hand rubbing the back of his neck. I peel my eyes away from him to the reason I have a chill down my spine. Hope is standing in the living room doorway.

6

I am pacing the kitchen making more coffee for my guests, wondering if it's too early in the morning to make mine an Irish one. Through the hall I can hear Devon being his usual hyperactive self, answering Hope's questions while showing great interest in her job at the magazine; it seems some things have stayed the same: he's still a people person and a chatterbox when there are no cameras about.

When I had initially seen Hope in my living room, I had hastily excused myself to allow my best friend and former best friend to get better acquainted; and to avoid the onslaught of questions. When I hear Hope laughing – a high pitch giggle – I'm not quite sure if that was a good idea, especially when I re-enter the room and she shoots me daggers; apparently all her warmth and charm is being saved for Devon this morning.

I place the tray on my coffee table, a black coffee with one sugar for Devon. He smiles when he sees it. Hope grabs her peppermint latte in her cacti-print mug and crosses her legs on the deep turquoise chair to the side of the couch. All iciness evaporates when she takes her eyes off me and secures them on Devon once more.

I pick up my own coffee, glancing from Devon to Hope

as I take a seat, back in my spot on the couch. Devon simply watches me. I can hear what must be his phone buzzing in his pocket; it's beeped like twenty times, but he doesn't make to answer it. Then Hope speaks up.

'So, do you get to have a break over the holidays or are you working right through with these press junkets?' she asks.

'Oh shoot.' Devon stands up rapidly, looking at his watch, towering over both of us. 'So sorry, Hope, I've got to go. You just reminded me I've got two interviews today and need to show the producer around the village.'

'I totally understand,' Hope says waving away his apology, pushing her round spectacles up her nose as she stands to say bye. She gives Devon a hug.

Devon squeezes her cheerfully, meanwhile I'm sat rather comfy on my couch and am momentarily stunned at the scene I am currently witnessing.

What is going on? What is happening? I look to Eddie for answers. I swear he gives me a coy smirk before he swims to the other side of his tank.

Then Devon turns to me and gives me a nervous look. He quickly bends down to take a sip of his coffee, smiling when he does so, before giving me a tentative nod, clapping his hands together like he's unsure what to do with them and then he walks towards the door.

'Right, OK, well I best go. Hope, if you and Scarlett want to catch up for drinks later, just let me know – you have my number.' Now he sends a more confident wink and an Academy-Award-worthy smile my way. What the…?

Devon then retraces his steps to collect his coat, while patting down his jeans to check he's got everything – keys, phone, wallet – before Hope shows him out. When I hear the front door close, I wander back into the kitchen and collect all the ingredients I need for my original task for today that didn't involve ex best friends and best friends having a good old chinwag in my living room.

'Scarlett Davis, you have some explaining to do,' Hope exclaims, as she marches into the kitchen, hands on hips, her black leggings and crisp white shirt combo looking stylish and fresh at just gone eight-thirty a.m.

I nurse my cold brew wondering if I am in fact dreaming, have hit my head really hard or am in some parallel universe. I don't want to explain things to Hope but even if I did, I'm too dazed at this moment to do so and I really do have to get a move on with my gingerbread for the Christmas fair. Hope plonks herself down at the kitchen table.

'I came to tell you that Devon Wood had sent me flowers as a thank you for a lovely interview and that Jess is out of his mind that I didn't tell him sooner and smuggle him out of work, then I get here and...' She doesn't finish her sentence; she just gawks at me as I drizzle golden syrup into my mixing bowl. The fact that Devon sent her flowers chips a minuscule edge off my wall. 'I can't believe you used to have baths with Devon Wood and you never told me. You've seen that man naked,' Hope says dreamily as she pinches a gingerbread from the plate on the table.

'Oi, I need those for the fair and I think that crosses a professional line, thinking of one of your interviewees naked. I'd watch that if I were you,' I say, sternly, not best pleased that visions of new Devon in a bath suddenly swarm my brain. 'And, Hope, we were babies – please never say that again. Don't turn it into something gross – and what exactly did you guys talk about?' I add, the words coming out quick, trying to dispel the images of Devon in a bath by attaching negatives to them.

'I didn't turn it into something gross. I don't think there would be anything gross about having a bath with Devon Wood,' she says moving her eyebrows up and down over the top of her light gold frames.

'Hope, please, no one is having baths with Devon Wood. That was a ridiculously long time ago,' I say, exasperated with my BFF. This is all too much at such an early hour. I whisk the gingerbread mixture with vigour, inhaling the perfume of nutmeg and ginger, and in my mind start constructing the gingerbread house and what it will look like when it's finished.

'I'm sure a lot of people would like to,' Hope says, interrupting my happy thoughts. I drop the whisk and brush a hand through my short bob, flicking back the thicker side part that falls in my face. Hope's comment hits me right in the chest, reminding me that Devon and I are not babies anymore. Having baths together is not part of our secret club where we build caves and mountains with bubbles; that was a lifetime ago. Devon is now a Hollywood heartthrob, he's not my nerdy best friend, he's not my Devon, he hasn't been mine for ten years.

I rub a hand over my heart. This is why the past should stay in the past. This is why hanging out is not a good idea. My heart hurts.

'Well, he should go and have baths with any one of those people instead of waltzing in here like the past ten years haven't happened. Who does he think he is? The guy does a bit of acting and suddenly he thinks he can do whatever he pleases?' The hardness in my tone from earlier is making a comeback. I'm talking more to myself than Hope, but I see her watching me, a quizzical look on her face.

'What?' I snap. 'You can't just surprise people like that, not take their feelings into consideration. It's rude, turning up unannounced.'

Hope gets up from the table and walks over to the counter. She picks up the whisk and starts whisking while I take a sip of festive coffee to calm myself down. She then opens her mouth to speak before closing it again, like she's choosing her words carefully. I turn away, then turn back to her again, waiting for her to back me up.

'I imagine it was all a lot to take in yesterday. At least you weren't ambushed by him being there. He had no idea you were coming,' she starts, softly. I can tell she is aware of the whirlwind of emotions spinning through my head and is trying her best to be diplomatic whilst still being understanding and show she's on my side. 'He had no time to prepare for your unexpected entrance at the pub, but isn't it lovely that he wanted to see you. And, Scarlett, I'm sorry you were so anxious yesterday with me springing the interview on you, but you lied – you told me you didn't know Devon. You didn't let me in. All these years you've had me thinking Jess and I were too nerdy for you, and all this time your aversion to superheroes is because of Devon Wood. Yes, he told me all about you two growing up thinking you were Springhollow's superheroes.'

She lets out a small "this is unbelievable" kind of laugh. 'I understand this is all a bit of a shock, given what Devon told me about you two, but I don't think he came here to upset you or because he's throwing his Hollywood weight around, he simply came to see a friend. And by the looks of how content he was sat on your couch, you two have unfinished business.' She resolves.

The mixture now looks creamy, so I take over adding the flour, distracting myself from having to look at Hope and deal with her words of wisdom. She gives me some space and leans against the island.

Her words are buzzing around my brain as I fold the mixture. Hope doesn't say anything else; instead she moves to busy herself with pulling yoghurt from the fridge along with orange juice and a bag of granola from the cupboard while I form a dough with the mixture, wrap it and place it in the fridge to rest for thirty minutes.

'Devon left, Hope. Ten years ago, he left, and I couldn't face superheroes when he was gone,' I admit, taking a seat at the breakfast bar. 'I was so mad at him for leaving, it was easier to hate it all and push it away than deal with it.'

Hope places a glass of orange in front of me. I absent-mindedly wipe the condensation off the glass.

'I know you struggled at school, Scarlett, but why didn't you tell me you were hurting? Why didn't you tell me about Devon?' Hope asks, taking a seat next to me with two bowls of yoghurt and granola. I leave the glass and move to twirling the spoon between my fingertips.

'I was done with school. I hoped for a fresh start at college and you and Jess were a godsend after dealing with Ruby and her gang. I don't know what I would have done without you. Devon always had my back when the other girls laughed at me for liking boy stuff and boys didn't think I was cool enough to play their games. God it's so stupid when you look back, but I always had Devon; no one could

LUCY KNOTT

come between us. Then he left in the blink of an eye. He was the loud one, the one who would get us into other games or occasionally have other kids want to play with us. When he left, I became invisible and I liked it that way. I didn't want to play with anyone else and I didn't talk about him because that would have made him real.' I mutter my story – even now it hurts recalling my school days. The village folk might have been a tight-knit community but that didn't stop school from being full of cliques and bullies, many of whom moved away over the years.

'He said you were like Batman and Robin,' Hope says through a warm smile.

'Oh yeah.' I chuckle. 'Did he say who was who?' I take a bite of granola, not wanting to dwell in my sad memories for long, I've done that way too much over the years and knowing who was who when we were kids, I am curious to know what Devon said.

Hope laughs. 'He said he was Robin. I can only imagine the fights. With your stubborn heart I imagine Devon has a strong dislike for Robin now.' She nudges me playfully. I laugh at how accurate her statement is. I certainly got my use out of the Batman costume; I think I let Devon wear it once. 'So, if you were so close, why didn't you stay in touch? Did your parents not encourage you to write or arrange phone calls?'

The bite of granola I have in my mouth suddenly becomes hard to chew. Ten years is a long time to keep a story buried; digging it up isn't easy. I take a drink of orange to help the granola go down before pushing my bowl away.

'Our parents were not very fond of each other. My mum struggled with Devon and I being glued together all the time. She didn't always do a great job of hiding her disappointment that I didn't enjoy going to ballet like the other girls. Our mums thought we needed other friends too, often arranging play dates with other kids, but we always figured a way out of it, playing out on the street, gravitating towards each other. That and we should have had our own ward at the hospital with how much we frequented the place. They were at a bit of a loose end with our antics.

'So, when Devon's dad got a job out in New York, they didn't think twice. Devon didn't tell me until the night before he left, and the news completely blindsided me. I was angry and didn't want to talk to him. My mum never pushed the matter, instead I guess she looked at it as a chance for me to grow without him.' My shoulders slump as the words come spilling out. My chest suddenly feels lighter, like pressure has been removed in opening up to Hope.

'That's a bummer,' she says, rubbing my forearm. 'I'm sorry.'

'Don't be, I have you and Jess. I got over it,' I lie. One look at Hope and I know she sees right through me, as she looks at me from under her long lashes with a pointed stare.

'I can see how that would have hurt, but he's here now and he seems to want to hang out, so why not catch up on lost time? High school was tough for so many people, college too. You saw what Jess had to contend with,' Hope says, going back to her breakfast.

I play with the hem of my tee. Because of her style Hope often escaped the wrath of bullies whereas in college Jess and I enjoyed plenty of snide remarks and our group was collectively known as "Beauty and the geeks" and that was without me wearing comic book tees or sharing my love of art. I just didn't seem to fit in.

However, Hope and Jess liked me. They, along with their families, moved to Springhollow a month shy of each other when they were starting college. Being the new kids in the square they sort of gravitated towards each other and clicked. But it was only four years ago that they started dating. I couldn't have been happier for them both. Hope sat me down one day to ask if it would upset me if she and Jess started dating. I was pretty puzzled at first. I guess I just took it as a given. In fact, I think I told her that I would be more upset if they didn't. Hope and Jess, Jess and Hope – it simply fit. I've never really felt like a third wheel. It was more frustrating when they invited me to everything, especially when it was things I was pretending not to like.

'I just…' I start and then pause. While opening up to Hope feels somewhat healthy, it's scary and I'm worried as to how much I can or should say. 'I just don't want to get attached again. I can feel it already, even when I'm mad at him, it's like I like being mad at him as long as he's here,' I confess, which is huge for me. I take a breath in; my head is spinning. I take another sip of juice. Hope rubs my back. 'He's not going to be here for long. I know I hurt him too, so it's better if I just keep him in the past, and then I can stop missing him once and for all.'

'You never stopped missing him, you still miss him and you're always going to miss him,' Hope informs me nonchalantly. I look up at her, confused by the abruptness and insensitive tone of her statement, which really isn't going to help my current sombre mood or positive intentions of forgetting about him. 'Unless,' she adds, 'you acknowledge to

Devon that you made mistakes too, like you've just done to me, and you open your eyes and realise that your former BFF is in town right this second and you have some lost time to catch up on.' I see the sparkle of mischief in Hope's cat-like green eyes.

'I can't though,' I say putting my guard up straight away, like I did earlier with the man himself. There's no way I can do it. There's no way Devon and I can be friends again. 'He's moved on, Hope, he doesn't need me, which he has clearly demonstrated over the past ten years. He's done mighty fine without me. He's a bloody superhero for crying out loud and I don't need him either,' I say slathering on the excuses. Anything to make her see that this is a bad idea.

'Oh my God, you're like Captain America and The Winter Soldier. He's more Steve Rogers and you're more Bucky because you've got Bucky's evil glare down to a T and you don't want to remember all the amazing times you had with Devon and you won't let yourself believe your friendship with Devon can be resurrected and that's without having had some mad scientist manipulating your brain. Oh, but we all know how that story ends.' Hope claps her hands together, ignoring everything I just said, a delirious smile on her face. 'Uh, Cap and Bucky, Bucky and Cap,' she adds a little more sarcastically.

I know what she's doing. She's downplaying my anxiety over this whole situation; she thinks that I'm being overly dramatic. She thinks that just because Devon and I were best friends for sixteen years and that I've missed him so much these past ten that our friendship can just pick up where it left off. She thinks she's right, that she knows what's best for me – that all these years this is all I've wanted and have been waiting for. OK, so she didn't exactly say all that, but I can see it in her face. I can read between the lines: she somehow thinks I still care about him, that I'm just putting a wall up because I'm scared of my emotions, but I don't and I'm not. I need to tell her this and make it very clear to her where Devon and I stand.

I get up from my chair and look Hope in the eyes. I go to tell her that she needs to understand that Devon and I are no longer friends; that too much time has passed, when instead I say, 'Why does he get to be Captain America?'

Damn it.

Hope lets out a high-pitched squeal. 'Oh my God, wait till I tell Jess you're a closet nerd. He's going to freak out. Scarlett, we have like ten years of superhero movies to catch up on and you are going to love them all. And you need to come and see Devon's movie with me – you're actually going to die.'

'Hope, have you not been listening? I'm not into that stuff anymore. Devon coming back doesn't change any of that. I'm a grown-up. I don't play with action figures anymore,' I say, firmly, even stomping my feet a little.

'Oh please, Jess and I are grown-ups too and believe me when I tell you, if you loved the comic books, wait until you see what they did with the films. Oh, this is like the best day ever,' Hope exclaims, before taking a big bite of her yoghurt and granola, like she requires all the energy for this momentous day. 'I understand this might be difficult for you, Scarlett, and I'm not dismissing your emotions, but maybe Devon coming back is a sign. You work so hard, you let your mum dress you, and your idea of fun is watering your cacti and going for walks. You need to allow some of that inner child out and embrace who you are. And don't get me wrong I love who you are, and I love your plants, but I love you even more now, so please don't be scared,' she says, turning to face me, bowl now in her hand as she takes smaller bites in thought.

I stop still and wrap my arms around myself. I don't know what to say, it's all so much to take in. While yes, I can feel the excitement bubble in the pit of my stomach over talking about comic books with Hope and Jess, I can also feel the undercurrent of nerves. Suppressing my love of comics all these years has helped me keep my focus at work and be the best personal assistant I can be to Hope.

If I allow myself to get too caught up in that world it will only be a matter of time before I get the itch again – the itch to dream bigger – and I can't do that to Hope. I can't do that to my mother. If I start sporting Spider-Man tees again, she'll have kittens and deem me unmarriageable. She will be the talk of the town; I can't put her through that.

And Devon, what did Devon want? What did he expect from me? OK, so we say our sorries, put it down to being young and stubborn, then what? Devon leaves again. I can't get attached. Sometimes you just can't be the person you want to be or do the things you want to do because you end up letting people down or getting hurt.

'I'm not scared,' I mumble stubbornly as Hope pops off her chair and quickly rinses her dish in the sink. 'Just have a think about it, OK? I'm here for you,' she says, giving me a little hug and skipping to the front door. I walk to the kitchen door and watch her bundle up for the cold. 'I'll be back later to check on you.'

As Hope closes the front door behind her, a cold blast

sweeps through the house. The last superhero movie I saw was *Captain America: The First Avenger*. If the rest of the films are anything like that one, I know I'm in for a treat and I feel a tiny thrill at the idea of getting to watch them with Hope, but at the same time I feel like Steve Rogers – after years of being buried in the ice, I've been uncovered. I tiptoe into the living room to switch off the lamp now that the sun is out among the grey clouds while my brain tries to decipher if my past and present colliding is a Christmas wish come true or a gift I need to return.

7

Alone in my house I'm distracted from the emotions that have been overwhelming my mind and body since I got out of bed this morning as I tune in to the lyrics of Wham! and sing my heart out in the kitchen. The Christmas fair project is coming along nicely, and I get a thrill every time I think about the village coming together to decorate their own gingerbread and share their own labour of love, whatever their heart's desire; maybe they make a hotel, a Christmas tree or a building that holds a special place in their heart. I've enjoyed stepping away from the Styrofoam and paints and, though I know that most of the folks in Springhollow have enjoyed my arts and crafts themed stall each year, I hope they will love this idea just as much; if not for the fact that these creative tools are edible and delicious.

For my gingerbread house, which I will be using as the example piece, I'm going to be doing a replica of *The Village Gazette* building. Our office block is made up of a three-storey old-fashioned town house that dates back to 1923 and the magazine has been running out of there from the very beginning. It's one of our town's most beloved buildings along with the village library and Mr and Mrs Rolph's bakery. I will say that, though my job doesn't always set my soul on fire, working in the building is something I like about it. It's cosy and homey, each section of the magazine having a different room, the walls holding notice boards of inspiration for each writer. The horoscope room is a lot of fun. All the artwork pinned to said boards often mesmerises me: the paintings, the colours, the galaxies and their glittering specks.

The top floor, where Hope's office is, is more open plan, the walls having been knocked through to make just two rooms, one big square with rows of desks, leading to Hope's office at the end. The ceiling is high and the patterned skirting makes it rather regal-looking and vintage, which it is, but it's stood the test of time and is still on trend. There are wall-to-wall bookshelves and old-fashioned radiators – those white curvy ones – and grand bay windows that from the street make it look magical, like one of those fancy toyshops. I'm hoping to capture the essence of the building in gingerbread form.

I scour my dining table, looking over the bags of icing sugar and the tray of gingerbread pieces I had made on Wednesday night, to look for my plan. I drew up a rough sketch of what I wanted this thing to look like with a few notes of the dimensions I would need each biscuit piece to be so it would fit together snug. I must have left it in my spare room to ensure no eyes but mine could see it.

I take the stairs two at a time, reaching the landing slightly out of breath. The door to the spare room is the only door that is closed; I don't like for people to snoop, and by people I mostly mean Hope and Jess. I promise I'm not a bad friend but whenever Hope sees something I've crafted, she second-guesses my position as her personal assistant, and I don't want her to worry about me. Art is my hobby and whenever I feel in the mood to pursue it, I come into my spare room. My "storage room" as it's known to everyone else, which is just a tiny white lie. My love of superheroes might have been revealed this morning but my dream job I am keeping guarded. Hope needs me at the magazine, especially now that we're on the cusp of possible closure.

I push open the door and navigate around the cardboard boxes I stacked either side of the door. Twinkling lights are strung around my desk with more potted plants by the window. I wander straight over to my cluttered oak desk that is littered with all different-sized sheets of paper, half-finished sketches, doodles, and pencil crayons that need sharpening. I get the same familiar itch of desire to pull up my chair and get lost in my imagination, which I used to get as a child when Devon and I would draw for hours; creating other worlds and dreaming up our own comic books.

My fingers tingle, my hands ball into fists. I'm transported back to the hospital room when I told Devon he would need to draw for me. The sparks in my fingertips that burned underneath my casts with my want and need to draw as it had been taken away from me due to my injury, is the same feeling I get now. I haven't drawn in days and I haven't attempted to sketch my beloved characters and comic book ideas in years.

I see my gingerbread blueprint and pick it up, turning to walk away but I hesitate. I backpedal and take a seat at my desk, hands trembling with both fear and excitement. I open the top drawer of my desk. From under a blanket of scrap paper I remove a wad of drawings, drawings I haven't looked at in three years – to be exact.

One night at the annual Springhollow summer fair Hope and Jess had had a few too many glasses of wine and were arguing over which Marvel superhero was superior. I had remained silent. However, once home and with my brain infused with a healthy dose of pink gin, I had stumbled into my spare room and started drawing. Somewhere around four a.m. I had succumbed to the land of nod and abandoned my comic strip. When sober and clear-headed the next day, I hadn't been able to finish it.

Now though as I flick through the pages of colour and fine lines, I find myself grinning from ear to ear. I find my Faber Castell pencil tin and immediately pick up where I left off. The magic, the other realms, the heroes, and villains, they all fly from my brain and straight to the page. My brows are drawn, my tongue sticks out with every swish of my wrist and stroke of my pencil. Though I'm still wary of Devon being back, I can't help the inspiration it has unleashed inside me.

'Scarlett, Scarlett.' My hand stiffens and freezes above the page. I swear I can hear my name. 'Scarlett, are you ready?' I automatically look down at my attire – the vintage tee and shorts from this morning. Where the hell did the time go? My heart starts hammering when I realise I'm not on Planet Naelea but in my spare room. 'Scarlett, are you OK?'

'Shoot,' I mutter to myself. My hand flies to the switch on the wall. I turn off my fairy lights and run to the door. Whipping the door closed behind me, I turn and smack straight into Hope on my small landing.

'Why aren't you dressed? What were you doing in there?'

she says looking me up and down, noticing my rapid breathing.

'Whooo,' I breathe out, making a dramatic show of bending over, placing my hands on knees, the tell-tale sign of an unfit person having just exerted themselves. 'I was just moving around some boxes, cleaning and dusting. It was due a tidy, all those stacked boxes just collecting dust,' I say, moving my hands from my knees to Hope's elbows and guiding her and her puzzled expression to my bedroom door, to distract her with my apparent need to change.

'You've been cleaning for five hours?' Hope asks taking a seat on my bed. Had it been that long? Holy moly. I can't remember the last time I sat down and spent that long drawing, let alone the last time I spent that long doing something I truly enjoyed. Oh sugar, I left the gingerbread in the fridge and all the ingredients out. I silently count to three, not wanting to panic Hope. I might now be behind schedule for my Christmas project, but I will finish it. I have to.

'I had a lot of stuff to sort through. You know what it's like, you come across pictures, old childhood stuff and get distracted. Boxes get heavy, it takes time moving them around.' I'm rambling as I rifle through my cupboard for something to wear. 'Where are we going?' I add, trying to gauge what outfit I require. These days I don't often pick my own ensembles. Between work, dinners with my parents and spending time at home, I'm usually in whatever outfits my mum has picked out for me or my favourite baggy tees and PJ's.

'Oh yeah, you stumble upon any photos of you and Devon?' Hope asks, a smirk playing at her baby-pink lips.

'Speaking of Devon, we're going out remember? He invited us out this morning. I texted to tell you I accepted. Jess is meeting us at the pub. He needed longer to get ready. He'd already changed three times before I left – he's kind of freaking out over meeting him,' Hope tells me through a chuckle, amusement behind her eyes.

I stop rooting through my clothes to look at Hope. 'I wasn't looking nor did I find any pictures of me and Devon,' I say firmly. 'And, oh gosh, tell Jess to relax – it's just Devon.'

'To you maybe but not to the rest of us. I mean, of course I'm not going to go all fangirl on him or anything. I'm cool.' As if to demonstrate her coolness, she flicks her blonde hair over her shoulder. 'I know how emotional this is for you and I know I said I'll be here for you but pretty please for one second can you let me have this moment and try to understand how freaking awesome this is for us comic book nerds? Your friend Devon is part of the superhero franchise and your two best friends happen to love superheroes. Whether you want to admit to liking them or not, this is a fantasy come to life for me and Jess. I know deep down you know that.' She sort of squeals at the end of her sentence as my stomach explodes with a swarm of tiny ant men.

'Fine.' I huff, turning my attention back to my wardrobe. I will point out that in the ten years that I have known Hope and Jess, I never actually said I disliked comic books. I just always happened to fall busy when they wanted to watch the movies, or I remained quiet whenever they had one of their deep discussions on where they would rather live: Asgard or Wakanda? So, really, I've not totally been lying to them all these years.

And sure, I thought it was ridiculously cool that Devon was a superhero. I just couldn't quite believe it, share my emotions or be outwardly giddy over it just yet. His reintroduction into my life hasn't exactly been subtle, he'd *Doctor Strange*'d it out of nowhere; I am going to need more than twenty-four hours to digest it all.

I stop my search when my hands land on my olive-green maxi button-up dress and pull it off the hanger. A small smile curves at my lips as I throw the dress on to my bed and watch the fabric crinkle slightly. It seems like an age since I wore something that felt like me, besides my lounge wear. But with my mum and dad being on holiday, it's not like I'll see them at the pub and be given a once-over or disapproving stare from my mother. My stomach flips with a tiny jolt of excitement. I feel a little dangerous defying her – not that I'd ever want to hurt her feelings but to be free of ruffles and pink for an evening will be incredibly liberating. I wander back out into the hall and into the bathroom to turn on the shower. Hope continues talking to me through the open doors as I make quick work of putting shampoo and conditioner through my hair. As I move in and out of the water, I hear her muffles.

'So, what was Devon like as a child? What did you guys do together, besides take baths?' I don't even have to glance at the bathroom doorway to know that Hope is wearing a coy grin; I can hear it in her voice.

'We did the same as every other kid who lives in a small town, rode our skateboards round the square, played at the park, nothing out of the ordinary,' I say casually turning off the shower and wrapping a towel around me.

Hope flings a pair of underwear at me – my lacy set

of matching bra and knickers from my date drawer. 'And played Superman and Lois Lane?' She winks.

'Hope,' I gasp. 'That's my good set – I don't need them tonight.'

Hope tuts and taps at her watch. 'Scarlett Davis, you put them on now. We're late. Stop dawdling and complaining. Wearing pretty underwear should not be saved for special occasions; life is a special occasion. Every single day is an occasion to celebrate. Now chop, chop,' she says, clapping her hands.

I throw her a sarcastic smile and shut the door in her face. I sigh at the underwear, thinking of my silly drawer of what I deemed "sexy underwear" appropriate for dates. Why did I feel the need to wear uncomfortable clothing to impress the people in my life and feel worth it? It's not like the men stuck around after they saw me in lace. Another sigh comes out a little heavier this time, but I do as I'm told, before raking serum through my short hair.

'I thought you said you were going to let me think about all this, go at my own pace an' all,' I shout through the doorway, hopping on each foot as I step into my knickers.

'I am. That's why I thought it would be good to have a group hang-out, take it slow, have me and Jess there for support. I'll wait downstairs,' Hope says through the door, gleefully, and strategically ending the conversation so I can't argue with her reasoning.

Twenty minutes later, after a quick layer of foundation, a dab of lip-gloss, a sweep of rosy pink blush and a swipe of mascara, I'm ready to go. When I reach the bottom of the stairs it occurs to me again that in the whirlwind of Hope arriving, me trying to hide my art room and getting caught up in conversation and arguing over underwear, that the plan is to meet up with Devon tonight and I'm a grown woman. I don't have to go, no matter what my best friend says. I really don't know if I'm ready to see him again.

As I walk through the corridor, I spot my excuse on the dining room table; all my gingerbread house supplies I had left out earlier.

'Oh shoot, why don't you go ahead, and I'll catch up. I completely forgot I'd left everything out after baking. Oh, dear and I left the butter out an' all.' I go to step into the kitchen when Hope grabs my wrist with one hand and holds my coat out with the other.

'I already put the butter away. I think the rest will be fine,' she says, her green eyes boring into mine suspiciously, telling me she can read me like a book.

I take my coat and grab my Doc Martens, when the smile vanishes from Hope's face and she pauses, her hand hovering over the door handle.

'Tell me, did Devon do something horrible to you?' Hope asks. I can feel her pointed glare on the back of my neck as I bend down to lace up my boots.

'What? Other than move to New York at the tender age of sixteen, leaving me best-friendless and then proceeding to enjoy his life without me and becoming a bloody superhero? No,' I say, not hiding my sarcasm as I stand up straight, brushing my bob behind my ears.

'Did you have a thing for him, or did he have a thing for you? Did one of you try it on with the other but get rejected, making all this awkward?' she says, gasping all dramatically at the end.

'What? God no. Hope, we were sixteen and we were

utter nerds. I never liked him in that way,' I say, screwing up my face in disgust.

Hope shrugs looking pleased with herself, like she's Bruce Banner and she's just figured out an equation. 'Well then, that's good. I see no reason why you can't come out tonight, loosen up a bit and catch up with an old friend. Maybe tonight you can find closure – plus we never go out anymore. Tonight, I don't want to think about work. Let's just hang out with our men, I mean my man and your friend,' she says clutching my forearm as she shoves me out of my front door.

It's hard to say no to her when she sneaks in comments like that. She works so damn hard; she needs to let her hair down every once in a while. The "men" comment, I skim over, not taking her bait. 'And remember, I'm here for you,' she adds, beaming at me, but her eyes grow too wide and I don't believe her innocent look; I'm pretty sure she's the one who's white-lying now.

I believe my current best friend is getting lost in her own fantasy of the man that is Devon Wood. I think she might need time to process my being former friends with him too and stop envisioning him suddenly slipping into our group. *It's called "The Three Musketeers" for a reason; there are only three of us,* I think to myself, but I don't want to burst her bubble this evening. She had asked me earlier to let her and Jess have this moment. I'm not about to be a spoilsport and ruin their own personal Comic Con.

8

The giant spruce tree lights up the square as we make our way towards the village pub. The twinkling multi-coloured bulbs that have been strung around it bounce off the shop windows, illuminating the library steps and the flowers on the lawn by the florist. It's my favourite time of year here in Springhollow. Sparkly bunting is hung between shops, garlands drape from streetlamp to streetlamp. Every house proudly displays a homemade wreath on their front door, some of which I helped make at our stall last year.

I look up at the deepening navy sky and cross my fingers for snow as we cut across the village green, which surrounds the beautiful Christmas tree, crafted presents and reindeer.

At the door of the village pub Jess ambushes us, causing both Hope and I to jump. He rakes a hand through his curly black locks and begins pacing right in front of me. 'Scarlett, what should I do? How should I act? I'm cool right? I'm hip, I'm fly, it's all good, yeah it's all good,' Jess stammers, grabbing my biceps, his words reaching me on his cold breath that fills the space between us. He's twitching nervously and does some awkward attempt at a confident shrug. His brow is damp with sweat; it's freezing out here.

'Dude, did you just say "I'm hip, I'm cool"?' I ask, barely containing my chuckle.

Hope splutters, trying to swallow down her laughter, before prising Jess's hands off me. Jess is giving me a pleading look, fear in his eyes, a look that says to go easy on him.

'Scarlett, if you want a loaf of cinnamon bread for Christmas morning or someone to fix your radiators ever again, you'll be nice to me – not to mention that I'm not mad at you for hiding your love of comics from us all these years,' Jess mutters as Hope hooks her arm through his. *Touché, Jess, touché,* I muse to myself. I feel that little ball of guilt in my stomach. I do appreciate with all my heart that Hope and Jess have been more excited than angry about my lie, so I will myself to behave, plus Jess makes cinnamon loaf better than Mrs Rolph at the bakery and that is no easy feat; it has become my Christmas morning tradition over the years, and as far as those pesky old-fashioned radiators, they remain the only thing in my house I struggle to get my head around and fix.

'OK, OK, just don't be a dork – or be a dork. Devon loves dorks – or maybe he doesn't. Ooh which one was it?' I really can't help but tease Jess, even with my cinnamon loaf at risk. I raise my eyebrows at Jess playfully but jokes tonight are going completely over his head. Hope shoves me hard towards the door but not before giving me a stern "stop making Jess hyperventilate" glare and warns, 'You two, stop it now. Jess, hon, be yourself; he'll love you the way you are.'

Inside the pub it seems like fairies visited overnight as more decorations have adorned every surface. Red and green paper chains now link each wooden beam, comical Santas drinking beer sit along the bar and the famous gold and white Christmas tree proudly stands by the fireplace, which tonight is sending its warm and cosy smell of burning logs throughout the pub.

I automatically go to make my way to the corner booth, near the fire, when I spot Devon out of the corner of my eye by the bar. He's dressed far more casually than the suit and tie combo he wore for yesterday's press and how he had been this morning before his interviews. Now he sports a long-sleeved denim shirt with a few open buttons at the top showing a white cotton tee underneath. He has the same bright smile that I remember so well that causes my own lips to curve into a grin, but his posture is more confident and rugged.

'Wow, he looks handsome dressed a little more casual,' Hope notes.

'Hmm, yeah, I mean no, whatever,' I mumble in a daze, unable to take my eyes off him.

'Tell me again why you never tried to kiss him?' Hope queries, pulling me right out of my daydream.

'Don't do that, Hope. It's Devon. It's still just Devon. He doesn't see me like that,' I tell her in a hushed but firm whisper.

'I'm just putting this out there but maybe if your friendship is on the rocks you could try something else,' she suggests.

I turn to her, incredulous, my eyebrows have shot into my hairline. She wiggles hers at me.

'One, that's gross and I told you to stop it and two, did you really just suggest a relationship built on anger and lies?' I retort.

'He's too cool for us,' Jess pipes up. He's ogling worse than I was, but his words sting and hit a nerve that makes me feel queasy. Devon is talking to Ryan and a group of other boys we never spoke to when we were at school, and he looks relaxed and at ease in their presence. I can't just walk up to them. I never fitted into that crowd, but new Devon looks like he's fitting in just fine.

And then like a sucker punch to the gut all the air is knocked out of me as I witness Ruby saunter up to Devon, wrap him in a hug and kiss both of his cheeks.

If I had thought life couldn't possibly throw anything worse at me after Devon left, Ruby stepped in to challenge any shred of optimism and prove me wrong. Maybe I shouldn't be blaming Devon for my failed GCSEs and for my locking my dreams in a cupboard and throwing away the key; maybe Ruby deserved that title.

'Oh my God, what the heck is that? It's so gross. No one in their right mind would want to look at that,' Ruby says from over my shoulder with a cackle.

I'm sitting on the field in the playground flicking through my unfinished comic strip, my hand and arm itching in my cast. I haven't been able to draw for weeks and it all seems pointless now anyway.

'Leave me alone, Ruby,' I try, keeping my head down.

'No guy is ever going to want to go out with an alien-loving freak like you,' she adds, stepping on my book bag that's resting by my feet and walking away.

★

My mouth drops open as I watch Ruby's five foot seven, curvy and stunning frame lean into Devon. Her hand moves over his forearm as she throws her head back and laughs at something he just said. Ruby is girlie to a T and her tight-fitting dress that clings to her body perfectly is pressing up way too close against Devon. I find myself looking down at my favourite olive-green dress and black Doc Martens and feel my insecurities bubble in my gut. What was I even thinking coming here? I suddenly feel foolish and vulnerable.

'We should go,' I say, turning back towards the door, but Hope grabs my wrist.

'You are not leaving because of her,' she says seriously, all the humour in her voice from before having disappeared. 'We don't have to say hi yet. Look there's a space over there where Autumn is serving,' Hope points out, linking one arm around Jess and one arm around me as she guides us towards the other end of the bar, away from Devon and Ruby. Just thinking their names together causes my chest to tighten. I do my best not to look at them while we walk but it's hard not to keep glancing their way, especially when Ruby lets out another cackle. I can't believe Devon is fraternising with a supervillain.

'Sup, gang, what can I get for you?' Autumn asks in her soft, dreamlike tone when we reach the bar. I'm distracted for a moment by her outfit of a long black skirt and white turtleneck combo. It suits her beautifully and I find myself wishing I could wear more clothes like that.

'I love your outfit tonight, Scarlett,' she says, catching me looking at her. 'I think you should wear that more often,' she adds, making me blush. I'm occasionally told I look nice at the office, but it feels different when someone says it when I'm wearing something that I picked out and not my mum. It means more so I'm never quite sure how to handle it. I just end up feeling anxious, like they're seeing a piece of me that I've been keeping buried for years.

'Thank you,' I reply. 'Can we get the usual, please,' I add, feeling better when my attention is on Autumn and her pretty outfit. I've always liked Autumn; she was the bookworm at school, always had her head buried in a book. She'd sometimes join in with mine and Devon's games in primary school or we'd sit together while she read the latest in fiction as Devon and I pulled out our comics. She's as sweet as they come, a natural beauty on the inside and out. I wish she had gone to the same high school as us, then maybe I would have had an ally when Devon left. She works during the week at the library, then helps Ryan out here over the weekend when it gets busy.

'Have you seen Devon since he's been back?' Autumn asks as she prepares our drinks.

'We have and we've said our hellos – lovely man,' Hope answers for me, waving the question away casually, like the awesome best friend that she is. 'How are things at the library? Have you and Mrs Bride had chance to think about my suggestion? I know it's a busy time, but I'd love to hear your thoughts,' Hope says, changing the subject smoothly, though now I feel bad because she's thinking about work. She had mentioned something about our magazine distribution and finding more ways to sell it and make it visible. I know she had been talking to Mrs Bride a lot on the phone last week.

'What's on your Christmas list this year, Autumn?' I ask, making both Autumn and Hope chuckle. Hope shakes her head at me, as I make a mental note to pop in to see Autumn and Mrs Bride before the holidays and go over ideas with them, so it's one thing Hope doesn't have to worry about, though I must also focus on the gingerbread project if I want it to be ready in time for the fair on Saturday.

'What? We're letting our hair down. No talking about work – least of all when we can talk about Christmas,' I remind Hope as Autumn places our drinks in front of us.

Hope's eyes flicker with a little fear. I can tell she's anxious to hear what Mrs Bride thinks but she doesn't want to appear desperate for an answer and spill the magazine's secret. I wink at her and raise my glass to signal I've got her back and we're in this together. Her shoulders visibly relax.

'I'm thinking of giving myself a holiday, maybe surprising Willow with a cosy cottage somewhere. And just to put your mind at ease, Hope, I've read through your idea and think it's great. I just have to go through it with Mrs Bride,' Autumn tells us with a kind smile and then she does a zipping motion across her lips signalling no more talk of work.

'Thank you,' Hope mouths, squeezing Autumn's hand.

'A cottage sounds gorgeous; Willow will love that. No hustle and bustle of the holidays – just you, her and nature.' I nod my approval.

'That's what I was thinking,' Autumn replies, flashing a giddy smile, in between serving a couple of Guinnesses to a few locals.

'We're getting a dog,' Jess chimes in and almost the second he finishes his sentence Hope says, 'No we are not.' Causing me to choke on my gin.

Autumn chuckles. 'Aww finally.'

'Don't encourage him, Autumn,' Hope warns.

'I shall say no more,' Autumn adds, winking at Jess before she gets caught up serving the growing crowd. The village pub is the place to be on weekends. Hope, Jess and I have spent many an evening here after long days at the office winding down with a glass of gin and joining in with the pub quizzes. My general knowledge isn't too shabby for someone who failed her GCSEs.

'What are you going to call him or her?' I take over from Autumn, teasing Hope. Jess has wanted a dog for the longest time, but a dog doesn't quite fit into Hope's organised and clean living space or their busy schedules.

'I'm not sure. It depends if he or she already has a name and likes it. I want to adopt from the shelter. They've just put an add out that they are desperate for more families to give some pups a home this Christmas and to think we have such a warm, cosy home and good jobs that would allow us to look after and support them in the best way. It just feels right, you know,' Jess tells me, casually draping his arm around Hope's shoulders and dropping a kiss on her temple. I'm finding it really difficult not to choke on my gin as I try and keep in my giggles watching Hope roll her eyes as Jess squeezes her shoulders tight. 'Hope would be such a great dog mum. She's so kind and loving and nurturing.'

'You're laying it on thick tonight; you can stop anytime,' Hope says, turning to face Jess, who gives her a huge puppy-dog stare. 'Stop it,' she says affectionately before giving him a kiss. The two of them truly make a cute pair.

'When did I say it was OK for you two to become an item?' I joke, fiddling with my straw when someone clears their throat behind me. Hope and Jess stop their canoodling and when Jess looks up, he looks as though Thanos has just collected the last of the infinity stones and Hope is smiling encouragingly at me.

I smooth down my dress with my gin-free hand and roll my shoulders back, the image of Ruby looking gorgeous in her figure-hugging dress engraved in my mind. I turn around to greet Devon.

'Hi,' I say, awkwardly giving him a wave, even though he is less than a metre in front of me. I was going to go for the handshake, contemplated a hug, but it came out as a wave. Devon takes an awkward two steps forward and one step back as if he was going in for a hug too, so I don't feel as embarrassed.

'You came,' he says, giving me a side smile that makes a dimple pop in his right cheek. He looks different to earlier when he had been stood with Ruby and the boys from school, almost shy and less intimidating. I try and shake off thoughts of Ruby and think of something to say, but it's hard when Devon is studying me. His brown eyes scan my dress and then fall on my eyes, creating a flutter of butterflies deep in my belly.

'Nice to see you again, Devon,' Hope says stepping forward and giving him a quick hug. Her voice sounds more authoritative compared to this morning. I can see she is still gobsmacked over casually getting to hug a superhero but she's playing my best friend card and doing her duties now that she knows mine and Devon's story a little better. I welcome her interruption and take a refreshing sip of gin.

'You know Hope; this is Jess. Just give him a minute, he's a little bit in love with you,' I say, stepping aside and introducing Jess. My shoulders relax a touch when I see how ecstatic Jess is. It's hard not to be transported back to being my sixteen-year-old self freaking out over the thought of one day meeting Robert Downey Jr. Though that was another dream I never pursued after turning my back on the whole comic universe, I can empathise with how awesome this moment is for one of my best friends and I'm behaving myself, like I promised Hope I would, and I'm letting him have his moment.

'Hi, Jess,' Devon says but I can't help noticing it sounds a little icy. It stops me in my tracks. Ten years goes out of the window along with whatever awkwardness I felt moments ago as I whack Devon in his thick bicep. 'Devon, this is one of my best friends, Jess.' I nudge him again harder and give him a pointed glare.

Devon's mouth opens wide and his eyes light up. 'Your friend?' he reiterates, resting a hand over his chest.

My brows furrow and I look down to check my glass to see how much gin I've consumed. I'm not even halfway through my glass yet, so it's definitely Devon acting weird.

'Yes, my friend,' I repeat slowly.

'And my boyfriend,' Hope chimes in merrily, squeezing Jess's shoulders. 'He's been terribly excited to meet you since I told him about you last night.'

I look at Hope's glass, which is empty.

'You're one of Scar's best friends – sorry, hi, Jess. It's so great to meet you and thank you for being a fan too. It's loud in here. Should we get a table?' Devon says, shaking Jess's hand and bringing him in for a hug, putting him at ease instantly, his voice now filled with warmth once again.

'Hi, erm, yeah that sounds good,' Jess manages as Devon guides him to the booth by the fire. Hope and I follow, me ignoring Hope's side elbows and giddy winks and wondering why Devon had for a split second come across a little hostile to Jess. Had Hollywood turned him into an egotistical man who felt superior to other men?

9

'*D*on't tell your mum,' my dad says with a wink, placing two glasses of lemonade on the table – one for me and one for Devon. Then he scoots up next to me in the booth with his pint of Guinness. I smile up at him, then get back to work concentrating on my colouring.

'I'm nearly done, Dad, don't look yet,' I say, my tongue sticking out as I try really hard not to colour outside the lines.

'I'm done,' D announces, turning his sheet over so I can't see it before taking a sip of his lemonade.

I colour in the last golden edge of the crown and carefully put my pencil crayon back in my precious Spider-Man pop-out pencil case. I take a big slurp of lemonade, the bubbles tickling my tongue, before I clutch my paper to my chest.

'OK, I'm ready,' I tell the judge.

'Mr Davis, remember you have to tell the truth – you can't choose Scar because she's yours,' D notes. He says this every Saturday but we're actually drawing five-five, since my dad started bringing us to the pub for colouring competitions while my mum works at the hairdresser's. I love this time with my dad; every week he surprises us with different superheroes to colour.

'I promise I won't, kid,' my dad assures nervous six-year-old Devon with a hearty chuckle. 'Are both contestants ready?'

I brace myself, my hands sweaty against the crisp white paper. D and I nod. Dad closes his eyes. 'One, two, three, what've you got?' Dad says opening them as D and I flip our papers around. I'm so pleased with my Wonder Woman colouring page. I only wobbled outside the line on one tiny bit. I hope my dad doesn't notice.

'Whoa, D,' I say, looking away from my dad's excited face to see what D has coloured in. He's holding up an epic colouring of Captain Marvel. 'I think D wins this week, Dad,' I whisper turning back to my dad.

'I might have to agree, Scar, but I think they both look fantastic and deserve a spot on the fridge,' he replies, encouragingly.

D and I high-five.

'I love yours too, Scar,' D says. His cheeks are red with pride.

'What would the winner like for a prize this week?' my dad asks Devon. Devon looks at me and grins.

'Ice-cream,' he exclaims without much thought. I cheer. We both love our ice-cream.

The four of us are sat in mine and Devon's old hang-out spot, the conversation is flowing, and my shoulders have relaxed more than I had intended them to this evening.

'What else did Scarlett here get you to do?' Hope asks, sipping her second gin with a broad grin on her face.

I sit up straight on the cosy booth seat and playfully

throw a coaster at Hope. 'We were young and stupid and this one was the bossy one – don't let him fool you. I just couldn't say no,' I protest, my voice a higher octave than normal.

Hope's face turns from amused to mischievous. I wish I had superpowers that meant I couldn't read her mind. Her clear "I wouldn't say no either" wink makes me sweat.

Devon has spent the last forty-five minutes regaling them with stories that make it look like he spent his childhood being forced into doing the craziest stunts and always playing the sidekick. He's become wildly enthusiastic, engaging and attentive, asking just as many questions to both Hope and Jess as they are asking him. So much so that by the time our third round of drinks arrive, I feel I could give them all a pop quiz on where each of them grew up, family history, brothers, sisters, pets, and holidays they've been on.

'I don't believe that for a second,' Hope says with a laugh.

I narrow my eyes, tilt my head and pucker my lips in a perfect pout. I look at Devon as if to say, "you asked for it," as I prepare to knock him off the pedestal that Hope and Jess now have him on after the picture he has painted of me just now.

'Devon, please tell my dear, dear friends here which one of us jumped out of a tree when they were twelve years old and fractured both their wrists?' I say, slowly and purposefully, leaning forward and looking Devon straight in the eyes.

He smirks and shakes his head at my nerve. 'That would have been you,' he says, unable to stop himself from snorting.

'And, Mr Wood, won't you please tell my best friends here who later skated off an icy roof, landed in the concrete bowl and broke their arm and fractured their wrist again?' I go on.

Devon matches my stance, leaning forward with his forearms on the table, his face inches from mine. Hope and Jess seemed to have stopped breathing, waiting with bated breath for Devon's answer, as they go quiet and still.

'That answer would also be you,' he notes, closing his eyes when Hope gasps.

'No way,' Jess mutters, cringing. 'Ouch, Scarlett, you never told us that.'

No, I did not. Both memories were too painful to ever bring up and the pain had nothing to do with the injuries. I can't help but laugh at mine and Devon's idiocy and because of the pang of joy I feel at being able to share such goofy memories and important pieces of my childhood with two of my best friends.

'And who came up with those such clever ideas?' I add, just to really hit home.

'Oh, are you blaming me? Are you sure it was me?' Devon says, pointing at himself and scrunching up his face to make a silly expression.

'Not quite the perfect poster boy now, are we?' I tease before moving away from Devon's face and leaning back in my seat to allow myself to breathe my own air.

'I can't believe you two. Your parents must have been nervous wrecks,' Hope comments. Devon and I both shrug in unison but remain quiet. We catch each other's eyes, and both let out a chuckle. He's obviously on the same page as me, not wanting to discuss our parents, and for a moment that connection feels nice.

'Oh my gosh, Devon, have you been to New York Comic Con? Have you seen the cosplay there?' Hope asks eagerly flapping her hands about and then they're off discussing cosplay, Jess and Hope giving detailed accounts of outfits they have worn and Devon's eyes lighting up after hearing about every one. I swirl the ice around in my glass and can't help but wonder if this is how it would have been throughout the past ten years had Devon not left. If the four of us would have cosplayed together.

'I've been a few times, but I've never cosplayed. I'm ashamed to admit this movie is the first time I've worn spandex since I was twelve,' Devon says shaking his head.

'Not a bad way to start up again, mate,' Jess notes, clinking bottles with Devon in agreement.

'Not at all.' Devon beams. 'I'm terrible when it comes to designing though. Scar was the brains behind our costumes and then our mums would make them for us, after much begging.' He laughs gently nudging his knuckles against mine, which are around the rim of my gin glass, resting on the table. I feel a slight fizz and move my hand away quickly.

Hope leans across the table and wags her finger a mere inch away from my face. I think she's had enough gin for the night. 'OK, since he got here, I am starting to love you more and more. No offence.'

'None taken,' I say with a nod.

Hope sits back down. 'She's always crafting and baking, but I've never seen her draw. I want to see these superhero costumes,' Hope says, talking to Devon now.

Devon's face goes from relaxed and full of laughter to

bewildered, like he's missed some form of inside joke. I ignore the straw in my glass and down the rest of my pink gin and lemonade in one long gulp.

'I can't believe you've never seen her draw. Scar draws – that's her thing. Right, Scar?' Devon nudges my knuckles again. His brows crease and he's looking a little worried now, like maybe something bad happened to me, like I hit my head and am suffering from amnesia and can't remember my childhood, when really it's not as dramatic as that. I may have just lied and kept my drawing a secret.

'Not this one, dude. I mean she's crafty and can make and build anything, but we've never seen her draw. She's never so much as glanced at my comic book collection, which I now have to give her credit for. That must have taken a hell of a lot of will power,' Jess chimes in unhelpfully. I'm getting that uncomfortable knot in my stomach that occurs when Devon's features do that thing where his bottom lip starts to stick out and his eyes go foggy. It's like Thor in the dryer all over again. He's upset and no doubt embarrassed that he doesn't get the joke.

'What are you guys chit-chatting about?' a shrill voice cuts through my friends' chatter.

'Oh, nothing that concerns you,' Jess informs Ruby.

I notice Devon shift uncomfortably in his seat. I dare not look at my enemy. Nothing Ruby ever says to me is pleasant and I'd rather her not spoil this unexpectedly happy evening.

'You here with the girls tonight? I'm sure they're missing you right now, but thanks for saying hello,' Hope says turning her back to Ruby who isn't remotely fazed by her lack of subtlety in her attempt to shoo her away. Hope's always stuck up for me whenever we bump into Ruby and her minions. Fortunately, Ruby travels a lot with work these days so that's not an everyday occurrence.

'Aww, so cute,' Ruby says, a fake smile plastered on her face when she sees Hope and Jess's hands intertwined on the table. 'Oh my gosh, how long has it been since you guys have seen each other?' Ruby asks, looking at Devon and I and making her eyes wide like this is all some exciting celebration and her questions are all spontaneous, when if I know Ruby, they're not. She's come over here with a purpose.

'It's been a while.' Devon nods.

'No, it can't be that long. It was only what, two years ago now that you were back here for the summer fair. We had those cheeky shots – yes, you must have seen Scarlett then I'm sure. Now I best go, but don't you stay out late; we have a busy day tomorrow,' she says with a wink, and a swish of her hips and a look that suggests she would devour Devon in a heartbeat if she got him alone, then she saunters off.

I can feel my nose tingling as I try and curb the tears that I feel any second now are going to spring from my eyes. I'm glad I'm in one of my own outfits tonight and not one of my mum's tight-fitting choices as the booth suddenly feels claustrophobic. I need to go.

The atmosphere at our table has gone from joyful to tense in a matter of minutes. In my blurry vision I can see Hope looking over at me with a sad expression on her face. Even in her slightly drunken state I know she understands what's going on. After all I confessed to her about Devon being the closest thing to me, how much his leaving hurt me and how confusing it all is with him being back. I know she didn't miss Ruby's comment about the summer fair. She waves at Jess urging him to move so I can get past. I nod my thanks as Devon mumbles something behind me.

How could I have let my guard down and have been so silly to let Devon, Jess and Hope get to know each other? And worse still let myself relax and actually enjoy the warm feeling in my stomach of them all getting along?

'Thank you for a lovely evening, everyone, but I've got so much to do tomorrow. I'd best be off,' I say as I stand, not wanting to make a scene.

'Scar, can we talk?' I hear Devon ask, but I don't have the strength to look at him.

'I've got to go,' I reply and then turn to leave.

IO

When I step outside the pub, I sense snow flurries will be upon Springhollow soon. The sky has turned a misty grey, with plumes of wispy white clouds, and there's a peacefulness to the air, like the calm before the magic. I take quick strides in my boots as the chill seeps through my coat, clashing with the heat of my body. When I near Mr and Mrs Rolph's bakery, I feel something tug at my coat and hear panting from behind me. My heart starts thumping in my chest, though I know everyone in Springhollow and crime is a once a year occurrence – if that – I start waving my arms manically and picking up my pace against the force. That is until I hear a groan I recognise and turn around to see Devon grabbing at my wrist.

When our eyes connect, he lets go and I stop still.

'I love you, little Steve Rogers, you're so cute. Yes, you are,' I say, kneeling on Devon's bed as Steve Rogers scurries around on the duvet.

D jumps onto the bed as the little hamster curls up into a ball in the middle of the cushy blanket.

'D, careful,' I say, watching the ball move up and down in tiny bounces.

'He loves it, it's like he's flying,' Devon tells me and so I stand up and start bouncing too.

'Scar, who do you love more? Me or Steve Rogers?' D asks as our jumping gets a tad crazier, but Devon's right, the little hamster seems to like it, squealing with glee and stretching out his tiny paws.

'I love you both the same, but I will probably love you forever. I don't think pets last that long. Autumn's rabbit died last week, and he was only three,' I say, matter-of-fact. Just then Devon slips on the duvet and goes flying off the side of his bed. I scream and jump down beside him.

'D, are you OK?' I whisper, suddenly aware that I don't want his mum running up the stairs to check on us.

Devon lets out a grunt. 'Ouch, yeah, I'm OK,' he says, wiggling his toes as I check him over. 'Scar?'

'What?' I reply, kneeling next to him and frantically looking around.

'I think I love you more th...'

'D, wait, move, move, move. I think your squashing Steve Rogers,' I interrupt panicking and fearing for the little guy's life when I don't see him anywhere on the bed.

If I knew one thing when I was a young, naïve twelve-year-old, I knew I loved Devon – at least in the same way I loved a hamster. I trusted him. I liked spending time with him. He made me laugh and looked after me and I did the same for him. He was always there when I needed him and always stood up for me when Ruby and her gang called me names.

He was cool and liked awesome stuff and unlike my mum – who didn't quite get why it was so important to add wings to my skateboard – Devon never questioned my antics or ideas; he joined in and helped me bring them to life.

The thing is I must stop pretending I am twelve years old; romanticising the past with the belief that it can somehow be my future. I'm angry with myself for being so stupid and mad that all these years later Devon can still hurt me like this. I need to put an end to all of this now. Despite what my twelve-year-old self assumed, I can't love him forever.

Devon goes to speak but I cut him off. 'Don't you dare,' I start. The words come out hard but contained. 'So, what, you turn up at my door this morning having a go at me for acting strange, blaming me for not writing to you; like I was the one who ruined it all? You came here two years ago, and you didn't think to say hi? To check in? You had all the time in the world for Ruby, but your supposed best friend wasn't worth a visit? I don't want to hear it, Devon. I've managed fine without you for the past ten years. Please just leave me alone.' I sigh a heavy sigh as the words lift off my chest. I pull my coat tighter around my body, aware now that my skin is no longer hot and sweaty but icy and stiff. In our time apart we've managed to build a web of resentment and more lies; it's no good for either of us.

'That's not fair. I tried, Scar. I wrote to you – how many letters did I send? How many? I made a mistake; I should have come to see you that summer but that doesn't take away from the fact that you ignored me, and I was scared. I didn't know if you wanted to see me again. How could I have possibly known? I didn't get one response, Scar, not one.' Devon's eyes are welling up now. He runs a hand through his dew-damp hair before rubbing his hands together. His shoulders are curved slightly to ward off the dropping temperature. I'm controlling my tears with the discipline I have practised over the years.

'Yes, well you can keep throwing that in my face, D, but I was young and hurt and you lied to me. This is all your fault. You left.' My voice escapes a little louder this time. I'm fed up of hearing that line; of him throwing my mistakes in my face. My hands begin to tremble. I know I am doing the same to him; trying to throw all the blame his way, but I can't help it. It's like my only protection. If it's Devon's fault he will know how to fix it. He got his life in order when he moved to New York. He did fine without me, scored his dream job and dream role. What have I done in his absence? If I acknowledge any part of it being my fault, then I will have to fix it and I don't know how.

'Scar, I'm sorry, I'm truly sorry but I was sixteen. Are you ever going to forgive me?' Devon says, waving his arms at his sides. It's only now I realise he has run out here without his coat. The tip of his nose is red, his brown eyes clear and twinkling from the cold air.

I look at the ground as I think back to the hospital bed when I was twelve and how Devon didn't leave my side until I had eaten and we had made up, but at sixteen it had been a whole other story. He didn't stay, he couldn't stay, and my life was changed forever. Suddenly Ruby's words ring out in my brain. I see her laughing with Devon, her hands on his body. My mind conjures the image of Devon stood with the popular boys.

'I don't think I can. We're two different people now. You don't know me and I sure as hell don't know the guy who just sits there and allows Ruby to stir up trouble and patronise me and my friends. You're not my best friend anymore,' I say firmly, finally releasing what I've needed to say out loud for the past ten years; to make it clear to him and to myself that he can't just turn up and muscle his way into that role again.

When I look up Devon's eyes are glistening, and his bottom lip is trembling. He goes to take a step forward but someone steps in. Hope puts her arm gently on his forearm. 'I don't think this is the time nor place,' she whispers to him and that's when I notice a few people have stopped in their tracks to nosy in on tonight's village entertainment courtesy of Devon and me. If it was ten years ago, Devon and I battling in the street would be just another day in the neighbourhood, but this isn't some make-believe fight – Spider-Man vs. the Green Goblin – this is real life and it's another harsh reminder that too much has changed.

Devon nods at Hope before Jess guides him back to the pub and Hope tucks her arm in to the crook of mine and starts walking. She doesn't speak; she simply strolls calmly by my side all the way to my house, lets us in with her key and potters about turning on lamps and flicking on the kettle. My bones ache from the cold and my eyelids feel too heavy for my face. I slothfully shuffle into the living room and fall onto the couch, my eyes battling to stay open. I tap Ed's bowl, but he's not swimming. I can see his glowing orange tail peeking out from his bed cave. 'Night night, Eddie,' I whisper, not caring about the mascara tears that are falling on the cushion as I give in to sleep.

★

I don't remember falling asleep or what time it was when we got back from the pub, but I twist and turn, my eyes slowly opening at three-thirty in the morning to find that I'm fully clothed on my couch with a blanket draped over me.

I lie awake staring at the shadows on my ceiling and my Christmas tree, cast by the moon's glow. The curtains are still wide open, and the shadows suddenly start dancing with small specks. I turn my attention to the long rectangle portrait window and see the first signs of snow. It's slow at first, just the odd dot flying past the glass, but after only a few minutes it grows heavy, the dots blurring with the speed at which they are falling. My heart skips a beat.

I sit up and notice a note on the table in addition to a glass of water, a cold cup of tea and toast and makeup wipes. A smile tugs at my lips and, though the toast is a little dry and stale now, I pick up a piece and take a crunchy bite, followed by a large gulp of water to reduce the thumping in my head. Then I reach for Hope's note.

> Take some time for you today. It's been a busy two days.
> Jess and I are here if you need us. Hope x
> P.S. Don't freak out. Also, it's supposed to snow tomorrow. Love you. xx

I pop open the pack of makeup wipes as more tears threaten my eyes. I chew on my tongue to steady my breathing and repeat Hope's favourite mantra, "don't freak out" from her favourite TV show and smile at how much I love her.

Once I've accumulated a stack of dirty makeup wipes and

my clock ticks over to four a.m., I move to sit at the edge of the couch to get a better view of the snowfall, not feeling sleepy anymore. Looking out through my window I can see the snow sticking to the ground, creating a white layer of crisp and crunchy ice. In the magic of the falling snow, my busy mind becomes calm. I'm going to be OK without Devon, I tell myself. After all this time spent dreaming about seeing him again, it's happened now, and we've said all we need to say to each other and though it was painful, it was a good thing. We got everything out in the open and now I can start living my life, properly.

I reach over to the arm of the couch and grab my pink and white woolly throw and wrap it around me. I tiptoe to the tree, not wanting to wake Eddie, and turn on its golden lights, which instantly make me feel better. I simply stand and stare at it.

'I can't believe you just did that.' D's not shouting, he says it softly with tears streaming down his face. D never gets angry with me; he cries instead. Sometimes I wish he would just yell.

'I didn't mean it,' I say, my voice louder. I'm mad at him for being upset. I don't like him being upset.

'Well it wasn't funny. You're not supposed to play tig with sticks, you're supposed to use your hands,' he explains matter-of-fact, his Superman cape lying limp in his small seven-year-old hands.

'Oh, come on, D, that stick was cool. I couldn't just leave it on the ground. And how did I know it would rip your cape?' I retort, folding my arms across my chest.

'You didn't even say sorry,' Devon says before running inside and leaving me alone with said cool stick and my stubborn pout.

With the glow of the tree lights, I walk into the kitchen and feel around for the light switch. The tools for my gingerbread house remain scattered on the table after I deserted them yesterday. I realise I never brought my blueprint down from my office but am too scared to venture in there right now. I can't have my unfinished comic book luring me back in, with a week to go until the Christmas fair I can have no distractions; this gingerbread house needs building. I remove the dough from the fridge and make quick work of cutting out Christmassy shapes and getting them in the oven before focusing my attention on decorating my building.

I look over my decorations and decide to work from memory, either that or just make it up as I go along. I'll need to make another batch of biscuits but with this being the main feature I think I'm going to decorate each piece and let them set and dry before piecing it together to ensure it all fits snugly and that way if I break any parts of the house I can double up my dough and make new ones along with reindeers and gingerbread people.

The front door of *The Village Gazette* building seems like the perfect place to start. It's a thick deep oak door with a brass door knocker and a round gold doorknob. The wood is grainy and worn, which I think gives it character. During the holidays, the addition of a large holly wreath only adds to its charm. I pick up my fondant and begin to roll out the shapes of red and green that I need to make the wreath in edible form.

Concentrating on the tiny details, painting each wooden knot and dusty red brick keeps me distracted well into lunchtime, when I put my brush down and have a rummage through my fridge. My appetite is non-existent; between my lack of sleep, which has just started catching up with me, and my fight with Devon last night, my body doesn't know what it wants. I content with making myself a peppermint coffee and powering through. The kitchen smells delicious and I'm pleased with how my shaped gingerbread have turned out, but I've only managed one side of the Gazette building. It's going to take longer than I thought. But it's a task I'm more than up for and helps keep my mind off replaying my argument with Devon.

Though the words "I'm sorry" keep repeating themselves in my brain. I shake my head and breathe in the aroma of peppermint and gingerbread and take a minute to sit down at the breakfast bar with a piece of paper and pen.

I scribble out a note to speak to Autumn this week and check in with Hope's library idea, in addition to some ideas of how to present the baking competition working with *The Village Gazette* to Mrs Rolph. But I feel like we need something bigger to keep the magazine afloat. As I sip my coffee and twirl my pen around in my fingers, I wonder if there is a way of making our magazine monthly rather than weekly and still have it profit. It would cut down on production and save on costs and maybe give people something to look forward to each month, so much so that they would treat themselves and not think twice about buying it.

Stretching my arms above my head I let out a little "mmm" sound, feeling excited by my idea. I then rub at my eyes and release a yawn I had been trying to hold in. The sound of tapping draws my attention to my living room window, so I pick up my coffee to go and investigate.

'Afternoon, sunshine,' I say to Eddie as I spot his little fluorescent body swimming around his tank. I sprinkle in some food before moving towards the window. The snow is falling once more but this time it's not feathery snowflakes but icy pellets thundering to the ground below. I smile. I love this time of year, being wrapped up indoors with the fire going, listening to the elements outside, the house in a sort of moody yet warm and peaceful darkness.

Devon and I used to make snow forts back in the day. When the weather turned anti-skateboarding on us, we'd build forts, take all our action figures inside with us and smuggle snacks from the kitchen, not coming out until it was time for dinner or home time for one of us.

"I'm sorry" mocks me in my mind again. I turn away from the memories the snow is eliciting and decide I should probably get out of last night's clothes and wash. A lazy Sunday in pyjamas was one thing, a smelly, icky, lazy Sunday in yesterday's clothes was another. I deposit my empty mug in the kitchen and twist my short hair into a topknot that becomes more a half up, half down topknot as I make my way up the stairs.

To divert my brain's attention from Devon, I run through my "to do" list. The chimney for my replica building needs whipping up, so I'll do that this afternoon with the next batch of cookies I make. I need to start on another wall of the building in order for construction to move forward this week on my Victorian-style house. I always prefer decorating each slab before piecing them together – that way more detail can be added without icing and fondant slipping out of place or drizzling down the roof and making a mess.

The hot shower melts away the tension in my shoulder blades. I can do this. I will finish this project in time, and it will be the best Christmas fair stall Springhollow has ever seen from *The Village Gazette*. The villagers are already getting excited. After the flyer went out on Thursday informing every one of the Gingerbread competition, I'd seen to a few emails Friday morning with people wanting to triple check the rules, eager to get started on their entry.

I wash and rinse with both shampoo and conditioner and when I step out of the shower, my warm fluffy towel is like a welcome hug. But when I catch myself in the mirror, I don't recognise the person before me. Something doesn't sit right. *You didn't even say you're sorry.* The words buzz around more forcefully in my head. When I go to retreat from my own evil glare, I pause on the landing. I hug my towel tighter to my body and slowly push open the door to my office/fake storage space and immediately start rummaging through old boxes I haven't looked through in years. This will make it up to him. This will be my apology, then I can truly put the past behind me and both Devon and I can stay out of each other's way and get on with our lives once and for all.

When I find what I am looking for, I go to leave, but before I know it, my fairy lights are aglow and I'm scribbling and sketching at my desk like my pencil never left the paper.

11

After rolling into bed at close to midnight I barely sleep a wink. My comic book had stolen all my attention for the evening; I felt like my hands couldn't keep up with the pace the ideas were coming to my brain, which had continued to fire on all cylinders while I tried to sleep. That and my plan for today kept spinning around my mind. I shower in the darkness and dress under the light of the moon. I dress in my sleek black trousers with long-sleeved light blue button-up blouse, eyeing up my denim dungarees as I do so, and sigh. It's just work clothes. Everyone has a uniform for work; it's no big deal and it makes my mum happy, I tell myself and quickly grab my mustard yellow beanie, to claim a little piece of myself.

Bundling up with my scarf and navy fleece I creep out of my house and into the freshly fallen snow. It crunches under the pressure of my boots, making me smile into my woolly scarf. I wave at Mr and Mrs Rolph as I pass the bakery on the corner of my street. Already the smell of baking loaves fills the square. I nod at Mrs Bride fiddling with her chunky keys to open the library doors. It's early in Springhollow – the whole the village isn't awake yet. It's not often I witness the first signs of life but as I need to walk to the edge of the village before work, I had to make an early start.

This morning I'm choosing to follow my instinct, which is something I haven't dared to do in a while, but with my package in my backpack I'm feeling brave. My plan is to nip to The Sunflower Inn, about five blocks from me, and see if I'm correct and that Devon and his entourage are staying there, what with it being the only inn in our quaint village. I don't think the smaller B and B's could accommodate the press crew. There I will leave my parcel at the front desk with Willow. That's it, simple as that and then I can be on my way.

I make it three blocks before the clouds decide to sprinkle generous heaps of snowflakes on me. I can't complain though. It's a beautiful sight watching the sun come up through snow showers. The moonlight and slowly rising sun make the snowflakes glisten and give the sky a stunning halo effect that projects rainbows of colour to guide my way. I skip a little faster hoping to keep the chill they bring at bay.

Whereas the village square was blanketed with quiet this morning, The Sunflower Inn is abuzz with life. There are people on mobile phones pacing the decking and I can see a camera being set up through the reception area in the dining room. It's a little odd seeing these sharp-suited and booted folks in the inn, not to judge, but the lack of Wi-Fi and the mobile service being spotty at best, we don't get many businesspeople bar the few regulars who come to switch off. The people I am currently observing look far from switched off.

'I take it you're here to see Devon.' Willow's soft and

airy voice snaps me out of my nosy people-watching and reminds me that I can't hover for long because no, no I'm not here to see Devon and I don't wish to bump into him either.

I turn my attention hastily away from watching the camera crew fiddle with lighting, to Willow. She's beautiful with sandy shoulder-length hair that naturally waves around her heart-shaped face. Her deep hazel eyes greet me with a smile. Willow and I went to primary school together, but she always kept herself to herself, picking flowers in the school playground or sitting with her eyes to the sky, lost in a daydream. We got on well enough, though I sometimes think mine and Devon's action-packed games terrified her. She didn't attend our high school, her parents choosing to home-school her instead.

'Hey, Willow, no erm no, I'm just here to drop this off for Devon and see if you could give it to him for me,' I say, rummaging through my backpack to retrieve the soft brown bag.

Willow stops fluttering around her desk plants and eyes me curiously. 'Do you not want to give it to him yourself?' she asks before her cheeks turn a rosy shade of pink and she hastily adds, 'I mean of course I can pass it on to him, Scarlett, but it sounds important. I just thought he'd prefer it coming from you.' There's a nervous flicker behind Willow's eyes that suggests she's worried that she just offended me by being rude, but Willow couldn't sound rude if she tried. And I'm not offended by her question, just a tad inconvenienced by it; meaning I really don't want to answer it.

I chuckle and wave my hands to make light of the conversation, to show that it isn't that important and to put

Willow at ease over her anxiety at possibly speaking out of turn. She is a sweetheart and really hadn't offended me. 'Erm, no, no. It's fine. I've got to get off to work, so I'd be truly grateful if you could just give it to him, please,' I say handing her the bag.

'OK, no problem. I can give it to him when he gets back,' she says, her worry lines vanishing, a bright smile in place as she takes the bag from me.

'Oh, he's not here?' I ask, unable to hide the curiosity in my tone. Willow is so busy placing the bag safely under the desk that she doesn't notice or think anything untoward of my query.

'No, he didn't check back in over the weekend. I thought he was with you,' she says standing upright and waving at customers coming down the stairs and into the breakfast room. They have to follow the peg boards to the dining area, which isn't in use by the documentary crew.

'Why would you think that?' I ask. How could the village just expect Devon and I to pick up where we left off when they saw the aftermath of what I became when he left?

'Because you were always glued together at the hip when we were kids and I know you missed him. I thought you had a lot of catching up to do and you'd just gravitate to each other like you're supposed to do,' Willow informs me with her airy grace and a gentle smile as she goes back to fussing over her potted desk daisies.

OK, so I guess some of them did think that, but they are wrong. It can't be like that for Devon and me anymore. I shake my head. I'm just here to make peace, to say sorry and that's it. Before I can respond to Willow a lady with her phone hovering between her lips and ear, so I can't tell if she's talking to someone or not, appears at my side.

'Excuse me, did she just say that you and Devon Wood spent the night together?' The lady is nowhere near as innocent as Willow, as in she's not innocent at all, her pencilled-on eyebrows move up and down. Willow giggles and sees to helping a customer who is asking about breakfast and I take a step back from the front desk.

'That would be a no, nope, no way. I have no idea where he is. Nice to meet you.' I nod and take another step towards the door. The lady follows.

'But she just said you were glued together? Childhood sweethearts, I take it. Did you do everything together? What do you make of Devon's shoot to stardom? Do you think he still remembers you?' With the lady's barrage of questions, I can feel a dull throb developing under my beanie. She's adamant about what she overheard and determined to get an answer. I feel like I'm suffocating with my many layers on under her hawk-eyed gaze.

'No, no I'm not answering your questions. Sorry, not the girl you are looking for,' I tell her boldly trying to allude to confidence but trip up over the rug as I walk backwards, only stopping when the doorknob digs into my back. I wiggle it to open it but it's stiff and won't budge. The lady is closing in on me.

'We're doing a documentary on Mr Wood. It would be fascinating to interview his childhood sweetheart; the media will eat that up,' she says tapping her mobile against her lips, dollar signs in her eyes. What is wrong with this bloody door? I can't seem to twist it and I feel like the woman is about to gobble me whole. I am having no luck navigating the simple invention of a doorknob behind my back so I whip around, ignoring the lady and make one desperate attempt to pull the knob when a shadow through the frosted glass chooses the exact moment to give the door an almighty push.

The clipboard lady takes a comedic step to the side, like that time I got paired with Ruby when we were doing trust exercises in school and Ruby did the same, allowing me to hit the floor with a hard whack; in fact it's exactly like that as my elbow greets the wood sending a sharp pain through my arm and I hear a smattering of laughter.

'Careful now, Scarlett. You always were such a bull in a china shop.' Ruby looks down at me as she makes her way over to the desk, a smirk on her red lips. 'Willow, Willow,' she shouts, ringing the bell. Willow is stood less than a metre away with another customer. I pick myself up off the floor and straighten my beanie. Clipboard lady is looking from me to Ruby and back again, but I can't quite tell what she's thinking – her face is neutral. 'Willow, what room is Devon in? I have some clothes for him.' I don't miss Ruby's quirked eyebrow, sly grin, the fact that her words were aimed more in my direction or the feeling that my stomach has just been put in a dryer on fast spin.

'Oh, so you're the one Devon was with last night.' Clipboard lady doesn't miss a beat and is next to Ruby in one giant stride. 'So, are you his childhood sweetheart?' I can't help the snort that escapes my lips. Even Willow scoffs and Willow never scoffs. Ruby hesitates for a second at the lady's assumption and stares at the small case of clothes. I can see her brain ticking over before she puffs out her bosom, flicks her hair back and flashes me a wild grin, more than happy to play along.

'Ruby – a pleasure to meet you.' Ruby sticks out her hand, which clipboard lady happily takes; she's found her golden ticket. I stand on the spot dumbfounded. Ruby just said she had clothes for Devon. That doesn't mean she spent the night with him, does it?

'Tell me, miss, have you always been the apple of Mr Wood's eye or has he got two women after his heart? Is there competition in these parts for Devon?' the lady asks, almost salivating at the gossip she is about to receive from a clearly willing-to-impart Ruby.

My coffee threatens to make a reappearance as Ruby cackles. 'Oh, honey, there's no competition. Men like Devon need a real lady.'

Since when did Ruby think Devon was a real man? In school she thought he was a snotty nerd and didn't give him the time of day. What had changed her mind now? Oh yeah, Devon's money, fame and camera crew – that would do it. My supervillain alarm goes off. I don't care for this lady and I've never been Ruby's number-one fan; together I am fearful of what damage they can do to Devon's reputation. Ruby just proved that she's game to whip up lies to get her fifteen minutes of fame, but how far will she take it? And why am I bothered? For all I know Devon spent the night with Ruby. They seemed pretty cosy in the pub on Saturday night. She's here now with clothes for him and looks like she belongs in his new world. I need to leave and forget about it, all of it.

I send a small smile Willow's way, ignore Ruby's comment and step out of the front door. The last thing I hear is 'Ooh, do we have ourselves a man in demand? Where did the other woman go?' as I close the door behind me. A shiver runs through me as the frosty air nips at my nose. I haven't the first clue about social media – I only hear snippets from Hope – but I know celebrity gossip is a big money machine. Is that what is going on here? Did Devon need a juicy headline to help sell his movie? Is that what clipboard lady is trying to find? Is Devon OK with that?

I walk down the path, past the line of baby conifers bearing strings of white fairy lights. The snow has calmed now, occasionally a light shower sprinkles my coat, falling with the breeze off the trees. I need to put this all behind me and not get involved. Devon has my apology now. If there are still any remnants of the Devon I once knew in him then he will understand my peace offering and we can get back to being worlds apart. The new Devon in his extraordinary world that involves clipboard men and women, camera crews, parties and smart suits. Me in my hometown, with my nine-to-five, secret office and clothes I don't like.

Speaking of clothes, Ruby would not look amiss on a red carpet, and she'd love every minute of the flashing lights and constant attention. If Devon has come here to make headlines and find his golden girl maybe Ruby is the right woman for him.

I push open the door of *The Village Gazette* with extra oomph and hear the doorknob connect with the wall as it swings open. I'm met with a wall of warmth; the heating must be on full blast. Normally, this would be welcome to aid in thawing me from the freeze outside but today it makes my chest tighten and I feel like I can't breathe. Something – anger, frustration, sadness, happiness – is stirring in my gut and I can't place it. My emotions feel all pent up and I'm not sure what to do with them. I don't need a door; I need a punch bag.

I unravel my scarf and whip off my beanie as I ascend the stairs. It's hard to miss the murmurs and eyes on me as I walk across my floor towards Hope's office, but I try to keep my head down and smile as brightly as I can muster to pretend like it's any ordinary day. But my co-workers, those who I went to primary school and high school with, know that's not true. They are all behaving the same as Ryan, Autumn and Willow, some smiling nervously, some with wide eyes full of excitement and some with smiles so docile you'd think they were up to something.

OK, so Devon is back in town. We all know it and we can all get over it now.

When I step into Hope's office, she's busy tapping away at her laptop and doesn't look up. That's when I realise in my mad rush of this morning that I'm ten minutes late and forgot to pick up our coffees. I go to turn around and leave when Hope pipes up.

'It's OK, I can wait until lunchtime for my caffeine fix. How are you doing?' She stops typing and looks up from her screen, with a soft smile, her green eyes twinkling at me.

'I'm good,' I say as I start to peel off all my layers and switch my own laptop on. 'Sorry I'm late – I lost track of time running an errand. What did I miss? Is there anything I should know?' I add, wanting to rid my brain of this morning's events and get straight to work.

'Don't worry about it. I'm happy you're feeling good,' she replies a little distracted. I can see that she's trying to give me attention while trying to read her screen at the same time. I chuckle. She waves a finger at me as if to say, "one minute".

When I sit down, I notice a brown bag on my desk. Curious as to what it could be, I pick it up and peek inside. It can't be the doughnuts Hope knows I like because whatever it is is wrapped in red tissue paper and there's a small note attached to it. I worry that I'm taking advantage of Hope and should wait until lunchtime to further investigate when I catch sight of the handwriting. My stomach does a one-eighty flip. There's no mistaking Devon's scrawl. I pull out the note.

Scar, I'm sorry.
P.S. Your apartment is severely lacking in action figures.

I pull and tug at the tissue paper to reveal a superhero, with a white cape and red spandex. What they can do with technology these days is unreal. I'm looking at Devon's face on an action figure and the resemblance is uncanny.

'No freaking way,' I say out loud, unable to help the bewildered laugh that escapes with the words: 'Devon has a freaking action figure.' I can't help looking to Hope who I notice has stopped what she was doing and is already looking at me with a smile on her face. 'A bloody action figure.' I gasp with a grin. Well, now my cape seems outdated. How is that fair? I give Devon an old, ratty, but not ripped cape and he gives me his very own action figure.

'Does this mean you two have made up now?' Hope asks, still studying me from across her desk.

I sink back in my chair, looking at all the details on my new figure. Was this proof that maybe my Devon still existed? But what about all the evidence with Ruby and the boys, the smooth-talking, the lies and ten bloody years between us? How can that be so?

'It's complicated,' I say, a little of the excitement in my voice from moments ago vanishing.

'What's so complicated?' Hope asks, getting up, walking around her desk and leaning against the front of it so she can really talk to me. I'm shocked. It's past nine a.m. This is unheard of for Hope. I sigh, the least I can do is answer her.

'I was at The Sunflower Inn this morning. They were setting up for filming Devon's documentary and Ruby came in with a case of clothes, said she needed to give them to Devon. Then she walked off with one of the clipboard ladies talking about being the love of Devon's life and spending the night with him. Hope, we're not kids anymore. I said some things on Saturday night that I know upset him and he upset me too. We're two different people now and I don't know if I could support him being with someone like Ruby, after all she put us through at school and how she treats us now. Devon being friendly with her, it hurts. And he's a big action hero now. What's he need with me? You're my best friend and Devon probably has loads of best friends in New York.' I spill my doubts and worries, and it feels like a release to be able to say Devon's name to Hope. Hope is quiet for a moment, just listening.

'Ruby came to The Sunflower Inn with a case of clothes and you think she spent the night with Devon? What, you think Devon streaked back to the inn in the nude?' Hope lets out a laugh. My brows draw in. I guess I didn't think of that. She gives me a "you're an idiot" smirk.

'You do remember that our dear friend Ruby is a stylist?

Maybe she's working with him this week – did you ever think of that? However that lady twisted it was probably music to Ruby's ears, especially if she knew you were listening,' Hope adds.

'How can you be so sure?' I say, still feeling a little shaken, and stupid, about the whole thing.

Hope leans back and crosses her legs. She has a vintage grey Thor tee tucked into her cream trousers, which she has paired with peach kitten heels. The whole outfit makes me happy. She narrows her eyes at me and purses her lips. 'Don't be mad. Because Devon spent Saturday and Sunday night with me and Jess and he wasn't at the inn this morning because he was dropping off your gift. It seems like you two had the same idea?' With her last words she quirks an eyebrow in question.

I stare her down for a moment. 'I once ruined his Superman cape and I never said sorry. I was dropping off mine as an apology. I left it for him with Willow. I never said sorry on Saturday night either,' I confess.

Hope makes an "awww" sound and I feel my cheeks get a little hotter.

'How come Devon stayed with you guys? Am I being replaced? That's kind of like picking sides, you know,' I say, a little humour in my tone but a little wary and hesitant about their newfound friendship at the same time.

'Hell no, don't even say that and please don't be mad. He didn't know where to turn after your fight on Saturday and he certainly didn't fancy going back to the inn to face security guards, media chaperones and the like, so Jess and I took him in and he ended up staying last night too. He's kind of obsessed with our comic collection,' Hope tells me, her face creased with empathy, concern, and a touch of amusement.

'Oh, the poor and lonely little superhero,' I tease, not feeling quite as mad as I thought I'd be hearing about my ex best friend and best friends hanging out without me. I'm sure the colourful figure in my hand is harbouring magical powers, for it's making me feel like a kid again and keeping me calm.

'Why did it bother you so much? The thought of Devon spending the night with Ruby?' Hope asks. Her voice is soft as she folds her arms across her chest.

I glance out of the window; the snow is starting to trickle down again, as I ponder her question. 'I've never had to think about Devon and other women before,' I reply, the words coming out quiet.

'I can't believe you're making me do this,' I say, trudging up the path to the town hall where tonight our school is hosting a summer dance.

'Oh, come on, Scar, all our friends are inside. It'll be fun,' Devon argues. He's wearing slim-fitting jeans and a tight-collared polo. It's hard not to notice he's growing, and his clothes are fitting snugger.

'You're my friend and you're out here, so I don't have to go in,' I note. Devon pushes open the door and loud music attacks my eardrums.

'And now I'm inside, so you do.' He smirks and grabs my hand.

I shuffle nervously in my black boots and denim playsuit as Devon pulls me along. I spot a few people from year ten but they're all busy dancing and mingling. I don't want to do either and tug at Devon when I find an empty table.

'I'll grab us drinks,' he says confidently as I sit down. The older we get the more I notice how Devon isn't as fazed by the looks we get, or the mean comments people make. He's friendly to everyone and is always smiling.

'Nice outfit.' I hear the all too familiar voice from behind me followed by the sniggers that usual accompany it from Ruby's bodyguards. 'Did we just miss the line of boys begging to dance with you?' Suddenly Devon appears at my side as if I just sent out an invisible Bat Signal. 'Oh of course not – it's just this one,' Ruby adds with a cackle.

I see the blush creep up Devon's neck but he doesn't retaliate; instead he puts down our drinks, grabs my hand, pulls me up and leads me to the dance floor, shooting Ruby a wink as he spins me around.

'We weren't the kind of kids that played Mummies and Daddies or sent Valentine's Day cards or giggled about crushes. If I'm being totally honest, seeing Ruby all over him at the pub was the first time I've thought about him being with other women. I guess it was always just the two of us. I never had competition,' I confess and immediately cringe at what I've just said. 'I didn't mean it like that; there's no competition, I'm not in a competition, I don't want Devon in that way. It's just weird,' I ramble, the words rushing out as I try and explain to Hope what I mean. I'm confusing myself right now but sharing Devon is not something I'm used to. I keep that thought to myself though because

I'm not really sharing him when he's not mine in any way, shape or form.

'I just feel protective towards him, which is stupid, but I'm going to stop and forget about it right now. He's a grown-up and who he dates is none of my business,' I say, matter-of-fact. My hand brushes over plastic Devon's hair and cape.

Hope stands up straight with a kind smile on her face. 'It's more than OK to feel protective. You felt the same with me and Jess remember? It's totally normal to feel this way. Totally just a friend thing,' she says, turning back to her desk. I'm sure I see a flicker of a cheeky smile as she sits down.

'You're right and there's no point in thinking about it anymore. I've made my peace and I don't have to see him again,' I say with a confident nod. It feels good to air all this out and get it off my chest. I can finally let go of it, so I don't have to harbour it or think about Devon for another ten years.

'Exactly. Now stop touching up Devon and get to work – you were late this morning,' she mock scolds me with a wink and I immediately throw action figure Devon on to my desk before sending an eye-roll her way and getting to work.

12

'My place for dinner tonight, no later than six-thirty and don't be late,' Hope says bounding over to me as the clock strikes five, and then she rushes out of the door before me, which is a first. We often leave together, or I take the lead if Hope needs to work late or I have dinner with my parents. I don't get chance to tell her that I can't and that I really need to get some work done on the Christmas fair project tonight.

Speaking of my parents, I should probably call by and say hello to mine before heading to Hope and Jess's. We've missed our weekly dinners due to them being away and I know my mum will be expecting me; it wouldn't be respectful for me not to greet them after their absence and see how they are. My dad, not being the tyrant my mother is, will just be excited to see me and catch up on all that has been going on in my life while he's been away. I try and pop round to his building site during my lunch hour with a coffee at least twice a week so we can chat. I love learning all that I can about building, woodwork and tools, and spending time together – just the two of us. It's nice not having to put on a pretence for my mum and occasionally getting to help and get my hands dirty.

I finish typing up my idea for a monthly *Village Gazette*, which I plan to put to Hope tomorrow. Now that I've written it down and hashed it out, it seems plausible and like this could be great going forward. Then I pick up mini Devon and tuck him into my backpack. Maybe mini Devon can work his magic and get me through a visit with my mother unscathed.

I love both my parents. They're my parents – they raised me, fed me and kept a roof over my head – but it's safe to say that though one should never show favouritism, I'll always be a daddy's girl. While my mum works at Duncan's hairdressers and is forever trying to organise me, change me and wish me that little bit more girly, my dad is a builder and even now I don't think he'd stop me if I tried to shimmy up the scaffolding to see if I can fly. Though one doesn't need any more broken bones and I think I've learnt my lesson there.

He was always letting Devon and I run around the building sites making dens with wood and planks, when there was no work going on of course, and we wore our helmets. My dad is the only one, other than Devon, who supported my comic book aspirations. He was heartbroken when I gave it up and will still, every now and again to my mother's disappointment, bring it up.

I put one foot through the half-opened front door when my dad swings it wide open with a big grin on his face. 'Scar, do you know who's back in town?' he asks, pulling me in, ruffling my hair and slapping me on the back with great enthusiasm. Word sure travels fast around these parts; they've been back less than twelve hours. I kiss my dad's cheek before my mum enters the hallway and gives me an air kiss.

'Oh, she doesn't need to concern herself with Devon – she's a grown-up now,' she says bluntly, waving my dad's comment away while ushering me into the kitchen. I think my mum has always felt outnumbered by Dad and I, and that was only heightened when Devon was around. I think she thought Devon leaving would mean she'd get more time with her only daughter and with less of a bad influence around, that maybe I'd start taking interest in hair and fashion, but that wasn't to be and the whole incident only put a strain on our relationship more and we've never been especially close.

I see Mum around the village and have dinner with her and Dad once or twice a week, but it's never the most casual of affairs. Mum usually talks of her need for grandkids, asks about promotions at work, when I'm going to start dating and tries to get me to go shopping with her. Dad usually sits back, only occasionally giving me the "why did you give up drawing?" speech. It's hard to be mad when I know his heart is in the right place and I have to admit, it's nice to have someone around who appreciates that about me and gets me, even if I can't act on it.

'Nonsense, Pam. Of course, she's going to see Devon and say hello. You'll bring him around won't you, Scar? My favourite tag-team duo back together again. Ooh you two sure did keep me on my toes.' My dad beams fondly.

I can't help the grin that spreads on my face with my dad's words. He knew how much I struggled when Devon left. He's never forced me to be something I'm not and back then he was always there with a positive word, telling me to keep my chin up and that Devon would be back, whereas my mum took to suggesting I try this and that, pushing me into different clubs and telling me I'd make new friends.

'Did you know that Richard just broke up with Rachel? You two always looked so cute together way back when you were in nursery. He's a vet and so handsome. His mother is coming into the salon this week. I'll have a word,' Mum informs me, getting straight to business when I visit. She's busy making tea while Dad and I are sat at the kitchen table. He rolls his eyes at me behind her back and gives me a small wink, so she doesn't see. 'You need a sensible man, darling. Someone sophisticated who has their life together,' she adds and I know this is her way of saying I need someone to knock some sense into me and bring a little decorum and purpose into my life. 'And, where's that pretty polo neck I got you for work last week? Did you go to work like that today?' she questions, giving my attire a disapproving once-over.

'You know Devon's a movie star now, Mum? He's probably got loads of money. He even wears suits; I mean he can't be wearing his Superman pyjamas on the red carpets, now can he?' I say, sending a wink back my dad's way, as my mum turns around and places two cups of tea on the table. 'And this *is* the blue polo neck you got me,' I add, tugging at the restricting neckline.

'Oh, honey, celebrity is such a fickle business,' she says, looking at me sympathetically, like I'm being serious; she never did get my sarcasm. 'Oh, well, it looks beautiful on you, darling,' she comments waving at my blouse. It clearly didn't look beautiful if her expression was anything to go by; there is obviously something wrong. 'Are you going to grow out that hair of yours?' Ah, there it was. It would no doubt look better if my hair was longer; my mum is pushing my last nerve today and I've been in the house less than ten minutes. I'll wear her clothes, but I am not about to let her style my hair too.

'Well, you will have to be sure to tell D on Thursday when he comes for dinner,' I say suddenly feeling like a child again, wanting to stand up for Devon and ignoring my mum's ambush about my hair. My mum falters as she sits down.

'Thursday?' she questions. I stand up, not in the mood to further debate with my mum and not wanting to be late for dinner with Hope and Jess.

'Yes, Thursday. He's coming for dinner on Thursday night. He wanted to say hi to you both while he was in town,' I lie, feeling a little woozy with the words coming out of my mouth. Before my parents can see me turn pale, I turn and leave the kitchen. 'I'm glad you got home safe; I'll see you Thursday evening,' I shout as I let myself out.

I quick-march to Hope and Jess's while the reality of what I have just done sinks in. Devon and I are in the middle of a fight, well, no, not even in the middle of a fight. We had a fight and now it has ended, we have made peace and have no reason to talk. I have my mini Devon and he has my Superman cape. It was all going to plan, where we could fly off into the sunset and not look back, so why on the earth did I go and invite him for dinner with my parents? He doesn't need me to stand up for him anymore.

The snow crunches beneath my feet as I push open Hope's gate and walk up her path. Wait, I can just tell my parents that important movie star stuff has come up and Devon won't be able to make it. OK, my dad will be a little gutted, but my mum can just add it to her list of reasons why Devon is trouble and a disappointment.

As a plan is swirling around my brain, the snowflakes are swirling around me under the moonlight when Jess answers my knock on the door.

'You're early for a change,' he informs me, teasing. I smile in response, a bright and sarcastic smile, as I shiver and step into the hallway. 'Go through, Scarlett. Hope's cooking.' He takes my coat and hangs it up.

I hear nattering in the kitchen between clatters of spoons and pans and wonder if Hope needs help, not least because she's talking to herself but because cooking usually makes her frazzled; she's a great cook but tends to panic when cooking for guests, even when it's only me.

When I enter the kitchen I freeze on the spot and my stomach takes a rail spill. Devon is sat at the dining table. He's wearing a relaxed white cotton shirt with long sleeves, slim jeans and his hair is making curly shapes that stick out every which way; like it used to do when we were kids risking the damp and rain for the sake of keeping a lookout for any supervillains in Springhollow.

We say "hi" in unison before Jess claps Devon on the back. 'Let me show you my action figure collection,' he says. Devon gets up off his stool, relaxed and at ease with that slight jerk of enthusiasm he does when he gets excited about something. 'Yeah, man, sure.' He nods at me as they walk into the living room.

I'm still glued to my spot while Hope continues cooking casually, like this kind of evening is a daily occurrence.

'What's he doing here?' I ask in a hushed, fast whisper,

making my way over to the small island where Hope is dicing tomatoes.

Hope's eyes go wide under her giant glasses. She stops with her wrist movements and looks at me.

'Don't be mad,' she pleads.

'I feel like you're saying that to me a lot this week,' I reply.

'It's just we were having such a good time on Saturday until Ruby spoilt it. I'm not standing up for him for what he did, and I know there's still hurt there but after listening to your fight, it felt like there was so much more you both needed to say. And then your eyes lit up when he gave you that gift. You both still care. And besides his press finished early today, and I couldn't risk him sitting alone in the pub or wandering the streets of Springhollow where anyone could get their paws on him, like you-know-who,' she says, putting the back of her hand to her mouth as she says the last bit in a whisper.

'That's what his security guards are for,' I say, still a little shook up from shock.

'You know what I mean. If he's with us, then Ruby and the paparazzi can't get to him and weave their fake little stories,' Hope finishes explaining her plan, which is actually not a bad one. But after our big row and exchange of toys I'm wondering if Devon and I will be able to co-exist in this plan.

'Why don't you go check on the boys. Dinner's nearly ready and I'm certain you're itching to see Jess's comic book collection up close and personal, having resisted all these years.' She winks, throwing the tomatoes into a bowl with lettuce leaves and olives.

For a moment I hang my head in an apologetic and embarrassed bow but with Clark Kent's secret identity having been revealed – that's me, I'm Clark Kent in this instance, with my love of superheroes officially out in the open, thanks to Devon's return – I can't help the bubble of excitement that shoots through my veins at what Hope just said and I grin at her broadly.

I make my way towards the living room, a bundle of nerves because a) Jess and Hope's living room truly is a treasure trove of awesome memorabilia and this will be the first time I'm stepping into it not under a false facade but as the nerd that I am, and b) Devon's presence makes something shift inside me. All the childlike inspiration bursts forward and joy bubbles in my gut, yet something about that terrifies me at the same time. I want to act like ten years is no big deal but just like at the pub I'm scared to let go – feeling like nothing good will come of me letting my joy free, well maybe expect for a finished comic book.

'Scar, look at this.' Devon strides over to me the minute I enter the room, holding a vintage 1984 Superman Kenner figure. All nervousness evaporates along with any notion of being sensible and guarded, as I take in what Devon is holding.

'Whoa, I never noticed Jess had one of these.' I hold it delicately; Devon's fingers graze mine as he eagerly examines the object too, giving me an electric shock.

'Ow,' we say in unison, not taking our eyes off the figure.

'I'm going to check on Hope.' Jess leaves us to ogle and drool over his vintage toy collection.

'So, I saw your office today,' Devon notes when it's just us. When I look up, he's right there, our noses inches from each other. My breath catches. Devon turns away sharply, catching his shin on the coffee table as he does so. His dorkiness is only accentuated by his now-tall frame.

'Oh yeah, thank you for my voodoo doll, saved me the hassle of making one.' I smirk. He scratches the back of his neck and chuckles nervously. 'I'm kidding, D,' I add, looking around at the shelves and shelves of comic books.

'I know,' he stutters, just watching me. 'Thank you for the cape – it meant a lot.'

'No problem. So, what did you think of my office – well, Hope's office?' I ask placing Superman back in his glass cabinet and trying to keep the conversation light and void of too many feelings.

'Er, yeah, it's good,' Devon mumbles bending down to rub his shin.

'It's good?' I question and roll my eyes.

'Yeah, it's nice. Can I ask a question?' He looks at me with his deep brown eyes. I look away and ogle the colourful comic books instead, trying not to salivate at the condition they are in.

'Hope and Jess said you don't draw. You didn't answer me when I was at your house. Did you ever send your work to those publishers?' he enquires, his hands running up and down the front of his shirt, toying with the buttons. I pick up a mini figurine of the Batmobile and examine it like it's an extremely rare and delicate dinosaur fossil.

'No, no I did not. Do we have to have this conversation? I didn't become an illustrator, OK, D? Can you drop it? I already get the "what happened to creating comic books?" spiel from my dad at least once a month. I don't need it from you,' I tell him firmly, carefully placing the Batmobile back and looking at the movie posters that line the walls. *Captain America: The First Avenger* came out when I was sixteen. I'd seen all the Marvel movies before that one with Devon and then Devon left. I stare in amazement at the collection on the walls, the movies that followed look incredible, but I've never seen them.

'OK but...' Devon starts.

'But nothing, D. I'm happy. I work with Hope. You've met her, and you all seem well acquainted now. You know how cool she is. Oh God, you haven't told Hope about my wanting to be an illustrator, have you?' I ask, turning to him, my eyes wide with fear as I wait for his answer.

He holds up his hands and bows his head. 'No, Scar, I wouldn't do that. I could tell how nervous you were when I brought it up at the pub. What I don't get is why you're hiding it.' There's a sadness in his eyes that I really don't want to deal with right now.

'Well, what I don't get is how you act all smooth in front of the cameras and how you can possibly be so friendly with Ruby, but you don't hear me asking questions and being all judgey and bringing that up,' I say, casually waving my hands and turning away to caress Jess's Iron Man helmet.

'That's because you don't like talking about your feelings,' Devon says, but his tone is playful, like he's pleased that he knows me so well.

I pry my eyes away from the gold and red metal to look at him. My hands go to my hips. 'I think I showed that I'm more than capable of sharing my feelings the other night. Forgive me for not wanting to argue with you tonight. And forgive me for not being the next Stan Lee. I might not be off saving the world like you but I'm the best personal assistant Hope has ever had. She needs me and my dad needs me and though I still don't quite live up to my mum's expectations, life is good here. I'm doing all right.' That's the most I've shared my feelings in years, purely for the sake of shushing Devon and not because he's easy to talk to.

Devon looks at me with furrowed brows. His eyelashes flutter wide open and I know he wants to ask more questions about my mum, talk about my needs and delve deeper into my emotions but that's all he's going to get for tonight, so I hastily change the subject.

'Any new best friends in New York I should be worried about? Huh?' I half-smirk. That sounded funnier and more chilled in my head, but even I can't miss the wobble in my voice when I say it out loud. I distract myself by getting comfy on the couch. Devon paces a few steps before he brushes his hands over his thighs and sits down next to me.

'Oh yeah, like Hope and Jess?' He quirks an eyebrow, his big grin even more prominent with a full set of adult pearly whites.

'Oh please, they were just filling in…' I hear Hope's footsteps and Jess's not far behind.

'I heard that,' Hope says carrying a tray of pita, olives, and hummus into the room. My stomach grumbles its appreciation.

'Is school the same as it is here?' she asks taking a seat on the chair opposite the couch.

'No, it's a lot more over the top and dramatic, but I guess passionate too. The cliques you see in the American movies are no joke – it's all heightened when no one is wearing a uniform. It was hard finding my place in the high school coming in halfway through the year, but once I got settled with the drama club, it wasn't too bad.' Devon sits on the edge of the couch when he speaks and gives his undivided attention to Hope when answering her question.

For the first time in ten years I picture him stood lonely in the school hallways, with no one to hang out with, away from home, instead of my usual imagery of him swanning off to New York, becoming fast friends with every kid on the playground and happily forgetting all about me. My stomach knots guiltily.

'Any American girls capture your British heart?' Hope asks boldly. Devon blushes a deep shade of red.

'Dude, you probably have girls throwing themselves at you,' Jess comments, tucking into the olives.

I try and settle the sudden weird, uncomfortable feeling of guilt and I don't know what in my stomach with a piece of pita. I haven't eaten since lunch and my stomach is suddenly scolding me for it with all its odd rumbles and squirming. I catch Hope looking at me from the corner of my eye and smile and raise my pita at her in thanks, while Devon mumbles through an answer.

It occurs to me to save him from being put on the spot like this, like when we were kids and he forgot to do his homework. I was used to his mum's disappointed looks, but Devon was not. His mother had high and strict standards and Devon hated to upset her. It was usually my fault his homework had been forgotten. Forgive me for thinking that the safety of Springhollow ranked as a higher priority than maths. But I don't say anything and there's a small part of me that is intrigued by his answer. He's grown rather tall. He's got those dark features and looks handsome in a suit, which is what women apparently go for.

'Erm ha, me? No, not really,' Devon humbly replies.

'So, there's no special someone in your life?' Hope pushes. Devon shuffles on the couch, his shoulders stiffen and his hand rubs at the back of his neck.

'No, no special someone,' he replies quietly, cheeks ablaze.

'Do you prefer Christmas in New York or Christmas in Springhollow?' I blurt out, sitting up straighter, unable to sit back and watch Devon sweat for much longer. He used to be a lot better with the mushy-gushy, best friends for life stuff, but talking about women has him looking hot under his collarless shirt.

His shoulders fall a few inches as he helps himself to some bread and when he turns to face me the red in his cheeks slowly starts to fade and he relaxes once more.

'You're going to hate me but, well, both,' D answers, all excitement back on his features. I gasp, mock horrified.

'No, it cannot be. There is nowhere on earth that does Christmas like Springhollow,' I protest.

'Ahh, but, Scar, New York has this magic and the Rockefeller tree is spectacular; like nothing you have ever seen before.' Devon's eyes light up in wonder.

'We have a tree,' I argue, playfully, nibbling on more pita.

'Yeah, I know.' Devon tilts his head from side to side, the dimple in his right cheek growing more prominent. 'But it doesn't quite compare to the Rockefeller tree. It's gigantic and sparkles from every branch.'

I pop an olive in my mouth. 'Our tree sparkles and it doesn't have to be big or the biggest to be awesome. It's not the size that matters.'

Hope chokes on her hummus and Devon's cheeks return to a lovely rosy hue.

'And with that, I think dinner is ready,' Hope says, standing. It takes me a minute to register what I just said and how my wonderful friends could have turned it into something inappropriate. I nod awkwardly at Devon who lets out a laugh, shakes his head and stands.

'After you,' he says with a smirk. It's my turn to blush as I clamber off the couch, only meeting his chest when I stand. I automatically punch him in the bicep and tut at his teasing smugness.

'What was that for?' He laughs, rubbing his arm. 'You always did have a way with words,' he adds shoving me towards the door before I can respond with another playful jab.

13

Hope hands me a glass of wine as I take my seat at the table. Devon sits next to me, Hope and Jess across from us. I take a few big gulps to cool the burning in my cheeks and see Hope smirk out of the corner of my eye.

'To second chances and new beginnings,' she announces, raising her glass. I clink mine against hers and the boys' pint glasses, rolling my eyes at her toast, but my stomach rumbles again so instead of analysing her words I choose to dig in.

Hope has made a delicious feast of salmon, asparagus, roast potatoes and cauliflower cheese and every bite is scrumptious. There's a big quiet as we all take a couple of moments to simply enjoy the food before us. Before long I'm on my second glass of red wine and have loaded my plate with a few extra trimmings of roast potatoes and cauliflower cheese and everyone is chatting merrily.

'You two must have had some fun Christmases together when you were kids?' Hope sits back having finished her one plate. I finish my bite of potato, its buttery flavour and the wine make me feel deliriously happy.

'Remember that Christmas we tied Thor to the neighbourhood cat, and she didn't like it too much and took off through my house, knocking all the baubles and pines off the entire bottom half of the tree?' I reply, leaning back in my chair and looking at Devon. He too is relaxed, beer in hand, eyes glassy from yummy starchy potatoes and creamy veg.

'Then your mum banned the real trees after that, and you were only allowed fake ones.' Devon lets out a laugh.

'She wasn't best pleased.' I shake my head, laughing, and take a sip of wine.

'What about that time on the construction site when we got stuck on the roof and your dad got mad at us for peering off the scaffold?' Devon reminisces with a smile on his lips.

I cringe. 'I don't know who took the heat worse for that one: us or Dad. Our mums were fuming.' I can't help chuckle at the memory and the fact that my dad still calls us his favourite tag team and likes the idea of seeing the two of us together again, when I'm pretty sure Mum didn't talk to him for two weeks after that particular incident.

'You two sound like right troublemakers,' Jess notes. Both him and Hope are sat grinning at our misdemeanours.

'Arrgh, it was all in the name of fighting the good fight and keeping down the crime rate in Springhollow.' Devon shrugs.

Hope bursts out laughing. 'I've never known Springhollow to even have crime,' she says.

'You're welcome,' I say with a nod of my head, holding up my wine glass, which causes Devon to laugh his loud and hearty laugh that has grown deeper with age.

I see Hope studying both Devon and me. Her lips are pursed her eyes are narrowed and then a smile spreads across her face and she stands. 'I'll get dessert.'

Devon helps her clear the table while I refill both mine and Hope's glasses before Jess places two cold beers on the table and takes his seat, looking all the more relaxed in Devon's company now than he did two nights ago at the pub.

'So, what's it like having a superhero for tea?' I ask, teasing him only a little.

'By the sounds of it we have two. Why did you keep it from us all these years?' Jess asks, a thoughtful, concerned look on his boyish face. I've briefly explained myself to Hope and even though I have no problems turning to Jess for advice on day-to-day problems or asking for his help when say there's a giant spider in my house, it's hard for me to admit that I kept Devon and my love of superheroes from them out of anger and fear. That and it was hard to explain it to them when I couldn't even understand it all myself. Thinking about it now, it seems absurd that I punished myself with no drawing or comic books and abstained from all the movies I once loved, but it had become a coping mechanism, my way of trying to get Devon out of my head. Would Jess understand that?

I'm saved from having to explain myself when Hope places a lemon cheesecake on the table and Devon plonks down a tub of ice-cream from Salvatore's, our local hole-in-the-wall ice-cream shop. You've never had ice-cream like it before. All the ingredients come from the local farmers and Salvatore only makes a limited number of batches each day so it's rich, creamy, divine and guaranteed freshness.

'I bet you don't get ice-cream like Salvatore's in New York,' I say proudly as Devon takes his seat.

'You would be right. Springhollow gets a point there,'

Devon replies with a soft smile. I think the wine has officially gone to my head as I get a warm feeling in the pit of my stomach when he smiles like that; his eyes sparkle and his features are at ease. He's looking at me with an expression you would give a spectacular sunset, a mixture of awe and gentle appreciation. Suddenly, I get a feeling of falling and jerk in my chair. I shake it off with a giant bite of lemon cheesecake, needing the food to soak up the alcohol in my system. No more wine for me tonight. Why is Hope allowing me to drink so much wine on a work night?

'We're on a point system, now, are we? Springhollow vs. New York?' I ask casually, hoping that everyone is just as tipsy as me and didn't notice my awkward jerk. Hope hasn't taken her eyes off me, which I take to mean she didn't miss it. Jess is devouring his ice-cream and Devon is still slightly twisted in his chair facing me. Reverting to sarcasm is my default. I need to get the conversation flowing again to show that I'm cool, but my heart is thumping a little too fast. I'm worried that everyone can hear it.

'So, what does Springhollow get if it wins?' I say teasing and laughing at my own words; the epitome of cool that I am.

Devon doesn't play along; instead he gives me a thoughtful look and then turns to his dessert and licks his lips. 'This looks amazing, Hope. So, are there any new traditions I shouldn't miss while I'm here?' he asks, his voice sounding a little strained at first and then more normal after his first bite of cheesecake.

Hope looks at me. I offer her a bright smile, like Devon ignoring my question wasn't anything unusual. She looks back at Devon then excitement floods her face.

'Oh, Mr and Mrs Rolph only recently started a cookie competition. Every Wednesday you can enter a cookie and then the town comes together to try them, and you pop your winning number in a ballot box. The cookie with the most votes throughout the year will be the cookie that we leave out for Santa on Christmas Eve. It's really cute. The kids love it and it gets families baking together, which is gorgeous. We're thinking of asking for small donations for the magazine and then running an article every two weeks on the winning recipes and talking to the families involved next year. It's really fun. Hmm, what else?' Hope ponders, her fast-talking clearly showing her passion for what she does and for our village's festivities.

Jess sits back after finishing his dessert and reaches his arm over the back of her chair absent-mindedly playing with her hair. He looks at her with clear admiration. I'm used to witnessing these looks and I still haven't tired of it. I love the two of them together.

When I turn to take in Devon's reaction to this beautiful new tradition, I see he's already looking at me. I hope he didn't catch me and my silly wine-induced longing look at Jess's movements. That soft smile spreads across his face again. He moves his arm in my direction and for a moment I think he's going to put his arm around me, mirroring Jess's position, and a rush of heat floods through my body. What the? But his hand brushes past my shoulder and rests on the back of my chair.

I must look the picture of deer caught in the headlights right now because Devon squints his eyes at me, assessing me – my cheeks feel like they are on fire. What is wrong with me? I sure as hell do not want Devon to know of my mushy-gushy desires. It's getting late now and Jess and Hope are getting to that cosy stage; doing that thing that couples do where you can tell they are ready to curl up for the day in each other's arms after a long day of work and other appointments that have kept them apart.

Normally when it's just me it's fine. I like seeing them so loved up and happy together, after all these years, but in Devon's presence it feels weird. It feels too personal. We never talked crushes, boyfriends, girlfriends or relationship stuff so I feel like a kid again, like I want to stick my tongue out and say "gross", just to avoid the romance in the air.

'These two put on a different stall each year at the Christmas fair too. The Christmas fair isn't new but the stuff these two come up with always goes down a treat,' Jess says proudly, moving up closer to Hope. She rests a hand on his leg and nestles into his side casually.

'I can't really take the credit; it's all this one,' Hope responds, pointing in my direction, sleepily. 'Last year Scarlett had everyone making wreaths, the year before that it was snow globes and this year it's... wait for it... gingerbread houses. It's going to be amazing,' she finishes with a clap.

'It sounds it,' Devon concurs. 'Creativity has always been this one's forte.'

'Oh yeah, tell us more about her drawings,' Hope says eagerly.

Devon hesitates and looks over to me. I try and telepathically communicate that he better remember our conversation from before or I will kill him, by giving him my most subtly evil stare. 'I, erm, where to begin?' he starts but I can't take any chances with what he's about to say. I move to uncross my legs and accidently manage to tip my wine glass onto his lap as I go to stand up to clear the table.

'Oh shoot, sorry. I was just going to clear up. It's getting late and it's a work night. My boss hates it if I'm late.' I laugh as Devon starts patting his trousers with a napkin. Hope and Jess are both on their feet, gasps having escaped their mouths. Hope races around the table with a tea towel, offering it to Devon. She gives me an evil glare mixed with a confused look at my jittery behaviour. We've had enough talk of the past tonight; I knew what she was doing. If I won't open up, she now has Devon to interrogate and supply her with the information she desires, but not on my watch. There are just some things she doesn't need to know.

'No worries, Scar. They're just trousers. I'm good, guys,' Devon informs the table. I'm busying myself carrying plates back and forth to the kitchen while the others fuss over him.

'See he's fine, you two. It was an accident, just a little wine spill. I think he'll live,' I say, loading my arms with more plates for the sink.

Hope catches my eye and straightens herself up. 'Of course, yes. Sorry, Devon. Scarlett can show you to the spare room. Jess has a drawer of old clothes. Please help yourself to some fresh trousers and I can get these in the wash for you.'

I freeze on my way to the kitchen counter. 'I can get them for him, honey,' Jess says.

'Oh no no, it's OK, *dear*. You can help me clear the rest of the table before Scarlett makes any more mess. She knows where to look. Off you go,' Hope says, suddenly sounding like a desperate housewife as she relieves me of the glass in my hand and ushers Devon and I towards the kitchen door.

'Thanks, Hope,' I say confidently and casually, to show her that being alone with Devon in a bedroom does not faze me in the slightest and she has got it all wrong. 'I can do that, no problem.'

In the small box room, I make a beeline for the chest of drawers, pull out any old pair of Jess's trousers and throw them at Devon. 'There you go, D,' I say in a sprightly manner, trying to ignore the fuzz in my brain and the tingle down my spine when Devon hesitantly brushes past me in the confined space. Is it just me or is it warm in here?

Before I can leave to give Devon some privacy, he stops in front of me. I'm not used to his towering over me. At sixteen he was maybe a couple inches taller than me; now he's like three heads taller.

'What was that all about?' I say, feeling a wave of dizziness wash over me. I really want my bed right now.

'What was what all about, Scar?' he asks clutching the trousers in his hands, tilting his head to try and engage me eye to eye. 'I wasn't even going to mention you wanting to be an illustrator – you can trust me you know.' He sits down on the bed, his knees touching my thighs when he does so – the tiny room not quite accommodating his size. I stand in front of him feeling a little trapped in between his legs.

'I'm sorry, I just couldn't risk it. You say that to Hope and it will upset her. She'll blame herself like she's the one holding me back and she'll worry that I'm not happy.' I plead my case for my dramatic actions, able to look into Devon's eyes better now that he is sitting. They match mine a little in the glazed department and I know he's had one too many beers too. It's time to call it a night. I hope he will be able to remember his way back to The Sunflower Inn, because I really don't want to have to be his escort. I want my bed; this night is making my head spin in more ways than one.

'Just try to understand that when you're long gone, I'm still going to be here and I'd like to keep my friends and know they are happy, if that's OK with you?' I add. Jeez what do I sound like? I sound like Devon, that's what. Since he got here, my emotions and feelings are running amok. I need to get them in check. I ignore Devon's therapist-style gaze and silence that has me wanting to fill the gaps with more of my own words and tell him everything; even after ten years I'm struggling to hide things from him.

'You're angry with me again,' he notes. It takes me a minute to register his words, having spaced out staring at him. He takes one hand from the tight grip he has on his borrowed trousers and it hovers by my wrists, like he wants to comfort me but doesn't know how. When we were kids and I was poorly, like the time I fractured both my wrists, he would simply rest his hands on mine or lie next to me, so I didn't have to be scared on my own. Now though, he's not touching me, and instead of comfort I feel a static in the air, like I'm about to get an electric shock. It's enough to cause me to step backwards, catch my heel on the dresser and snap me out of my thoughts.

'I'm not angry, just thinking. We need to get to bed,' I say, hastily changing the subject, whilst bending down and rubbing my ankle. There's no more opening up and letting him in. He will be gone in a week. I need to stay strong.

I hear his mock dramatic gasp and laugh through gritted teeth with the pain in my ankle – it's not going away no matter how gently I rub it. I don't get to put Devon at ease and explain that I did not mean that we need to get to bed together but our own separate beds, because he jumps up off the aforementioned bed and knees me in the face as he does so. I automatically straighten up to grab my nose as Devon bends down frantically to check on me and I nut him in the chin.

A range of curse words fly out of my mouth while Devon groans in pain. My vision is blurred with the water that streaks down my face from the sting in my nose. Devon has one hand on his chin, yet his other hand has somehow made its way on to my cheek like he's still trying to protect me or look after me in some way, even though the damage has already been done. Strangely enough, this time his touch works; his hand on my cheek begins to settle my heart rate and ease the throbbing in my face. We lock eyes and I swallow down hard. Devon's lips are parted and there remains a faint look of shock on his face. I can see that his eyes are streaming too.

Suddenly there's a knock on the open door. Two figures are hovering, a mix of amusement and curiosity etched on their faces.

'We didn't want to disturb you or anything, just in case, you know, you needed some privacy and whatnot, but if you're OK, then we'll leave you...' Jess trails off, waving his hands and shrugging apologetically like he's interrupted something. He then tugs Hope by the elbow, trying to guide her back to the stairs, but she's too stubborn to move, too enthralled with gawping at the scene of Devon still holding my cheek.

When Jess finally gets her to move, I hear her chuckle and

mumble, 'Who knew superheroes liked it rough.' There's no doubt that Devon heard this too as he snaps, albeit gently, his hand away from my cheek and starts fumbling to find his spare trousers to create distance between us. I nervously fiddle with my hands, stepping from foot to foot.

'I'll, erm, I'll be downstairs. I'll let you change,' I stutter and jog the short distance to the door.

'Yeah, erm yes. Scar?' Devon stutters and I pause at the door.

'Do you always wear clothes like that to work?' he asks, his tone serious but softer and clear now as he nods at my blue blouse and grey skirt.

I lean against the frame and bang my head against it. 'Yes, D.' I groan, wishing he would stop analysing my entire life. 'Lots of people have "work clothes",' I add using air quotes. While that was true, I'm sure Hope would be more than fine if I wore my more favourable denim dungarees or jumpsuits. She allows everyone in the office to wear what they feel good and comfortable in. I guess by now she thinks my outfits are of my choosing for the office. I groan again, not liking Devon's ability to somehow know me when it feels like I don't know myself anymore.

'OK, well I liked what you were wearing at the pub the other night. It was very you, but that looks nice too.' His tone becomes a tad husky, he coughs to clear his throat at the end.

'Thanks,' is all I manage, my own voice feeling a touch restricted at the idea of D noticing my outfit. My mind flits to what I had been wearing underneath my olive dress that night and suddenly I wonder if he would like that too, which makes my cheeks heat. I quickly turn away.

I take my time walking down the stairs so I don't make a scene and so my cheeks can cool down. I did not need to concern myself with what kind of women's underwear rose Devon's hammer. Did I just use the term "Devon's hammer"? How much wine had I had tonight? *OK, stop it,* I urgently tell my brain. The more carefree I act, the quicker this whole incident will be forgotten. I will not speak of it and therefore it shall not become a big deal.

When I get to the doorway of the kitchen, both Jess and Hope are leaning against the counter, mumbling to each other in a hushed whisper – I can't make out what they are saying – the sink is overflowing with bubbles and plates piled high.

'Everything OK?' Hope asks merrily when she spots me – a beaming smile on her face, a dish cloth in her hands. Jess is eating another bowl of ice-cream.

I rest my hand against the arc of the doorframe. 'Of course, yeah, everything's fine. Do you need help with the dishes?' I ask, silently praying that Hope and Jess will have the clean-up covered so I can get home to bed and sleep this night off, though I'd usually clean up with Hope having done all the cooking. Footsteps creek on the stairs to the left of me and Devon appears, creating a shadow next to me.

'Can I help with anything?' he asks, seemingly reading my mind and going with my plan and choosing to move past the silly bedroom ordeal – my nose is still throbbing. I'm sure I need ice but that will have to wait until I get home.

'Don't be ridiculous. No, no, you two go and rest, the dishes are no trouble,' Hope assures us, waving in the direction of the living room.

'OK, then, well it's getting late. I'm going to head off. Thank you so much for the food – it was amazing.' I jog to the counter kiss Hope on the cheek and give Jess a one-arm hug. 'Love you both, see you tomorrow.'

I squeeze past Devon, and, in the corridor, I gather my coat and scarf, then look up to address him. 'See you around, D. Be safe getting back to the inn.' I throw on my beanie, make quick work of the lock and am out into the welcome, refreshing, crisp air in a flash.

The multi-coloured twinkles from our grand, maybe not as grand as the Rockefeller, tree light my path, as does the glowing moon. I only have to cross the square, turn right at the bakery and I'll be on my street. As I round the bend, I nearly skid on a pool of ice when I hear my name. There's no mistaking who the voice belongs to – even now with its older, deeper, baritone, I'd recognise it anywhere, and because only Devon and my dad call me "Scar". My stomach does that horrible tornado of mixed emotions that seems to be a new thing since Devon arrived. It's a swirling concoction of joy, confusion and fear. But I can't exactly run; he knows where I live.

'Scar,' he shouts again.

I spin around as he catches up with me. 'Are you trying to wake up the whole village?' I ask. Surprisingly a laugh escapes my lips – I must still be a little tipsy, even with the icy air nipping at my cheeks, but really it's the memories of us sneaking out of our houses after dark to ensure the safety of the village that makes me giggle.

'If I remember correctly that used to be one of our powers: talk loudly and the baddies will know someone's watching.' Devon smirks, once again reading my mind. "Can I walk you home?' he adds, hands in his pockets, rocking back and forth on his toes and ankles.

'Sure,' I find myself saying, through another chuckle at Devon's words – yes, he had remembered correctly, and he only came up with that power because he couldn't ever stop talking, even when it was paramount to our mission to creep around and be silent.

'I've missed this place,' he notes, as we walk side by side. Coming up to Mr and Mrs Rolph's bakery, I glance at Devon whose eyes are fixed on the window. For the second time this evening my stomach flips with guilt. I never once thought about him missing our village and all its comforts. Every time I thought about him I pictured him excited to leave me, thrilled about making new friends and getting away from me. I never did stop to think about how it had all made him feel; his first few letters had been happy ones, telling me all about his new house and new school.

'When you wrote to me, you always seemed so happy?' I say, as we pick up the pace again, having slowed for Devon to stare longingly at the cake counter, which at this time is empty.

He shrugs. 'I was a kid. Mum and Dad had made it all sound so exciting and I guess I thought if I went along with it, if I was happy and enjoyed myself, pretended it was a holiday, did what they asked, that it would all be over quicker, which sounds so backwards now saying it out loud. And, I was happy, Scar. My parents were happy, so I couldn't burst their bubble,' he says, his hand finding its way to the back of his neck.

'You're good at making people happy, D. I'm glad you

are happy too. You deserve all the happiness living your dream,' I say, looking up so I can meet his gaze.

That's what Devon did when we were kids: he made people happy. He was always being goofy and trying to make people laugh even if they weren't always laughing with him but at him. He wanted to see them smile. Whereas he used this huge change to excel and look at the positives, go into theatre and make something of himself, I became an introvert, buried my feelings and stopped believing in myself and my dreams. But that didn't mean that Devon hadn't struggled. I truly meant what I said – he deserved to be happy and with or without me I was so glad that he had found his happiness.

Devon's eyes grow warm, still a little glazed from too many beers. He rocks back on his toes, hands in his pockets.

'You do that too, you know, Scar,' he says, bending over slightly so I don't have to crane my neck too much.

'Do what?' I ask, aware that we have stopped walking again.

'Make people happy,' he answers causing me to howl with laughter. In the distance I hear the faint hoot of an owl and quickly put a hand over my mouth. It's late – we don't need the neighbourhood snooping out their windows and speculating on Devon and I being out late together.

'Why the laughter?' Devon asks, confusion spreading across his face, his eyes narrowing as he bends down further, getting a little closer, like he's examining my features.

'Oh, D, I wish that were the case. My mum is never happy with any decision I make. I'm a complete failure to her. I can't even pull off this blue blouse. My dad wishes I would draw again – it's always disappointed him that I stopped. I guess I make Hope and Jess happy sometimes – we laugh, we have a good time together – but I'm boring and have missed out on movie dates, game nights and upset them both over the years making them think they were uncool in their nerdy ways,' I say, spilling my insecurities out into the night. Thank you, wine, and thank you, Devon.

'I don't believe that for a second. Our mums will always be our mums, but I saw the way your dad looked at you – every day for sixteen years in fact – and not once did he not have a smile on his face. Hope and Jess love you and Hope never stops raving about how much you keep her life organised at work and how lost she would be without you. You put everyone around you first; you just need to remember to think of your own happiness too,' Devon states, sounding like a wise old Yoda, which makes me giggle. This is all getting too deep.

'I do think of my own happiness,' I mumble, tripping up over my thoughts as we reach my front door. Did I really or did I think too much about what made everyone else happy?

I yawn as Devon gives me a cheeky, 'Mmm, hmm.'

'Night, Devon,' I say with a roll of my eyes.

'Goodnight, Scarlett,' he replies and his whole face looks like it's radiating happiness. Away from the cameras, away from the world, just standing on my doorstep, he looks like my Devon.

14

Tuesday at the office whizzed by in a blur of Christmas fair planning, gingerbread house competition prepping, emails and sitting down with Hope to discuss the magazine potentially switching to monthly. Today at work was pretty much the same except after an evening of baking, chimney making and decorating in a mad rush to get my project finished for Saturday, I had struggled to keep my eyes open. Now, it's Wednesday evening and I'm stood behind a *Great British Bake Off* style workbench under a gorgeous tent behind Mr and Mrs Rolph's bakery, which is littered with pastel bunting, strung tinsel and twinkling fairy lights with a Christmas tree in the centre decorated with all kinds of beautifully carved kitchen utensils and brightly coloured cake ornaments. Festive music is humming in the background and half the village – couples, kids, singletons, and families – are packed in like cranberries in cranberry jelly.

I've managed to scrape my short black hair into some resemblance of a ponytail in order to keep it out of my face as I focus on dicing up slivers of peppermint bark. The smell wafts around me with every crack of the bark, causing a flurry of snowflakes to dance in my belly. I've not had one drop of alcohol since Monday night and I'm not going to lie, I love this time of year even more when I glance over to Hope at her table where she is insisting on teaching Devon how to use the stand mixer while I get our cookies underway. Yes, with no alcohol in my system I'm admitting that having Devon home for Christmas is the Christmas present I've always wanted. This confession suddenly has the flurry of snowflakes in my stomach forming a blizzard; it's a dangerous confession I know, when I must remember that he will be leaving again in four days.

'I don't think I've ever seen Scarlett this happy.' My ears prick up to my name, but I don't look up, afraid of catching Hope's attention. She is talking in a low voice purposefully, so I won't hear her, while she has Devon to herself. I keep busy but I can't help straining my ears, earwigging into the conversation.

'You and Jess make her happy and I know her parents do, even with all her mum's weird expectations. She loves her family; she loves this village.' Devon hits the nail on the head; Hope should know this. I'm very happy with my life – OK, OK, parts of it.

'It's a different kind of happy,' Hope explains. I pretend that my furrowed brow is because of the precision I am using to get my slivers of chocolate. I bend down with my eyes narrowed, looking over my chopped chocolate. Is there a different kind of happy? I don't think so. As far as I am aware happy was just happy and though, yes, drawing and creating comic books makes me ridiculously happy, so does working with my best friend.

'Can I ask you something? Has Scarlett had many boyfriends?' I barely catch Devon's question. His voice goes so quiet I have to pretend I need another bar of chocolate that rests at the edge of our table, closer to Hope and Jess's. I really don't need any more chocolate; suffice to say the Mount Everest of peppermint bark I now have on the chopping board in front of me is enough. Devon has his back to me. I chance a glance when I hear Hope bustle around her oven, bending down to switch it on. He has one hand resting on the work top, one hand picking at some mint leaves Hope is using.

'If you want to call them that.' Hope doesn't hesitate or mince her words. I can feel my face flush. With all these people around and ovens getting ready to bake, it's certainly heating up in here. 'Scarlett seems to fall for the wrong guys. They have their fun and then leave her heartbroken. She hasn't dated in years,' Hope tells Devon gently.

I'm trying to measure flour, aware that it's going everywhere as I'm concentrating more on their conversation and looking at them through my peripherals. Devon turns slightly and I can see his cheeks ablaze too. Oh gosh, did Hope really just tell him that?

'She's not really someone guys fall for, so she tells me. They want someone more elegant and more womanly and she ain't that, apparently. She doesn't believe in fairy-tale love; she says it doesn't last. But I think she's wrong and just hasn't met the right person.' She scoops up cookie dough onto her sheet. Meanwhile, she's pinched my partner and I'm yet to form a dough; however, I can't bring myself to interrupt their conversation. I'm not sure I want Devon to know all this, but at the same time I can't help wondering why he's interested.

'But I see the way she looks at you and Jess,' Devon

argues. 'She knows love and her parents are childhood sweethearts.'

'And I see the way she looks at you.' Hope pauses and leaves that statement lingering in the aromatic air for a few moments before Jess appears, straight from work. 'Hi, hon,' Hope starts, before wielding a spatula at Devon. 'I'm aware that Scarlett's words are just a front. I've just never been able to get through her protective armour. Maybe you could talk to her.'

'You want me to talk to Scar about love?' There's no denying the croak in Devon's voice.

'She talks to you,' Hope pushes.

'Yeah, about caped crusaders and stakeouts – we don't talk about love.' He clears his throat.

Hope shrugs. 'Then why did you ask about boyfriends, Mr Wood?' Hope winks at him and I take that as my cue to save my dear ex best friend from further questioning. And even though Devon was partly to blame for engaging in this conversation I can sense he wasn't prepared for the direction Hope is about to take it.

I march over. 'Hope, I need my partner back please. D, I'd love it if you could fold in the peppermint slivers,' I say confidently, as Jess dons his own apron and starts helping Hope.

'I thought we were making cinnamon cookies?' Devon queries.

'Oh, we are. We're combining all the flavours of Christmas into one cookie.' I squeal. 'You'll *love* it.' I emphasise the word "love" causing both Devon and Hope to roll their eyes; Devon turns a considerable shade of pink as he does so while Hope swipes flour across my nose as punishment for listening in to their conversation. It's better I tell them though; that way Devon knows he most definitely does not have to adhere to Hope's wishes and try to conceive a conversation about "love" with me.

I receive a wide-eyed, awkward smile before Devon walks off to deal with the peppermint bark. I watch him for a second before turning my attention back to Hope, giving her a mock evil glare.

'It's rude to eavesdrop on people's conversations you know,' she informs me, licking her spoon.

'You know it breaks all kinds of best friend codes to fraternise with the enemy?' I counter.

Before Hope can respond Mrs Rolph announces that we have twenty minutes left and best get our cookies baking as she gives Devon and I a pointed glare.

'Yes, ma'am.' Devon nods politely, which softens her very serious expression. 'Oh, it's so good to have you back, Devon dear. You mustn't be a stranger,' she says, closing in on our spot and pinching Devon's cheeks, her eyes crinkling with a warm smile. I snicker. Devon gives me the side eye, but I can see his lips twitching with a smirk.

'Hope, please keep an eye on these two when they use the oven.' Her tone is back to serious as she addresses Hope.

'Oh, come on, we weren't that bad,' I protest, pushing a loose strand of wayward hair behind my ear with the back of my hand.

'What is the oven used for?' Mrs Rolph asks Devon and me. I feel as though I'm back in school, or on an army base. I stand a little straighter and hold my head up. Devon does the same next to me.

'The oven is for cooking and baking the most

mouth-watering eats; it should not be used to melt action figures.' Devon and I recite in monotone unison. Hope and Jess burst out laughing. I give Hope a hip-check. Her counter is all clean and Jess keeps checking the oven, whereas with all these distractions ours is covered in flour and our four different fillings and flavourings. Once we are dismissed from our lesson for the evening Devon pops our cookies in the oven under Hope's supervision and I get to clearing away our – OK, mostly my – mess.

Everyone is respectful of Mr and Mrs Rolph and so conversation is kept to a minimum while every participant focuses on getting their areas tidy while the cookies bake in the oven. I don't even know how to describe the smells to you but it's pure Christmas overload and it's delightful. From warm vanilla sugar and mulled wine inspired flavours, to cinnamon, eggnog and peppermint; there are currently so many festive aromas dancing around the tent. It's heavenly.

As the chimes of oven timers begin to go off in jingle-bell-like fashion, one after the other, excited gasps and joyous hand clapping can be heard all around and the smell becomes even bolder as the oven doors open, revealing their precious cargo.

Mine and Devon's is the last oven to ping and I anxiously step from foot to foot while Devon sees to taking out our creation. I love cooking and I love to experiment with food. I think it's been my way of getting my creativity out over the years without drawing – that and these Christmas craft stalls. The smell of the peppermint hits me first, making me lick my lips, followed by the hint of cinnamon, a faint hint of vanilla and, finally, a dash of Baileys, because really nothing quite says Christmas like a glass of Baileys.

Devon places the tray on the counter and sends me a smile, which I can see is confident mixed with surprised impressed. The cookies look great: perfectly round, with a few bigger and smaller, the odd lump and bump, but I could bottle their smell and make the next number-one Christmas fragrance guaranteed.

'I should trust you more often. These smell incredible, Scar,' Devon notes as we both plate up the cookies ready for the judges and pop the majority in a Tupperware container.

'You haven't tasted them yet,' I say playfully.

'True,' Devon responds, giving me a side glance and laughing. I have to say I was nervous when my dad mentioned the tag team being back together. I still am, but if I just take this evening for what it is and nothing more, no thinking about him sticking around when I know he can't, then I've had a truly wonderful time teaming up with Devon again. Watching him place each cookie neatly in the snowman tin, I note he looks relaxed. Crinkles around his eyes give evidence of his laughter from moments ago. His hair is threatening to wave from sweat – it's hot inside this tent even with the snow falling outside – and there's a look in his deep brown eyes that tells me he really wants to eat one of those cookies.

I don't know what life is like for him in New York, sure I assume he's landed on his feet with this movie role; living his dream and playing a superhero. But besides the strong desire to devour a cookie, his eyes are sparkling the way they used to when we were kids and we'd just learnt that Superman was Clark Kent. Considering the last time I saw those eyes was when we were sixteen and they were streaming with tears, seeing that twinkle is much preferred.

'See something you like?' I jump out of my skin as Hope creeps up beside me, her not so innocent words frightening the life out of me. I had well and truly disappeared into my own world, or more accurately a world where nothing had changed between Devon and I; where it was still simple, and we were best friends again. I shake my head to compose myself.

'I do in fact. Those, my dear Hope, are the winning cookies,' I proclaim, taking a step closer to Devon to try and walk off my sudden shakes from Hope scaring me. Hope eyes me suspiciously. Devon breaks a cookie in half and hands me one half.

'No, Devon, you're not supposed to try them now. We wait until Mr and Mrs Rolph judge the first bite.' Hope informs Devon of the rules in a hushed and urgent whisper. He already has his half of the cookie hovering by his lips. He looks from me to Hope then back to me, worry lines creasing in his brow, then just like the spoon of gloop at the hospital all those years ago, I go to speak and before I know what's happening Devon stuffs his cookie half into my mouth.

'She did it first,' he says. My eyes go wide. Devon shrugs at Hope and points at me tutting, before taking my cookie half out of my hand and helping himself to neat bites. I'm momentarily stunned, cookie crumbs falling from the corner of my mouth. I consider spitting it out, but my tongue is too happy with the flavours that it just allows them to hang around for a minute before I start chomping unattractively to break up the huge bite Devon force-fed me.

'I wonder what punishment Mrs Rolph will give the two of you should she find out about you breaking the rules.'

Now I know Hope is just winding me up by the smirk on her face.

'Ready to give these in, babe?' Jess asks, wandering over with their plate of cookies. When he catches sight of me, he gasps. I'm stood stock-still trying to manoeuvre the chunks of cookie in my mouth without choking and making too much of a mess, but crumbs are going everywhere. Unable to form the words 'I know, I know' I wave him off, nod my head and roll my eyes instead.

Jess heeds my gesture and takes Hope with him to the front of the tent where everyone is starting to gather for the cookie tasting. My eyes water when with one giant gulp I free my mouth from the festive treat. I promptly turn around and whack Devon in the chest, making him cough on his own bite of cookie; that serves him right. He gives me an innocent, 'What?' with his eyes, his shoulders rounding, his forearms coming up to shield his chest from any more blows.

'These are bomb, Scar, like amazing. All the flavours are awesome.' I see Devon eye up the tin and before I have time to overthink or really know or understand what I am doing, I'm scanning the room to check that all eyes are now on Mr and Mrs Rolph and that no beady ones are interested in Devon and me or looking our way, then I grab the tin of cookies and dash to the door; hoping that Devon doesn't leave me running like a loon through the square in the snow, on my own, with a tin full of hijacked cookies.

Letting my feet guide me I don't stop until they find their intended destination. Squinting through the shower of snowflakes and the dimming light of the sky – the sun having long since set – I come to a halt at the park. I'm standing in front of an overgrown wintergreen boxwood that takes up one length of the fence at the edge of the park. A chill sweeps over me now that I've stopped running as I study the shrub.

'Are you not going to go in?' I nearly send the tin of cookies flying but Devon grabs my shoulders to stop me from falling. His strong grip warming my skin.

'Holy moly, D, don't do that.' I exhale. When I turn around, he's got both our coats tucked under his armpit and he's wearing a grin of pure joy as he looks from me to the shrubbery. I steady my breath staring at his chest a minute longer while I focus on breathing in and out.

'Have you got your phone on you?' I ask. I left mine on my desk at the office. Devon fumbles in his pocket excitedly.

'Got it – stand back, Scar,' he says handing me the tin and stepping forward. OK, right, so it was all right getting me to jump out of that tree first to test our ability to fly and it was perfectly fine for me to allow the spider we captured to bite me first that one time, but grown-up Devon got brave and when it comes to crawling under a totally safe bush he's one hundred per cent got my back. I suppose I should be grateful. There is a possibility all sorts could be lurking in the shadows, so there's a chance Devon could be scratched or bitten. Not that I'd want that or anything, but I have had my fair share of injuries on his account.

'Are you sure this is a good idea?' I ask, as D sets fire to the small bundle of twigs and branches we put together in the middle of our new den.

'Every den should have a campfire,' D replies watching

in awe as the twigs catch alight with ferocious speed. The
smoke quickly fills the small space and embers spark off
the branches and land on the shrub that surrounds us.

'D,' I say, panic in my tone. 'D!'

'It's working, Scar – did you bring the marshmallows?'
Devon says enthusiastically.

'D, our whole den is on fire. Forget the marshmallows,
get out, get out,' I yell, shoving him and kicking him to
crawl faster. By the time I reach the entrance and breathe in
the smoke-free air, the ends of my hair are scorched, and my
jumper has a hole in it. I lob the whole bag of marshmallows
at D's head like I'm pitching a baseball.

With Devon's phone now lighting up our path he bends
down to where there's a small arch between the soil and the
branches. His butt is in my face and I can't help ogle. Forget
Man of Steel, Devon has a butt of steel. What am I even
thinking? I cough and shake my head and thankfully my
ogling is short-lived as Devon disappears within a matter of
seconds. I clear my throat and scold myself for objectifying
a man like that, least of all my ex best friend – a guy I used
to take bubble baths with – ewww, I cringe.

'Are you coming in, Scar?' the bush shouts.

'Grab the cookies,' I croak, clearly not fully over my view
from moments ago. I bend down, grateful that Devon has
no clue of the reason for my shaky tone, and hold the tin
out under the branches. Once Devon has relived me of it,
I get down on my hands and knees in the damp earth and
scuttle through the bush. My heart rate starts to pick up
when I suddenly start to feel like this is a very bad idea.

There wasn't a whole lot that scared me when I was a kid running wild with Devon. Now though I have just willingly crawled into a spider's haven. How much Baileys had I put into these bakes?

The bush becomes a clearing being lit my Devon's phone flashlight, and oh my gosh if it isn't tinier than I remembered and extremely cramped. I can feel a breeze on my backside that is still sticking out of the tree, but I have no more room to move. Devon is sitting cross-legged with his neck tilted to his right, his ear touching his shoulder, and there is absolutely nowhere for me to straighten out or sit, without sitting on Devon's knee or getting tangled up with him in some way and I'm definitely not doing that. Without warning laughter barrels out of me.

'D, I don't think this is going to work,' I note, my face inches from his face when I look up. Suddenly there is a flash of light and my laughter seizes. 'D, I am not getting stuck under here in a stor…'

'Shhh,' Devon cuts me off, his face having gone from humorous to panicked. He hastily switches of the flashlight on his phone, rendering our space pitch-black.

'What's going on?' I ask, getting nervous now.

'Shhh,' Devon repeats. There's another flash, which causes Devon to yank my wrist and pull me into him so I'm sitting on his lap.

My breath hitches. 'What on earth are…' This time when Devon tells me to shush, I can feel his warm breath on my neck and his finger on my lips. Goose bumps prickle my skin in an instant and that shuts me right up. Can he hear how hard my heart is hammering? I can feel heat radiating off him with the one hand I have resting on his shoulder to keep myself steady. Is this as uncomfortable for Devon as it is for me?

After what feels like a light year Devon pushes me off his lap. 'Let's get out of here,' he urges me.

I'm back on all fours and need to focus on something other than the feel of Devon's solid thighs and the heat in my cheeks from seconds ago. 'Don't forget the cookies,' is all I can manage.

'Er, yeah, er huh. I got them,' Devon croaks and stutters to get his words out, sounding rather frazzled. Outside the shrub, I stand up, stretch out my legs and brush down my mum's choice of pencil-fit skirt. Though the frost is settling in now, just looking at my coat that Devon pushes through the arch first has me burning at my cheeks again. For something to do other than watch Devon and his strong limbs emerge from the boxwood, I gather our belongings, shaking off the mud and leaves, and look around for signs of the flashing light.

'What was that?' I ask, handing Devon his coat and doing my best to ignore the flustered state that I find myself in after being in such an unexpected confined space with Devon after all these years. I don't know what's wrong with me. I think my emotions are all over the place. It takes D a moment to recover from being contorted in our old den, his eyes darting around the park and seemingly avoiding my line of vision, before he rakes a hand through his hair and puts on his coat. I can only assume that was as awkward and weird for him as it was for me, if the lack of eye contact and blush I can see even in the dark are anything to go by. So, moving on.

I take a cookie from the box and start walking to the exit

of the park. 'Cameras. Someone was taking pictures, though I can't exactly say for sure it was of you,' Devon replies stepping into line with me, reaching out and snapping off some of my cookie for himself. A shiver runs down my spine.

'Why would someone be taking a picture of me?' I ask innocently. No one has ever taken pictures of me without my consent here in Springhollow.

'They must have seen us dive into the bush and wondered what we were doing? That will be a fun one to explain,' Devon says through a nervous chuckle. I munch my biscuit thoughtfully.

'Oh gosh, sorry. Right, I sometimes forget. It wasn't me they were after; it was you. I'm sorry, D. I thought all your people were back at the inn and I hadn't seen any suspicious outsiders around here, but I wasn't thinking.' It finally clicks. The business of The Sunflower Inn over the weekend, the security, the filming crews and entourage that Devon now requires had been lost on me tonight. For a short time baking cookies and running off to escape to our old childhood den had seemed like an innocent enough adventure, not with a movie star but with my best friend.

Something squirms in my gut; the little niggle that, just like our boxwood den tried to tell me, is warning me that a lot has changed in ten years and I'd do right to remember that. I try to dispel it with another bite of peppermint heaven.

'It's OK, Scar. I liked that you remembered our den; it's just a shame we can't fit in it anymore.' This time, his chuckle is more relaxed.

'D, what will they do with the photos? You know, the

paparazzi?' I ask, my voice coming out small. I've never had to think about something like that before, but surely my face doesn't match up to the likes of the actresses and actors that Devon is usually pictured with. It makes me queasy just thinking about it. The twinge in my stomach is back in full force but this time it's not the worry that things have changed between us but a fierce protectiveness that I can't place.

'Oh, don't worry about that, Scar. Whoever took the photos only managed to score shots of your butt. Our faces were inside when the flashes went off. So, I don't think there's really much they can do with them anyway,' Devon says chewing his cookie and shrugging nonchalantly. When I look over at him, I can see the corner of his mouth twitching and know full well he's doing his damnedest not to laugh.

'Oi,' I say, mock annoyed. The smirk on his face making me forget what moments ago I had just been anxious about. I pop my last bite of cookie in my mouth and shove him in his bicep with all my might. It has no effect; Devon has since morphed into The Hulk and is no longer the skinny kid I once knew. 'Well, at least I don't have to worry about the shots being worth anything then and being plastered on international magazines around the world,' I note, relieved.

'Oh, I'm not sure about that. I think they'd be worth plenty,' Devon says making me laugh. The snowflakes and light raindrops hitting window ledges are the only sounds I hear in the peaceful night, when I realise my own laughter is ruining it as we reach my front door. Devon's gone quiet, hands in his pockets, just watching me. Was he being serious? There's no way Devon would be thinking about my arse; that's not part of the best friend code. OK, so I might have taken a cheeky glance at his earlier, but it wasn't exactly my fault – he had gotten on all fours in front of me. It had been right there. Suddenly my cheeks flush red hot. I had my butt in Devon's face when I crawled out of our stupid den. Had that been why he had looked so flustered, stuttering over his words upon exit? Surely not.

'I think I'm going to call it a night. I'm sorry that I pulled you away from the cookie tasting and that our den was a bust. I'm not sure what I was thinking,' I say, my words coming out fast as I jangle my keys into the lock.

'Not at all. I miss our adventures. I had a good time, though I'd suggest we find a new den. I've grown a couple inches since we were twelve,' Devon says, his eyes now focused on mine, a slight hint of a confident smirk tugging at his lips. The night sky's golden stars reflect in his warm brown eyes and for a moment I feel completely content, like I'm home. Keys hitting the concrete with a musical note snap me from my trance.

'Erm, ha-ha, I hadn't noticed,' I joke regarding Devon's growth spurt as I bend down to retrieve my slippery keys. I force myself to concentrate on the difficult task at hand: opening my front door. It's not like I haven't done it a million times before. However, with Devon at such close proximity it would be a first, so I guess my shaky hands aren't that unreasonable. 'Night, D,' I force enthusiastically. I really need to get my feelings in check. Hadn't Lois Lane and Peggy Carter taught me anything? Falling in love with a superhero was a dangerous game. I step into my house as Devon salutes me and wanders down my path to the gate; he's a gentleman and waits for me to close my door – knowing I'm safe inside before he walks away.

I push the door to and lean my head against it. Without Devon by my side, my body shivers. My feet feel like blocks of ice in my boots. Finally a night of running around the park without a coat on catches up with me and – hold on a minute, the goose bumps are back in full force. Did I just say love? Did I just say I was falling in love with a superhero?

15

'You're a star,' Hope says as I place her coffee on her desk. The two paper cups had been keeping my hands warm beneath my gloves.

'What did I do?' I ask as I place my hot peppermint coffee on my own desk – I switched to hot from iced lattes this morning as the chill from last night's escapades has yet to leave my bones.

'I just got an email back from the production team and the governors and they are keen on the idea for us to move the magazine to monthly. With the drop in profit right now we'd be having to do that anyway within the next month, so it makes sense. They're going to run some numbers and talk in more detail then get back to me to go over the plan, so we're not out of the clear yet. However, I'm staying positive. Devon's interview will be running in the January issue and there's already been a buzz online with the website having more hits thanks to his picture advertising the issue, so I'm keeping my fingers crossed for a boost in pre-orders, that could swerve them. And, I had chance to speak to Mrs Rolph about your donation idea and merging the competition with the magazine and she said it was a marvellous plan and they'd love to be a part of it. Which brings me to where did you disappear off to last night?' She lets out a breath after her monologue and quirks a brow under her golden frames.

'Oh, that's amazing, Hope. I knew you could do it. Things are looking up,' I say cheerfully, feeling a touch of stress leave my body.

'It had nothing to do with me – those were your ideas. And?' she says, giving me a pointed stare.

'And I just needed some fresh air and wanted to show D something at the park,' I try with half honesty. I don't truly know what came over me. One look at Devon and his playful behaviour with the cookies had made me feel like a kid again and I just got the urge to run, to be free, to go off on our own adventure, like we used to do. It was random and silly and the sniffles I have this morning prove why adults don't tend to get on their hands and knees in the cold, wet earth to hide in bushes.

Surprisingly, Hope doesn't press any further; she just smiles. 'Sounds fun. The park's beautiful this time of year.' And she turns her attention back to her computer. I take a sip of my coffee and let the velvety liquid heat my bones, while my laptop loads. I look over at Hope, my best friend of almost ten years, and contemplate her rosy, sweet complexion. This morning she's wearing high-waisted corduroys with a simple beige blouse tucked in, which compliments her golden-framed glasses and sandy blonde hair. I spent most of my life fearing girls thanks to Ruby, but Hope changed all that and I'm not quite sure what I did to deserve someone as cool as her in my life.

*

'I've got pizza in the oven, but I've got ice-cream, chocolate buttons, Galaxy Ripples and Minstrels right here,' I announce closing my bedroom door behind me and trying not to drop everything, the ice-cream freezing my forearm.

'Just pour the whole bag of buttons in my mouth,' Hope says, her voice coming out muffled with her face being buried in my pillow.

'One at a time,' I suggest. 'He should be the one to choke to death, not you,' I add, feeling a little mean but my best friend is in pain – I'm allowed to be mean and I want to show my support. I don't have many girlfriends and I've only known Hope for six months. I really like her and want her to know she can come to me and count on me. And in truth, the guy did cheat on her; he deserves something bad to happen to him, maybe not death, but like a severely sprained ankle or something.

'Why are boys so terrible?' she asks, sitting up and reaching for the ice-cream. I pass her a spoon, not really knowing how to answer, my seventeen-year-old self not having had any experience with boyfriends.

'Chuck Bartowski's not terrible,' I say thinking of a way to make her smile and spotting her notebook on the floor, which bears the character from her favourite TV show.

'I wish all men were like Chuck Bartowski.' She sighs and shoves a huge spoon of ice-cream into her mouth.

'Imagine if we were spies,' I start and quickly get lost in creating an epic fantasy, bringing Hope along with me. By the time I finish my story, she's had brain freeze four times, eaten a Galaxy Ripple, cried twice, laughed so hard she has dribbled ice-cream all over my sheets, told me I'm the best and can't remember why she was sad in the first place.

*

'Scarlett? Scarlett?' Hope bends down in front of me, her owl-like eyes peering over my laptop screen. I jump nearly spilling coffee down my pale yellow spotty shirt – actually that might not be a bad thing, why hadn't I thought of that before?

'What? Yes, sorry what?' I stutter, trying to remember where I am.

'Are you OK?' Hope asks, eyes narrowing, her fingers now tapping the edge of my laptop.

'Me? Yes, I'm fine,' I croak, forcing a wobbly smile. I want to tell Hope all about my confused, unwarranted and unwanted feelings about Devon, but I don't know where to start; plus there is far too much going on at work that I really should be focusing on.

'I don't need you in the office today, Scarlett. I'm giving you the day free to work on Saturday's booth – that OK? You've been busy with all the magazine ideas this week and I know you need time to put together your showstopper,' Hope tells me, studying me with great curiosity. I could do with a day to really focus on this project, what with all the distractions this week.

'Yes, that sounds perfect. Thanks, Hope,' I say, now more confident and cheerful.

'Good, it's two days away. I can't wait to see what've you done and thanks again for all your ideas and hard work.' Hope matches my cheerful tone and skips off back to her desk.

I gather my belongings and just as I'm about to leave, my stomach does a backslide.

'It's Thursday today,' I say, to no one in particular.

'It is, yes,' Hope mumbles but doesn't look up from her screen.

With the excitement of comic books and distractions of dinner, school talk and bedroom incidents on Monday night and cookie competitions and shrubbery antics last night, I had completely forgotten that my parents are expecting Devon for tea tonight, or rather I'd forgotten to ring them and let them know that Devon wouldn't be able to make it due to work. I compose myself so Hope doesn't have further need to worry about me and merrily tell her I'll catch her later before calmly walking out of the office and into the December chill.

I rummage around my bag in search of my rarely used mobile phone and ring my mum. She answers on the third ring.

'Scarlett dear, I'm in the middle of a cut and blow,' she says, exasperated, yet she still answered – she didn't have to answer, but it would be very unlike her to miss an opportunity to tell me that I hadn't been thinking about what I was doing.

'Oh, sorry, Mum. I'm just ringing to let you know that Devon won't be able to make it tonight. He's busy filming this documentary and filming is running into the night,' I say quickly, my words matching my footsteps as I fast march to my house.

There's a pause on my mum's end. 'Well, it was expected, dear. What did I tell you about that boy being unreliable?' she says and I can practically see her standing with her hands on her hips, lips pursed.

'OK, well I'll pop in and see you another time, Mum.'

Just like I did when we were kids, I get a strong surge in my chest to stand up for Devon, but I don't want to rise to Mum's bait and deal with this right now. It's how I got in this mess in the first place and I'll never change her. It's best just to get off the phone and keep my white lie simple before I put my foot in it again and end up inviting Devon for Christmas or something ridiculous.

'Don't be silly, Scarlett. The food is already prepared – you can still have dinner with your dad and me. I'll see you at seven. Now I really must get on, poor Margret.' My mum clicks off mumbling about some poor old lady that's catching her death with wet hair. I'm left with my mouth open fumbling for my keys on my doorstep. That had only partly gone well. I had been looking forward to an evening by myself, but I suppose it would be fun to get Dad to show me some vacation pictures and have a proper catch-up. If I can avoid Mum being rude about Devon and tolerate her and the latest gossip from the hairdresser's today, I will be fine.

Once in the house, I fire off a quick text to my dad to tell him I won't be round at the site during lunch due to my project but that I'd see him later for tea. Then I get to work.

The aroma of syrupy, cinnamon, gingerbread goodness floats around my kitchen. There isn't a surface that is not covered by edible decorations, colourful fondant and sprinkles of every kind. With the Christmas fair being only two days away I must focus today to get some more work done on the centrepiece of our booth. So far, the foundation of the building is erect and looking sturdy with its brickwork carvings and edible paint wash that gives it texture and dimension; making it come to life with the rusty purple and red stone shades.

Now, my mission is to touch up all the final details like the window decorations, wreaths, the dusting of snow around the chimney, snowflakes that have settled on the roof and the little pots of holly that line the steps up to the big oak door. The occasional bite of broken gingerbread pieces keeps my mind focused on the task at hand and helps put my mum's phone call to the back of my mind as well as any itching I get to go upstairs into my office and finish my comic book. Hope was so excited earlier to see my creation that I can't possibly let her down.

As the afternoon rolls on I relish being tucked away in my cosy home, getting to unleash my creative streak. I love being able to stretch my legs, move around the table and bring my imagination to life. I assemble tiny flowers and add some gold edible dust to them to make them sparkle when a light bulb pings above my head with an idea. Along with the centrepiece I had made tons of gingerbread biscuits in the shapes of houses and gingerbread men for both kids and adults to decorate but what about those who want to make a gingerbread house but might not have all the special ingredients at home or the time to make one to enter for the competition? Our booth is all about getting creative, coming together and making sure no one is left out. It's interactive every year and I love it.

My new idea buzzes in my brain, making me jump with excitement. If I can put together a simple house structure, I can get people to add a small decoration to it when they stop by our booth and we can raffle it off at the end to ensure that one family gets to go home with the ultimate gingerbread treat for Christmas Day, and it will be a whole village effort; something I think would get everyone ducking into our booth and something extra to raise a bit of money for the magazine.

I leave the snowflakes and holly to set while I potter around the kitchen getting my stencils ready for the communal gingerbread house, that I think will be everyone's favourite activity this year, and my stomach vaults with a weird mixture of joy and nerves. This will be the first time in ten years that Devon will get to experience the Christmas fair. My mind starts racing with all the things I must show him. He needs to indulge in Mr and Mrs Rolph's Christmas cinnamon roll while having a mooch around the handmade vendors. He must try Ryan's mulled wine while listening to the carollers. He certainly has to have a go at the winter games in the park; the sled obstacle course is my favourite. And he will absolutely be decorating his own gingerbread man on our stall. Just thinking about it all makes my heart pitter-patter with elf-like urgency on a busy Christmas Eve. That is if he can make it and it doesn't clash with his filming schedule.

I roll out my gingerbread dough, making a mental list of all these activities when my Christmas bauble bursts. The closer it gets to the Christmas fair, the closer it is to Devon leaving again. Sunday he will be on a flight back to New York, out of my life for another ten years or now that he's a giant movie star, starring in his own bloody awesome movie, more likely forever. If you were wondering, since my inner nerd was found out, I have watched the trailer to Devon's superhero movie, only like five times and yes, like

Hope had said, it looks freaking amazing. This is going to catapult him to the top of whatever casting lists they have in Hollywood for sure.

I carefully cut out the sides of my house, using a ruler to ensure all four sides are equal, though I know they will need further shaping after they've baked. No matter it being the same dough mix, each piece will have a mind of its own under the heat of the oven. This takes my mind off Devon for a few moments as I work on getting everything as symmetrical as possible. I don't pause to further investigate my feelings over Devon leaving town again. I know it's just the feeling of fear creeping up again; that fear of re-enacting what happened all those years ago.

But it doesn't have to be like that. For one, I'm a grown-up now. I can keep my emotions in check and understand reality and logic. And two, it's no big surprise. I know Devon is leaving. I've known it since I first laid eyes on him again last Friday, so it's no massive deal; life will go on just as before. Something wobbles and feels unsteady in my gut like I've just rolled over a stone on my skateboard. Devon is going to leave again and just like before there's nothing I can do to stop him.

The timer on the oven beeps letting me know ten minutes is up and also that it's six-fifty and my mum and dad are expecting me at seven. I pull out the biscuits from the oven, settle them down on the mat and hastily put away anything that needs to be refrigerated before racing up the stairs and throwing on the frilly pink polo my mum bought me. Then I rush into the hall, grabbing my coat and my beanie and leg it out of the house.

With my head down against the harsh wind I round the

corner and am sent flying as someone steps up on to the kerb – their long leg outstretched. I reach my hands out to stop myself face-planting the snow.

'Shoot, are you OK, Scar?' Devon's hand is around my waist like he's scooping up a tiny chihuahua off the floor with ease within seconds. I feel his strong, warm hand on my stomach. My back is pressed to his solid frame, and I swallow hard, not sure if I can turn around and face him, for fear he might actually see my heart trying to leap out of my chest. Clearly nearly falling to my death on the corner of a dark street at the dead of night – I know it's only seven, but it's winter, it might as well be midnight – with dangerous ice all around me has caused my body to go into shock. I'm way cooler than this. Danger was my middle name growing up. Devon would laugh if he thought a little trip had frightened me.

'What are you doing here?' I round my shoulders out, push my beanie back up my head from where it had fallen over my eyes a touch and take a small step back as I turn around; to avoid being nose to nose with Devon. Never mind a thank you for catching me. There's no time for pleasantries – I need to shake off my shock and remain strong.

Devon's cheeks are rosy, and his lips are slightly parted when I finally look at him. His eyes are glued to the hand that rests over my hip and lower back now that I've turned towards him. I didn't think it possible, but my heart rate seems to pick up speed as my whole body gets this ridiculous and overwhelming urge to kiss him; to kiss Devon. I force my eyes away from his perfectly plump and red lips and stagger backwards, putting my hand on his chest to push myself away and snap Devon out of whatever daydream is going on in his frozen and quiet state.

Our eyes connect and I feel a sizzle through my fingertips and heat where Devon's fingers are touching my body, like lightning bolts are flowing through my veins. Suddenly Devon starts blinking furiously like he's got something in his eyes and he quickly moves his hand away, like I did in fact give him an electric shock.

'Erm, er, your dad popped into the inn earlier on his way back from work, said something about seeing me at dinner tonight,' D stutters, no longer meeting my gaze. I pat down my coat where I suddenly feel a cool draught now Devon's hand isn't there and I breathe slowly in an attempt to pull myself together.

'And you came? Why would you come?' I ask, my brows furrowing, the question distracting me from wanting Devon's hands on my body again.

'Well, yeah,' Devon answers, his eyes crinkling as if I just asked a really stupid question. I guess when dinner together with our parents was a regular occurrence growing up and never an odd happening, it kind of is. He tucks his hands safely into his coat pockets after we both check our watches in unison. It's ten past seven.

'Shoot,' I say out loud and Devon starts to walk, reading my mind.

'You can't blame me for this evening. I gave you an out – I told my mum you couldn't make it, so don't say I didn't warn you,' I say to Devon matter-of-fact, walking quickly and pointing at him sternly.

'How was I to know that? I know your parents, Scar, it will be fine,' he says, his voice sounding like he's trying to reassure me. 'And what are you wearing?' He flicks at my frilly collar as we close in on my parents' house.

I look up at him and ignore the flutter in my belly when we reach my parents' gate. I sigh. 'My mum may have got a little crazier in the last ten years,' I say.

Devon shrugs a casual shrug, like he's telling me not to worry; he's got this, just like he used to do when we were kids. It was usually me who did the talking when trying to win over his mum and him who did the talking when we needed to sweet-talk my mum, but oh how times have changed.

'Oh, and she doesn't like you very much,' I add nonchalantly, as my dad opens the door with a beaming grin on his face. Out of the corner of my eye, I see Devon's eyes mist over with fear and his lips twitch. I can't help the smirk that tugs at my own. After ten years of facing my mum's disapproving speeches, there's a comfort in knowing that at least tonight it won't just be me taking the fall for being late but my partner in crime too.

After my dad fussed over Devon with plenty of manly pats on the back as he showed him through the corridor and into the dining room and my mum greeted us with unsubtle tuts while gesturing to the clock and the table where the food was already plated up, we are now all seated around said table. My dad is currently working overtime; chatting to Devon all about his acting career and not letting my dear mother get a word in edgeways. I can tell by my mum's piercing eye contact between the two of them and the robotic, slow pace at which she is cutting her steak, that she's bursting to butt in and make a comment.

I'm internally grateful for my dad. The fear in Devon's

eyes has slowly dissipated and the sparkle is back; golden flecks swirling within the deep brown. He's full of energy when he talks about things he's passionate about and as I sit back chewing on a roasted carrot, I once again feel happy in the knowledge that my bubbly, hyper, forever a kid at heart best friend is still there; just in a bigger, broader and more muscly frame. All the worries I had that evening seeing him so cool and smooth with the boys at the pub have evaporated the more time we have spent together.

'Are you married, Devon?' my mum asks, not holding back the punches, the minute my dad takes a bite of his food. Why did my dad need to eat too? I look over at him and he casts me an apologetic look as he munches on a small tree of broccoli. I give him a side smile to tell him it's OK. I wasn't exactly expecting us to manage a whole evening without my mum talking.

Devon neatly places his knife and fork on his clean plate. 'That was delicious, thank you.' He says politely. I look from D to my mum and by the small twitch in her right eye I can see she's trying with all her might not to smile at the very gentlemanly way Devon is acting. It's a far cry from our rushing to get away from the dinner table and talking with our mouths full when we were kids. But being children and not knowing any better back then was not a worthy excuse according to my mum.

'I'm not married, no, Mrs Davis.' Devon barely gets his words out before my mum starts her barrage of questions.

'And why not? Is marriage not your cup of tea? At your age do you not think it's wise to be thinking of settling down or is marriage too much of a responsibility?' She keeps her voice in a neutral tone and doesn't take her eyes off Devon, finishing her inquest with a soft and innocent smile. I feel Devon shift a little in his seat, but my eyes are on my mother while I try and figure out what to say to her. Normally, I'd simply shrug off her embarrassing and patronising questions. I know deep, deep, deep down that she means well and wants what's best for everyone. She simply doesn't understand that what's best for someone might not be what she thinks is best, but it's not coming from a place of ill intent.

The room is silent. My mouth is so dry I feel as if I've just eaten chalk and not a lovely steak dinner and no words are forming in my brain to defend Devon. My mum's questions play over in my mind and I find that my intrigue has piqued.

'Do you think we'll always be best friends?' Devon asks. He's sitting in the corner of my bedroom on my Spider-Man bean bag; it's more his Spider-Man bean bag really as that's where he always sits.

I jump up and race to the bottom drawer of my dresser, awkwardly trying to pull out the layers of A4 paper that are held together with colourful paperclips and ribbon that make up our book, with my bandaged hands. Each page clearly depicts our superhero costumes: what they will look like, where we will keep them in our mansion ready for an emergency. I've also drawn a room that's filled with paper and crayons and one of those big tables where you see adults drawing storyboards on for movies – kind of like those little booklets the teachers have us make at school. I want a big space for one of them so I can write books and comics when I'm not saving the world.

Devon's pages show the garage we will need to keep our magic cars and he put in a movie room and stage so he can act and do shows, kind of like the ones we do at school. He's good at them. I like to be at the back, but Devon isn't scared of standing at the front and having lots of lines. It's all here on these pages: our plan for when we grow up together, side by side.

'Of course we will, dummy,' I reply. 'It's going to be so fun living together; you can have all the hamsters you want,' I say bouncing on my knees and nudging Devon to flip to a clean page.

'Do you think it will be like our parents?' Devon asks, turning the pages to get to an empty one.

'Yeah, I guess so,' I say nonchalantly, getting distracted by all the bright colours.

'I'd like that,' D replies, picking up a crayon with a smile on his face. I attempt to draw but it's difficult with both my hands being in casts.

'But with none of the gross kissing stuff they do,' I add, sticking out my tongue to make a "yuck" sound as I try to add an ice-cream parlour to our dream home.

Devon straightens up in his chair, glances down at the tablecloth before clearing his throat. 'I'd love to get married and settle down. Err, I guess I just haven't found the right girl yet.' Devon's voice remains polite and he looks at my mum when answering. I find myself watching him as he speaks, his voice sounding different, more serious than I'm used to hearing, sweet even.

'Don't worry, lad, some things are just right under your

nose...' my dad starts but is interrupted by my mum who stands up with some speed and clears her throat.

'Who's ready for dessert? Dear, can you help me clear the plates?' She gives my dad a pointed glare. My brows furrow at my dad's choice of words. Did he know something about Devon's love life that I didn't? I'm not aware of them having been in touch over the years.

The chair next to me creaks as Devon leans back and rakes a hand through his dark hair. When I turn to look at him, he's already looking at me with a contemplative expression on his face.

'What about you, Scar?' he asks, fiddling with the edge of his napkin. I cross one leg under the other and twist myself so I can see him better.

'What about me?' I ask, unfurrowing my brows, a little yawn escaping my lips. I forgot how tired being in the kitchen all afternoon can make me in addition to dinner with my mother. I cover my mouth with my puffy sleeve before resting my elbow on my chair's back and leaning my head against my hand.

'You ever thought about getting married?' Devon copies my stance, twisting around so he's fully facing me. For a moment I get lost in his chocolate button eyes and feel as though I would be happy staring into them forever. They send a warmth through my body and a tingle up my spine, giving me a sense of home and exciting newness all at once. My head lolls to the side, feeling heavy; my side parting making my long fringe fall across my eye. Devon reaches out ever so casually and tucks it behind my ear and it's extremely difficult to deny the way my body reacts to his touch. That electricity floods my veins once again.

'What? You mean like us getting married?' The question was meant to come out teasing and playful, instead it comes out wistful and a little husky; the words lingering in the air when neither of us laugh it off.

'Why so serious?' My dad's voice and prompt laughter cause Devon and I to snap back around in our seats. Devon being the better actor of the two of us immediately starts laughing and congratulating my dad for that classic while I force a chuckle and busy myself helping my mum dish out dessert.

The rest of the evening goes by smoothly, mostly because I spend it shovelling Eton mess in my mouth and Devon concentrates on keeping the conversation with my dad flowing while occasionally sending a quick compliment my mum's way about the food. There's no more talk of marriage and surprisingly no more interrogating questions or snide comments from my mum; it's quite pleasant. I wonder if my dad had words with her in the kitchen.

We say our goodbyes and reach my front door in a comfortable silence. My eyes are growing steadily weary; my bed calling my name. I unlock the door and we both step inside, peeling off our layers and making all the typical shivering sounds a person makes when stepping out of the icy air and into central heating, before we make a beeline for the couch and flop down upon it. The tension in my shoulders relaxes and I breathe out the anxiety of the evening, feeling free to be myself in my own space. I lean forward and check on Ed and see his little tail wagging in his cave. He always sleeps with his tail sticking out. Knowing he's there makes me relax. I lean back and rest my head against a cushion.

'So, your mum really doesn't like me?' Devon notes, more than asks with his head tilted to the ceiling, his neck resting on the back of the couch. I chuckle, a delirious, tired sort of chuckle. 'I thought out of the two of us, I was her favourite growing up?' he adds, making me laugh harder. I elbow him in his ribs.

'Hey! You wish. You were the bad influence. You may have been able to sweet-talk her occasionally back then but I had being her only child in my favour, kind of, she had to like me a little.' I say through my giggles. 'And you lost more points when you left. I think she thought it would be great for her and I to bond, maybe have some girl time together but I was miserable and angry about everything for a long time. I could probably try a little harder; go to the salon, allow her to pamper me rather than cut my own hair, but the thing about walls is that once you've built them, they're not very easy to knock down,' I add, my giggles having subsided; my thoughts pouring out of me without fear. 'Oh gosh, I'm turning into you. What are you doing to me?' I say out loud, again without thinking, the giggles creeping up my throat once more.

Devon is looking at me, soft concentration on his face, eyes slightly narrowed, a smile tugging at those rosy lips.

'What?' I say, shoving him lazily.

'I don't think that wall is as sturdy as you think. And what's wrong with turning into me? I am pretty fantastic you know,' he replies, going from serious to playful by the end of his sentence, which I know full well is to stop me freaking out and dwelling on his "wall not being sturdy" statement. It works. I rest my head on his shoulder, tuck my feet up to the side of me and give in to my sleepy eyes, closing them tight while a smile dances on my lips.

'I know,' I whisper, referring to Devon and his being rather wonderful. Of course, I'd known that when I was a kid and saying it now despite all we've been though still feels right. I've only had a handful of men join me on my couch over the years and this is the first time I'm not picking at my nails nervously or rambling about the kind of fish flakes that Ed likes. Not that Devon is like those men because this evening hasn't been a date, but the thought makes me smile so much that I succumb to the land of nod.

16

I wriggle my body, burying myself deeper into the warmth of my bed, arching my back into the curve of my duvet. My cheek tingles against my pillow, the scent of it inviting and delicious. I move my hand up underneath it wanting to wrap myself up in its cosiness when instead of smooth fabric connecting with my fingers, I feel a smooth palm and a sizzle beneath my skin when long fingers interlock with mine. I hear a low grumble from behind me.

My eyes dart open as my brain starts to compute the situation I am in. Am I using Devon's forearm as a pillow? Are Devon and I holding hands? And holy moly, did I just wriggle my butt against Devon's crotch region? My mind is screaming at me to jump off the couch and get a safe distance away from the superhero currently spooning me on my couch, but my body is deceiving every signal my brain is giving it and does not want to move.

I lie still as Devon begins to stir; one arm moves tighter around my waist and pulls me closer to him. His foot moves up my calf, his toes gently nudge my tights, my skin heats everywhere with his caressing movements. My heart starts beating to the rhythm of John Williams' 'Love Theme' from Superman. Oh gosh, really? I can't breathe. My hips involuntarily twist into him, making his hand drift along my stomach. I need to wake him. I carefully manoeuvre myself, prying my fingers out of Devon's grip, so I am on my back, then turn my head to gaze up at him. He looks handsome when he sleeps; peaceful and content with a little morning five o'clock shadow defining his jawline.

Before I can open my mouth, his eyelashes flutter and I am greeted by his rich brown eyes that sparkle almost caramel under the sun's morning glow through the window. I expect him to freak out and sit up in shock, but he doesn't move. I follow his gaze as he looks over the length of my body, that is snug against his, his hand resting on the base of my torso and back up to my face. His eyes linger on my lips first and then meet mine once more. The arm under my head shifts slightly as I feel his fingers in my now-frizzy hair.

'Morning,' he says lazily, as a smile curves at his lips. The huskiness in his voice and the way he moves, keeping me close, deliberately now that he's awake and staring right at me, catches me off guard. The way he looks at me stirs something deep in my belly. I don't feel judged by his eyes – they always hold such warmth, but why isn't he freaking out? And why am I still in his arms? I should have moved by now. He's awake; getting up will not disturb him.

'D?' I whisper, but my thought process is cut off as his hand plays with my hair that meets my collarbone and my body tingles. He's delicate in his movements causing my stupid body to shiver with pleasure.

'Scar?' Devon croaks. I make a noise, too distracted to speak. 'Did you just groan?' At what point did I close my eyes again? When I open them, Devon is wearing a teasing smirk and somewhere in the distance my alarm clock starts ringing. I roll off the couch, hit the wooden floor, bounce up onto my feet and throw a cushion at Devon's head.

'Put the kettle on please. I need to shower and get ready for work,' I shout as I take the stairs two at a time.

We don't talk about this morning's wake-up call when I enter the kitchen. Devon simply hands me my coffee, made just the way I like it, then we both excuse ourselves – Devon remembering he has an early interview and me needing to get to the office.

I'm in my chair just as the clock strikes nine a.m. and it's only then I realise Hope's not sat behind her desk. She rushes in wafting papers in her hands five minutes later as I'm booting up my laptop and looking over the day's mail.

'Is it just me who gets the paper jammed every time I touch that machine?' Hope asks as she settles behind her desk. I usually do the photocopying for her and I'm usually a little earlier than I was today. My cheeks flush and I feel bad for my tardiness – see this is why Hope needs me. She has more important things to do than dealing with photocopier malfunctions.

'It is, yes, and I'm sorry. Did you need me to copy some things for you?' I reply, tucking my hair behind my ear.

Hope stops shuffling her papers and actually stops working for a moment to look at me.

'No, no I've got it. I'm a big girl; I can figure out the photocopier,' she says taking her glasses off and chewing on the frame, elbows propped up on her desk. 'How is the gingerbread house coming along and where were you last night? Jess said he saw Devon leaving your house this morning.' She slides the last statement in in a more mumbling tone.

My face contorts into a huge grin at the mention of the gingerbread house; I feel it's my best work yet and can't wait to share it with her.

'It's looking amazing and so festive; I think everyone is going to love it,' I answer, before clicking my mouse over my emails and pulling my eye contact away from Hope.

'I'm sure it's gorgeous. I can't wait to see it. And the what did you and Devon get up to last night part of that question?' she urges raising a brow.

'Oh, we just had dinner at my parents'.' It's not like I have to hide the fact that I hung out with Devon to Hope. She knows he's my ex best friend and she's the one that has been inviting him to dinner dates and cookie competitions. I just don't want her to start overanalysing things and getting excited about double dates or planning all our future cosplay outfits because I'm certainly not doing that. 'We got in late and fell asleep on the couch. You know how exhausting it is having dinner with my mum,' I add nonchalantly.

After the bedroom debacle and Hope's wiggling eyebrows after too much wine on Monday night and my disappearing act with Devon on Wednesday, I don't want her to get the wrong idea and think that Devon and I could be anything more than we are. I don't want her bubble to burst when he leaves on Sunday. A part of me wants to let her in on my wayward thoughts but I'm scared that talking about my feelings will only make them more real. I swallow down the lump in my throat and focus on checking over some article submissions for January.

'You didn't text me back. I got no goodnight text,' she

says, still stood up and looking my way, a small smile tugging at her cheeks and her eyebrows halfway up her forehead, like I'm about to divulge some kind of magical night with Devon to her. I squint my eyes not even wanting my brain to go down that lane and start giving me visuals of what that would be like, especially not after this morning; I can already feel my cheeks redden.

'Hope, you know I never look at my phone,' I say matter-of-fact, forcing my words to come out firm and not lost in a sexy daydream.

'So, I take it you didn't see the latest article on your roomie?' she asks, shuffling papers on her desk.

Why is she not working? It's so unlike Hope to be this unprofessional.

'Since when do I read celeb gossip?' I reply, though I have to admit, there's a small part of me, like a tiny weeny part of me, that's interested to know what the world thinks of Devon; how he comes across to the masses and if they love him as much as I do. Did I just say love again? You know what I mean.

'It seems our good friend Ruby managed to stir up a heap of interest in Devon's love life – her taking centre stage of course, over the whole childhood sweetheart thing.' Hope is looking at me expectantly; I wish she would sit down. I shuffle in my chair making it squeak and creak as a knot forms in my stomach.

'Hope,' I start with a sigh. 'D is a grown-up – we are all grown-ups here. He can protect himself now and if he can't see someone like Ruby from a mile away then that's on him.' I lean back having clicked send on an email to Clark about the winner of this week's cookie competition and about collecting their information for January. Oh, and not that Clark – that would be pretty neat though wouldn't it? Both work at a newspaper, both wear glasses, only one is hiding a secret superhero identity but it's not the one who works with me, unfortunately.

'So, you're good if the whole world thinks that Ruby is his girlfriend?' Hope presses.

Cue more chair creaking from behind my desk. 'If that's what Devon wants the world to think, then of course I am. As his former best friend, I just want him to be happy. He and his people know what sells movies, I don't.' I nod. It's the one name I haven't been able to bring up when spending time with Devon. We always end up having so much fun that I just don't want to talk about her. In my mind I'd settled on Hope's assumption that Ruby is styling Devon for the documentary and then I had pushed her to the back of my mind.

'OK, fine.' Hope finally sits down and gets back to work.

'Great,' I say occupying my brain with an email on "How to keep Chickens" for a sponsor of ours. It's rather interesting and maybe Eddie could do with a friend. But it's difficult to really take any of the words in. I don't believe that Devon could fall for someone like Ruby, not after all she put us through at school. My Devon didn't fit with someone with such a mean and malicious streak but then again maybe I don't know the real Devon. People said fame changed people. I don't think it has changed D, not after the time we have spent together, but how could I be sure? I still don't know what happened two years ago; how he managed to pay Ruby a visit at the summer fair but not me.

An email pings into my inbox from our governors

requiring more detail on how we plan to proceed with a monthly magazine. I scan over the words, grateful that they can keep my mind busy and off thoughts of "would the real Devon please stand up?" but at the same time my palms grow sweaty. There's a lot of talk of more content and filling the pages. If it's to be a monthly issue, then it will require more substance to justify a slight price increase. Hope is copied in to the email too.

'What are you thinking?' she asks, chewing on the end of her pencil. I immediately go through our staff register and try to come up with a way to expand people's skill sets and give them multiple areas to cover. We're only a small team. It might be tricky, but surely we can make it work.

'We can send people out in the field more, see if they can find more hidden gems of Springhollow. It will be a meatier issue so the more stories the better. Maybe Billy can add an extra feature on horoscopes, focus on a specific one each month,' I say, not feeling all that enthusiastic or inspired by my off-the-cuff ideas.

'Yeah, maybe we do more interviews, ask the villagers about their favourite memories of Springhollow or favourite era,' Hope suggests, her tone a touch shaky. As I read the bottom of the email, I understand why. The governor goes into detail about how they would like to see a mock-up of our plan going forward so they can approve our new vision. If they don't see it creating a rise in subscriptions or it being beneficial and viable to produce, then it's likely that the magazine will be scrapped. Oh, and they want our proposal on Monday.

'That sounds good. See, we have ideas; it's all going to be fine,' I tell Hope with forced positivity, but she's now well and truly in Business Hope state of mind and so I bring up the file of our current magazine's formatting, side by side with a blank Word document and I will my fingers to type out the answer to our magazine woes.

I return from a coffee run and a quick visit to the building site to check in with my dad, as my lunch hour draws to a close. It's always nice to get out and stretch my legs. It's never bothered me fetching coffee for Hope, as I adore popping in to see Mr and Mrs Rolph at the bakery; they make the best coffee in town, and it feeds my own coffee addiction. I also love surprising my dad each day with a new flavour and seeing him in his element at work. He loves what he does and it's a pleasure to watch him on the job. Today I picked up a few extra Christmas specials for Dad's work buddies. I think the peppermint is now a favourite of theirs too.

As I go to place Hope's coffee on her desk, she takes it from my grasp as she stands up, walks around her table and ushers me back towards the door.

With her hand on my elbow she says, 'I need you to do a quick job for me, pretty please. I know it's not in your usual job description but I can't send anyone else with all the changes and altered deadlines looming and you know how much I love your writing, so can you please go to the address on this paper and cover the events taking place. We just got a phone call. Someone mentioned we might want to get the local news on it and well, we're the local news.' Hope barely takes a breath and it's not like I can say no when she's already guiding me out of the office and she's my boss. Hope always got a kick out of the articles I used to submit to Alfred, but after being turned down so many times, I'd just stopped submitting them, even when she became the person in charge.

'Erm, yeah, OK,' I say, a little hesitantly, taking the piece of paper from her hand, my eyebrows drawn in; my nose scrunched up at the vagueness of my new task.

'Thanks, I owe you one,' she says cheerfully, giving me half a hug before returning to her seat. I appreciate her compliment and confidence in me to cover a journalist's job and can't hide the sudden excitement I feel getting to escape the office for a little while. I smile as the peppermint-chocolate coffee I'm holding in my hand wafts up to me, the contents swirling and sploshing inside the paper cup. I make my way down the stairs, a little extra pep in my step, and out into the cold once more. Opening the folded sticky note my feet automatically walk in the direction of "Daffodil Lane" the minute my eyes scan the message. It reads that I am to report the happenings that are occurring on the corner where Daffodil Lane meets Riverbend.

It's been a while since I have ventured over to this side of town. Thinking about it now I'm actually surprised that we got a call reporting newsworthy activity. Apart from houses, a small community centre and the skatepark, there's not much there. I backtrack my thoughts and return to skatepark as I reread the paper in my hand. On the corner of Daffodil Lane and Riverbend is the skatepark. What on earth was happening at the skatepark? Kids are still in school until – I check my watch – three-thirty, which is an hour and a half from now. I quicken my pace as my mind starts whizzing with possibilities. I can see the headlines now "Kick flips and Zimmer frames", "Ollying old ladies", "Heel-flipping hedgehogs".

A good fifteen minutes have passed by the time I reach the iron-gate entrance of the park. I'm panting slightly from my brisk walk. Over my panting I strain to hear noise, but I can't hear any commotion or wheels hitting the ramp and worry that I've messed up my one job and missed all the action, letting Hope down. I desperately don't want to let her down, not with the current state the magazine is in. I push the gate and it creaks open. I toss my coffee cup into the recycling bin before pulling out my notebook and pen, ready to jot down any sudden movement. But there's no one about. I take a few steps towards the bowl, my heart rate picking up when I hear the familiar sound of someone crashing and burning on their board. Adrenaline is coursing through me when I realise it's been ten years since I stepped foot in this place.

The memory constricts my chest. My hand holding my pen rests over my heart as I try to rub away the tightness. Why do we have to grow up? Or why is it that when we grow up, we have to stop doing all the things we love in order to come across as sophisticated or professional? And where on earth had my mum hid my board?

As these thoughts play on my mind, the occupant of the skate bowl rolls closer to me and up the side of the bowl. He's a few feet in the air above me, grabs his board, twists his body impressively before connecting with the bowl again and rolling away. I make a note that maybe our town will have their first ever participant in the X-Games one day; that would be an awesome headline and one I think our town should get behind. I find a low rail and sit on it, content that

I'm not in the way considering no one else is here when the skater lands with another impressive manoeuvre in front of me and throws down a bag. My skin begins to tingle when I look over the scarf pulled up around their mouth, beanie hat pulled low, but eyes big and bright and reflecting the afternoon sun's bold orange glow. How is it that my best friend and former best friend have only known each other for five days and they are already in cahoots, aiding each other in secret missions? I let out a chuckle.

'Am I really here to report the latest news?' I say with an eye-roll as I place my notebook and pen on the ground, give Devon one more mock annoyed look and open the backpack.

Inside is a brand-new Element skateboard. I gasp, yanking it out of the bag and rushing to my feet. 'Seriously?' is the only word I can manage as I take in the pristine board with its bright colours and smooth deck, turning it over in my hands and looking at it with great adoration.

'Seriously,' Devon replies, muffled through his scarf. 'There's something else in there too.'

I pry my eyes off my new board and dive into the bag, pulling out a pair of cargo pants and Converse. Only then do I register my black pencil skirt and boots. 'When did you get so smart?' I tease. Hastily, I step into the trousers, pulling my black boots off, Converse on and shuffling out of my pencil skirt and shoving it in the backpack. I can feel my toes tingling with anticipation as I drop the board in front of them, stepping onto it with my left foot.

'Oh, I don't know about this. I'm sure reporting the news would be more fun,' I say sarcastically, shoving Devon to get past him so I can drop into the bowl, which is covered by a concrete structure, keeping it free of snow. The minute I drop into the bowl I feel exhilarated. My feet are thanking the shoe gods for Converse and I feel like I'm on top of the world.

It's only when a trickle of young teens start chatting and taking over the ramps that I finally look up and jump off my board. I'd been following D around the course, tracing the curves of the bowl, catching a few rail slides and seeing if I could still do a trick or two on the half-pipe that I wasn't aware of the time. I'm pleased to say that muscle memory has been on fine form this afternoon and I can't wipe the windswept grin off my face.

Devon kicks up his board beside me while I catch my breath at the top of the pipe.

'I can't believe you got Hope to let me have the afternoon off work to skate, especially considering we're currently in crunch time with saving the magazine,' I say, stunned.

'I have my uses. What seems to be the problem with the magazine? Anything I can help with?' Devon says with a grin and flash of concern. I look him up and down, appreciating his offer, but he has plenty on his plate. I don't want to add worrying about a Springhollow treasure to his busy schedule. I shrug.

'The weeklies aren't selling so we thought about taking it monthly, giving people something to look forward to, but that means packing it with more... well, I don't quite know. Springhollow is a small village. I'm sceptical to how many stories we can possibly dig up in this place. You already ruined my "Skateboards and Zimmer frames" headline,' I confess to Devon, unable to keep from spilling my truth. He lets out a hearty laugh at my last comment, which makes me scrunch up my nose and rub a hand over my chest.

'I like that – maybe that's what you need, to think outside the box. Think like Scarlett. Also, I don't believe you haven't skated in years; you didn't miss a beat,' Devon notes casually. His scarf is now around his neck so I can see his rosy lips as he speaks.

"Think like Scarlett," echoes in my brain. What on earth does that mean and why did D make it sound so easy?

While I contemplate his words, I hold the tip of my board and line my back wheels up against the edge of the half-pipe. Not having figured it out yet, I glance at D and shrug, taking his skateboarding compliment, which makes me feel good. 'I came back two days after you left, but I couldn't do it. Mum went ballistic when she saw me carrying my board home, told me it was bad enough that I was a smart, pretty young girl but I should certainly not be skating with a broken arm and fractured hand. She gave me the whole speech about being an adult, getting a job and being respectful and professional around town. It was fun,' I express, with a laugh, not unaware that that's the most I've said about that ever. I really was turning into Devon, letting my emotions sneak out like that.

'Sometimes you can't worry about what everyone else thinks,' Devon starts, with a look that holds so much sincerity that I almost want to reach out and hug him, almost, but my brain gets the best of me, too scared to open up too much, to ask him more about his hurt in case it stirs up my own again. But there was certainly something unsettling about his advice. Was he worrying about what people thought of him?

'That's easy for you to say when the whole world thinks you're a superhero,' I tease, nudging his elbow. Catching his eye, the flicker of pain vanishes. He shoves me back, making me wobble. I very nearly lose my balance and fall into the half-pipe but recover quickly.

'Race you to the gate,' he shouts, dropping in and leaving me up top. I momentarily get distracted. I may not like sharing my own feelings, but there's something unnerving about Devon not pushing to share his because – whether I like it or not – that's never stopped him before. Just now he shut down quick and for the first time, I feel bad for resorting to a joke instead of addressing whatever hurt he is harbouring. Ruby may be a bully, but maybe she listened to Devon; was there for him in ways I couldn't be. I could be the fun friend, a piece of childhood nostalgia, but maybe he needed a woman, a woman who opened up to him and didn't hide behind walls.

The thought of not being all that Devon needs makes my stomach turn. It used to always just be me and him. There's a sharp longing in my chest for those days; I want them back. But does that mean I want Devon as more than a friend?

My face must be a picture when I reach Devon at the gate; he beat me by a long shot, my thoughts having kept me glued me to the half-pipe for a good five minutes after he declared the race.

'Why so tense, Scar?' he asks looking over my features.

'I'm not tense.' I shake my head with a laugh.

'You were pouting – that means something's on your mind.' Devon looks up at me through his long lashes as he stuffs both our boards in his backpack. Should I talk to him, tell him what's on my mind? There are now a bunch of things on my mind, but one thing is standing out above the rest, which makes me feel guilty about work. Should I ask about Ruby and tell him that I'm feeling wholly confused about our current friendship status after all these years apart? Would he laugh?

'I was just thinking that this has been the best day ever. I'm definitely going to be doing this more often,' I say merrily, allowing the happy words to replace my heavy thoughts and totally chickening out when it comes to my emotions. Devon's eyes linger on mine. I know he can sense I'm not telling the truth, but again he doesn't push. Do I want him to push?

'OK,' he says in a way that confirms he can still see right through me. 'Ice-cream?' he questions, with a side smirk, moving past my sudden awkwardness.

'Yes please,' I answer, forgetting my woes with one thought of Salvatore's gingerbread ice-cream with hot chocolate sauce in a cinnamon waffle cone.

'Does Salvatore still do his gingerbread ice-cream at this time of year?' D asks, making me beam as we leave the skatepark behind and walk along Daffodil Lane.

'He sure does, but you can't order the same thing as me,' I say with a wide smirk on my face, feeling my shoulders relax over my confusing thoughts as we walk our familiar route to the ice-cream shop.

'Oh yeah, so you can eat mine too?' he replies, grinning just as big as me.

'Exactly.' I nod. With Devon by my side now the walk back to the village square doesn't seem as far. We chat about the new tricks he has learnt on his board – New

York has plenty of skateparks and the big kid in him never stopped skating – it makes me miss the big kid in me all the more. I cave and ask one or two questions about his acting gigs and in typical Devon style he gets super animated and enthusiastic, talking about his passion for his chosen art form; not once does he touch on the fame and he doesn't speak at all like he did in front of the camera when I first bumped into him.

By the time we get to Salvatore's window I'm ready for all the ice-cream – skateboarding for an hour has made me ravenous. I order my gingerbread ice-cream with hot chocolate sauce in a cinnamon waffle cone and can't help digging in before Devon has placed his order; I don't even care that my hands are slowly growing as cold as the ice-cream in their mitts.

Devon orders a peppermint chip ice-cream with a chocolate cone and my heart skips a beat – it's just the excitement over ice-cream I tell myself, and getting to share this festive treat with such a good friend, but as we thank Salvatore my eyes survey Devon as he takes his first bite. His chocolate brown eyes grow wide, he has a slight rosy hue in his cheeks and his hair is making animal shapes with sweat and dew. When he smiles his nose crinkles and his eyes narrow making room for that wide grin that can dazzle from miles away; he looks like a man and every bit a Hollywood heartthrob, yet a boyish charm remains.

As he savours his first bite, I rise to my tiptoes for a sneak attack; taking a bite out of his ice-cream. He lets out a howl of a laugh when I lick my lips and wiggle my eyebrows.

The remainder of our walk to The Sunflower Inn consists of Devon trying to take a bite out of my cone and me trying to dodge him until I finally relent and let him have the best bit; the butt of the cone filled with the last remaining gooey and melting bit of gingerbread ice-cream and thick chocolate sauce. That scores me one of those dimple-incurring smiles followed by a smug look. I give him an eye-roll and a hefty shove into reception where Devon's face falls serious as he looks around, taking in the surroundings. There's no one in the lobby except Willow who eyes us curiously when Devon puts a finger to his lips, signalling for me to keep quiet before he makes a ninja-like move towards the stairs and waves for me to follow. I see the mischievous twinkle in his eye like we're about to embark on one of our childhood missions, so I copy his movements bending low; spy mode activated.

We make it to his room after plenty of three ninja-like manoeuvres; a cartwheel here, a roll there, and burst through his door in a fit of giggles.

The glow of the moon lights up Devon's tidy room. I can see that's he's unpacked, making himself at home, his suitcase put away neatly in the corner and for some reason that makes me smile. He switches on the bedside lamp and pulls off his hoodie. I go to do the same with my coat, my clothes damp from the afternoon chill, making me shiver, but get caught, unable to untie the knot in the toggles. My fingers are frozen and sore in contrast to the heat of the room, making it difficult for me to get a grip, and I keep going cross-eyed looking down at my chest to untie the top one.

I look in the mirror to avoid the dizziness and locate the knot when Devon steps behind me and reaches over my shoulders to help. Instantly my body heats. He must have turned the heat on full blast, noticing my struggle with my icy fingertips, but as his hand brushes over my collarbone to the base of my neck I feel my spine tingle and I can't be one hundred per cent certain the temperature of the room is the reason for my flushed cheeks. I can feel his warm breath on my ear. I watch his movements in the mirror, his lips graze my earlobe and I feel like I'm floating with his gentle touch. When he lets out a low groan my nerves get the best of me.

'D?' I say, turning to him before my eyes threaten to roll back with pleasure. I lift them up to face him. He looks like home, his features soft in the dim light. I want to pull him close, the only person who seems to be able to knock down my wall and make me want more, to give more of myself, but the foundations I have built are still there, the layer that remains terrified that makes me divert to casual chit-chat and humour to put distance between us.

'D? Did you just groan?' I chuckle and smirk playfully, patting him in the chest. His eyes fly open, my voice not quite filled with the sarcasm I was relying on and instead more of a croaky longing and wistfulness.

He pulls at my toggles, successfully undoing the knot and laughs, clearing his throat.

'Err, ha no. Are you wearing perfume? It caught in my throat.' He makes a choking noise.

Our eyes remain locked on each other's and I can sense we're both trying to read what's behind them when there's a knock at the door, snapping us out of our trances. Devon jumps and turns away, sliding a finger over the neck of his T-shirt as if to loosen it.

I play with the now-untied toggle and make to take my coat off, its dampness now seeping into my skin, but I freeze when Devon pulls open the door and Ruby is standing there in a silvery shimmering dress, her eyelashes fluttering manically as she announces, 'They need you downstairs, Devon.' And barges into the room with a clothes rack in tow.

'OK, can you give me a minute?' Devon stammers but his question goes unanswered as she swings the rack next to the bed. When she looks up and her eyes finally find mine, her lashes stop fluttering as a perfectly evil scowl takes over her face. I manage a smile as I pull my coat back over my shoulders and suddenly want to be anywhere but here.

I start to gather my things as Devon comes over to me. He bends down so he is closer to my ear. 'I'll see you tomorrow at the fair, Scar.' His breath tickles my ear and my stomach flips at the excitement in his tone. He's quiet enough that it's like our little secret but I can feel Ruby's hawk eyes watching his every move. Then out of nowhere he leans in and hugs me. It's the warmest hug I've ever received. When he moves away, I half expect to see two hearts on his tummy; like he's Love-a-Lot Bear in disguise, sent to spread joy and love to everyone with hugs alone.

I nod, smile and walk to the door. I'm not even out of the room when Ruby makes a big show of grabbing Devon's forearm and placing one hand on his chest and says, 'We need you out of those clothes, mister, try this on first,' with a tight smirk on her face. Does Devon know that she's flirting? Does he like it?

The thoughts wander through my mind as I make my way back to my house. My insides are a ball of confusion. My body still tingles from Devon's touch and I get a ridiculous spark of electricity rushing through my veins when I think back to Devon's lips being so close to mine earlier. What would I have done if he kissed me? Did I want him to kiss me?

Devon had been the most special person in my life for sixteen solid years; we'd done everything together, but that didn't equate to romantic love. We were just kids having fun. Seeing him now after all these years, it's just a piece of nostalgia, a comfort zone that I am slipping back into and you're not supposed to fall back into your comfort zone – everyone knows that. Then again, since Devon has arrived, I have been taking more steps out of my comfort zone – drawing again, skating again, dreaming again – and it feels amazing. There is something new, exciting, and different about our grown-up relationship, something comforting yet wild and inspired.

But then there is Ruby. Ruby, the kind of woman who would fit into his new life; she would flourish in all the glitz and the glam and she is clearly making an effort to put herself out there and let Devon know she wants him. The gossip mill certainly ate them up as a couple if what Hope is telling me about the latest headlines are anything to go by.

Stepping into my hallway, I lock the door behind me, check on Ed and follow my feet up the stairs and into my office. Without thinking I sit at my desk, pick up a pencil crayon and get lost in drawing; allowing all my conflicting emotions to melt away with each pencil stroke, while "Think like Scarlett" ricochets around my mind.

17

I toss and turn in my fluffy sheets as my brain registers the familiar constant beeping of my alarm. Taking in a deep breath I can smell the last batch of gingerbread cookies I had made last night dancing throughout the house, which makes me less cranky about my alarm going off at six a.m. on a Saturday after I'd not long since fallen asleep. I'd stayed up until I finished my comic book and then my mind had wandered back down the dangerous half-pipe of thinking about Devon and Ruby together and reminiscing about mine and Devon's more intimate moments that we have shared since his reintroduction to my life, so I had ventured in to the kitchen.

Wanting to avoid, with every fibre of my being, what I didn't want to admit were jealous bubbles when I thought of Ruby and the tingly feelings the latter evoked, I had set about adding the final touches to today's centrepiece and baking two batches of cookies to keep my mind occupied with much safer thoughts. One cup of molasses, two cups of flour, a pinch of this and that, until my eyelids were practically lead, and I knew I probably shouldn't be operating an oven and that I'd drift off without a second thought.

My forearms prickle with goose bumps as I make the first move to get out of the warm confines of my bed. I scrape my sweeping fringe back into a grippy clip and stretch my legs out in front of me, my toes tickling the wall, just as I hear a knock at the door. Then it all goes quiet and I wonder for a minute if I had just been hearing things, but then the knock comes again and this time there's more thought behind it.

Two knocks, one knock, a fast three knocks, followed by two more slow knocks and then silence. A grin spreads faster than the Flash across my face before I can catch it. I shoot out of bed ignoring the iciness that meets my toes the minute they connect with the wooden floorboards. I only just avoid a collision with my wall as I race down the stairs.

Whatever conflicting and confusing thoughts were flying around my head last night disappear as quick as Susan Storm as I hear mine and Devon's secret childhood knock. I feel like a kid again, which makes my stomach perform a triple flip, causing me to misstep and career down the last three stairs like an avalanche.

'Scar?' I hear from the other side of the door.

'I'm good,' I shout, jumping up. I pat myself down and tell myself to play it cool as I yank open the front door with a bright smile. Devon is stood on the step wearing a black parka, striped scarf, five o'clock shadow and one of his beaming smiles. His nose is a little red from the cold and snowflakes fall in light flurries behind him. I notice the lines and crinkles around his eyes and mouth from the way he talks so expressively all the time, and his deep brown eyes are twinkling under the early sunrise. This time I don't think I can blame my stomach for the uncomfortable shift inside me. I'm pretty sure the sizzle and pounding is coming from a little higher up; in my heart.

Devon's grin widens as I just stand there, my legs turning to icicles.

'I brought breakfast,' he announces holding up the bag in his hand, which snaps me to attention with the mouth-watering cinnamon aroma of its contents.

'You didn't?' I start, waving him and the bag in. 'You bought us cinnamon twists?' I ask, closing the door and practically skipping around him as he heads for the kitchen.

'I sure did,' he replies, shaking the bag above his head, teasing me as I hear the cinnamon sugar crashing around inside it.

'Good morning, Mrs Rolph,' Devon and I say in unison.

'Good morning, my dears, what can I get you today?' Mrs Rolph asks us. D and I are bundled up and ready for the Christmas fair, coins in our hands that our mums gave us for our Christmas fair breakfast tradition.

'Please can I have a cinnamon twist,' we say again in sync.

'Sure thing,' Mrs Rolph replies. She takes our coins and hands us our warm, delicious treats then eyes us suspiciously. 'Have either of you seen Bonny lately? My old cat seems to have wandered off,' she asks, peering over the counter causing both Devon and I to take a massive bite of our twists, shake our heads with our mouths full and run away.

My heart does another flutter at the memory as I watch

Devon pouring the contents of the bag onto a plate. His tall and grown-up stature doesn't seem out of place in my kitchen. He somehow, after only two visits, knows where everything is; which I can only attribute to him knowing how my brain works in regards to where I would keep things, and I find myself smiling at the thought as he takes a seat at the table.

My stomach rumbles, reminding me that the cinnamon twists are to be eaten and not admired. I immediately flush as that thought takes a naughty turn, making me avert my eyes from Devon and busy myself with the kettle to make coffee.

By the time I turn back around Devon has placed a cinnamon twist on to my plate but has yet to start eating. He's just staring at me, holding his fork aloft, elbow on the table, dimple in his right cheek. I place our coffees by our plates and take a seat, grabbing my fork and diving in.

'What?' I say through a mouthful of delectable flaky pastry.

'Nothing,' Devon says, using the side of his fork to cut the twist, his head bowing down like he's suddenly gone shy.

'Your cheeks have gone red,' I point out, smiling now because he looks kind of cute when his cheeks go red. There must be way too much sugar in this twist because I should not be thinking of Devon as cute.

He chews thoughtfully and then shrugs casually, a cheeky glint washing over his eyes.

'Do you own a pair of pyjama pants?' He chuckles and now it's my turn to blush furiously and in front of him this time.

★

After we devoured breakfast in comfortable silence, I excused Devon to the living room first so as to not flash my knickers further from under my baggy tee and got ready in record time so that we would make it on time to the fair for early set-up. I was even more grateful for Devon's presence this morning when he helped carry the gingerbread houses while I carried the plethora of bags holding my boxes and boxes of gingerbread cookies and pieces.

It was only a short walk but not having to make a dozen trips was appreciated with the snow falling heavier and the ice glistening from some precarious spots already in the early hours.

Hope and Jess were already milling about our booth, twinkling lights strung and an array of *Village Gazette* magazines expertly decorating one of our tables. Hope had left a space in the middle and placed a cake stand ready for our gingerbread house to take centre stage. I left the bags on top of the adjacent table while Devon helped set the house down to do the big reveal for Hope.

'What's in that box?' Hope asks eagerly when Devon gently pops the other box next to my biscuits that I have yet to unwrap. Her cheeks are positively red from the morning air's icy nip and no doubt her buzzing around trying to get everything perfect.

'Hold your horses, I want to show you this one first,' I say mock exasperated, but her excitement is contagious. The sunrise, the sparkling lights, the glittering Christmas trees huddled in every one's booths, this morning's throwback to childhood eating cinnamon twists with Devon on the best day of the year – sometimes the fair is better than Christmas Day, with all its joy and magic – and Hope smiling at me expectantly, I get a flurry of snowflakes whizzing around in my stomach. Hope gathers closer to me. Devon and Jess are stood back, hands in pockets watching us both in our giddy states with grins on their faces.

I take the lid off the box on the stand and carefully fold down the sides and slide the box from under the silver tray the house is iced onto for security measures. Hope gasps and I feel a swell of pride looking at my replica of our office building made in gingerbread form as all the intricate details are exaggerated with all the highlights and shadows caused by the sunrise and festive lights shining around it.

'Oh, my goodness, look at that wreath and look at all the bricks, oh and you got the front door simply perfect. Didn't I tell you she was amazing?' Hope is walking around inspecting each side of the gingerbread building. Jess steps closer, putting an arm on her shoulder. I'm not entirely sure who she told I was amazing because she doesn't look up; her eyes are trained on taking in the features of our centrepiece.

'It's awesome, Scarlett, everyone's going to love it,' Jess tells me with a smile.

'OK, OK, I had another idea while I was baking.' I start moving around to our other table where everyone will be able to decorate a gingerbread cookie; I made gingerbread men, houses and trees for them to choose from. Jess and Hope follow me; Devon is stood close by near the tree, a smile on his face watching my current performance. He's quiet, which is unusual, and his eyes look a little misty but I'm wary of the time and that soon there will be giddy kids and cheery adults swarming our booth. We need to finish setting up and putting up all our signs. I will have to check in with him later and see if he's all right.

'So, I thought, when everyone comes to decorate a biscuit, that they could add some decoration to this house.' I repeat the box number one process with box number two, to reveal a plain undecorated house. 'That way at the end of the day we will have a house that has been created by the whole village. We could do a raffle to raise money for the Gazette and the winner gets to take it home for Christmas Day.'

I barely get the word *day* out of my mouth when Hope attacks me with a hug. 'You are a genius – a festive, Christmas fair genius. I love it so much. The village is going to love it. Have I told you before, your creative genius is wasted being my personal assistant? Talk about village spirit, oh I can't wait to see what everyone creates together,' Hope says, clapping her hands, squeezing me again and then bouncing off to get our banner, tugging Jess with her to help. I adjust the communal gingerbread house on its silver tray, better to leave this one flat on the table so the kids can reach it, rather than on a cake stand. It will help avoids wobbles too. I begin to unpack the boxes of gingerbread cookies, icing and decorations and spread them across the table in an inviting way, when Devon wanders over.

'I know I haven't been around for your previous Christmas escapades, but I think you've outdone yourself this year. Everything looks awesome, Scar, way beyond awesome actually, like beyond awesome,' he says, putting one arm around my shoulder and dropping a kiss on the top of my head as I step back to admire the table. From the top of my head right down to the tips of my toes I feel a rush of warmth. Such a kind and gentle gesture feels intimate coming from Devon. I automatically rest my head against his chest, a sense of contentment overwhelming me.

'I was feeling extra inspired this year,' I say smiling at him. It's the truth. With Devon around my creative juices are flowing freely again. While baking last night, after finishing my first comic book, all the ideas I had as a kid came flooding back and then some. My hands are itching to get back to the drawing board again. But if I'm not careful, right now, I'm close to falling back to sleep nuzzled up in Devon's parka. Saving me from doing so I feel a tug on my coat, which snaps me back to attention. Looking down I see two green eyes staring up at me.

'Miss Scarlett, can I do a biscuit please?' I recognise the girl to be the daughter of Mrs May from the sweet shop. I know Mrs May will be busy getting her stall ready and I'm pleased ours is just about done. I have a few signs to pop up around the decorating table, but I can do that while Penny is decorating; she shouldn't be a problem.

'Of course, Pen, let me get a spot for you. What would you like to decorate?' I ask, unfolding a chair for her to sit on and retrieving one of the paper plates I brought with me. They're Christmas ones with little snowmen and Christmas trees on them.

'A Christmas tree, please,' she replies her eyes growing wide when she gets closer to the table and sees all the yummy sprinkles. I pop a tree on her plate and encourage her to help herself and to have fun before turning to Devon.

'I'll be busy on here for a little while, but you go and explore. You're under strict instruction to enjoy every morsel of this festive gathering. By time you come back you should be stuffed to the brim and nearly Christmassed out, though save the mulled wine for me and I can maybe join you later if Hope and I can get a short break each,' I say wagging my finger at him, grinning from ear to ear, Christmas joy well and truly weaving its way through my veins now.

'Excuse me.' Devon and I both turn to Penny who is looking at us both through puppy-dog eyes. 'Can superheroes decorate cookies for Santa too?' Without missing a beat Devon's already animated nature becomes extra enthusiastic but with a more soft and gentle approach, when he takes a seat next to her exclaiming, 'They absolutely can.'

'You're a superhero. I saw you on my TV,' I hear Penny say, leaning in a little closer to Devon and speaking in a hushed whisper. I think my heart just melted quicker than an ice lolly on a scorching sunny day.

'He's cute with kids,' Hope says coming up behind me and making me jump. I hastily turn my attention away from Penny and Devon and pat down my coat, freeing it of falling snowflakes as the wind blows a small flurry under our canopy.

'Yeah, well he's a superhero; all kids love superheroes,' I remind her. It's not hard to win over kids when you have a plastic action figure made of you, I find myself thinking, trying to weigh down the butterflies that are attempting to flutter around in my belly at the sight of him decorating cookies with Penny.

'Yeah, that's it,' Hope says, shoving me in my bicep. 'Right, come on, get your signs up and help me with the banner and let's get to work,' she finishes with a smirk.

★

Where once lay an array of naked and plain gingerbread trees, houses and people, there is now a multi-coloured, sparkling, sprinkle-covered table of unique festive master-pieces that I can't stop smiling at. I need to gather them up and clingfilm them now that most of them have set and move them to the back of our booth ready for the kids to pick up on their way home, so I can make room for the afternoon's customers.

I've been overseeing the decorating table and encouraging the children and adults alike to add their famous scribbles or artwork to the communal gingerbread house. It looks positively enchanting with everyone's different ideas. One side looks like a fairy garden with butterflies, wings and tiny flowers creeping up the side and lining the bottom edge. Another side, one of the adults drew Santa climbing up the house to get to the chimney and it looks fantastic. At the front door, one of the older children decided they were going to draw a dog; they wanted the inhabitants to own a dog. It was the cutest thing. And the roof is crammed with so many jelly tots, dolly mixtures and chocolate buttons, I'm not sure Santa would be able to find the chimney. It's glorious. It's up to the afternoon fair-goers to finish off the last side of the house and maybe decorate the small path that I made up on the tray. I can't wait to see what they come up with. Even my dad added his penmanship, drawing a tinsel-covered scaffolding on one side.

I'm moving the last few plates when one of them catches my eye. It's two gingerbread people and their outfits make my eyes blink fast and furiously and immediately an image of mine and Devon's book springs into my mind. One gingerbread is wearing a pink all-in-one spandex-like attire.

Emblazoned on the chest is a bright yellow star surrounded by lots of smaller stars. She has white wrist cuffs that match a pair of white boots; they have extra sparkle added to them with silver balls and edible glitter and a pink glittery headband is in its black hair. The other wears a red all-in-one, a lightning bolt taking centre stage, a little less glitter but a few extra stars around the lightning bolt. I think back to our book and our drawings. I had made Devon have some stars on his costume too when we were little.

'It's me and you.' Devon's whisper tickles my ear as he comes up beside me.

'I know,' I instantly whisper back. 'You remembered our superhero costumes,' I say, taking my eyes off the gingerbread Devon so I can look at the real Devon.

'Of course.' He smiles, hands tapping his pockets, looking a little nervous. 'I think we make for cute gingerbread people,' he adds, making me laugh. I look back to his designs again and my eyes narrow in thought.

'D, your childhood dream costume doesn't look that different to your current real-life movie superhero costume,' I note, mouth open and looking back at him to see his nose crinkle, his eyes crease and all his pearly whites on show.

'I know, right?' he says excitement all over his features.

'Oh, my goodness, aren't they adorable.' Upon hearing the fake shrill voice, I turn my head away from Devon to see Ruby standing next to him, her arm weaving its way through his. Devon's cheeks burn bright red as he gives me a look I can't quite read before giving Ruby a sort of half-smile.

'The children do such a great job with these little craft things and messy kids play. Come on, I'll show you what the adults get up to for fun,' Ruby says, gripping Devon's arm tighter. I want to tell her that Devon loves messy play then realise it was twelve-year-old Devon who loved getting messy and the words don't make it out of my mouth. I take a step back. Devon opens his mouth to speak but I get there first.

'Oh, yes sure. He's all yours, Ruby. You won't be able to move around here in a minute with all the kids enjoying themselves – arrgh, you best get away quick. Who'd want to be around that?' I say, through a fake chuckle, flailing my arms in mock fear. I'm sure I see Devon smirk, but it's only small before Ruby is dragging him away. He goes to speak again but Ruby cuts him off with talk of the documentary. I shrug and wave him off as cheerfully as I can muster before he looks away, getting lost in the packed afternoon crowd.

'Have you asked him about her yet?' Hope asks from behind me, startling me once more.

'Jeez, would you stop doing that?' I say, hand on my chest as I leave the kids decorating and wander over to her table where more than half of *The Village Gazettes* on display have gone – making me feel proud. They have been replaced by family's entries into the gingerbread house competition. This town sure is imaginative. They all look fantastic.

'Why so jittery today?' she asks coyly, munching on sweets from a pick a mix bag then offering the bag to me. I retrieve a fizzy cola bottle and bite it in half.

'I see you're eating sweets – something's up,' I note, grimacing slightly as the sourness tickles my taste buds.

'I see you're avoiding my questions,' she responds, stoically not letting the fizziness affect her or taking her eyes off me.

LUCY KNOTT

I shrug, popping the other half in my mouth, only to repeat the pursed-lip, shiver process.

'Christmas can be a stressful time of year,' she says pointing a milk bottle at me, her eyes assessing me knowingly. With my brain being so consumed with thoughts of Devon and the Christmas fair last night, I had completely forgotten to check in with Hope and see how she was coping after yesterday's email.

'Hey, I'm sorry I didn't check in with you last night. I can't believe you let me have the afternoon off to go skateboarding with Devon when you needed me. Are you feeling OK about the magazine?' I ask, my voice softening.

Hope looks at me and lets out a chuckle. 'Don't be daft, you've gone above and beyond with all your ideas and have kept me sane. Let's enjoy this magical weekend and then Monday, we'll Tony Stark it and put our heads together the minute we step foot in the office, OK?' Hope says with a slight wobble to her voice.

I nod my support and not try not to let her see me gulp. I believe in us – we'll figure it out.

'Besides, Devon is only here for a short time. You deserve to enjoy him and I'm fine – it's just this damn dog,' Hope explains, putting a handful of assorted pick a mix in her mouth.

'You've got a dog?' I say loudly, then hastily look around for Jess. How had he not told me yet?

Hope hunches over and scans the tent too. 'No and that's the problem. I'm actually really considering surprising him for Christmas but look at me. I've not even got the thing yet and it's already stressing me out,' she whispers.

'Aww but you're going to be great doggy parents and you

know Jess is going to love it and squish it and take care of it,' I say, unable to hide the teasing in my tone as I wrap my arms around Hope and snuggle into her.

'You're not funny,' she tells me, pushing me off her. 'But you and Devon would make for great kiddie parents,' she adds, getting me back. I pinch another cola bottle and pull a face. She shakes her head at me. 'If you don't want a dog, you could always adopt Devon, I think Jess would be just as thrilled.' I chuckle.

How I had managed to keep Devon a secret for ten years, I have no idea. I have to admit it feels good being able to have that part of my life out in the open even if it does mean Hope wants to talk more about my feelings. Before Devon, it had been easier to just pass off that I was simply not an emotional person and was happy keeping myself to myself. Hope knew my mother could sometimes get me down, that I had been bullied at school, and I wasn't very lucky with men, but I was happy around her and Jess, so everything was cool. I am who I am and all that, but ever since Devon showed up it's like she keeps testing the keys to see which one fits in the lock. She certainly gets best friend points for recognising that maybe there was more to my often-guarded state, and that more came in the form of a six-foot-four superhero.

'Uh, take these off me,' Hope says, as we both go quiet, eating pick a mix and staring into the distance contemplating parenthood.

'Would you prefer an avocado doughnut?' I tease. 'But really? Healthy doughnuts – I can't believe the thought even crossed your mind when we have Mr and Mrs Rolph if we want doughnuts,' I say, pulling a gummy ring from the bag as I take it off her and glance over at the children who are happily singing Christmas songs and throwing handfuls of sprinkles on their creations, which look marvellous and magical.

'You certainly get points for avoiding questions. Do you not think you should talk to him about how you feel?' Hope says, referring to her initial question that I have done a rather brilliant job of avoiding.

'What? Mr Rolph knows how much I love his doughnuts.' As my words hit the airwaves, I clock how they sound and nearly choke on my candy ring. Hope doubles over, hand on her side, cackling like a hyena and tears are streaming down my crimson face.

'What's so funny?' Jess asks, making his way over to our table with a tray of mulled wine and Devon by his side. I wipe at my eyes as Hope tries to stand up straight but when she looks at me, another cackle and snort let loose between the two of us. We haven't even had a sip of mulled wine yet.

I do a double take of Devon, wondering why he's not with Ruby and then I shoot a look at Jess who gives me an innocent grin. 'He's off the clock today and I don't think the man needs anymore fashion tips,' he says patting Devon on the back.

'Thanks, man,' Devon replies, his hands together, as he nods in gratitude with a shy smile on his face. I am just about to pop a fizzy peach in my mouth, content with the four of us together, when Devon walks over to me, leans down and bites the whole thing out of my fingertips.

18

'OK, here it goes. Is everyone ready with their tickets? The number is: 5264,' Hope announces to the gathered crowd. The adults are sipping on their cocoa or mulled wine; the children are already munching on their decorated gingerbread which Devon, Jess and I have just been giving out; and the sound of Cliff Richard singing can be heard softly in the background. Our stall is all nearly cleared away, but we've taken a brief pause to round up all the raffle entrants to see who the winner of our communal gingerbread house is. Everyone is smiling and looking around as we wait for the winner to wave their ticket in celebration.

'Wave it, sweetheart. Tell Hope it's you.' I turn to my left and see Emily, with her little boy of two years old in her arms, encouraging him to hold aloft their ticket. Emily is a single mum and our town's seamstress. All those gorgeous handmade pieces I have been telling you about are her creations; she is simply magic with a needle and thread. Her beautiful little boy Barney, with his shocking white hair and blue eyes, is as cute as can be. They couldn't be more deserving of this treat. I clap my hands feeling elated when Barney shyly waves the ticket and Hope spots them. It's

234

clear to see Hope is pleased with this outcome too as she makes her way over to Barney and gives him a high five and Emily a giant hug.

Today has been a huge success. We had so many entrants into the competition and I think pretty much everyone in town stopped by the stall to decorate a cookie. The winning gingerbread house had been announced earlier along with the winner of Emily's craft competition and Mrs May's "guess how many sweets in the bottle" game. Our winning house was a family of four who had just moved to village and were eager to join in with the festivities. They had created a gorgeous replica of the village square with fluffy grass frosting and a beautiful tree and you could see the kids had been allowed to do most of it. It was a sure-fire winner and a lovely way of welcoming the family to Springhollow.

As the crowd begin to disperse, I congratulate Emily and Barney with hugs and high fives of my own while Devon introduces himself making Barney come out of his shell as he tugs Devon's leg – Devon immediately squats down to the little boy's level as Barney whispers, 'Are you Superman?'

'What makes you say that?' Devon asks in playful whisper and a beaming grin.

'You look like a superhero. You're big,' Barney replies poking Devon in his broad chest. Devon chuckles as Barney then pokes at his bicep through his parka. 'You got muscles.'

Emily and I both giggle watching the scene out of the corner of our eyes while I help Emily tuck the gingerbread house into the bottom of their buggy.

'Well, thank you. It looks like you've got muscles too. Are you a superhero?' Devon asks gently squeezing Barney's little arm. 'Whoa, you're very strong,' he adds, making Barney laugh.

'When I'm big like you,' Barney responds, making my chest swell with pride. He's a little boy after my own heart and is just like Devon and I were at his age. And Devon went out and achieved his dream. I couldn't be prouder of him either.

'I think you will be the best superhero,' Devon notes causing Barney to fling his arms around his neck and squeeze him tight. Barney's heart-warming actions create a little domino effect and when we say bye to him and Emily, a small crowd of children form, all wanting autographs from Devon. Hope and Jess nip over having folded up the last of our signs and having cleared up my baking bits and pieces. Hope gives me a heads-up that she's going to get a head start dropping our stuff off at my house on their way home and I tell her we will catch up with them shortly.

Ten or so families later and Devon and I each have a takeaway mulled wine for the short walk home. Snowflakes are teasing the navy blue sky, drifting along the evening breeze as we crunch the heavier snow from earlier underneath our feet.

'Am I not going to get to see you in all your spandex glory?' I blurt out, feeling deliriously joyful. With all the superhero talk it occurred to me that I haven't yet got to witness Devon in his costume besides the posters and the trailer I have watched a hundred times.

Devon splutters on his wine and gives me a side glance.

'I mean, aren't you wearing it right now under all those clothes? Isn't that what superheroes are supposed to do?' I say, grinning so hard my eyes crinkle as I skip along.

'Ooh the secret nerd is now telling me what superheroes are supposed to do,' Devon teases, wiggling his eyebrows at me. I stick my tongue out and shove him in the ribs.

'We always said we'd never take our costumes off, so, I have to say I'm rather disappointed. I guess Superman will just have to remain at the top of my list as my favourite superhero of all time then,' I tease back.

'Oh yeah,' Devon says with a smirk, throwing his mulled-wine-free hand over my shoulder and bending down to whisper in my ear. 'Does that mean we need to get you in spandex, or will Spider-Man forever remain at the top of my list?' His warm breath tickles my ear sending a shiver down my spine. I just want to wrap my arms around him and keep him close but instead I let out a laugh, hip-check him and race to my front door as I spot Hope and Jess coming up my path.

'Great timing,' Hope says. 'I'm shattered. We're going to call it a night and head off. Let us know what you guys are doing tomorrow,' she says, wrapping me in a quick hug. Jess gives me a fist bump and repeats the action with Devon before scurrying out the gate. Something inside me stirs when Hope ever so casually says "let us know what you guys are doing tomorrow". I like the way it sounds, like Devon being here is a more permanent and normal thing.

'Was that a yes or no on the spandex?' Devon says as he steps up next to me on the front step as I unlock the door Hope had just locked. I turn to look up at him and give him a dramatic eye-roll in response. But when I meet his mischievous gaze, the child within me starts jumping with glee.

'I have an idea.' Pushing open my front door, I quickly

step out of my black boots and unravel my scarf. My house feels nice and toasty as I make to dash for the stairs. Devon follows suit. 'Arrgh wait.' I pause thudding into Devon as I turn round and make my way back down the stairs. Devon isn't fazed by my smacking into him; he's filled out a lot more since we were sixteen, but I ignore that and pop our empty mulled wine cups in the recycle bin. 'We will need snacks.'

'OK,' Devon replies, simply watching my movements and holding out his arms as I begin to pile chocolate chip cookies, leftover gingerbread men, bags of popcorn and a box of mince pies in them. Then I collect a bottle of red wine and two glasses and march back up the stairs.

'Are you moving?' Devon asks when I push open the door to the right of my landing. I place the wine and glasses on one of the boxes and duck through the narrow gap towards my desk. Devon follows and frees his arms of the treats, placing them on the chair, looking around in awe. Switching on my twinkling lights, I survey the floor space and look over the mix of empty and full boxes.

'No, no, it just keeps people from snooping around and seeing my drawings and stuff,' I say, waving off my confession like it's been no big deal harbouring that secret for ten years.

'You made yourself a secret lair? Cool,' Devon notes. He wanders over to my desk, looking over all the drawings I have pinned to the wall and the piles of drawings and papers sprawled out on my desk. I can tell he doesn't want to burst my current glee-filled bubble and start questioning my need to keep my artwork a secret for all these years again and for that I'm grateful. I'd like to move past that now. He's here and Hope and Jess know all about him now and I feel a sense of relief. Plus, I'm too excited for my plan to be distracted by heavy conversation.

'Ha-ha, I guess I did.' I smile as it dawns on me that yes, I guess this has been my superhero lair all these years; a secret den unknown to the world around me. 'And speaking of lair…' I start throwing blankets at Devon and moving boxes '…I think it's missing something.'

'A fort?' Devon catches on making me smile. For the next ten minutes we busy ourselves stacking boxes and throwing blankets and throws over the top until we have a cave-like situation. I only pause to put on some Christmas music and pop open the wine. We have to adjust the height of the boxes a few times to accommodate Devon, and finally I nip out to change into my pyjamas and collect my duvet off my bed, so the floor is cosier and squishier, completing our fort and making me a thousand times more comfortable and fort ready.

I sit at the entranceway allowing Devon to hand me the pile of treats, followed by the wine, then I hear him shuffling around, opening a drawer or two before his face appears and he crawls in holding our childhood book.

'How did you know I'd still have that thing?' I ask, taking a sip of wine as he makes himself comfortable. I'm surprisingly not fussed that he found it. It makes sense to look at it in our fort. Maybe we could add a few things, I find myself thinking. Like what, I'm not quite sure. Devon has achieved the ultimate goal of becoming a superhero and I imagine he has a nice big house in New York. I'm unaware of the tree situation in Long Island so I can't say if a tree house would be on the cards in future for Devon, and I'm just here in Springhollow being an assistant, not exactly saving the world, but I suppose a tree house could be possible for me. The park has enough trees, though I don't have a superhero outfit like Devon has.

I let Devon flick through our book and reminisce as I lie back on the blankets enjoying the peacefulness of our fort that's lost to the world, while I mull over such thoughts in my head. A few moments pass when I register that Devon is lying beside me, our book held in the air above his face as he continues to read and look at the pictures.

'Does it bother you anymore how Ruby used to treat us at school?' I muse, the question casually finding its way out into the open as my thoughts move in and out of childhood while I study the colours of the Christmas throw we're using as the roof of our fort. I can feel Devon's elbow against mine and hear the swish of him turning the page of our childhood book. Maybe it's the mulled wine, maybe it's the magical time of the year, but I feel the last remaining foundation of my wall shatter as I allow myself to enjoy the feeling of this amazing day – well, amazing besides the Ruby bits and my sudden remembrance of the way she gripped on to Devon earlier today.

I do suppose Hope was right at the cookie competition, more than anyone I do feel I can talk to D about everything and anything and I guess now is as good a time as any to talk about our love lives, we are grown-ups now after all.

'I don't know, I tend not to think about the negatives anymore. Sometimes that's easier said than done being in the public eye now. I have to work a little harder, but I much prefer to see the positives.' I can feel his shoulder move up and down as he shrugs against me. His feet are most certainly sticking out of our fort with his head almost level with mine and I wonder if that's what he had been upset about at the skatepark, that he had found himself worrying too much about what other people thought in his new world of fame.

'But you obviously like the person she's become. I saw you laughing with her, how she's always clinging to you. I have to be honest with you though, D, she's not changed the way she treats me, but if she makes you happy and she somehow shows a different side to you then I'll just have to learn to accept it.' I smile at the cotton snowmen, wanting with all my heart to believe and act on what I just said, even though it feels like The Hulk has just inhabited my stomach and is thrashing around.

Devon shifts on to his elbow, placing our book on my stomach. I stay on my back tilting my head up so I can meet his gaze. Were his eyes always this vibrant, a deep brown with flecks of hazel in the low light?

'What do you mean if she makes me happy?' he asks, creases forming on his forehead, confusion etched on his face. I scrunch up my nose. Is he going to make me say it out loud?

'You know if you and her are lovers. Hope tells me that's what the magazines are saying, and you never seem to mind when she's all pressed up against you. I mean she is gorgeous, like on the outside. She looks like a woman,' I stammer, averting my gaze to the Christmas throw once more. It really is a pretty throw; handmade by Emily. She really does make the most beautiful things. A giggle escapes my lips as my brain registers the word "lover" lingering between Devon and me. I know I'm definitely high on Christmas right now, but also the pure joy I feel when Devon's eyes crinkle with amusement too. His cheeks flush and he gives me the toothiest, cheesiest smile.

'Lovers?' he questions, an eyebrow raising like he's that man in the action movie Hope and Jess had me watch. What's his name? The Rock. Then a smirk replaces the awkwardness and if I wasn't lying down, I think I would have been bowled over by how sexy Devon looks right now. How dare my nerdy ex best friend look so sexy propped up on his elbow with a slight red flush in his cheeks, those brown eyes huge and sparkling. What's he playing at? He pokes me above my heart with his finger, which causes a firework to explode there, in all its green and red festive glory.

'You think I want to be with Ruby? And did you actually just use the word "lovers"?' He pokes me again, which sends a firework shooting towards my stomach. I try and ignore the embers heating my body and making my own cheeks a Christmassy shade of red.

'Well, yeah, I guess, I don't know. Are you not? I mean you came to see her two years ago – I thought you two might have kept in touch. And she's glamorous and perfect for your red-carpet life,' I say, only a little bit confused but determined to state out the facts and saying them out loud, getting them out in the open makes me feel more like I can come to terms with it if it's actually true.

D bends his knee, now resting it over my shin. He shuffles to get comfy on our mound of blankets on the floor. He doesn't seem bothered by our limbs touching and neither am I, though my body is deftly aware, distracting me ever so slightly from my attempt at a serious grown-up conversation.

'Scar, you do know Ruby is a stylist – that's why she's been on set and hanging around,' he says with a half-smirk and a small chuckle like he can't believe what I just thought, but then his entertained features soften to a more serious tone, his eyes become slightly hooded as he absent-mindedly plays with the hem of my baggy tee and he lets out a heavy, "here goes nothing" kind of sigh.

'I didn't come here to see Ruby two years ago. I was nearby for a shoot and I wanted to see you. All these years I've wanted to see you. I've thought about you every day, but then I saw you. At the summer fair, I caught a glimpse of you. You were laughing with Jess and well, obviously I didn't know who Jess was back then and I assumed he was your boyfriend.' The blush creeps back on to his cheeks. His hand is now fiddling with the bow of my shorts. I seem to have forgotten how to breathe.

'I saw you happy and I didn't want to ruin that happiness. The last time I had seen you I had put a hurt behind your eyes I couldn't bear. He made you laugh, and, in that moment, I knew everything had changed for good and we could never go back.' I take my eyes off his dimpled cheeks to look him in the eye. He's already looking at me intently and I suddenly feel like I've caught the kerb with the edge of my skateboard causing me to hurl towards the ground.

'What do you mean, D? You don't think we can be friends anymore?' Our eyes are locked on each other's and I find my hand tracing over his fingers that are messing with my bow. Devon clears his throat.

'Not quite, Scar. You were wearing the sweetest denim pinafore with a yellow tee and your yellow pumps. Your hair was a little longer than it is now, maybe touching your shoulders, and I could see your blue eyes glistening in the sun. I couldn't take my eyes off you, all grown-up. I realised then that I still loved you and that love had somehow grown, in all our years apart and through all the growing up, into something so much stronger. I wanted to be the one to look after you, like when we were kids, but so much more than that. It felt wrong seeing you with someone else. But I couldn't fool myself. We'd spent so much time apart and seeing you with him – so radiant, so beautiful, so happy – I panicked. I worried I would only mess up again, that too much time had passed, and my feelings were just confused. Then you crashed into me at the press junket last week.'

His brown eyes are glistening now under the moonlight that's sneaking in through the cracks in our fort and with the tears that are forming puddles on his lash line. But no more words leave his lips.

I'm trying to process all that he has said. He'd used the word "love" but I knew that. I knew I loved Devon when we were kids, just like I knew I loved my mum and dad and little Steve Rogers. But what did he mean stronger? Did it feel stronger, different somehow now? I want to reach out and stroke his cheek to assure him it's OK and there's no need for tears, but nervous laughter bubbles up inside me as I go over everything he said. 'Wait, you thought I was with Jess?' Giggles erupt and I swat D in the chest, making his shoulders relax as he joins in with my laughter. I may have ruined the moment a little but if we're clearing the air, I feel nothing is off limits or an invalid point to make, and I need a second to make sense of my thoughts.

'Well I didn't know who Jess and Hope were then did I? I just saw you with a guy.' He shoves me back playfully before lying back down so he's staring at the snowmen on the roof of our fort once more. This allows me some space to breathe.

'Just to clarify, Jess and I have never been together. It's been him and Hope since day one.' I lift our book from my stomach and place it to the side of me carefully then swivel my hips so it's my turn to prop myself up on my elbow. I watch as Devon closes his eyes and breathes in deeply and then I take a brave breath myself.

'I never apologised for shouting at you and letting you leave the way you did. I wanted to run after you, but I felt defeated. I couldn't stop you going. I messed up, D. I should have replied to your messages, but I thought it was better to just forget about you. I wanted more, I didn't want to be pen pals; I wanted you with me. I just sort of retreated in on myself and was angry with everyone. If it wasn't for Hope and Jess, I don't know what I would have done at college. I dated guys but I never felt like I could be me. I didn't know how to act, so my relationships never worked out.

'All this time I haven't been able to get you out of my head. But I was so confused. I wanted you back, I wanted you here, but I was still mad at you. I wasn't myself around other men. I guess I was thinking about them leaving before they'd even left.' I pause, scared to say more and so I lie back down to gather my thoughts.

Back then, when I was dating, my thoughts would often drift to Devon. I thought relationships were supposed to be easy, comfortable and bring a sense of familiarity. I missed being able to be completely myself around a guy and at ease in their company. Then the guys would leave, and it would hit me again – that's what they all did, that's what Devon had done too and I would feel hopeless.

But then when I bumped into him a week ago, it felt like something more was bothering me. Had I been angry because of something other than his simply leaving? When dating, did my brain turn to Devon because it was Devon I wanted to be dating? This whole week my feelings have been all over the place. Having him next to me just feels right. He fits. Is this what he means by our love being stronger? More than friendship?

My heart rate begins to pick up as I feel Devon's fingers interlock with mine down by my hip. His thumb brushes over my hand. Does he understand it too? That electricity is back. A powerful surge of passion takes over my entire body and mind. I sit up ready to make the boldest move I have ever made: I want to kiss Devon, I really want to kiss him. I turn, move forward and bend down towards his face when Devon mirrors my actions causing us to meet halfway with a cracking headbutt.

I blink as my eyes fill with tears, my forehead pounding. I let out a yelp, which again Devon matches, though his is more of a deep grunt.

Trying to balance with one hand on my forehead and the other on Devon's chest, I shuffle my weight so I'm sitting cross-legged and when I open my eyes D's are but an inch away. I send a prayer to Odin himself that Devon had been thinking the same thing as me, as with the throbbing in my forehead I don't think I will be quick enough in making up an excuse to get me out of this one.

'Were you about to kiss me?' we ask in unison, our voices turning to a whisper at the end. Heat radiates off both our cheeks. Devon's hand is now gently soothing my forehead. A dimple forms in his right cheek, his eyes crinkle with a smile that lights up his whole face and then his lips find mine. My hands find his face and hair as I melt into the softness of him. His movements are gentle. One hand moving to the back of my head, the other on my waist pulling me closer to him in a way that's both passionate and sweet.

Our kisses are a slow and steady rush as we tumble down into the blankets. Devon's hand moves to the top of my shorts as our hips connect. 'I prefer the tiny pants.' He breathes, rubbing his nose against mine. His eyes look at me so attentively as he runs a finger over the drawstring of the shorts I remembered to put on this time. A laugh escapes my tingling lips as I trace my palm over his five o'clock shadow. Stronger? I do believe our love may be surpassing the strength of Hercules right about now.

19

Arush of heat sweeps over my body. My eyelashes flicker until I manage to force them to stay open – my twinkly lights catch me off guard with their brightness in the dark room. I don't have a clock in my spare room so I have no idea of the time. All I know is that my stomach is rumbling after the evening's events. I don't fancy any of the snacks Devon and I brought up to the fort, so as quietly as I can I wriggle free of Devon's sleeping limps that are wrapped around me, securing my warmth. I push myself up off the floor and sneak to the landing, grabbing my shorts on the way out.

The heating hasn't come on yet, so the house is chilly. I rub my hands together and do a little shiver as I make my way to the kitchen. The clock on the cooker reads four-forty-five, which surprises me as I don't usually see this side of six a.m. if I can help it, but this morning I feel oddly sprightly. I rub my hands over my arms to warm myself up as I set about boiling the kettle and pulling out ingredients from the fridge and cupboard. I know what I'd like for breakfast and the thought simultaneously makes my stomach growl and my lips curve up into a small smile. Pancakes: my dad used to make Devon and I pancakes whenever we had sleepovers.

They'd fill us up and give us plenty of energy to battle any bad guys throughout the day, my dad would tell us.

While I let the batter rest for ten minutes or so, I retrieve some blueberries and raspberries from the fridge along with whipped cream, then some leftover chocolate slivers and a jar of Nutella from the cupboard and place them on the dining table before I grab my coffee mug and wander through to the living room. I flick on the switch and my Christmas tree illuminates. A gasp escapes my lips. Every. Time. Eddie isn't awake yet so I leave him to rest and perch myself on my favourite spot – the cushion on the window ledge, so my view is either the tree or my street, and well, both when I catch the reflection of the tree in the glass. Outside, snow lays thick on the ground and there are more flakes falling. I smile into my coffee feeling the peacefulness of the season when I hear shuffling.

The tree demands all the light leaving the rest of the room in a shadowy darkness, but my Spidey sense is tingly. I can feel Devon's presence. Sure enough his large figure appears from around the tree. He doesn't talk, just stands behind me wrapping his arms around me, taking in the scenery out the window. The holly wreaths and colourful bauble wreaths on the rows of houses make the street look idyllic enough for a Christmas card – maybe that could be next year's Christmas fair idea? A few moments pass before Devon drops a kiss on the top of my head, making my toes curl under. I turn to him and wrap my legs around his waist, which receives a low groan and a flustered smile. I know he's blushing, but contradictory to his rosy cheeks I can just make out his features under the gold glow of the tree and there's a confidence in his eyes that is ridiculously sexy.

'Breakfast?' I croak out, unable to take my eyes off him, even though I'm sure it's going to leave a crick in my neck.

Devon takes the coffee mug from me and places it on the window ledge then slides his hands under my bum, scooping me up with ease. My legs are still wrapped around him like a koala. 'Yes, please,' he says, before kissing me. His kiss is tender yet passionate, a mixture of a slow but hungry pace. It sends goose bumps over my entire body. One of my hands rests against his chest; the other I have on the back of his neck. He's gorgeous and strong and home.

The sunrise has slowly started to add a little more light to the room, making the Christmas lights more a soft twinkle than a harsh yellow glow. Devon's eyes are fixated on mine. I see a hint of naughtiness behind them and know he was thinking of a totally different kind of breakfast – just as I had been.

'I thought you said you didn't have telepathic powers,' I joke, raising an eyebrow and brushing my lips over his. I like that I can do that, and I love how his body reacts towards mine. I'm not ready to move away from him just yet and will happily choose from the menu he is thinking of.

'I can't go around giving away all my secret superhero powers now, can I?' he notes through a mock modest smirk.

'So, these powers...' I start as Devon moves his hands to my hips and throws me over his shoulder. I shriek and try to get away but when my wriggling has no effect, I relax and let my head dangle admiring my view; it truly is the perfect view, hmm buns of steel.

'What did you say?' Devon asks, walking past the kitchen and up the stairs.

'Huh? What? Oh nothing,' I say, not realising I'd said that out loud and not sounding even the slightest bit innocent.

'You're not too bad yourself,' Devon adds tapping me on the bum; I don't hate it and I let out a giggle as he pushes open my bedroom door.

We eventually make it down for pancakes and I am very much enjoying the scene in my kitchen of Devon in his boxers helping prepare breakfast. We casually potter around the kitchen chatting about New York and Springhollow, what's changed over the years, what Devon misses, but how he loves acting. I find myself talking freely about comic books when the subject turns to Devon's new film.

'So, what was it like getting to wear the suit every day?' I ask, having held in certain questions before, simply out of fear of discussing our nerdy past and getting too attached, but this morning it rolls off my tongue with ease and excitement. 'I bet you didn't want to take it off.' I smile flipping a pancake.

He leans against the counter sipping on his coffee. I can see the huge smile forming from behind his mug.

'OK, besides all the wires and the awkwardness of going to the toilet; Scar, it was incredible. I felt invincible in that thing. It was so thick and detailed and comfy. I felt like if I fell, I would just bounce right back up again. It really felt like it was meant to be, all the curves and contours fitting to my body. I mean I know it was custom made for me but still – come on, it was awesome. Made to fit me,' he adds at the end with a wistful disbelief that makes my heart patter.

I slide the pancake onto a plate all while studying his

face. 'I'm so proud of you, D. I should have said it sooner, but I'm so bloody proud of you. You did it, you really did it and you make the absolute perfect superhero,' I say, trying not to let my emotions get the best of me but nearly choking on the joy that envelops my chest and restricts the words coming out of my throat.

Devon takes the plate from me, that spark, that unignorable static that fizzes whenever we are close catches my fingertips and we just stand there and smile at each other for a moment. 'You're really lovely, you know,' I say, feeling that familiar warmth and safety wash over me.

Devon grins that shy grin of his, where his eyes narrow and nose crinkles making the smile on my own face widen. My stomach rumbling interrupts the romantic moment and Devon gives me a gentle nudge towards the table.

'How are your parents doing?' I ask, pouring syrup over my stack of buttery, fluffy pancakes and trying to take my mind off the curves and contours of D's body.

'Same old.' Devon places his forearms on the edge of the table, knife and fork aloft in thought. 'I missed your dad a lot when we first got to New York – I still do. You know what my parents are like. I think they will forever be disappointed that I'm working on Broadway and not Wall Street. But I guess, like your mum, I know they mean well. They always said they would support me, and they did,' he finishes, placing his knife and fork down and grabbing the can of whipped cream. I watch as he throws his head back and squirts it into his mouth. When he catches my eye, he smirks and passes me the can.

I chuckle and swallow my last bite of pancake, taking the cold can as I give Devon a sympathetic shrug to acknowledge my understanding of his parents. I love my mother but for once I'd love for her to love all of me – failures, flaws and all.

'To never growing up,' Devon says nudging the can in my hand; always the sidekick encouraging me to misbehave and feed the child within me.

The squirty sound of the whipped cream can hisses as Devon pushes the nozzle. The scrumptious treat tickles my tongue as I quickly push back in my chair to stop Devon squirting any more into my mouth. He's got his hand wrapped around mine, doing the deed for me. He's now laughing while I'm trying not to dribble whipped cream all over the place.

'Oi!' I splutter, hands reaching for a napkin, while Devon casually goes to spray more cream into his own mouth. I quickly dab at my chin and then knock the can, causing him to miss his mouth and squirt it all over his cheek, in turn leading it to drip down his chest.

'Touché.' He laughs, quirking his eyebrow. A blush spreads over his cheeks as he looks down at the mess. I grab the napkins, pretending I need them all to wipe my face, which makes him laugh and shake his head further. I get back to eating my pancakes like nothing has happened leaving him to clean up after himself, but Devon isn't fazed. He simply stands up to the side of me where he pauses, giving me a face full of his lower torso. Satisfied when I cough through a bite of syrup-covered pancake, he walks over to the sink, nonchalantly asking, 'Everything OK over there?'

'Mmm yep. All good,' I reply with no way of hiding the lust in my voice. I don't turn around, instead I just focus on my food. The next second D's hands are on my shoulders and I can feel his breath on my neck.

'I'm glad to hear it,' he whispers in my ear. A grin spreads across my face but I don't look at him, I simply enjoy the giddiness that he evokes. The next second I am pushing myself up on my chair, so I reach Devon's height and I spin around to face him.

'I have an idea,' I exclaim. 'Popcorn and all the comic book movies I have missed, please.'

'Have I ever told you how much I love your ideas,' Devon replies, nodding his head at me. He then turns around allowing me to jump on his back as he walks towards the cupboards so we can retrieve our snack.

The tree lights sparkle, the fire is burning, *The Avengers* is on the TV and Devon is by my side; it's utter bliss and takes me back to our childhood Saturday mornings watching cartoons. The kissing and the pausing to get a little naughty under the mistletoe is a rather new and delicious grown-up version of fun that I can't get enough of. It doesn't feel strange or odd to be kissing my best friend. It all feels incredibly natural.

Looking at Devon now sitting by the coffee table on a mound of blankets we brought down from upstairs, his hair is a touch wavy and decidedly messy having had my hands in it most of the morning; his cheeks are full and rosy, a permanent smile procuring that effect; and his body that should be positively out of place in my small living quarters is every bit perfect. His biceps have grown tenfold and are solid as a rock; his stomach displays the subtle hint of abs but is toned and strong, and forget about those legs that lead to his peachy butt. He's like one of my action heroes come to life and well, he is now an actual action hero and is very much alive in front of me. As these thoughts are swimming through my head, I don't notice Devon move until he's nuzzling my neck, causing those scrumptious tingles to ignite my whole body.

There's an element of awkwardness to our movements with the occasional knock of the knees or fumbling hand or finger caught in a knot in my hair, which relaxes me. I feel I can be myself and so can he and there's no pressure for perfection. Devon has this shy yet confident approach, drinking me in and taking his time and it sets my pulse racing.

'Scar, you are awesome, do you know that?' he says, feet playing footsy with mine at the end of the blanket, his finger drawing pictures on my stomach with the lightest touch, his head resting on his forearm to the side of me.

'Thanks, so are you,' I say dreamily. He kisses my cheek before announcing that we need more popcorn. He gets up, grabbing the bowl, when there's a knock at the door.

'You get the popcorn; I'll get the door,' I say following him.

Unlatching the lock, I swing open the door, completely forgetting my state of dress, and am greeted by a freezing cold wind and Hope and Jess.

'Hey,' I say in a sprightly tone, ushering them in and out of the cold, while I jump from toe to toe, my feet turning to icicles on the wooden floor.

'Good afternoon,' Hope says cheerily taking a step forward and looking over my baggy tee and shorts combo.

'It's already afternoon?' I question. I had totally lost track of time, too busy focusing on the awesomeness that was *Avengers Assemble*.

'Yes, I've been trying to call you to see if you were going to head to the inn to say bye to Devon...' Her words trail off when she steps into the hallway as Devon walks out of the kitchen still in just his boxers, holding the bowl of popcorn.

Hope's jaw hits the floor and her eyes grow large underneath her even larger glasses.

'Oh God, we didn't mean to interrupt you... you guys... you both... erm whatever you were up to... together,' Hope stutters before peeling her eyes off Devon and looking at me. She gives me a coy nod, raising her eyebrows so they vanish into her hairline before her eyes find Devon again.

A moment passes and nobody moves or says a word until the door shuts behind Jess making me jump. Jess wipes his feet and steps forward past Hope.

'Bye then, mate. It was good to meet you. We're just going to get out of your way, and don't be a stranger, hey.' He pats Devon on the shoulder. Devon smiles and nods as Jess turns around, placing both his hands on Hope's shoulders to guide her back out the door. This seems to remind Hope where she is and what she's doing.

'Oh, merry Christmas.' She nods at Devon, her eyes lingering a little too long. Devon moves the popcorn bowl a little lower in modesty, causing my hand to shoot to my mouth to stifle a giggle.

'Popcorn. Devon was just getting popcorn,' I manage causally as Hope passes me and heads out the door, positively beaming like her Christmas has just come early.

'See you guys later,' I call after them, shaking my head in disbelief.

'Thanks for stopping by,' Devon shouts.

'I wanted to give him a hug,' I hear Hope say to Jess as they walk down the snowy path.

'Probably a bit of an inappropriate time,' Jess replies as he closes my garden gate behind them. I close the door and double over in a fit of giggles. I think I might have gone mad. I know Hope, I know what this scene looks like and I know what she is thinking and she is absolutely one hundred per cent right; it is exactly what it looks like and she would be right to think what she is no doubt thinking. I have no excuse and I'm not sure what to make of that yet.

A handful of popcorn hits me in the face and falls to the floor, the odd one getting caught in my hair. I wipe at my eyes and see Devon looking at me smirking and nibbling on popcorn yet still glued to the spot. I run at him and he dodges me running into the living room and over to the fire. Its heat is inviting after being stood in the chilly doorway. I abandon my attempt at getting Devon back with the popcorn, choosing to wrap myself up in the blankets and snuggle closer to the flames instead. Placing the bowl down beside me Devon slides into the duvet behind me, wrapping his arms and legs around me and resting his chin on my head. My body warms up within seconds.

'What happens now?' I ask, the flames hypnotic, calming my laughter as my brain registers why Hope and Jess had popped around; to say bye to Devon because Devon isn't staying. He is leaving today.

'We always wear pyjamas and check before answering the door,' Devon suggests, squeezing me tighter. I snort despite the blizzard of emotions whirring around in my stomach. All at once they have hit me hard and I don't want to speak for fear of getting angry with Devon for having to go or for bursting into tears, which is so not like me. Laughter is a safer bet and it's not exactly difficult to laugh or feel happy either when Devon's arms are wrapped around me and I can smell the mix of pancake batter lingering on his skin and his fresh, aftershave.

It's not until the final log burns to ashes in the fireplace that I realise Devon should probably make a move. The clock on the mantel is telling us it's three minutes past three and I know Devon has a nine p.m. flight. I imagine he's got to pack and I'm sure his publicists and assistants are keen to arrive on time to the airport and get back home before Christmas. I turn into Devon as a thought crosses my mind.

'What do your publicist and management team think you're doing today?' I enquire as the credits roll.

'I asked if I could be left alone to spend time with my family before we left, and they obliged,' he informs me, tucking my long bob behind my ear.

'You can just do that, like they let you have your privacy? I thought you'd have paparazzi running around all the time?' I question further, intrigued by how this all works. I haven't thought to ask until now as the whole celebrity culture isn't really my thing, but I've heard Hope talk about how tricky it is for celebs to lead normal lives with photographers constantly hounding them. But this week with Devon has been relatively calm besides all the action and filming at the inn.

'It's a little different in New York.' He shrugs casually. 'There are a few more posters, billboards and newspaper stands everywhere. Here everyone knows me, and they've allowed me to get on like I'm still just the little boy running around with my best friend. I like that. And there are certain rules and regulations paparazzi must adhere to these days. Plus, this documentary is relatively low key. They haven't announced it yet, so my publicist hasn't been too disgruntled by my disappearing acts and choosing what to keep private. I'm allowed to have a say,' he finishes, fingers still in my hair.

'Hmm, that's good,' I say, interested by the way in which he lives now. I can't imagine seeing posters of my face on walls or billboards, causing people to stop and stare at me; then again I've occasionally thought about how cool it would be to have my own booth at a comic convention where people would know me and come and buy my comics; but a giant billboard, that's a touch intimidating. I reach for the remote and switch off the TV. 'Do you have to date people in your world? Hope's told me stories about fake relationships for publicity. Do you get a say in who you date?' I ask, absent-mindedly stroking my fingers over his forearm.

'Yeah, I guess fake relationships have been known to happen. Publicists will try and have a say in everything and can get carried away if you let them. They're just doing what's best for business and if they think dating a certain celeb will put you on the map and get your movie more attention, then they can be pretty ruthless; but you don't have to worry about that. I'd never do that. Those Ruby rumours are not my publicist, just journalists trying to stir things up,' he tells me, making a lump form in my throat.

'That's crazy but that's good to know.' I nod, though

it won't put a stop to magazines gossiping and spreading rumours about his love life, knowing where Devon stands on pretending to be in a relationship with another woman does make me feel more at ease.

'Right, you best get moving,' I say, making to stand up. Devon looks at me with his lips parted like he has more to say or something he wants to ask. I know this because he's my very best friend and yes, I think I've claimed him back as that after this week.

However, he's not talking and he's not asking questions, which is very unlike him. 'Come on, you can't be late.' I try and muster all the chirpiness I can when thinking about going on with my daily routine without the excitement of seeing him at the end of the day or him being a part of any of it.

Devon shuffles in the blanket and drops a kiss on my nose as he stands up. 'Yes, I'd better. OK,' he replies looking a little flustered. 'Scar? Erm...' He shakes his head like he's thinking over what he wants to say. I've never seen him look so nervous.

'D, it's OK. Go and get ready,' I say gently, trying to soothe the anxiety I can feel radiating off him.

I set about tidying up the living room, folding the blankets and putting them on the couch, collecting our snacks from the floor and popping them on the coffee table.

'Scar, there's this really amazing art school in New York and I think it would be perfect for you,' he informs me. 'I know you love it here; I'm not asking you to move to New York – it would just be for a couple of months. This place, you would do awesome. It would be so good for you,' he adds, an excitement but nervousness in his tone.

I can't help the guffaw that comes out of me in disbelief as I sprinkle a few more fishy flakes in Ed's tank. 'Devon, I can't leave Hope for a couple of months. I have a job and my dad would miss me.'

'I know. Look, I know you work hard but I thought you could still work for Hope but you could start focusing on your drawing again, pushing a little bit to make your dreams come true and your dad would miss you but he's always wanted that for you,' Devon goes on.

'Devon, stop. I have plenty of things to focus on at work, especially with the magazine being in limbo right now. I haven't even thought about it all weekend. I can't give myself more distractions and I certainly can't just drop everything and leave Hope with all the work. It's fine,' I say, my voice coming out firmer as I feel a drop of anger bubbling in my stomach.

'But, Scar, it's not fine. You can't just go back to how it was before.' Devon is leaning towards me, hunched over with his arms out and bent at the elbows as he speaks, trying to catch my eye as I faff about with cushions. The drop of anger becomes a full on splash.

'Before what, Devon? I loved my life. I loved the people in my life. You have no right to come here and tell me what's fine and what isn't,' I say, my voice turning hard as I throw the cushions back onto their spots on the couch.

'But it wasn't fine, Scarlett. You're telling me your definition of fine was hiding who you were, working a job you're not truly passionate about, shoving your dreams in a dark hole and worrying about what everyone else thinks? That's fine?' he adds, causing the air to leave my lungs.

I feel attacked. Tears prickle my eyes. I turn my body

towards the blurry Christmas lights and blink a few times to encourage the water in my eyes to disappear. I don't want Devon to see me cry. I was stupid to let him in.

'Who you're calling "everyone" are people that care about me. They make me happy too. They are loyal and kind and they're here for me. You might have been able to turn your back and drop everything, but I can't. I can't leave Springhollow and I won't. That's not who I am,' I say, my voice breaking, my bottom lip trembling.

'That's not fair, Scar; I didn't drop everything. I tried to be a part of your life. You pushed me away. I'm not telling you to leave, I just don't want you to forget who you are and what you're capable of. You don't have to bury that part of you – you can have it all.' Tears well up in Devon's dark brown eyes. He steps forward to console me, but I step back, bumping into the plain silver baubles on the tree that jingle when I hit them.

'Scarlett, stop being so ridiculous, you're going to school. Could you please take that cap off? That boy was not the only person in the world – you have lots of other friends,' my mum scolds from the bottom of the stairs as she looks me up and down. I don't remove my cap. I walk down the stairs at a snail's pace and head to school and with every step I take I feel as if I'm going to be sick.

I sit quietly at the back of class trying not to look over at where Devon usually sits, distracting myself by trying to draw with my left hand. Mr Cassidy is talking about equations, but I barely hear a word, until he clears his throat in front of me. 'Miss Davis, I think you'll find that you will have more success in life if you stop with your silly doodling and actually pay attention to the lesson.'

The whole class sniggers.

The lunch bell twists my stomach into uncomfortable knots. I make it to the cafeteria door and glance around at the tables, trying to figure out where to sit when Beth, Ruby's right-hand bodyguard, swipes my hat off my head, before Ruby steps in front of me. 'Oh my God, she's crying,' Ruby says, her voice carrying across the large space.

'No, I'm not. Go away, Ruby,' I mutter, grabbing for my hat. How could my eyes still be puffy from this morning?

'You're so pathetic. I'm not surprised Devon had to go all the way to New York to get away from you,' she says and I don't stick around to hear the laughter. I turn and flee to the girls' toilets where I hide until the bell indicates it's home time.

'I know who I am. You don't get to come here after ten years and tell me who you think I am. I'm so happy New York was and is a success for you and I'm ridiculously proud of how your life has turned out. But I'm the alien-loving weirdo who failed her GCSEs and had to make them up in college because her mother made her. I'm the girl who went on dates in dresses her mother picked out for her and who barely ate because said dresses were too tight. I'm the girl who keeps Hope's life organised so I don't have to spend too much time dwelling on mine, the girl who loves nights in with her goldfish and staring at the sky from a park bench while comic strips swirl around in her head.

I'm the girl who, since you left, has felt too afraid to

dream too big because sometimes when you take too big a leap you end up with broken and fractured pieces of you that you don't quite know how to put back together again on your own,' I tell him, tears falling down my cheeks, my choppy hair getting stuck to them. I shouldn't have let Devon in. This week was a mistake. I don't know what I was thinking. 'It's time to go now, Devon,' I add hastily when he goes to speak. I walk past him and gesture towards the stairs. 'I don't get to have it all. You've got to get back to your world. I'm not good enough for you,' I mumble.

'Scar, don't...' Devon starts but I don't want to hear it. I don't want sympathy or pity for my insecurities or my truths. There were many reasons why Hope and Jess didn't know about Devon Wood or my desire to be an artist and that would be one of them. If they didn't know, they didn't have to feel sorry for me for my lack of accomplishments.

'Please, D, you're going to be late,' I say and turn my back on him and walk into the kitchen.

By the time I've tidied up the plates from breakfast, he's standing in the doorway, head scraping the arch, cotton long-sleeve shirt hugging him in all the right places making him look delicious but at the same time cuddly and soft. 'Scarlett, you can't keep blaming me and pushing me away like this. You are...'

'Don't worry about it, Devon, I'm not blaming you,' I say rather forcefully. His face is serious, no beaming smile on his lips; instead they curve down at the edges, his eyes cloudy under the dimming sky in the grey afternoon.

'Then stop this and listen to me,' he pleads walking into the kitchen. I walk out and stand by the front door.

'Stop what?' I ask, shielding my still bare legs from the icy breeze by hiding them behind the door when I open it.

'Jeez, this, this whole pushing me away thing. You can't be doing this right now,' Devon says, and I can hear the anger rising in his tone. 'You're just going to throw me out. You don't care what I have to say or how I feel. You're simply happy to see me go?' Devon says, his tone growing sterner and stronger as he rakes a hand through his hair. I don't say a word. I simply look ahead at the path. Behind me I hear shuffling and huffing as Devon puts on his shoes and grabs his things.

'I get it. It didn't matter how I felt back then, and it doesn't matter how I feel now. All this time you've only thought that it was you who was hurt and you're doing it again. Have I ever made you feel not good enough? Because I'm truly sorry if I have, Scar, but I think you've put that on yourself. Maybe you need to ask yourself if you are good enough for you.' The anger in Devon's tone scares me. I've never heard him sound like this before. I catch the puffiness around his eyes when he storms past me. 'Dreaming big doesn't mean there aren't ups and downs you know. At least when you leap there's a chance you can fly; if you never leap you will never know, and you end up stuck and weeks like this would have never happened,' Devon says as his tears start up again. He wipes at his face and shoves his hands in his pockets.

My emotions are running wild in my gut when I think over the joy I have felt this week. 'Maybe this week shouldn't have happened. Bye, Devon,' I say closing the door, unable to look at the pain in his face for much longer.

20

'Do you think she'll like this one?' I whisper to D as I fold my piece of paper in half. On the front I've drawn a robot that is holding a heart that says, "I love you."

'Put some more glitter on it,' he suggests, passing me the tub of pink glitter from the craft pot.

'How are you getting on over here, my loves?' Mrs Bride asks, coming over to the children's corner of the library where kids can sit and read on bean bags or craft at a large oval table. She always makes sure it's stocked up with all sorts of glitter, colourful paper, glue, paint and crayons.

'Does it look good, Mrs Bride?' I ask, proudly holding up my mum's surprise birthday card. Mrs Bride bends down and gives my card a good look.

'My dear, it's fabulous. Did you draw that robot?' she says, peeking at me over her spectacles. I nod enthusiastically. 'I think your mum is going to love it. You have a real talent, Miss Scarlett.'

I giggle at the praise. 'I really hope so, she didn't like the alien last year. I thought a robot might be better.'

It's teeth-shatteringly frosty outside on Monday morning.

Christmas Eve is on Thursday and I think there's a strong chance it's going to be a white Christmas. I pull my maroon beanie tighter over my ears and stuff my gloved hands inside my coat pocket as I quick-march to the library. With the fair and then having spent the weekend with Devon, I haven't given much thought to Hope and my proposal for the governors and it's due today, which only adds to my shaky state. The heating envelops me in a welcome hug when I pull open the door and jump inside. I dance on the spot for a moment to warm up.

'Good morning, Miss Scarlett.'

'Hey, Scarlett.'

I'm immediately greeted by Mrs Bride and Autumn who are stood behind the gorgeous oak desk with coffee mugs in hand. I can smell the peppermint aroma as it wafts over to me on the hot steam. 'Good morning,' I reply, loosening the top button of my fluffy parka and wiping my feet before walking over to them.

'How are you, lovely?' Autumn asks me with a warm smile. Her tight curly auburn hair is loosely atop her head in a pretty messy bun and today she's wearing a yellow knit jumper with black leggings; she looks gorgeous.

'I'm doing great, thank you. How are things? Did you manage to organise your holiday?' I return with a cheery smile.

'I did, please keep your lips sealed. I've actually managed to keep it from Willow. I've just got to keep it a secret for another night. We leave tomorrow,' she tells me with a soft chuckle. I mimic zipping my lips like she had done that night at the bar.

'And how are you, Mrs Bride?' I say a little louder, turning to the little old lady to Autumn's right, who looks demure and elegant in her light blue fleece, white polo neck and a touch of pink blush on her cheeks.

'I'm wonderful, dear. Now this magazine of yours,' she replies, getting straight to the business of why I'm here early on a Monday morning. 'You and Hope are doing a fine job and you know I will always support our villagers and I will of course be happy to carry it in here with the option to buy, but, Miss Scarlett, I know there's more to you wanting to stock it here than either you or Hope are letting on and, well, I think it's time for a change,' she tells me coming out from behind the desk.

She lays a hand on my elbow and guides me to the children's area and gestures we should sit down at the table. I oblige and pull out my notebook to jot down her ideas to report back to Hope, trying to think over my conversations with the village folk over the last week. Apart from my blunder at the bakery early on, letting it slip about trouble with the magazine, I feel that I've done a stellar job of keeping its struggle a secret.

'You girls have been working so hard and Hope did a beautiful job taking over from Alfred and continuing the magazine's traditions, but many of his ideas are dated now. While yes, we all love the horoscopes and coupons, notes about town and articles on the village's history,' she says this while waving her arms around as if to show me it's a tad boring and monotonous, 'Mable was telling me you're going to be including recipes from the bake offs each month, which I think is gorgeous. It's nice to include us folk but we want that imagination of yours. I know you and Hope have plenty of it,' she finishes, her blue eyes opening wide.

She rests a delicate hand on mine, the one I have atop my notebook where I haven't actually written anything, being distracted by her words and just listening.

'Hmm,' is all that comes out of my mouth as I squint in thought. I thought tradition and village news was what the people of Springhollow wanted.

Mrs Bride chuckles and shakes her head. 'Sometimes we get so caught up in thinking we know what people want that we forget to ask them or we do what other people want and end of up losing ourselves, and we never can grow when we do that. No, dear, we get so stuck being what everyone else wants us to be that we don't get to show them who we are. And who we are might actually be just what they need – they just don't know it yet. You need to show them. You need to open their eyes,' she says patting me gently on the hand.

I swallow down the lump in my throat, afraid that if I speak, I will cry. So, I just sit there and stare at her hand in mine.

'You know, it's been a long time since I've seen a birthday card with a cyclops holding a love heart and balloons. There's plenty of teddy bears out there but sometimes I just don't want a teddy bear. You and Hope have all these empty pages at your disposal; you get to create the stories those pages tell,' she adds.

'That's not really up to me, Mrs Bride. Hope's in charge but I will pass on your advice,' I say, finally finding my words, though they come out small, full of excuses, and I can't look directly at her friendly face.

'Nonsense, sweetheart. Hope would be lost without you; she tells everyone so. True, she has a lot on her plate in running things and yes, she has creative control, but she sings your praises from every rooftop. Why do you think that Christmas stall has been handed over to you for the past four years? You took a leap, you let her see a special side of you. Now, Miss Scarlett, there's plenty more special in there – you've just got to let it out,' she tells me, pinching my cheek when she's finished before slowly standing up.

I say my farewells to Mrs Bride, giving her a tight hug because I still can't quite find the right words to express how much what she said meant to me and I wave to Autumn, quickly wishing her a wonderful getaway, before I'm out in the icy air once more. The threatening blizzard has calmed in the cold air and has decided to take residency in my head instead. Could what Mrs Bride just said be the something big that I was looking for? "Think like Scarlett," choruses in the back of my mind.

Have Hope and I been going about this magazine all wrong? Subscriptions have dropped over the last year as had single purchases. Surely, that was a sign that it had grown stale and the people wanted something new. My heart starts racing as fast as quicksilver. Mrs Bride talked about empty pages. She remembered my drawings growing up and she was right: since Hope had taken over the magazine I had taken leaps in sharing my ideas each year for the Christmas fair. I may have hidden my drawings, but I had expressed my creativity in a different way and the village had loved it. Could it be that they might accept more of me if I dared to show them? I don't have to leave Hope, but I don't have to give up on my dream either. How had I never thought of it before?

Empty pages. Empty pages. The words keep ringing out

in my brain. I pay attention to those ones and choose to ignore the other voice that's reminding me that Devon had said that very thing only yesterday and I had gotten angry with him.

I supress thoughts of Devon and race up the stairs, practically skipping across the floor towards mine and Hope's office. My palms are sweating but I have an idea. When I walk into the room, I'm greeted by Hope waving a letter in the air and squealing. Her eyes are enormous through her giant glasses and she's grinning like a child who knows Santa will be visiting in only three days.

'What's going on?' I ask, hand on my chest, tired from my skipping excursion.

'You won!!' she shouts, with enthusiasm. 'You won!!' She grips onto my shoulders.

She makes it difficult for me not to smile when she begins to jump up and down on the spot; her excitement contagious, but I have no idea what I've won or why I'm now bouncing up and down.

'What did I win?' My brows knit together in confusion, contradicting my lips that are smiling a happy yet nervous grin for Hope.

'You won the opportunity of a lifetime. The School of Visual Arts runs a summer program and you just won the opportunity to attend next year,' Hope explains, slowing down her jumping up and down so she can do so.

My brain already being a flurry of activity is finding it hard to let this new piece of information in to comprehend it. I stop bouncing. 'What? But I didn't enter a competition.'

Hope shrugs like there's a magic fairy going around just granting people's wishes that shouldn't be questioned. 'You just won a spot on a prestigious art course to hone your craft. This is amazing, can you please look more excited,' she says, shoving me gently.

I walk over to my desk feeling dumbfounded and take a seat. 'Hope, what's going on? You can't expect me to be excited when I have no idea what you're talking about,' I say, looking at my best friend as her bright smile is replaced by a sigh and a nervous grin. She pulls up a chair from in front of her desk and sits down next to mine.

'Don't be mad,' she says, and I give her a pointed stare from under my lashes. I have heard that too many times this week. My stomach somersaults. 'Devon kept referring to you drawing. I know you are creative. I love the way you build and craft and decorate your house, but I've never seen you draw. I was dropping off the chairs and bits and pieces from the fair and thought I'd take them up to your storage room for you.' She pauses and I shift uncomfortably in my seat and close my eyes.

'You shouldn't have gone in there,' I say, but strangely enough I don't feel angry or mad, just defeated, like the fight in me to hide that part of myself has grown too tired.

'Scarlett, your artwork is out of this world and I'm sorry that you felt you couldn't share it with Jess and me. I'm sorry we failed you as friends and you felt you couldn't let us see that side to you. We never would have judged you or laughed.' Hope's face is crestfallen; her cheeks are as white as the snow outside. I immediately sit up in my chair.

'Don't be stupid, Hope. You and Jess have never failed me, not once. I love you both so much,' I say urgently, not wanting to see her look so heartbroken. She looks up at me, her eyes glistening.

'But we didn't see you, not like Devon. When he's around, you have this spark, this smile that I've never seen before. He pushes you and challenges you and I just accepted you.' She flicks a hand over the collar of my ruffled baby pink blouse.

'He's had a few extra years than you and Jess to push me and my buttons – that's for sure,' I scoff, tears pooling in my eyes. Hope chuckles and passes me a tissue, getting one for herself too.

'I saw the comic book on your desk. I couldn't put it down. When Jess saw it, he said it was competition-worthy and spoke to his friends at work to see if anyone knew of any. I looked on the internet and found "The School of Visual Arts" and the best part is it's in New York,' she informs me, wiping at her eyes and smiling now, excitement creeping back on her face. My stomach plummets to my feet.

'I can't leave you,' I say, feeling the same wall go up I felt yesterday when Devon was encouraging me to do the same thing.

'You're not leaving me, Scarlett; I wouldn't let you,' she says, playfully shoving me in the shoulder. 'But I do know that this is an incredible opportunity for you and as your best friend and boss, I think you should take it and actually I'm demanding you take it – look at it like I'm sending you on a work course. You are wasted just being my personal assistant; from now on I'm pushing you. Consider this me pushing you,' she declares, determination back on her face, confidence finding its way back in her tone. A small smile tugs at my lips but fails to fully form.

'I can't go to New York,' I mumble, looking to the floor.

'Sure, you can. Things are changing around here and, considering we've got six months to plan for it, I think we can make it happen,' Hope counters. I look up and meet her gaze. So much has happened this past week and Hope has stood by me every step of the way. Being able to express myself and join in with talks of superheroes has felt like a piece of my childhood spandex being stitched back together but to create a brand-new costume. I don't want to hide anything anymore.

'I got so angry with him and pushed him away,' I confess and for once I let Hope see the tears that fall as I explain what Devon had said about me pursuing my art and how I'd told him he didn't know me and that I wasn't good enough for him. Hope wraps her arms around me, and I feel closer to her than I have felt in ten years.

'Well, that's dumb,' she says when she releases me, and I can't help chuckle because actually when I say it out loud it does sound pretty dumb. 'Scarlett, has Devon ever once made you feel not good enough?' she asks.

I sit up straight. 'No, no I don't think so. He makes me feel like me but, Hope, he's a movie star now – surely he needs someone womanly and glamorous the likes of Ruby or, as my mum would say, someone more feminine and elegant – and that's not me.' I tell her.

'Wait, stop. Scarlett, what does your dad think about you?' Hope asks, waving a finger in my face and then grabbing my hands and shaking me. I think for a moment, confused by her questioning.

'Erm, I think he thinks I'm cool and fun.' I stumble a little over the words.

'And what do Jess and I think of you?' she asks, tugging at my hands and sitting on the edge of her seat.

'I don't know – that I'm awesome and a creative genius,' I say, blushing and shrugging but they are their words not mine.

'Exactly. Look, I know Ruby gave you a hard time in school and she's still not much better now and your mum can be a handful. There are always going to be people who put you down but you've got to stop letting those people in and shutting the people that love you out.' I feel as though Thor's hammer has just smacked me right in the face. Hope's right. She's right. It had been easy to shut out the negativity when Devon was right next to me because he was there, and he loved me, and in turn, I loved me. I loved my imagination, I loved who I was with him by my side.

When he left, I had no shield. I let the bullies get to me and I stopped loving me; I stopped loving who I was and became someone else entirely. For the past ten years I have kept all my childhood memories in boxes marked "do not open", not forgetting to put the boxes marked "dreams" at the bottom of the piles, making them impossible to get to. I blamed Devon for so long and did what I thought I was supposed to be doing, becoming the person I thought I had to become, through fear of people not loving me. I lost all sight of the person I wanted to become, of the person I loved, until Devon came back into my life. It wasn't his fault when I was sixteen that life got a bit messed up and it isn't his fault now. He's the only person who knew of all my hopes and dreams and who encouraged and supported them. I only have myself to blame.

I wipe at my tears and shoot out of my chair. 'Hope, I think we have been going about this magazine all wrong. I was talking to Mrs Bride this morning and she said the magazine is boring. She said people want something fresh, something new and exciting. That's the reason sales are dwindling, and people aren't buying it anymore. Donations, raffles, and recipes are all well and good but there's no longevity in that. This magazine isn't Alfred's anymore; it's yours.' I say, boldly, pacing the office.

'It's ours,' Hope states, standing up to join me in pacing the floor. 'What are you saying?'

'I'm saying it needs a revamp. You read what the governors wrote the other day. A monthly magazine needs more content. We can still have sections dedicated to the village but let's give them stories, colour, news they can't see or hear on the street corner. I think you were on the right track looking into social media and bringing in new and fresh ideas. Putting it out monthly will give us more time to put it together, to research, write and source all kinds of information and give them something they can't wait to get a hold of each month,' I ramble.

'That's brilliant. You can do a monthly comic strip or an ongoing story that they want to know what happens next,' Hope suggests.

I stop pacing, hands on my hips. 'What?' I object.

'It's perfect. Devon is on the front cover of the January issue. You should do a comic strip. I can get Clark and Becky to write a short story, oh gosh you could do a colouring page too. Maybe a superhero one for Devon. We can still do horoscopes because everyone loves them, but we can make it more inclusive for all ages,' Hope says with a nod before running behind her desk and scribbling on her big open-faced notebook.

'Seriously?' I say, standing stock-still.

'Seriously,' Hope confirms, dazzling me with her grin. I start to feel the excitement bubbling in my gut; for the first time in ten years I feel like I'm getting the chance to really contribute to the magazine and, though a part of me is terrified, I feel a bigger part of me is thrilled at the opportunity. If Billy Batson can stand up to the seven deadly sins to become the superhero he was destined to be, I think I can pick up a pencil crayon and draw a comic strip for *The Village Gazette*. A laugh escapes my lips, but it is short-lived when I think of Devon.

'Hope, I screwed up big this time,' I say, not keeping my emotions bottled up and letting her know what I'm feeling. Her face softens as she registers what I'm talking about. She walks back around the table and pulls me in for a hug. I snuggle close and rest my head on her shoulder.

'Did Steve Rogers ever give up on Bucky Barnes?' Hope asks, brushing my long fringe out of my face.

'No,' I mumble as a tear falls and I sniffle.

'Well then, I don't believe you, Scarlett, are going to give up on Devon.' She drops a kiss on my head.

'I get to be Cap this time,' I say softly, causing Hope's shoulder to bob up and down as she lets out a laugh.

'Yes, yes you do,' she confirms.

21

Somewhere around the late afternoon, the cute flurry of snowflakes transforms into hail and sloppy rain bangs harshly on the office window. Hope and I had called a meeting around ten a.m. to discuss the change of direction with the magazine and to hear everyone's thoughts and ideas going forward. By the end of the meeting the atmosphere in the office had drastically changed to a much more inspired vibe, yet an exhausted one. Everyone had pulled together to add a new element to our proposal for the governors. Some people had expanded on their skill and suggested how to spruce it up; for example, instead of just half a page with one crossword, taking two pages and including quizzes, dot to dots and puzzles. While others had spoken up of their passions and leapt at the opportunity to write short stories and worldly articles that didn't focus on Springhollow.

I had sat on the edge of Hope's desk with my fingers and toes crossed when she had hit send on the proposal. Now, we simply had to wait.

With the Christmas issue done and dusted last week and with everyone's efforts this morning, Hope wants everyone to take it easy over the next few days, to enjoy their time off over the holidays and come back feeling fresh and rejuvenated, if we have something to come back to that is. She nipped out to the bakery at lunch and bought a delicious selection of treats for everyone and I can see them through my window all mingling and chatting over gingerbread doughnuts and peppermint coffees. I'm finishing up some emails when the clock ticks closer to three p.m. I find my fingers hovering over my keyboard as I'm in the middle of emailing Autumn to thank her and Mrs Bride for this morning and to give them an update when I get a now or never kind of idea that I need to run by Hope.

'Do you fancy taking a trip to New York with me?' I ask, pulling up Google and typing in flights to New York.

'I could maybe swing it as a business trip for the both of us next year; it will just depend on if we get the go-ahead and then how everything goes with the January issue and if we're still in business,' Hope tells me, shuffling around some design ideas on her desk and then tapping her mouse to refresh her screen for the twentieth time to check her emails.

I scroll through some of the options that come up on my screen to see if my spontaneous plan is actually doable. 'I wasn't talking about next year, I was thinking of maybe taking a trip, say, tomorrow,' I reveal to her. She drops all the papers on her desk and rushes to my side.

'Oh my gosh, yes, you should go. That's such a romantic idea and at Christmas time too – it will be the perfect apology.' She swoons.

'So, you're coming?' I say, feeling relieved that she doesn't think I'm crazy.

'No, I'm afraid I can't but you need to go. You can do this on your own. Wait a minute,' she says, throwing a finger in the air before rushing back over to her desk and frantically typing at her keyboard. My stomach sinks. New York is not Springhollow. New York is concrete buildings, high-rise offices, fast-paced, fast-talking, sophisticated men and women who travel around via subway. How does one work out those subway maps or cope being crammed into spaces when they are used to Springhollow's fresh air and walking everywhere? I gulp, not quite sure this is a good idea if Hope can't come with me.

'You really can't come?' I try one more time.

'I really can't. I might be picking up a dog tomorrow from the shelter,' she tells me casually, like it's no big deal.

'You're what? No way.' I gasp, swivelling my chair around. Hope clicks at her mouse and then looks up at me, biting at her bottom lip. 'You could look more excited,' I say, using her words from earlier this morning against her.

'Oh, I am, I am,' she says, flapping her hands up and down. 'I will be fine once I get used to it. Don't tell Jess though. It's going to be a surprise. I'm keeping it at my mum and dad's until Christmas Day.'

'Eeek,' I squeal. 'He's going to be so excited.'

Hope rolls her eyes. 'The things we do for love.' She mutters before dashing out of the office door. I don't have time to question where she's gone when she's back in seconds waving a piece of paper she's just collected from the printer.

'What's that?' I ask with curiosity as she drops it on my desk.

'Wednesday is the last day of New York Comic Con. You can surprise him there,' she explains.

'Oh, that's brilliant, Hope. Thank you so much,' I cry.

'How were you planning on finding him? I don't want to spoil your plans; you can surprise him your way,' she adds.

'I have absolutely no idea,' I say with a laugh. 'I hadn't thought that far ahead.'

Hope bursts out laughing and leans over my shoulder to help me search for flights.

I spot one that leaves tomorrow morning and will get me to New York with enough time for me to get a good night's sleep and be up bright and early on Wednesday to face Comic Con and tell Devon exactly how I feel. My stomach triple-flips at the thought, but I'm not sixteen years old anymore and I am no longer living a life of secrets or creating obstacles for myself out of fear. I am twenty-six years old and a little bit in love with my childhood best friend and this time I'm not letting him get away without a fight. I know we already had a fight but I mean like a good fight where he knows how I feel kind of fight where I put it all on the line and don't push him away. And if Devon doesn't feel the same way, well, I'm just not going to think about that right now.

We book my flight and hotel and then Hope insists that I leave early to pack and get myself together. I hug her goodbye and she tells me she'll call by tonight to make sure I've got everything and to see how I'm doing. As I breathe in the frosty Springhollow air, I know there's something I have to do before I leave.

'Hey, Dad,' I say, giving him a big hug before stepping into the hallway of my parents' house.

'You're out early. Everything OK at the office?' he queries, walking into the kitchen and automatically flicking on the kettle. I take off my coat and take a seat at the table.

'Yes, everything's fine thank you. More than fine actually, we're taking the magazine in a new direction next year and I'm going to be more involved,' I inform him, helping myself to a custard cream from the biscuit tin on the table.

'That's fantastic, Scar,' he says with a huge grin as he potters about pouring the milk into our mugs.

'Yes, if we get the go-ahead then I'm going to be doing a comic strip for the January issue and if the January issue does well and we stay in business, I will be doing a comic strip for each of our issues,' I explain, which causes him to splash milk everywhere as he turns around to look at me, beaming.

'Oh, Scar. I knew you could do it,' he says, dabbing at the milk he spilt with a tea towel and bringing our mugs to the table. He then drops a kiss on my forehead before taking his seat.

'Thanks, Dad. I have some other news too,' I say and take a sip of tea for some British courage. 'I'm going to New York tomorrow. Don't worry, I'll be back on Christmas Eve, but I need to see Devon. He didn't leave on very good terms and I need to apologise to him. I said some things that weren't kind because I've been holding on to so much anger and resentment towards him for all these years and I need to put it right,' I say in one long breath, not wanting to chicken out of being emotional and letting my dad in. He leans forward in his chair, his hands wrapped around his mug.

'Just because you and Devon had a fight doesn't mean you're not meant for each other – you know that right?

We're not perfect people and you know that all that time apart means nothing when you've got something as special as you two have,' he tells me. I can feel myself getting choked up and so I take a comforting sip of tea, to stem the flow of tears, my eyes too sore to rub any more after all the crying I've done today.

'Thanks, Dad. You know, I think this might be more than just a friendship thing,' I add, feeling my cheeks flush, not knowing quite how to broach the subject with my dad. I've not really had to introduce many men to him over the years, so it feels slightly awkward.

'You don't say,' is his reply as he leans back and takes a knowing sip of tea, which makes me laugh and nearly splutter on mine.

'Will you tell Mum for me?' I ask. My voice comes out a little wobbly. My dad's smiling lips turn down in a frown. The creases in his brow deepen when he meets my gaze.

'Oh, sweetheart, I think she'd appreciate it if you told her yourself. She will be home shortly,' he informs me, and then his face forms a thoughtful expression. 'Scar, I know sometimes your mum might come across a bit much, but she cares. If she hadn't put her foot down at times when you were kids, I think the number of hospital visits you and Devon racked up would be triple digits. I wanted so much for you to fly and be all that you were, but someone had to teach you that jumping off scaffolding wasn't always a wise idea. She meant well and she still does.'

I'm grateful for my dad's words as I never really thought about it like that before. Someone had to teach me that if you touch fire it would burn you; someone had to teach me boundaries and respect for the world around me.

*

'I can't believe you, Scarlett Davis. What on earth do you think you were playing at? You can't tie up the neighbour's cat – it's not kind, nor is it respectful and we take our shoes off when we enter someone's home,' my mum shouts as I go to step inside the house. My shoes are caked in mud, my hands are sticky from I don't know what and my evening of playing out on the street with Devon has been cut short by my mum, who is currently livid and dragging me inside.

'You know your mother has always known it was Devon for you too. She knew how much it hurt you when he left. I think she focused on putting on a brave face, but she hated seeing you hurt knowing that she couldn't fix it,' my dad adds when I don't say anything, thinking back to all the times my mum shouted at me and realising that most of the tellings-off were warranted.

My ears prick up to rustling at the front door before it clicks, and my mum's perfume mixed with the aroma of hairspray and all kinds of lotions and potions wafts through the hall.

'Hi, honey, I'm in the kitchen,' Dad calls out.

'Hi, Mum,' I call after him.

'Scarlett, is that you?' Mum shouts back and I resist the urge to say something sarcastic. 'Is everything OK, darling?' she asks as she walks into the kitchen. She goes straight over to my dad to give him a hug and a kiss and then repeats the same action with me.

'I'll get you a cuppa – you sit down,' my dad says, standing up so my mum can take his place at the table.

Before I can back out, I take one giant breath and let it all out.

'I'm sorry, Mum. I'm sorry that I haven't been the most perfect little girl and that I spent most of my childhood giving you a heart attack with the all the hospital visits and mine and Devon's crazy antics. I'm sorry I didn't try harder at school. But I'm not that little girl anymore. I want us to try harder to fix our relationship and spend time together but you have to want to spend time with me, not some version of me that you see in your head, wearing pink and lace, pretending I don't love drawing or constantly looking me up and down like I'm a disappointment.

'I love you, for all your stubborn ways, neatness, cardigans and cooking, all the wonderful and odd things that make you you, but you have to be willing to do the same for me. Do you think you can do that?' I can feel the tension build in my neck as I look at my mum to try and decipher the expression on her face, and if she took it well.

After a few moments and a brief distraction of my dad placing Mum's tea on the table, she reaches out and takes my sweaty hands in her tidy manicured ones. She opens her mouth then closes it again as a tear falls down her cheek. My leg starts nervously twitching, anticipating her response.

'Scarlett, of course I love you.' She wipes at her wet face with the back of her hand. 'All of you.' She gives me a pointed glare and releases my hands. 'Oh, honey, I'm sorry. When you were a child, I just wished for you to enjoy the things that I had loved as a little girl. I know I was wrong to try and push those things on you and I am sorry. But darling when Devon left you became so quiet and watching you just plod through school and college with no passion, well I didn't mean to control you or push things on you, I just wanted you to have options. I wanted to see your face light up like it did when you were little – always excited and running around. And I do love your drawings, honey, maybe not the ones with those creepy villain things you would draw, but of course I see your talent. But you've never pushed for it and so I thought it best to try and give you different ideas.' My mum leans back in her chair, releasing her hands and fiddling with her nails.

I feel my own eyes growing wet. I never looked at it like that. Have I really been going through life so unenthusiastically? I don't know what to say.

'I know you need to draw; you need to be creative. Oh, sweetheart, it's a joy to see you at the Christmas fair each year; you do such a magnificent job of bringing people together. Maybe you could draw a happy comic book, fewer weapons and spooky monsters, some festive cheer,' my mum suggests, her eyes sparkling with a little humour now, causing me to laugh.

'A Christmas comic book? I think I like that idea, Mum,' I say, rubbing at my eyes. Had my mum just given me a suggestion for a comic book? Hello, Santa? Where are you hiding?

'Whatever it is, Scarlett, you've got to go for it. I promise to take a step back, as long as you give it all you've got. You don't need my help, but I will give you some space,' she says, taking my hands in hers once more.

'And the clothes, Mum, will you stop buying me clothes?' I plead, squeezing her hands in mine.

'Oh, but you look so pretty in pastel colours and bows,' she says, putting her gentle hand through my hair and sounding so sweet. I do not look pretty in pastel and bows.

'Mum,' I say more sternly.

'Oh, all right, honey. I will try, but if I see something with your name on it, you can't be mad at me,' she says with a smile, as I cringe, hating to think what else has my name on it in her eyes.

'Right. Now, Mum, don't freak out, but I'm off to New York tomorrow morning to go and find Devon. I've got it all planned out so there's no need to worry. I will be back on Christmas Eve, OK?' I say calmly and matter-of-fact as I stand up. She does a wonderful impression of Eddie for a few moments before composing herself and forcing what I know is a fake grin, because my mum loves me and no matter how many times I tell her not to worry, she's going to worry. This time instead of rolling my eyes, I retrieve something from my bag, step around the table and wrap my arms around her and give her a kiss on the cheek as I place my card on the table.

'What's this?' she asks.

'I made it for you when I was nine and then I think we had an argument over my not wanting to wear a bow for the school photos and so I never gave it to you,' I explain as she picks up the card and gently traces her fingers over the unicorns and teddy bears I had drawn and decorated with sparkles, lace, buttons, and glitter. I had really been trying with the birthday cards and, after seeing her face year after year with all the goblins and ghouls, I had known what to do to make her happy but after the argument I didn't want to give it to her and out of spite went back to my original designs from then on.

'Oh, I love it, Scarlett, and I love you,' she says, swivelling around on her chair to hug me properly.

'I love you too. Now, I best be off,' I tell them, hugging my dad and gathering my things before heading to the front door. It's getting late and I still have to pack.

'Be safe and say hello to Devon for me,' Mum says as she and Dad wave from the front door. I wave back and blow kisses as I precariously race towards the village green on the icy ground, rushing to pick up a few things before I need to head home. I manage to pull together a pick 'n' mix from Mrs May's sweet shop just before the clock strikes five – one that includes all Devon's favourite childhood sweets, just as a small peace offering for when I see him again, and when I close the door of the small shop behind me I almost bump into Ruby.

'Sorry,' I mumble, stepping aside so she can get past me, but Ruby doesn't move. She takes a step back blocking my path.

'You really think you stand a chance now that Devon's a big movie star? You really think his publicist is going to allow you two to date just because you jump on a plane and make some silly grand romantic gesture? Grow up, Scarlett, and get a clue. You wear beanie hats and your mum's clothes – you look like you're an overgrown child. Devon needs someone who understands the limelight and the glitz and glam,' Ruby informs me, looking me up and down the way she has done since we were running around in reception class. But instead of feeling my usual anger or shame, I hold my head up high. Today I'm done with letting Ruby make me feel so small.

Also, how bloody quickly does word travel around this village? How did she know I was going to New York?

'Oh, the whole town thinks it's so adorable, like they're rooting for the childhood sweethearts to reunite. But you're going to make a fool of yourself, Scarlett.' My stomach twists, no pressure then. I have no idea why Ruby hates me this much and feels the need to give me this much of a bruising, but it's time to put a stop to it.

'Devon's a man now, Scarlett, and he needs a real woman. He's grown up, unlike you.' She adds another dig in before I can open my mouth.

'You know what, Ruby?' I can feel my insides bubbling. All the years of allowing myself to feel worthless, not good enough for my mum, for men, for anyone, are over now. 'No, I don't dress like you, Ruby, and I don't like high heels. I know what the acronym Shazam stands for and I couldn't tell you anything about being the CEO of a company and nor do I have the desire to be one. I may get giddy at the sight of a pencil crayon and love riding my skateboard but I'm still a woman. I might not meet your standards of sophistication. I may not look like I've just walked off a catwalk. I might not always act like I have my crap together, and it's because I don't.

'This whole being an adult, paying the bills, working a nine-to-five – it's all terrifying to me. I want to be an artist, I want to draw superheroes every day and skateboard to get around – that's who I am. And I've been ashamed of who I am for far too long, trying to please everyone and be what everyone else expects me to be, but I'm done. You can believe what you want about Devon, but you don't know him like I know him, and you don't care about him like I do. This whole glitzy and glamorous lifestyle you keep harping on about, it's not him. Well, no actually I take that back, it is him, it's a small part of him now but you can't pick and choose the parts of people that you like – you have to love all of them,' I say defiantly, digging my boots into the snow and feeling like I should have stood up to Ruby a long time ago.

Ruby doesn't say anything; she just stands there, eyebrows raised, nose in the air, her lips pursed curtly. A few icy moments pass. I pop the brown paper bag into my handmade recycled cork shopping bag, made by Emily, and go to walk away.

'Oh, poor Scarlett, still holding on to the past because her future looks so bleak. I couldn't possibly burst your bauble so close to Christmas. I'll let you have your little fantasy; after all, what else have you got? But don't say I didn't warn you, that man needs a woman who can satisfy him,' Ruby says, her words sly and condescending.

I shake my head in sad disbelief at how someone can be so mean. But when I go to take another step I pause as her words hit me in full force.

'You do realise you are judging Devon based on his looks and new physique and his new career status? Just like you and so many people judge me because of the beanie and my tomboy ways. Inside, Devon is still Devon, a nerd with a heart of gold, and I am no less a real woman,' I say feeling well and truly like I could lead The Avengers into battle right now.

'You a real—' Ruby scoffs but I interrupt.

'Ruby, stop. That's enough now. This has got to stop. I can't stand here and listen to it anymore. What did I ever do to you that's caused you to hate me so much?' I ask, my voice firm, but soft.

Ruby's eyes dart to the snowy ground, then around the square. I don't move. I want to be patient; I want to hear her out. It's the first time I have seen Ruby speechless and when she doesn't answer for a long moment, I'm about to wish her a happy Christmas and be on my way when she opens her mouth and her voice comes out in a whisper so quiet, I have to lean in to hear her.

'You were always so yourself. You and Devon were always so happy and laughing and having fun, like you didn't have a care in the world about what other people thought of you,' she mutters.

I nearly drop my shopping bag on the floor, my whole body goes numb and the tears in my eyes quickly chill my cheeks in the icy air. 'But, Ruby, everything you said to me – the way you treated me, all those horrible comments – they hurt, they hurt so bad that I started to hide myself. I started to care.' I barely get my words out; my voice sounds so small.

'Yes, well, I'm sorry for that but at least you got to feel what it was like for me always having to be pretty and perfect,' she retorts, her voice becoming hard again.

'I'm sorry about whoever made you feel like you had to be pretty and perfect. I never thought you had to be pretty and perfect. I would have just liked you to be nice and if you would have talked to me, I would have understood. I was constantly battling my mum growing up. I was constantly battling you, Ruby, and then I let you win,' I tell her. I'm not angry; instead I'm more shocked and pained by her confession.

'Well, whatever, it doesn't matter now,' she replies curtly.

I grip on to my bag tighter, trying to process this conversation. It did matter, at least it had mattered to me for twenty-three years, but today has already taken a lot out of me and I need to start looking forward and not letting my past define me. 'Look, I've got to go but I hope you have a lovely Christmas, Ruby, and I hope you find who you want to be and have the courage to be her and love her,' I finish and walk off.

22

For someone who has never stepped foot outside of Springhollow, I think I'm doing a pretty decent job of navigating the Big Apple. Granted the taxi man helped a lot, bringing me from the airport to right outside my hotel and then scribbling directions on a piece of paper for me of how to get to the Comic Con convention centre tomorrow. I did receive an odd look at first when I explained that my phone didn't have internet access. Is that really such an alien concept these days? There's a lot of honking and loud noises when I do get out of the taxi and I find myself staring up at The New Yorker, A Wyndham Hotel. The building itself looks bigger than my whole village.

I find myself frozen to the spot; one, because New York is absolutely freezing and two, because I can't stop gaping at the thousands of little windows all lit up. It's like one humongous Advent calendar. A check to the shoulder and a wheelie bag running over my toe snaps me into action. It's early evening but there are people everywhere and they all seem to be in a rush to get somewhere. It takes me a second to make the two strides forward to the front door of the hotel without getting trampled on and muttering a plethora of "sorries" and "excuse me's".

The warmth of the indoors engulfs me when I enter the lobby. I feel like Ant-Man, like I have suddenly shrunk in size. My mind can't quite comprehend that the giant room I am standing in is just the lobby. It's glorious and gold, with chandeliers dangling from the ceiling and the architecture is stunning. I mean I love our *Village Gazette* building, but this New Yorker is something else.

I check in and find my room, which is all gleaming white with brown accents and a bed that screams bedtime the minute I lay my weary eyes on it. But it's the view from the window that knocks me for six. I'd heard people talk of the New York skyline; only last week Devon had been his animated, passionate self, telling me that it was something I had to experience one day and well, here I was, experiencing it in all its magnificence. Lights upon lights upon lights, everywhere I turn.

I kick off my boots as my right hand begins to tingle. Laying my suitcase on my bed, I open it up and pull out my sketchbook and make myself comfortable in the armchair by the window.

The next minute I wake up, scrunched up in the armchair, legs curled up underneath me, my sketchbooks sprawled out on the floor displaying only a few sharp grey lines depicting the many buildings before me. Glancing across the skyline, a few lights have been extinguished but it is still very much a sparkling beauty. Looking over to the side of the bed at the small alarm clock, I read three-thirty a.m. and think it might be sensible to have a quick wash and get into the comfy-looking bed to finish the remainder of my slumber, if I'd like to remotely not resemble a zombie tomorrow.

*

I fill up on a breakfast of pastries and fruit, not quite to the deliciousness of Mr and Mrs's Rolph's treats but they weren't bad, when I realise I'm mentally comparing Springhollow and New York in my head, almost like this is a test that will decide my fate next year and whether I attend the art school. If the art school has accommodation as good as the New Yorker, then count me in. The bed didn't just look cosy, it had felt so glorious and snug that I'd not wanted to get out of it this morning until I remembered the plan for today.

Now, I'm following the instructions the taxi man so kindly gave me yesterday while trying not to get bumped into by the stream of rushing pedestrians. This certainly would take some getting used to; I already miss the peaceful square back home and the fact that everyone stops and says hello to each other on any given day for any given reason. I've been walking a good twenty minutes when I start to see Spider-Man graphic tees and Pikachu bobble hats, which can only signify I'm heading in the right direction. My stomach doesn't miss this information when it gurgles with nerves.

I follow a small group of men and woman each sporting brightly coloured spandex outfits. I immediately think back to the cosplay Devon, Hope and Jess had told me about. On closer inspection I recognise that together they make up the five Power Rangers, and for a moment my nerves vanish as I revel in being this close to such ridiculously cool people. Is this the kind of stuff I have been missing out on with hiding who I am all these years? These are grown men and women dressed as Power Rangers and they look awesome. I tell them so and receive hellos and thumbs-up from each of them.

My confidence is steadily rising, my shoulders relax, and I stand taller as the line to go inside dwindles down and I pass more amazing costumes and cheerful people. Handing my ticket over the man at the door, I can barely contain my excitement when the entire convention room comes into view. Everywhere I look there are posters representing my childhood and signs informing me where I can meet comic book legends and actors from all the movie franchises I have managed to miss in the last ten years.

There's so much to take in. The worlds I loved as a kid have all come to life through the big screen and I have so much to catch up on. Devon had got me caught up on *The Avengers* before he left and I'd watched a couple of the movie trailers that followed that one, so I recognise some names, but otherwise it's the posters and the imagery all over the show that has me gawping like I've forgotten how to close my mouth.

A little to the right of me I notice a line and a sign reading "The First Avenger", a squeal of excitement escapes my lips and I jump in the queue. No way, it's my first Comic Con and I'm going to meet Steve Rogers. My insides are doing a happy dance. Hope and Jess will be so proud of me when I tell them, and Devon will have a heart attack.

'OK, I think I'm hyperventilating,' D informs me as we make our way into the packed movie theatre and take our seats.

'Here, have some popcorn,' I say, smirking. My insides are squirming with excitement too but I'm trying to keep it together so I can take in every morsel of Captain America: The First Avenger.

'I'm sure you're not supposed to offer people who are hyperventilating food,' D says shooting me a look with his hand on his chest. 'Scar, we've been waiting for this day since we were in nappies.'

'I know, I know. Shh it's starting,' I reply, gripping D's knee so hard my knuckles turn white.

'Oh my God, that was epic,' D practically squeals three hours later as we exit the cinema.

'Tell me about it. Hands down best movie ever,' I declare.

'Can you believe we have to wait until next year for The Avengers?' D moans, his sixteen-year-old brain not being able to deal with such torture.

'Scar?' I swear I can hear my name, but with each step closer I take to Steve Rogers, I get distracted thinking about what I'm going to say to him. 'Scarlett.' I hear my name for sure this time and my stomach triple-vaults when I register the warm voice. I turn around and see Devon standing there with a man even taller than him next to him; whom I take to be his security guard. He's broad and has a stoic face. The people in the line with me all turn too, immediately getting their phones out and snapping pictures and enquiring about selfies. The security guard raises his hands to calm them.

I smile at Devon but the speech that I had planned on the plane over here gets lost somewhere in my overstimulated mind.

'What are you doing here?' Devon asks. I know I wanted to tell him something but right now I can't focus.

'Erm, well right now I'm in the line to meet "Captain America". He's right over there, D. Have you seen this place? Holy moly it's amazing.' I'm barely able to contain the glee in my voice as I try and point discreetly at Steve Rogers himself. I'm sure I see a flicker of a smile tug at the corner of Devon's mouth, which gives me hope that he might not be as mad at me as he was when I closed the door in his face a few days ago.

Suddenly I start to feel a little claustrophobic as a small crowd begins to gather around Devon and starts pushing to get closer to him. I curse myself for being a scaredy cat and for getting distracted when I know I don't have much time. I leave tomorrow morning. I need to stick to my plan and tell Devon why I'm here now.

I step forward, getting an elbow in my sternum as I do so – ouch, I just want to get closer to my best friend; my best friend who to these people is a beloved superhero. Shoot, this might be harder than I thought. There might be a flaw in Hope's idea.

'Excuse me, miss, if you want a picture with Devon, the line is over there.' I follow the man's finger to where there is a line wrapped around one length of the convention centre, waiting for Devon. Yep, this was going to be way harder than I had imagined. This time there isn't a shadow of a doubt in my mind that Devon is smirking and there's no mistaking the mischievous glint in his eye. He shrugs as he gets dragged away. OK, so maybe he is still a little mad at me and is going to make me work for this.

I glance back at Steve Rogers, let out a sigh and go in search of the end of Devon's line.

So, if I thought Devon and I were hardcore superhero nerds when we were kids, it's nothing compared to the thousands of people in the line with me right now. An hour has ticked by and the line is moving terribly slowly.

'How come we're not moving very fast?' I finally pick up the courage to ask the girl in front of me who's wearing a T-shirt with Devon's face on it. It still hasn't quite sunk in that he's a movie star. I pry my eyes away from the shirt.

'Oh, it's just Devon. His lines always take forever. He likes to talk to everyone he meets, instead of the usual hi and bye most people stick to. He's really lovely. Is this your first time meeting him? Oh, you will love him. He's a sweetheart,' the girl answers enthusiastically, rocking back on her heels and clapping her hands.

Right now, I would love food, but I can't help the smile that forms at my lips and how my skin prickles with goose bumps when the girl speaks, and I know I can't lose my place in line. I have things I need to say to this nerdy sweetheart.

Can you believe it takes another hour before I can even see Devon's table? My stomach is well and truly growly at me, but we've made it this far and must go on. The squeals from fans are louder now and I can even make out a few happy dances from enthusiastic movie goers. This place is amazing, allowing everyone to interact, and I can hear Devon put everyone at ease, listen to their stories and oblige all the requests for selfies and photographs. And to think, only a few days ago I thought he had grown into a smooth, standoffish and smarmy man.

I'm now the second in line. My heart starts hammering

in my chest and I can feel the sweat on my top lip. It made sense to wear my cream chunky knit and denim flare combo when stepping outside of the hotel this morning but now it feels like I'm standing next to a heater and my jumper is sucking up all the heat. I concentrate on the girl in front of me and her awesome "Team Bartowski" Converse, making a mental note to get some for Hope and to try and steady the dizziness I feel in my head. This is Devon for crying out loud, the guy I can tell everything and anything to, so what's wrong with me? I tell him how I feel and then I'm done. He either feels the same or he doesn't. I'm no stranger to rejection, so all will be OK, I tell myself.

Yet somehow at that thought my stomach feels like I've raced down a half-pipe full speed, twisted my ankle and landed with a heavy thud at the bottom. Will I really be OK if Devon doesn't feel the same? Yes, I tell myself, yes. I have to be.

When he left me at sixteen years old I let it change my entire world, hid who I was, felt ashamed of who I was, but now, now I'm a grown-up, a grown-up who loves to draw comic books and watch superhero movies and skateboard and Devon's visit made me love all those things again and not be afraid of them. Devon made me see that it's OK to be an adult and still be passionate, still get excited and to still let our inner children out every now and again. I don't want to lose that again.

With that thought I feel my body temperature cool down and my heart rate slow down. Ever since we were kids Devon has worn his heart on his sleeve and I was always the tougher one, the tomboy with attitude, but as I look at him sitting against the edge of the plastic fold away table talking to the girl with his face on her T-shirt and making her smile as broad as The Joker, but in a nice way, I know my walls are once again crumbling but this time I know that's where I want them to stay. No more walls. I can be vulnerable and still strong, just like Devon has always been. I just never realised. Through his own heartbreak and troubles, he remains a light to everyone around him.

Now, it's not about him feeling the same way, though I'm still crossing my everything. I just need to thank him. I need him to know that I love him for all that he is and for all that he inspires me to be and I need to look him in the eyes and for once in my life tell him that it's me who is sorry.

'Excuse me, miss.' It takes me a second to realise that one of the assistants is looking at me, gesturing towards Devon's table. I suck in a deep breath and catch Devon's eyes on me as my stomach grumbles at me angrily. Even my happy thoughts are having trouble keeping my hunger distracted. As I make my way over I notice a security guard walk in from behind the curtain to the left of Devon, bend down, whisper in his ear and hand him a plastic bag that holds something delicious as the smell wafts up and hits me, before he stands up straight and offers me a nod. I smile back at the man and then get back to concentrating on Devon's brown eyes and not the idea of food. Devon gets up and edges around the table to greet me. My shoulders release their tension the minute he steps closer.

'Look, I didn't exactly come here to meet Steve Rogers, though you do owe me a photo op,' I say, which receives a small smile from Devon. 'I'm sorry. I'm so sorry for everything, D, and I came to see you. I came after you. I know it might be ten years too late, but I came after you.'

Saying the words releases a bunch of tightness in my chest. Owning my regrets but more importantly putting them in the past and rectifying them, doing something about them, makes me feel as light as feather.

Devon doesn't say anything. He turns away and reaches into the bag the security guy brought over and pulls out a box, like the ones you get from a food truck, and hands it to me. I smell a burger and fries. If I had any doubts before about loving this man, then they quickly dissolve.

'I knew you'd be hungry.' He shrugs casually, like it's no big deal to be so ridiculously thoughtful, when the reality is it means everything to me, and I really want to hug him right now. 'Do me a favour, Scar? Go eat something and enjoy every inch of this place and meet me at the Rockefeller tree tonight at seven, OK?'

'The big tree?' I ask in a hushed whisper, not taking my eyes off his.

'Yes, the big tree – you can't miss it,' he replies with a grin and a cheeky wink.

I shove him in the shoulder playfully, which causes the security guard to step forward. Devon quickly raises his hand and the security guard steps back. I jump and offer Devon an apologetic look then nod at his plan; a little fearful of my surroundings. I'm grateful that Devon understands how much I want to explore this convention and I now realise this is probably not the best place to talk. There's a lot I want to say but Devon's line is still wrapped around the building.

I raise my arms to wave at him or hug him or something but see the security guard out of the corner of my eye shuffle so instead I just awkwardly back away and shrug at Devon, waving the burger and fries box in thanks. His shoulders move up and down with a chuckle and he does a shy wave, which nearly causes me to topple into a camera set-up. It's getting rather hot in here again.

'Ooh wait,' I say remembering the sweets I brought with me. I jog backwards a little and once again cause the security guard to take a sudden step forward. I've really got this man on edge. This time I wave my hand. 'It's OK, it's OK,' I say, pulling out the brown bag from my shoulder bag. 'These are for you,' I say to Devon. 'You might need a snack,' I add, with a smile, glancing down the line.

He looks up at me from under his long lashes and gives me a proper smile this time but doesn't speak. 'Big tree at seven. See you then.'

I nod and retreat.

I find a small area with tables and chairs and take a seat to tuck into my food and calm down. This is all new territory for me and it's both exciting and terrifying at the same time. The salty and fluffy flavour and texture of the chips gives me pause. Devon brought me food, which was kind of him, and he smiled when I gave him sweets, so I can only hope it means he doesn't entirely hate me and that when we meet tonight it will be a joyous occasion.

In fact, no matter Devon's feelings for me, I feel like a new and revived version of myself and I'm determined that it will be.

23

The chatter in the convention centre is quietening down as the crowd begins emptying out, and many of the actors and artists have left their booths. I'm being weighed down by a few bags, having picked up some gifts for Hope, Jess and my dad that I simply couldn't resist, and my brain is just a happy inspired whir of colours and comic strips as I come to a standstill at the convention doors, contemplating if I'm ready to leave yet. I spent a good amount of time in the artist quarter chatting to an incredible comic book artist about her books and work. I even picked up a few of her sketches to hang up in my lair as a small Christmas gift to myself.

A quick look at my watch and I know I must make a move if I want to be on time to meet Devon at seven, but it's difficult to pry myself away from this sacred room that has breathed so much life and inspiration into my dreams. I'm so glad Hope had suggested I come here and that I don't have to keep my passion a secret anymore.

I quick-march to the hotel, feeling a little more like a local, where I deposit my bags and ask the concierge for directions to the big tree. It's now or never.

★

'Whoa, that was awesome, Scar, you did it.' D praises me after I hit my first ever rail slide. I swivel my cap back around, so the visor is at the front to keep the sun out of my eyes now I've completed my trick and give him a thumbs-up. The summer heat wave is not discouraging us today. We have a week left until we head back to school to start our last year and we are determined to master these tricks before the holiday's up.

'Nice moves,' I hear from behind me. I put down my bottle of water and turn around and am greeted by Tan and his friends.

'Thanks,' I say, suddenly feeling self-conscious with how much I am sweating in the heat. Tan's a regular at the park with his friends, but they've never talked to us before. They're college boys.

'What are you doing Friday night?' he asks, taking a step closer to me. Suddenly, Devon's arm is on my hip so fast as he steps up behind me, arm across my back. My knees unexpectedly turn to jelly.

'Erm, I'm not sure – we usually just hang here till late,' I stammer, but Tan's eyes take in D and he takes a step back.

'Is this your boyfriend?' he asks, nodding at Devon. With D's fingers grazing my hip bone, I'm finding it hard to form words. What's wrong with me?

'Yes, I am,' D says boldly, and I actually choke on air.

'Sorry, dude,' Tan says. 'See you around,' he adds before he and his gang turn around and skate away. When they are gone, Devon casually takes his hand off me and grabs his board.

'What was that all about, D?' I ask, confused by what just happened.

'They're college boys – you don't want to be going out with them,' he says, walking towards the bowl. I pick up my board and follow him.

'This coming from the person who knows so much about dating,' I say, not sure why I'm so annoyed. If I'd known Tan was asking me out, like on a date, I wouldn't have gone.

'I just wanted to protect you,' D explains, which only agitates me further.

'So what? You're my boyfriend now?' I ask, shoving him in his bicep.

'No, I uh…' he stammers, his cheeks turning red. 'No, not unless I don't know. Do you want me to be?' he asks, dropping his board to the ground, rolling it back and forth with his foot and looking anywhere but at me.

I choke on a gust of wind. 'Uh, no, I don't know. I don't…' I ramble. 'Should we just…'

'Race around the bowl and then grab an ice-cream?' D offers.

'Yeah, that,' I reply, shaking my head and dropping into the bowl.

I'm just walking past the cutest cupcake shop in search of the Rockefeller tree when I feel a hand on my shoulder. I spin round to see Devon in a tailored maroon coat and a black scarf. His hair is starting to curl with the dew in the air and he looks dashing. For a moment I forget that we're mad at each other and that I have a very heavy speech planned and embrace him with a hug. When he drapes his arms over my shoulders, I instantly relax into him and my words come pouring out.

'Devon, I'm sorry. I'm sorry that I pushed you away. I'm sorry that I never wrote to you and I am so very sorry that I never for one second thought about how much you were hurting too. It all could have been so different if I had tried, but I just gave up. I wasn't as strong when you left. The pressure from my mum got too much and I tried to be what everyone else wanted me to be. It felt good for a while pushing comics away; it helped me forget about you. The more I missed you the more I just got mad at you for not being by my side and I started hating everything that reminded me of you.

I lost myself and if today is any indication, I've missed out on so much. Did you see the guy who plays Thor? D, he's like a god, like legit he is Thor.' I take a step back and look up so I can see Devon's eyes. They squint a little in amusement.

'Sorry, I know, we can talk about him later.' I shake my head and take a big breath in, aware that my speech isn't quite coming out in the order I had planned, and that I am just rambling.

'I love you, Devon, I love you more than Steve Rogers and little Steve Rogers combined. I always have and always will. I love how you get me, and you challenge me while still loving all that I am, and I love how you make me want to be the me I want to be. I guess when you turned up in Springhollow I freaked out and couldn't shake the ten years that had gone by. I built a wall and kept telling myself that you'd changed, and we couldn't possibly know each other anymore because I wasn't the person I was when you left.

I had lost myself and you somehow flew right back in and found me, and it scared the heck out of me.'

I pause for breath as we shuffle a little closer to the window of the cupcake shop and out of the way of pedestrians. 'Now, you don't have to feel the same, I mean it would be nice and I'd like that, but I just want to thank you and tell you how much I adore you and think the world of you. You're the best superhero there is and not just in the movies but in real life too and you'll always be my favourite. I'd say you're an even better friend to me than Cap is to Bucky.'

Devon gasps and puts his hand on his heart dramatically before smirking. He looks ridiculously cute when he does that. I shuffle from foot to foot and laugh at his acting and feel like this whole getting emotions out in the open isn't so bad, though the sweat forming on my brow tells me otherwise. I remind myself that I will be OK, no matter what Devon says, but find my breath hitches when Devon opens his mouth.

'I'm sorry if you felt like I was barging into your world and acting like you should have been the same sixteen-year-old girl you were when I left. That was wrong of me, but I could still see that spark in your eye, and I didn't want to believe you had given up drawing because you are beyond talented. I guess a part of me just wanted to pick up where we left off and put the past behind us but that wasn't right nor fair. I want to know all of you and understand all of you and it pains me that you had such a difficult time when I left.' He clears his throat and eyes sparkle with tears.

'But that was on me, Devon. You were sixteen. I should never have blamed you and given up on what I wanted.

That was my fault. I should have fought for who I was, and I should have fought for our friendship. You had your struggles too. You moved to a brand-new place; you had to deal with new cliques, rejections, good auditions, bad auditions, your parents; and still you fought for your dream, and look at what you achieved,' I say, absent-mindedly playing with a button on his coat.

'I like us together, Scar. I like us grown-up and together. I want to fall asleep with you and wake up next to you. I want it all with you, Scarlett. Adult sleepovers are fun,' he says, wiggling his eyebrows.

I can feel my cheeks flush and I fiddle with the bobbles on my gloves, trying not to think about Devon in my bed right now when we are having a serious conversation.

'I like us together too,' I reply as Devon grabs my hands, which instantly warms my fingertips with that electricity again.

'Scarlett, will you promise to dance with me when everyone's watching, eat cookies with me under blanket forts and always be my partner in crime?' he says.

With Devon's words I feel like Christmas spirit just exploded in my heart; it's full of so much joy.

I look up into his beautiful brown eyes, that no matter where I am in the world, Springhollow or New York, make me feel like I'm home. I clear my throat to encourage my words to come out clear and not wobbly, but I can feel my whole body shaking.

'Devon Wood, will you promise to skateboard with me even when we're old and wrinkly, eat ice-cream for breakfast with me and always be the Robin to my Batman?'

'Yes, I do,' he says with a dazzling smile.

ONE SNOWY WEEK IN SPRINGHOLLOW

'Does this mean you're my boyfriend now?' I grin, a giggle escaping my lips.

'Do you want me to be your boyfriend?' he asks, matching my grin.

'Yes, yes, I think I do,' I reply, confidently this time.

'Well, OK then. I will... wait... why do you always get to be Batman?' he asks but I ignore his question and tug on his coat to bring him down to my level so I can kiss him. The minute my lips touch his that spark of electricity zips around my body and down to the tips of my toes. His kisses make me feel like the whole world disappears and we're the only two left. I don't want to pull away, but a Christmas shopper bumps into me with her giant bags, making me wobble on my tiptoes. Devon steadies me with his arms wrapped around my waist.

'You know, I still haven't seen this giant tree you've been boasting about,' I say, snuggling into the warmth of his chest. He drops a kiss on top of my head and my toes curl under; I love it when he does that, such a simple but sweet gesture that makes me feel safe and secure. Devon relieves my waist of his hands and moves them to my shoulders, turning me around on the spot. Then he wraps his arms around me and starts walking. It's a little awkward at first but we soon find a choppy rhythm as he guides me around the bakery and a short distance down the street.

Laughter and chatter grow louder. I can see golden reflections bouncing off the shop windows and when we make a slight turn to the left Devon is absolutely right: I cannot miss it. Right there next to the giant flags, gold poles, statues and gleaming white ice rink stands the most regal and mighty tree bursting with colour and magic.

'Wow,' is the only word I can form.

'Right?' Devon says enthusiastically, squeezing me tighter against his chest.

'Now, what would you say,' he starts after giving me a few minutes to enjoy the sight before me, 'to Christmas in New York and New Year's Eve in Springhollow?' he asks. I pry my eyes off the gleaming tree sucking me in with its enchanted glow and I turn to him once more.

'I'm supposed to be getting on a plane tomorrow morning,' I tell him. I can't possibly afford another night at the hotel and all the cheaper hotels had been fully booked. He quirks an eyebrow at me, like he can read my thoughts, knowing that I really don't want to leave him. 'Maybe you could accidently miss the flight and we can have a sleepover at mine instead,' he suggests. I have no desire to move away from Devon's arms or our spot in front of the tree anytime soon.

'I think we can make accidently missing my flight happen,' I say with an intrigued nod.

'I think we can too – we do make an unbeatable team,' he concurs, smiling down at me. I smile back but then my eyes crease as a little worry flutters over me. 'I must ring my mum and dad though and let them know as it will be their first Christmas without me, I hope my mum will be OK and I'll let Hope know in case she needs me; she and Jess usually pop round to escape a bit of the madness at their house and say hello and she's surprising Jess with a dog. I had wanted to see his face.'

Devon leans down and kisses me softly on the lips. 'We can call them right now,' he says, putting my worries at ease. 'And we can call them on Christmas Day and make sure you can see Jess's face.'

'Thank you,' I tell him, getting lost in his glistening eyes for a few moments. 'Can we just enjoy this big tree for a while longer and then I can call home? I quite like this new tradition.' I turn around so my back is now nestled into Devon's chest, his arms snug around my neck keeping me toasty.

'I think we're going to create lots more new traditions together,' he whispers into my ear.

'I think so too,' I reply, unable to help the wide smile that curves my lips and reaches all the way to my ears, where Devon's lips just grazed; making me tingle all over. With Devon by my side I don't feel so terrified of embracing all of me; the me that I have been hiding for so long. It's time for new adventures, a new job title and a new wardrobe... which might just include a cape.

24

Christmas Day saw Devon and I watch as many superhero movies back to back that it was possible to fit into one day, with a break around midday to pop over to his parents to exchange gifts and wish them a merry Christmas; which wasn't without the customary inquest as to what I was doing with my life, my plans for the future and the critical once-over of my mustard-coloured beanie-clad head. It seemed twenty-six-year-old me wasn't any better off than sixteen-year-old me in their eyes, but some things never change, I guess, and I kept a smile on my face as we tucked into the mince pies that I had bought at a World Market Devon had taken me to. I couldn't quite tell if Devon's parents cared for or missed the British tradition, but it had made Devon smile.

As he had gotten older, he often visited the shop when he was homesick. We hadn't stayed long at his parents'; Devon having spent the last few Christmases with friends and therefore having an excuse to leave before Devon's mum started berating me about my desire to fill the brains of both children and adults alike with mutants, time travel and bizarre creatures from fake planets. Devon had told his friends that for Christmas this year he would be spending the day at home and had arranged to meet up a few days later. So, the two of us had spent the evening video-chatting with my family and exchanging gifts. Devon surprised me with a new pencil case and a set of beautiful, sharp, crisp pencils, an awesome beanie and a jumper all emblazoned with his superhero logo and or face on them. I had laughed so hard I had cried but they have to be my most favourite gifts I have ever received.

In turn I had surprised Devon with a framed sketch I had done of him suited and booted in his spandex but instead of the original backdrop of his movie poster, I had replaced it with Springhollow and a shadow of him as a kid. He had also cried. Christmas Day had been truly magical.

Boxing Day followed with ice-skating in Central Park, a visit to Devon's favourite skatepark and Christmas cupcakes for dinner. I stayed in New York a total of eight days and, though I loved exploring the city and going on a tour of Devon's old school, theatre club and where he had his first audition, my favourite place had to be his small apartment in Brooklyn. Dotted around the walls were comic book posters that he had had framed and, to my surprise, upon initially stepping foot inside his place, drawings I had done as a child were hung up next to the greats. It made me feel like I could be someone and had taken my breath away that Devon had taken such care with them.

Whereas I had shoved all my childhood memorabilia in boxes, Devon's action figures took pride of place on a few sparse shelves in the living room and his comics littered the coffee table next to scripts that he was looking at. The apartment was colourful if not a little cold. There was a small fibre optic tree in the corner, but it was missing something; I just couldn't put my finger on it yet. We met up with a few of his close friends for dinner one evening, which was lovely. It sure was a whole lot easier not hiding who I was, especially when Devon's friends were that of the nerdy kind too.

The night flew by as I joined in with movie trivia and games, grateful for Hope and Jess and their conversations over the years, and mine and Devon's movie marathon, getting me through the tougher pop culture quizzes of today. The whole trip had been wonderful and inspiring and made my decision about attending the art school in the New Year that much clearer.

I'm now sat at our corner table in the village pub, Devon by my side and Mum, Dad, Hope and Jess also snuggled into the booth. Not to forget little Orion curled up at Hope's feet. The gorgeous baby St Bernard took a liking to Hope from the get-go and she's totally smitten. The look on Jess's face on Christmas Day had been priceless and I think he's now more in love with Hope than he was before, if that's even possible. I'm wearing my high-waisted denim flares with a festive Thor jumper, which my mum has only looked at disapprovingly twice tonight, but baby steps; I know change takes time.

As the clock ticks down to midnight and I glance over at Devon, the kid inside me is bursting with excitement and joy for the year ahead. I don't wish to silence her anymore or make her feel silly about where her passions lie. She knew from an early age what she wanted to do, who she wanted to be; I just needed to trust her and listen to her. I like thinking like Scarlett.

I've written down a list of agencies and publishing houses

and tomorrow will be taking my first giant leap in submitting my ideas and drawings to them. Suddenly my skillset and dreams don't feel so inadequate when I stop comparing myself to others or letting the world dictate what a twenty-six-year-old woman should look like. I can't wait to spread magic and encourage the imaginations of all who pick up my stories and to share a piece of myself with those who pick up *The Village Gazette*. Yes, Hope got the go-ahead on Christmas Eve and I can now honestly say I love my job. I hope my drawings and everyone's brilliant passions and ideas will be enough to make the January issue truly special so we can keep our magazine running because I am actually looking forward to going back to work on January 3rd.

The countdown gets more raucous. Glasses are raised into the air, champagne sloshing around and tipping over the edges, as we all stand to greet the New Year. As soon as the clock strikes twelve Devon's lips are on mine and I can hear the hollers and cheers in the background as I sink into his kiss. When he moves away, only but an inch, his eyes still trained on mine with that disarming smile on his ridiculously handsome, grown-up face, an actual giggle escapes my lips.

'You know I think this New Year might just beat that New Year we snuck out of bed while your parents were busy hosting that party and we watched the fireworks from our "treehouse" in the park.' Devon uses air quotes when he says "treehouse" for it wasn't a treehouse like you might picture it, meaning there was no actual structure nor house but merely a flat surface area where a few branches connected that were big enough for the two of us to fit in when we were ten.

'Hmm, how so? If I remember correctly those fireworks were pretty spectacular,' I reply, staring straight into his eyes, which shine brighter than any firework display and which grow more spectacular when Devon wrinkles his nose and his grin grows wider making them sparkle and beam with mischief.

'Well, back then I didn't get to do this.' And he kisses me again with his hand on my waist, pulling me close, closing the distance between us for the last ten years and cementing the bond that had never truly gone away.

Not long after the New Year chimes, Devon and I say our goodbyes to everyone at the pub and race each other across the square. It's safe to say I've not felt this free and happy in my hometown in ten years. My Thor jumper is keeping the frosty nip at bay as is the merry amount of gin I have consumed, not too much, but enough so I'm not concerned with the childlike glee etched on my face or how our childhood games might look to other people. I have my arms out at my sides like Falcon about to soar into the grey night sky and Devon with his long legs is leaping ahead singing Christmas songs.

I jangle about with my keys when we reach my step as we are both panting and inhaling the crispy air. I make a mental note that milk is the superior drink for superheroes and not alcohol as a stitch creeps into my side. Once through the door we shed our scarves, jackets and beanies and make a beeline for the couch. I had left the tree lights on, so the room is under a soft Christmassy glow before I add to it the low light of my lamp. We're both about to sit down when I notice something under the tree. Devon stops beside me, seemingly noticing it too. That's when I register a card

on the coffee table that wasn't there before. I pick it up as
Devon stares at the tree.

> *I thought I'd hold on to this. I had a feeling one day you*
> *might need it again.*
> *Love you always,*
> *Dad xx*

As I get to the end of the note Devon lets out a squeal and
dives on to his/my Spider-Man bean bag, while I try not to
choke up over my dad's words and his thoughtfulness after
all these years. I can't believe he had kept it. I had given him
a key to my house while I was away to look after Ed and
he most definitely scored points for using it well. He must
have snuck in on his way to the pub; we had gotten there
before them.

'Now that's more like it,' Devon comments, looking
relaxed and comfortable on his Spidey spot.

'Oh yeah.' I chuckle and quirk an eyebrow, already
sensing what he means.

'Yes,' he says with a wink. 'I love this place, but it needs
some comic books,' Devon adds, looking around like in his
head he is redecorating.

'Hmm, is that so,' I start, hands on my hips, looking over
the pretty pink walls and plenty of colourful throws and
furniture. Then I look back to Devon and have to laugh
at how much he has grown since he last sat on the bean
bag. Now he barely fits; there's just enough space for his
peachy bum. 'Well then, I think you missed one thing off my
Christmas list,' I say, making Devon's eyebrows crease and
nose crinkle with curiosity. He's leaning to one side on the

bean bag, propped up on an elbow, hands clasped, which makes his biceps pop. He looks all sorts of nerdy and sexy and he's underneath my tree. I clear my throat, nearly losing my train of thought.

'I'm going to need a cardboard cut-out, like a life-size one of this really awesome superhero who's recently taken the world by storm; he wears a white cape, with gold boots. He's quite the charmer with dashing good looks and I think he would fit perfectly into my space and add just the right amount of colour against the pink. Do you like the pink?' I say, confidently, hands still on my hips, thinking I'm going to need more pictures of Devon around this place when he must fly away to go and shoot all his movies and, you know, live in his New York apartment. We hadn't got around to discussing how exactly our new relationship was going to work, but I am keeping tonight's tone light as one thing I was sure of was that we would figure it out together, in time.

'You know, I really don't think you need a cardboard cut-out and yes, yes I like pink,' Devon replies before gently grabbing my wrist and pulling me into his lap, his cheeks a little flushed. I can hear more beans scatter and squeak under our weight and fear for our beloved Spidey bean bag.

'And why not?' I say, regarding the cardboard cut-out and give him a playful pouty look, our faces inches from each other's.

'Because why would you want cardboard when you have the real thing?' he questions, tracing his fingers along my cheek, making them flame under his touch.

'But you have an apartment in New York, you live in New York – you won't always be here,' I say, my voice now more of a whisper.

'About that... did you like the New York apartment?' Devon asks, and well if I can be so bold as to tell him my thoughts like he has shared with me about my home, I reply truthfully, 'It was cold. I mean it was nice and I liked that you had all the posters and our childhood stuff, but it was missing something.' I move my hand over the hem of his white cotton tee. A moment of silence passes.

'You, Scar. It was missing you. It's never felt like home. You are my home,' he breathes, his voice but a whisper, his lips brushing against my ear. The electric current is back and coursing through my veins.

'So, what you're saying is, that you would like to move in with me,' I whisper into D's ear. He laughs into mine, a laugh that makes my stomach volt a rail, it's so full of warmth and joy.

I move away so our cheeks are no longer touching so I can look my best friend in the eyes. My hand rests against his jaw, his hand moves to my thigh to keep me steady and balancing on his lap.

'I've missed you,' he says when our eyes meet. 'We have a million adventures to catch up on, thousands of forts to make up for and hundreds of pancake breakfasts to compensate for. You are home for me, Scar,' he adds, making me feel a little breathless.

I can feel the smile tugging at the corners of my lips. I wrap my arms around his neck. 'But won't you need to be in New York for work?' I can't help but query.

'I can travel and there's no rush in selling the apartment. I hear someone might need it next summer anyway?' Devon says with an encouraging, bright smile.

I wriggle on his lap so that I can wrap my legs around

him and stretch them out. 'I think that sounds like a plan, Superman,' I say, rhyming with happiness.

'I thought we were Batman and Robin?' Devon says with a grin.

'Right now, I'm feeling more like Superman and Lois Lane,' I note, pulling Devon close so are lips are nearly touching.

'Ahh, but do you know who I think my favourite duo of all time are?' he replies, his lips tickling mine.

'Who?' I ask.

'Me and you,' he answers, giving me the cheekiest and cheesiest grin. But it works, with those words I kiss him under the glowing lights of the Christmas tree while atop our Spider-Man bean bag and I feel like this time I've taken a leap and I'm doing it: I'm really flying.

Acknowledgements

I would like to say a massive thank you to Hannah Smith and the Aria fiction team for giving me this opportunity. I feel like I always have to pinch myself and will forever be grateful for this dream come true. Hannah, I am beyond thankful to be working with you again and for your belief in me, it means the world. I love bringing my stories to life with you and making them the best they can be, you are amazing. A massive thank you to Vicky Joss too for organizing my blog tour and for all the lovely social media posts and fun media stuff you do, you are awesome. Also, to the design team at Aria for creating the most beautiful, festive cover that makes me smile every time I look at it, you are incredible. Thank you, Helena Newton, for catching me when I decide to make up words, it has been lovely to work with you again on this book and I appreciate all you do.

To every single person who has picked up my books, messaged, reviewed, tweeted or shared my stories, I thank you from the bottom of my heart. Readers, book bloggers, friends, family and strangers a like, you are truly awesome in every way, please know how much I appreciate you.

To my wonderful author family, thank you, thank you, thank you. Thank you for giving me a place where I feel like

I fit, for your endless support and encouragement and for being a bunch of inspiring, talented, beautiful and positive humans.

To all those who have inspired me through movies, music, art and books, thank you for being guiding lights and for teaching me to never give up on my dreams. I'm grateful to all the superheroes that inspired this book, from Superman to Shazam, if we can dream it and have a little trust and faith, we can become it.

To my family, I try with every thank you section to sum up the love and gratitude I have for you but somehow words never seem to do how I feel justice. Thank you for everything. I love you all with every piece of me. Kelly and Jen, thank you for the laughs, the tears, the adventures, and the utter giddiness we shared that made 2019 so special and that made this book what it is. You are both amazing, obvi.

Nanna, thank you for loving me for all that I am, for believing in me and my dreams and for being the embodiment of love. I miss your smiling face more than I could ever express. I spent last year in a flurry of edits and excitement as my second and third book hit the shelves and then had the time of my life writing this fourth book. I told you all about it while I sat on your bed and scribbled down scenes in my notebook. You'd smile every time I said I needed to write and then you'd tell me "to write a good one." You filled my heart with so much hope, made me feel like everything would always turn out ok and taught me to "be happy" even through the ups and downs. Nanna, this book fills me with so much joy, memories of a year that brought so much happiness, and ended with a lot of pain, but I truly hope you'd be proud. I love you always, there's not a day that goes by that I don't think of you and Grandad, Nanna Knott and Grandad George too, you are always in my heart.

Dear Reader,

Thank you so very much for picking up my fourth book and for giving it a chance. I wish I could give you a hug and tell you how much it means to me, but please know it means everything. Hearing that my stories have connected with you and that you can relate to, have felt inspired by, or simply enjoyed one of my books is the absolute best feeling, so I truly hope you enjoy Scarlett and Devon's story as much as I enjoyed writing it. The two of them made my heart smile and bought a lot of love, laughter and joy into my life and I hope I can pass that on to you through these pages.

Remember, you are amazing and beautiful, and no dream is too farfetched or silly. You can do it. Live your passion.

All my love, Lucy xx

About the Author

LUCY KNOTT lives in Manchester England, just around the corner from her childhood home and less than five minutes from her twin sister Kelly and brother in law Chris. She loves spending time with her family in addition to writing, reading and cooking Italian food. When not buried in a book, scribbling in a notebook or having dance parties for one to Harry Styles in the kitchen, she works as a teaching assistant where the majority of her days are spent talking about dinosaurs and making Godzilla out of just about everything, from Blu Tac to cardboard boxes, and she loves every minute.

If she could up and move to the stunning Amalfi Coast, San Francisco or live in a cabin surrounded by fairy lights, she would, but for now she's quite content writing about those magical places. Lucy loves to write uplifting stories that she hopes will put a smile on your face, fill your heart with joy, encourage you to embrace the awesomeness that you are and believe that any dream is possible.

Hello from Aria

We hope you enjoyed this book! If you did let us know, we'd love to hear from you.

We are Aria, a dynamic digital-first fiction imprint from award-winning independent publishers Head of Zeus. At heart, we're committed to publishing fantastic commercial fiction – from romance and sagas to crime, thrillers and historical fiction. Visit us online and discover a community of like-minded fiction fans!

We're also on the look out for tomorrow's superstar authors. So, if you're a budding writer looking for a publisher, we'd love to hear from you. You can submit your book online at ariafiction.com/we-want-read-your-book

You can find us at:
Email: aria@headofzeus.com
Website: www.ariafiction.com
Submissions: www.ariafiction.com/we-want-read-your-book

- @ariafiction
- @Aria_Fiction
- @ariafiction